CHANCE
SONATA

The first of the *Sonata* novels

Helen Weygang

The *Sonata* novels

Chance Sonata

Fractured Sonata

Beautiful Sonata

Sonata: *a composition for an instrumental soloist, often with a piano accompaniment, typically in several movements* www.languages.oup.com

For Kate, my oldest friend

Chapter titles taken from the works of
Sir Peter Maxwell Davies CH CBE (1934-2016)

Historical inaccuracy for the sake of the plotline: The Sainsbury's supermarket in the Cromwell Road didn't open until 1983, two years after this story is set, and is still there today.

Fiddlers at the Wedding

Kathy Fairbanks didn't know she would change her life for ever the day her oldest friend got married. It was the last day of January 1981 and the innocent Kathy caught the early morning train from London Liverpool Street to Ipswich.

Kathy looked out of the window as the train rattled through Essex and the view didn't cheer her mood as it was barely daylight, the sky heavy with dark clouds. She leaned wearily on her violin case wedged between her and the window and closed her tired eyes. She and Emma had been friends since they had met at school. It had been Emma and her father who had encouraged Kathy to follow her heart into music as a career even though her own family hadn't understood. Music was in her blood. Always had been although she didn't know why. Three years ago Emma had finally persuaded Kathy it was time to stop running. She would be safe in their flat in Earl's Court. But Emma was now going to start a new life with her husband, and Kathy was going to be on her own again. Afraid of what the postman might bring and even more afraid of the ring of the doorbell.

The heating wasn't working on the early train so Kathy huddled closer into her fairly new blue duffle coat and pulled her knitted hat further down over her ears trying to preserve what little warmth her body was providing. She yawned to herself and thought maybe she should have travelled down the previous night but she had had the chance to play in a concert and Kathy, like Emma, was a freelance violinist so she couldn't afford to turn down any offers of work.

It was freezing at Ipswich Station on that raw January morning when the early train came in and Emma Mihaly was relieved to see the tiny, blonde figure of her childhood friend and waved her fur-coated arm rather enthusiastically. Collecting her bridesmaid was almost the last thing to do and she adjusted the collar of her coat as Kathy walked towards her.

"Kath! So glad you could make it!" she cried a little formally but this was a public railway station after all. She lowered her voice a little. "Don't suppose you met a cellist on the train? He would have got on it at Manningtree."

"No, should I have?"

"I just thought you might, it would save me the bother of hanging around here any longer. How was the concert?"

Kathy shrugged non-committedly, and stuffed her wind-blown hair more into her hat.

"Sorry, I forgot," Emma said apologetically. "You don't like Sibelius, do you?"

"Is that your cellist?" Kathy asked, glad of the diversion. She pointed rather rudely at a young man just walking from the station, trying to blow his nose while struggling with a cello in a very tatty soft case and a small bag which kept slipping off one shoulder of his sagging tweed coat.

"Oh my God," Emma groaned. "I suppose it must be. Wait here, I'll go and see."

Emma left Kathy standing beside her car, not even thinking to unlock it so her friend could get in out of the wind, and strode over to the young man who had put down his luggage and blown his nose successfully. What Emma said, Kathy could not hear but she knew from experience that when Emma's hands worked like that she was speaking Czech, not English. To Kathy's amusement the young man looked faintly startled at the arrival of a tall woman in a fur coat and put on a pair of round metal-rimmed spectacles then peered at Emma in a way that made Kathy think of Mole in *The Wind in the Willows* before wiping his hand on his overcoat in order to shake her hand in greeting.

Emma, slender and tall in her ankle boots, topped the brown-haired man by several inches but Kathy had to look up just a little to meet the soft, brown eyes that blinked at her in a face half-hidden by a turned-up collar and an untidy mess of curly hair. More like Moly every second she thought. She had always had a soft spot for Mole.

Emma dutifully performed the introductions. "Kathy Fairbanks, Jean-Guy Dechaume. Let's go, I've got to be at the hairdresser's in an hour."

"I've heard of you," Kathy told him doing her best to sound friendly while thinking there was something wrong about this. Jean-Guy Dechaume was a renowned cellist who, like Emma's father, was from Czechoslovakia, so what was he doing in Suffolk? And why was he travelling alone without hordes of security police round him?

He just smiled and sneezed and didn't answer.

Jean-Guy and cello sat in the back seat of the car while Kathy in the front seat had to listen to Emma's chatter about the wedding gifts she and Derek had received. Kathy guessed there must have been roadworks on the A12 again as Emma took a most peculiar route home. It was nearly an hour later they arrived at the track to the isolated old farmhouse where Emma's father had sought his refuge. Petr Mihaly had moved into that house just under twenty five years ago with nothing in the world except his baby daughter and memories of his murdered wife. He had had enough friends left to help him get out of Prague where he had been a well-known Professor of Music and settle where the North Sea hissed on the shingle and the wind could cut through you even in the middle of summer. When he arrived in June 1956 many of the local people had been selling up and moving out before the unknown demon of a nuclear power station was built on their doorstep so houses were cheap and people seldom strayed to such an unprepossessing place. Which suited the exiled man who had his own secrets to keep.

Emma stopped the car, checked her watch and realised she was running late. "Right, out the pair of you. I've got to bolt."

Kathy and Jean-Guy scrambled out of the car, the latter blew his nose again, and then they were left alone seemingly in the middle of nowhere.

Jean-Guy looked along the rough track that disappeared between some hedges, removed his glasses to see all the better and then said to Kathy, "The Professor lives here?"

That was the first time Kathy had heard him speak. He had a nice, quiet Moly kind of voice. "Yes," she replied and thought she had worked out what he was doing there. "Have you been invited to the wedding?"

This earned her a blank look and she wondered whether maybe his English wasn't as fluent as she had assumed.

"Emma is getting married today," she explained kindly.

"Oh. I did not know. It is bad time for me to be arriving. I'm sorry."

Kathy wasn't sure what to say to that as it meant her one idea had been wrong. So now she was back to the puzzle but it was way too cold to hang about at the end of a windswept drive and ask any more questions. She set off along the potholed track with Jean-Guy toiling wearily beside her and she wondered how long he had been travelling as he seemed to be exhausted. And where from? The track curved round to the right, hiding it from the road. It passed a pair of semi-ruined cottages, continued in a semi-circle then arrived at a house that was part red-brick, part timbered local pink and everything was totally hidden behind a riot of uncontrolled rhododendrons. Jean-Guy still looked bemused as Kathy banged the knocker on the oak front door, dark with age and studded with centuries-old iron.

A very tall, bearded gentleman whose white hair and lined face made him look a lot older than he was flung open the door, cried something in a language Kathy didn't understand but knew to be Czech, and rapturously hugged the young man in spite of the fact he once again had the grubby handkerchief up to his nose.

There was a shy, tentative reaction to this greeting, but Jean-Guy was obviously reluctant to let go of the neck of the cello.

"Come in, come in!" Professor Mihaly continued. "I presume that daughter of mine has gone to have her hair done? Good morning, Kathy, how are you? Please excuse my manners but I was with Jean-Guy's father at the Conservatoire in Prague and to see him here is something of a miracle. But here I am keeping you on the doorstep when no doubt all you want is a cup of coffee and a chair by the fire."

The Professor stood back to allow Kathy and Jean-Guy to step into the hall where Kathy peeled off her coat, hat, scarf and gloves, even though the house wasn't particularly warm. Jean-Guy, however, stood rooted to the threadbare carpet and didn't even let go of his cello.

Politely speaking English for Kathy's benefit, the Professor said: "Let me take your coat then you two go in and sit by the fire. We have almost two hours of peace before Emma comes home."

Jean-Guy looked as though he was about to cry. "I cannot, I should be too cold."

"Haven't you got a jumper?" Kathy asked, then realised that was a silly thing to say as this young man clearly had only what was in the shabby bag and no jumper of any description could fit into something so small.

"A...? I'm sorry, I don't know the word."

Kathy pulled at the sleeve of her Aztec-inspired bright sweater. "Jumper. One of these."

"Ah, no. I have none."

Kathy unzipped her bag and pulled out a too-large Aran sweater she had packed at the last minute as Suffolk always seemed to be at least ten degrees Fahrenheit cooler than London. She held this out to Jean-Guy. "Here, borrow this," she said unceremoniously, feeling sorry for poor Moly but not liking to show it.

Incredulous hands reached out for the sweater then paused. "Thank you, but I cannot. I have not bathed for too long."

Kathy hadn't liked to mention the young man's odour, but was relieved to know he was at least aware of it.

"Then you must bath if you wish," the Professor offered.

"That I should like," came the decisive reply. "Then, perhaps, I may wear the jumper." Jean-Guy was clearly pleased he had mastered another word in the English vernacular. He followed the Professor upstairs, taking his cello and the sweater with him.

Kathy moved into the sitting room, pleasantly untidy with books everywhere, a beautiful Broadwood concert grand piano in the window bay, and not a surface that was not occupied by sheet music, a book or a cat or sometimes all three. Kathy shared an armchair by the fire with the old tabby Brno, named after the birthplace of Emma's mother and so often mispronounced in the English language.

Brno and Kathy were carrying on a very one-sided conversation when approaching sounds of snuffling and sneezing heralded the arrival of Jean-Guy, smelling a lot sweeter and now wearing old jeans that Kathy was sure had once belonged to Emma, a shirt of the Professor's and Kathy's Aran sweater. Clean and not hunched with cold, Jean-Guy was, Kathy realised, probably not more than six inches taller than her, very thin, and looked as though he hadn't eaten a decent meal for weeks. The features of his pleasant, if not strikingly handsome, face were reddened and swollen thanks to his cold but his smile was warm and irresistible as he removed a score of a Dvorak piano trio from the armchair on the other side of the fire so he could sit thankfully down and finally give his nose a hearty blow on a clean handkerchief.

"Feel better?" Kathy asked, returning his smile and thinking she had seldom seen such a dreadful cold.

"Yes, thank you. Your sweater is very warm for me. Professor Mihaly is making some coffee for us. He says you are not to go and help him as you always make him muddled."

Kathy smiled remembering the countless times she had been politely asked not to help with the cooking as her calm efficiency always confused the Professor's well-tried, if absent-minded culinary tactics. But there was no doubting he was one of the best cooks she had ever come across.

Trying to keep her tone conversational rather than curious, Kathy enquired, "Are you French? I always thought you're Czech like the Prof and Emma."

"My grandfather was a Frenchman, my grandmother was Czech and so is my father. My mother is Russian," he volunteered and sneezed a lot more.

"Are you here to play in a concert?" Kathy asked still trying to work things out, then realised that sounded worse than stupid. No famous cellist would be in the UK to play without a press fanfare or entourage. Yet here he was with nothing but a cello in a scruffy case and a bag too small to pack a sweater. "Sorry, silly question."

Jean-Guy smiled sadly. "No, not a concert. Life is not good in Czechoslovakia right now and a French orchestra smuggled me from West Germany after my concert with them since last September. I have been travelling a long time. Now I am refugee and apply for asylum in England. I am allowed to tell you that aren't I?"

A log slipped in the fire and a pocket of pine resin flared and spat in the hearth. As though one of the house's reputed ghosts had walked across the room, Kathy shivered with a strange feeling at Jean-Guy's last few words. "I suppose so," she offered, although something in her mind said maybe he wasn't. "I hope you get your asylum," she offered brightly.

Jean-Guy had obviously decided he could trust her. "I hope so too. If I am sent back I will be punished."

Kathy caught her first glimpse of an unknown world and it frightened her. "But that's horrible."

Jean-Guy smiled at her as though envying her naivety. "It is their way."

Kathy had nothing to say. She had never met a refugee before. Never met anyone who had so little in the world and, it seemed, would leave behind everything they had and throw themselves on the mercy of strangers.

The Professor came in carrying a tray of mugs of coffee which he put on the coffee table. "Do you feel better, Jean-Guy?"

"Oh, yes, thank you. Do you hear from your Home Office yet?"

He looked at the young man sharply and was clearly trying to phrase his reply.

"Jean-Guy has told me he's a defector, if that helps," Kathy told him. "I won't tell anyone else unless you say I can."

The Professor looked slightly relieved if anything. "It is not public knowledge yet. But at least your knowing will make my life a little easier while you are here." He handed Jean-Guy a mug of coffee. "I'll have to write and let them know you have arrived. They've been very sympathetic so far and you have already been registered as an asylum seeker. Refugee status will take a little longer. Perhaps Kathy could help you try for a job which will show you want to become part of the economy but it can't be much as you are not supposed to work until you are at least a refugee."

Kathy's instinctive reaction was that she didn't want to step into this world of secrets that was now beckoning her. She looked across at Jean-Guy and he briefly caught her glance. She saw that terrible look in those eyes; it was the look of a man hunted in a hostile world and she knew how that felt. She changed her life for ever with her next breath. "Well, I'll do my best. But it'll probably just be a local café will want a waiter or something if you don't mind what you do. Could you live in London?"

The last glimmer of hope died. "No, I have no monies."

"But," the Professor declared jubilantly, "today Emma marries and moves out. If I pay the rent could Jean-Guy not share with you?"

Kathy looked at the young man who was reminding her more and more of poor Moly alone and lost in the Wild Wood. There was something so forlorn about him she suddenly longed to take him in her arms and hug him like a child.

"I'm sure the landlady won't mind and it is a two-bedroom flat."

His tired mind caught up with their conversation. "I am to share your flat?"

"Yes, if you want to."

"You are very good. Thank you."

Kathy felt a forgotten sensation that she could only have described as a warm glow around her heart.

She hadn't felt that for a long time and didn't want to feel it now.

"It's purely economic," she said lightly then looked away in case she should see any hurt in his eyes. She really didn't want to be cruel to poor Moly but she wasn't going to let herself get attracted to him. "May I take a bath too please, Prof, then I suppose I'd better start getting ready."

"Please do. I think it makes most sense if you take Emma's room as you will be here tonight and she won't. I have the small front room made up for Jean-Guy."

Kathy walked from the sitting room, steeling herself not even to look at Jean-Guy who was huddled in the armchair and sneezing again. Her mind was dogged by the sad, pale face of the young man with the French name who had departed so abruptly from the land of his birth. As she quickly bathed in the tepid water of the house's heating system and wished not for the first time there was a shower in the place, she thought out her own version of his story. A smile crossed her face when she got to the part where he was bundled into a double bass case. She was in Emma's room, her dressing gown over her underwear and brushing out her long fair hair when someone knocked on the door. Instinctively she tied her sash a little tighter.

"Come in," she called, "I'm quite decent."

Professor Mihaly's head popped round the door. "Glad to hear so. Are you having lunch? Jean-Guy and I will eat now."

He caught Kathy's eye and the two exchanged smiles. Kathy's appetite was notorious. "You know me," she said cheerfully.

"Come along then. Emma cannot be long now and the wedding is at three."

"Will Jean-Guy mind the dressing gown?"

"I doubt if he will even notice. He is full of being free and yet afraid they will send him back."

"Has he left family behind?"

"Both parents, and a sister."

Kathy lay down her brush and thoughtfully joined the Professor. "Then why did he ask to be brought out? You had nothing to lose when you came."

"Who knows what makes people go? I was so opposed to the communist system and I had contacts who helped me to bring my child out. But Jean-Guy's family are still faithful to communism so far as I know."

"Do you trust him?" Kathy asked curiously, thinking the Professor had never taken her into his confidence like this before.

"I have told the Home Office I will be responsible for him. There is nothing more I can do."

"And that was no answer to my question," Kathy challenged, feeling the spreading fear of getting tied up in something she didn't understand.

"I trust him. He has no love of the system either. They took him in not so long ago and held him for quite some time. No one knows what they did, he would never speak of it, but it was his father who got a message through to me last summer, at risk to himself, and told me that Jean-Guy wanted to run. When he is ready, maybe, he will speak of it. But we shouldn't ask."

"Of course, I understand."

Their conversation ceased when they went into the kitchen where Jean-Guy was sitting patiently at the table.

"Sorry," Kathy said perhaps a little too brightly. "I didn't realise you were waiting."

"It is nothing," came the polite assurance.

Kathy sat on Jean-Guy's right and dared not look at him too much. Her curiosity as to his story was starting to become a bit obsessive, so she kept her gaze firmly on his hands. He wore no jewellery; the fingers of the left hand were blunted through years of stopping cello strings and his hands and wrists were quite bony and, unlike the musicians' hands Kathy was used to seeing, looked as though they had done hard manual labour. The pity she felt for him surprised her. If she were not careful, pity would become affection and that wouldn't end happily.

"You are slacking, Kathy," the Professor remarked and his jovial tones jarred her back to her senses. "Jean-Guy has nearly finished his and you have barely touched yours."

"I have to get in to my bridesmaid's dress," Kathy pointed out and smiled, thankful to have been brought back to reality. She hurriedly finished her food, made her excuses and bolted from the kitchen. In the sanctuary of the hallway she tried to focus her mind, but she seemed to ache physically inside with an emptiness that had become her constant companion. Mental images darted in and out of her mind of traitors and torturers and Kathy knew she was heading back to her dark place.

"Not again," she murmured softly. "Don't let it happen again."

Emma found her friend sitting at the foot of the stairs in tears.

"Kath! Whatever's the matter?" she cried in concern and helped her to her feet.

"Same old trouble," Kathy sniffed and forced her mind to refocus. "Your hair looks nice."

Emma laughed. "Lamb to the slaughter. How's the waif?"

"Eating stew like it's his first meal for a month."

"It probably is. Come on, I'd better get into my dress and you'd better splash your face."

The two went up the stairs together and Kathy couldn't help remarking, "You seem to have taken Jean-Guy's arrival very calmly. He told me he's a defector."

Emma closed her bedroom door behind them. "You must never breathe a word about any of this, but Jean-Guy isn't the first that has passed through this house. It's just that he's Dad's first musician, and he unfortunately arrived on my wedding day and so did you."

"How exciting," Kathy sighed, her tears forgotten. "Has this been going on since I've known you?"

"All the time. I'm sure it's one reason Dad sent me away to school. I didn't really understand what was happening myself until I was about ten. It's a bit sad really as it means Dad can never go back but in a way this helping the defectors is his way of getting his own back for what they did to Mum. It probably means neither of us can ever go back." Emma smiled at Kathy who still looked slightly tearful and gave her a small hug. "But right now I'm going to take a bath without mussing up my hair, although I'm guessing both you and Jean-Guy have nicked whatever lukewarm water there may have been. You'd better change now. I won't be long if the water's as cold as I think it's going to be, and it'll take the two of us to get me into my dress."

Kathy was the only bridesmaid and as Jean-Guy wasn't going to the wedding, the vintage car took her to the church on her own before going back to the farmhouse for the bride and her father. She was glad of the company of Derek's family as she waited outside the church for her oldest friend to arrive. Ron and Sue were a down-to-earth couple from the unfashionable East End of London and they had found it definitely odd, but rather fun, that their only child should have found himself a Czech bride. But they were very fond of Emma, she had loved becoming part of a 'proper' family and they had also welcomed the friend who was more like a sister to her. Kathy thought Emma looked the perfect English bride in her beautiful white dress and carrying an unusual bouquet of white hellebores and ivy along with some mistletoe that always grew on the old crabapple tree in the farmhouse back garden. She loved the way Emma had taken that tiny part of the house to her wedding and looked at the white berries while she held the bouquet for the bride as well as her own little posy of ivy and a single pale pink hellebore. White. The colour of innocence and purity. She thought over the wild teenage years she and Emma had shared and had the ridiculous idea that maybe Emma should have got married in grey.

After the perfect English wedding the guests came back to the house for the buffet reception and meandered through most of the ground floor. In the sitting room Kathy played string quartets with some friends from her and Emma's days at music college not knowing that Jean-Guy was sitting at the top of the stairs, his head resting on the spindles, and listening to the music. His eyes were clouded and his nose would keep running but he blamed it on his cold.

Emma and Derek left for their honeymoon at five thirty, and by six the guests had all gone. Kathy put her violin away and joined the Professor in the kitchen where he was beginning the washing up, thankful the caterers had cleared away all they had brought.

"That's everyone gone home," she told him and started doing some drying up.

"You played well," he complimented her bluntly. "Will you go and find Jean-Guy for me, please and tell him to come and have some supper. He is supposed to be somewhere upstairs keeping warm."

Jean-Guy was still sitting on the stairs, by this time hunched up rather miserably and shivering.

"What are you doing?" Kathy cried as soon as she saw him and she paused half-way up the stairs with the skirt of her long blue dress lifted elegantly in one hand. "Come and get some supper," she ordered sharply. "You should be in bed, or you'll catch your death of cold sitting on draughty stairs like that."

Jean-Guy got stiffly to his feet. "I had to hear the music. Were you first violin?"

Kathy nodded, turned and walked down the stairs ahead of him.

"You are excellent violinist."

"Thank you. When do we get to hear you play the cello?"

"When I know I am safe."

"But that could be ages. You can't just not play."

"I shall play, yes. Scales and exercises. But no proper music until I am safe."

They reached for the kitchen door handle together and suddenly her hand was a prisoner under his. As she had guessed, the thin hands were work-roughened and strong. She snatched her hand away as though he had burned her and defensively crossed her arms across her body, hands tucked securely away. She wouldn't look at Jean-Guy but guessed he had found her reactions rather rude. She couldn't explain. He made no sound but opened the door and stood back out of her way.

Feeling relieved, Kathy managed to smile her thanks and stepped into the room.

The Professor looked round from the sink as the other two came in. "Jean-Guy that is a terrible cold. You will not be fit to travel to London tomorrow. Kathy, could you take his cello with you? He will stand more chance travelling alone."

"'More chance'?" Kathy repeated. "Is there any danger?"

The Professor smiled apologetically. "There is sometimes the chance of people looking for defectors at the beginning. I don't mean to imply there is any danger."

Jean-Guy started to protest that he was perfectly capable of taking his own cello but the common sense and experience of the Professor won the argument, and Jean-Guy ate his supper in sullen silence. He went to bed as soon as he decently could, leaving Kathy, still in her long blue dress, to help the Professor finish clearing up after the wedding.

"I don't think I've ever seen such a bad cold," Kathy remarked sympathetically.

"He is not at all well. Our contacts in the French orchestra could only take him as far as Strasbourg. From there he had to get to Paris and the safe house there as best he could. Of course he speaks fluent French, and we were going to leave him in Paris but already the Soviets were looking for him in France."

"And he speaks Czech too?" Kathy asked, wanting to bring the conversation back to things she could cope with.

"Yes. Russian, Czech, French and English." Washing up finished, the Professor took Kathy's arm and led her paternally to the sitting room where Brno had gone back to sleep in the chair in front of the fire and seemed to have forgiven the disruption to his routine that day.

"Kathy," The Professor said quietly. "I must talk to you very seriously. Jean-Guy will be staying at your flat, several people will be coming to check on him for the first few weeks. It will be very trying for you." The Professor paused, slightly embarrassed. "I have to ask you not to get too involved with Jean-Guy. I don't expect you will. At least not at first."

Kathy could have hugged the Professor for being so protective of her. "I'll try," she said and her head told her heart it wasn't going to happen.

"Perhaps," the Professor continued tentatively, "you may be able to tell me how Jean-Guy gets on in London? If he manages to make any friends or anything? Finds places to go instead of getting bored."

Something heavy was sinking towards Kathy's stomach. "You want me to spy on him?"

The Professor's laugh lacked true humour. "No, nothing so sinister. I am just concerned for the welfare of the son of a friend of mine, that is all."

"Oh, all right then," Kathy agreed quickly, trying to believe him.

Kathy was woken in the morning by the sound of rain remorselessly battering the ivy leaves round the window frame and was thankful it wasn't the forecast snow after all. She opened her eyes wearily wishing she could have had another couple of hours' sleep, and her blue gaze focussed on the articles in the room. Everything spoke of Emma. Most of the ornaments and books Kathy knew so well had been moved to the marital home but it was something even less tangible than the faint aura of perfume that still haunted the room.

A craving for a mug of tea made Kathy get out of bed and she dressed in her favourite pink sweatshirt and white dungarees but left her hair hanging loose as she often did. In the kitchen she found the Prof sorting through some papers which he pushed under the tea cosy when he saw her.

He looked at her over the top of his reading glasses. "Good morning, did you sleep well?"

"Yes, thank you." She got on with her breakfast and couldn't help hearing the sounds of sneezing upstairs. "I'll take some tea up to him in a minute, shall I? And get that cello off him so I can take it with me. I'll go up on the morning train if the ten o'clock bus still runs on a Sunday."

The Prof was a little surprised that Kathy should show such compassion to a man she had only met yesterday but he didn't comment. "Just about, but if you miss it there isn't another one until tomorrow but I can always give you a lift. I am sure he will be grateful for the tea. He can bring your violin when he comes to London as it won't be easy travelling with two instruments."

"I'll need it by Wednesday. Will he be fit to travel by then?"

"Yes. I don't keep people here for long."

"Emma told me you often help people like Jean-Guy," Kathy said quietly as she didn't like to have secrets from the Professor who had helped her too when she had needed it.

"Then Emma has told you too much. I am disappointed in her."

For the first time ever, there was a certain silence between the friends. "I'll take Jean-Guy his tea," was her only comment and she hoped she hadn't upset him.

"Will you ask him if he wants any breakfast? And tell him that if he dares to get out of bed before lunchtime I will send him back to Czechoslovakia."

The Professor's tone was light again and Kathy knew her indiscretion had been forgiven. She was still smiling as she knocked on the bedroom door.

"Enter!" Jean-Guy called.

Kathy stepped in to the room to see Jean-Guy fully dressed, just settling himself to play the cello. The instrument looked old and battered, and it was a dark, almost mahogany brown in colour.

"Some tea," Kathy told him. "And shouldn't you still be in bed?"

"I am not ill," Jean-Guy replied gracelessly as he took the mug of tea from her. "Thank you."

Kathy wasn't sure she totally agreed with that and watched as Jean-Guy gulped down the tea then began to tune the cello. Kathy, not having been told to go away, sat on the end of the bed to listen. She watched as he idly played a few scales and arpeggios. The sound seemed to flow out of the cello, filling the small room with the rich tones.

"Gorgeous cello," Kathy remarked. "Is it very old?"

"Two hundred, maybe two hundred fifty years old."

Kathy could have listened for ever to those simple scales and exercises but she was only too aware of the time and checked her watch. "Well, I'd better be going," she said reluctantly, "so hand over your cello."

There was something sad and gentle in the way he so carefully put the cello into its case and offered it to her. Kathy guessed he and the cello were like old friends who had been through a lot of joys and troubles together, and she gave him a slight smile as she took it from him.

He looked at the way she held the cello and his soft remark took her breath away. "Someone hurt you very much. Maybe one day we will exchange stories?"

"Maybe," Kathy heard herself say in a half-whisper. "I must go." She didn't want to talk about it right then. "I'll see you in London in a few days. With my violin but without your germs."

"Kathy!" the Professor yelled up the stairs. "It is time you were gone if you want to catch this bus for the train."

Jean-Guy acknowledged there were some things Kathy Fairbanks wasn't willing to talk about. "I shall take cello down for you if you want to fetch your bags."

Only the Professor and the cello were in the hall when Kathy rushed down the stairs, pulling on her coat as she came.

"Goodbye, Prof," she said as they hugged each other. "Thanks for having me."

"Lovely to see you, Kathy. And looking so much happier. You must come again, I shall always be pleased to see you."

"Yes, I think I may. I expect you'll see Emma before I do, so please give her my love."

"Of course. Take care of yourself."

"You too," Kathy cried in departure as she seized the cello and raced through the front door which the Professor had opened for her.

Kathy didn't get her breath back until she was sitting on the bus into Ipswich with the cello in the gangway beside her. Nobody took any notice of the petite blonde woman travelling with a cello in a tattered case until she was crossing Liverpool Street station to get to the Underground.

A tall gentleman, immaculately dressed, stopped her and addressed her in very courteous English. "Excuse me, and believe me I don't make a habit of stopping young ladies, but I happen to be looking for a cellist to do some session work. Do you play professionally?"

In spite of the gentleman's obviously good manners and his pure English, Kathy knew she had to lie.

"I'm sorry, I'm a bit of a fraud. I was staying with my aunt and I saw this at an antiques fair. I've always liked cellos so I bought it. I can't actually play a note."

"Oh, I see. I'm sorry to have stopped you. Whereabouts were you?"

"Nor far away." Kathy sensed that lack of information wasn't going to satisfy him. "Chingford way," she offered politely.

The gentleman was not that inclined to chat. "So sorry to have delayed you. Good day."

Kathy had a daft notion that if the gentleman had had a hat he would have raised it to her in the manners of her grandfather's generation, but he wasn't that old. She went on her way a little puzzled by the strange encounter, although that wouldn't have been the first impetuous booking she had taken, but when she looked back he had melted into the crowd..

The flat felt cold and cheerless with all Emma's things gone. It was on the first floor of a terraced town house and Kathy had always had the smaller of the two bedrooms, but the flat was hers now and she wanted the larger room which had the double bed in it and a view across the garden rather than facing the street. For most of the rest of the day she moved furniture around and did some frantic cleaning, until by evening all she could do was slump in an armchair and stare at a soppy film on the television. She had been dreading living on her own again but that wasn't going to happen. She cried at a film that was supposed to be funny and waited for her past to catch up with her.

Image, Reflection, Shadow

Kathy looked in her kitchen cupboards the next morning and realised that not only had Emma taken her possessions but a lot of the food seemed to have gone too. She realised she would have to go shopping before her new flatmate arrived and as she had just been paid for her last concert she decided to do a big shop and go to the new Sainsbury's which had opened in what had once been the West London Air Terminal on the Cromwell Road. She debated whether to take her car, but she had secured a good parking space last time she drove and she was reluctant to move the car as even a resident's parking permit was no guarantee of a space in the cluttered streets of Earl's Court where diplomatic cars seemed to think they could just take any available space.

She had been to Sainsbury's a few times but they had reorganised since she had last been there and in her quest for bread she went into the pet food aisle by mistake and there she saw a familiar face. She had no idea what the man's name was but they often met in the local 24-hour grocery at the end of her road very late at night and had got in the habit of exchanging the odd remark out of politeness. He was always very pleasant and friendly and, unlike most men, didn't make her feel threatened so she had decided he was a policeman as he always seemed to be wearing a white shirt under his jacket and had dark trousers and smart black shoes as though hiding a police uniform now he was off duty. She almost didn't recognise him this morning as he was wearing jeans and an old green sweater with a tatty waxed cotton coat nearly down to his ankles, and his hair was scruffy as though he had just got out of bed.

"Hullo," she greeted him, glad to see him looking less stressed than usual. "Any idea where the bread is?"

He looked up from the tin of cat food he had been studying and smiled distractedly. "Oh, hi. Bit of a change from our usual meeting place?"

"Just a bit." Kathy wasn't sure what to say and there was a short silence.

"Bread's a couple of aisles over. I think it's got eggs on the end." He looked back at the tin of cat food and asked almost shyly. "Do you know anything about cat food? I have no idea what I'm looking for here."

Kathy warmed to this quiet policeman who seemed genuinely confused by his shopping. "A bit. My parents always seem to have at least one cat."

He sighed almost audibly with relief. "I got home from work last night and there was a kitten on my doorstep. I've no idea where it came from but it was so thin I thought it was dead. I fed it some tuna last night as that was all I had but it just sicked it all up again. Thought it might need some proper cat food but really no idea as I've never had a cat in my life."

Kathy thought that was just too sweet for words. She reached past him for a familiar product. "Try this one. My parents use it for their new arrivals when they've just been weaned. Have you taken it to the vet to get it checked out?"

"I was just trying to keep it alive long enough to get there. Not working for a few days so I thought I'd fatten it up a bit then take it along and see if anyone wants to adopt it." He took the can of food and saw it was suitable for young cats and weaned kittens.

"Doesn't your landlord allow pets?" Kathy asked, feeling curious about this man who often seemed, like her, to be doing emergency grocery shopping at midnight and who had taken in a kitten that had nearly died on his doorstep.

"My job doesn't." He looked at the tin as though it held some deep mystery, and mused half to himself. "Not what I really wanted after a shift at work to come home and find a half-dead cat on the doorstep."

Kathy thought this was her chance to learn more about the lovely policeman. "Where do you work?" she asked politely.

He spoke as though he didn't want to say too much. "Oh, um, I'm out at Heathrow most of the time."

"Oh," Kathy replied, without thinking. "Are you airport police?"

She looked up and saw an expression somewhere between amusement and puzzlement on his face. "Why would I be in the police?"

Kathy felt herself getting redder and redder by the second. It seemed she had totally mis-guessed his occupation. But she had started the conversation now and it would be rude to run away and hide among the bread. "Sorry. I always thought you were."

He put the tin of cat food in his basket and remembered his manners towards this woman whose name he didn't know but who always looked so scared of something. "No, not a policeman," he said kindly. "Nothing so conventional. I just have the kind of job that most people don't understand."

Kathy's curiosity was getting ever stronger. He was playing with her now but some instinct told her she would be safe with him. He made her think of an elder brother. For all she knew he had a wife and a brood of children but he wore no wedding ring and the shopping she could see in his basket implied single living. She knew exactly what he meant by that remark and returned the smile. "Nor me. I'm a musician. What's your guilty secret?" She thought he really did have a lovely smile when he used it properly.

"Promise you won't laugh?"

"Promise."

"I'm an airline pilot."

"Why would I laugh about that? It sounds such a glamorous job."

"Wish it was. Probably got a lot in common with being a musician with its anti-social shifts."

They had both forgotten that they were supposed to be dashing round the supermarket, buying what they needed and then going home again.

"Probably pays better though. What sort of planes do you fly?"

"Oh," he said and sounded a bit startled. "Um, quite a few sorts really."

"I once had a flat under the Heathrow flight path, used to like watching the planes. Best one was Concorde. So beautiful." A sudden stab of memory made her wish she hadn't said anything.

He saw the change of expression in her eyes and knew she had touched on a dark memory. "Bloody noisy though," he offered lightly, trying not to scare her away. He saw the way her fingers tightened round the handles of her basket. "Sorry if we woke you up with all the noise."

Kathy was briefly distracted to notice he had a packet of noodles in his basket. "You fly Concorde?" she asked, thinking that wasn't very likely.

"For quite a few years now."

Somehow she believed him and couldn't help smiling back. "And you shop in Sainsbury's not Fortnum's?"

He wrinkled his nose glad she hadn't decided he was either a lunatic or a conman and run away. "Don't like their Cornflakes," he smiled and held out his hand. "Let's introduce ourselves properly after all this time. I'm Piers Buchanan and I fly aeroplanes."

Kathy formally shook his hand which felt cold to her touch and she hoped hers didn't feel hot and sweaty to him. "Kathy Fairbanks. I play the violin."

"Which explains why we are among the poor sods doing our grocery shopping at midnight. Well, good to have met you properly at last, Kathy. Don't forget to buy your bread." He stepped back from the cat food shelves as though he was letting her go. "I'm sure I'll see you in the corner shop soon. Now I'd better go and see if that moggy is still alive in my kitchen."

"Good luck," Kathy wished him and went off to find the bread. On the aisle with the eggs on the end, just as he had said. She stood looking at the bread wrappers for a while, mulling over that conversation in her mind. She liked to think that maybe he really did fly Concorde. It would be something to tell Emma anyway, just to make her envious. She hoped all went well for Piers' cat and reminded herself to ask him next time they met in the corner store. Groceries paid for, she went out of the shop into a bitter sleet which soon soaked through her coat as she trudged along the Cromwell Road.

Kathy didn't know whether she was delighted or mildly embarrassed when a sleek black Ferrari pulled up at the kerb just ahead of her and when she got level the driver yelled at her through the open window, "Oi, Catwoman, want a lift?"

She had never even been near a Ferrari before let alone inside one. "Thanks," she said as she did up her seat belt and Piers zipped in front of a taxi to join the traffic. "I'm afraid I'm going to make your seat soggy."

"Don't worry about it. Where to?"

"Hogarth Road. Thanks, I really appreciate this. I bought more than I meant to and it was going to be a long walk home. Flatmate's just moved out and taken half the pantry with her."

They stopped in a queue at a busy pedestrian crossing and Piers sounded genuinely apologetic. "Look, I don't want you to think this is some cheesy chat-up line, but would you come and tell me what you think of the cat, please? I don't know who else to ask."

Kathy's first impulse was to say she wasn't allowed to go round to other people's houses then she reminded herself that those days were gone. She hesitated just for a moment but her instincts told her this man wouldn't hurt her. "Um, well, I suppose so."

"Thank you. I don't know anything about cats."

Piers lived in a terraced three-storey house only a few streets away from her and, to Kathy's mild annoyance, part of the ground floor was a car port so he didn't need to hunt the streets looking for a space but backed in next to the house with the ease of practice. The kitchen was a large, bright room at the back with a door onto a small rear garden. To Kathy's surprise there was an obviously well-used but very small bright red Aga in a

35

former fireplace. Next to this, keeping warm, was a cardboard box. In the cardboard box was a tiny tortoiseshell cat, sitting up and yowling with an incredible volume for one so small.

"Litter box?" Kathy asked.

"What? Isn't that for the postman?"

"Litter box, not letter box. Just a shallow tray with some earth in it. Your cat wants the loo. And they're usually very clean animals who don't like peeing on their own floors."

"Oh God, I didn't even think." Piers rummaged in a couple of cupboards. "Will a roasting tin do?"

"Perfect. Just about a couple of inches of earth in it and she'll be fine. You won't as you'll have to empty it."

Piers went outside to the back garden with the roasting tin and was soon back with it. Tin on the floor next to the cardboard box and the cat was much happier. She even purred a bit when her chosen human put down a saucer with some of the food in it as Kathy had told him not to put it all down at once. The food was wolfed down and two people sat at the table to see if she was going to keep it in her stomach.

"Coffee?" Piers asked politely.

"Thank you," Kathy replied, although she hadn't intended staying. "I think your cat's OK, but I'd guess she's a stray looking at the state of her. You'll need to sort out fleas and worms and get a vet to work out how old she is so you can have her spayed." She unsubtly scrutinised the kitchen while she talked and her host skilfully made some excellent coffee using a rather elderly machine. Just the Aga, no other means of cooking she could see and a neat rail of utensils above it.

Cupboards were all fitted with white doors and wooden worktops, faintly Mediterranean tiles above the sink and cooker. Original tiled floor from the look of it. Old, round pine table big enough to have four mismatched chairs round it but otherwise no hints at family dining. He had brought her into the kitchen through a side door direct from the car port and there was a door in the wall opposite the back of the house which meant there must be another room at the front. There was yet another door which was open so she could see it led to a box staircase and there was an expected flight of stairs going up but also one going down, which implied a cellar. He hadn't said whether he rented or owned it but either way she didn't like to think what the monthly costs of such a place must be, and was dying to know how many bedrooms it had. It was a heck of a lot of space for a man who appeared to live on his own and she had clearly way underestimated his salary.

"I like your kitchen," she offered politely. "Looks like you do your own cooking?"

Piers put their coffees on the table and sat back with her so the cat could climb onto his lap where she started her ablutions. His smile was just a bit sad. "Have to. Don't be fooled by the big house and the car. The car's on finance and I'm mortgaged up to the hilt so can't afford to eat out. I just couldn't resist all the space. Or the car. Although technically I only own half the house as the rooms above the car port are a separate let which doesn't belong to me so it's all a bit lopsided. How old do you think Puss is?"

Kathy couldn't imagine what it must be like to own even half a house and she really wanted to explore this one. "Hard to say. Her eyes are green and her ears are up so at least eight weeks I'd guess but she is very small. And yes, I'm sure it's a she. No signs of the mother cat or any others from a litter?"

"Just her. I know she's only been here one night but I'm going to miss the funny wee thing when she goes."

Odd choice of words, Kathy thought as he didn't sound the slightest bit Scots as his name implied but more upper-middle-class Surrey than Sutherland.

"Sorry, that's the native Irishman in me."

Kathy had the most peculiar feeling as though she had known this man for a long time and they knew what each other was thinking and were perfectly at ease in each other's company. "I'd never have guessed. Whereabouts?"

"I was born in Drumahoe, not far from Derry, but mainly grew up in County Donegal."

He clearly didn't want to talk about it but just for those few names Kathy caught a slight inflexion in his vowels that wasn't perfect Home Counties. "You've moved further than me then. Born and raised at the end of the District Line in Wimbledon. And no Womble jokes please, I think I've heard them all already. Why don't you keep the cat?"

"With my job?" he asked incredulously as he tickled the cat under the chin and she gazed up at him in total adoration.

"Keep her as a house cat. Litter tray, water, food and toys, she'll be quite happy on her own for a day or so. Are you often away for long spells?"

"Can be. I do on-call shifts a couple of times a month as well as my regular lines so can get sent anywhere in the world on a moment's notice. Another appeal of this place, I'm only twenty minutes from Heathrow on a good day. Jesus! How can something so small purr so loud?"

"That's cats for you," Kathy told him and wondered how anyone could make flying an aeroplane sound such a mundane job.

He looked across and saw her coffee cup was empty. "Sorry, I'm keeping you. Thanks for the cat care advice. I'll run you home as it's still raining."

Kathy got almost reluctantly to her feet and wished she could stay in the cosy kitchen with its purring cat and the red Aga. "Well, I'm sure I'll see you in the grocery store one midnight. Thank you for the coffee."

"You're very welcome. Been good to have someone to talk to."

"You've got a cat now," she pointed out although it was a bit sad to think such a pleasant man was maybe rather lonely. She briefly wondered how long he had been living on his own.

He gently put the cat back in her box. "Yes," he said thoughtfully. "I rather think I have."

"Got a name for her?"

"Can't I just call her Cat?"

"Like Audrey Hepburn you mean?"

"Sorry, you've lost me."

"*Breakfast at Tiffany's*? Her character had a cat called Cat."

Piers looked at the tiny tortoiseshell now curled snugly round in her box. "I could always call her Audrey."

Kathy liked his sense of humour now he seemed to have discovered it. "Good idea."

He carried on looking at the cat as though not wanting to make Kathy feel uncomfortable. "You can come and see her any time you like."

She rather liked that idea. At least this sanctuary was only a few streets away if she had to start running again and this calm, quiet man would look after her. "May I?"

"Of course. I'm home for a few days now then off again on my travels for a bit. Just come and knock on the side door. If the car's at home the odds are I am too."

Kathy was quite sorry to climb the stairs to her first-floor flat and spent the next few hours feeling rather lonely herself. In the space of three days two men had come into her life and they couldn't have been more different. She was glad she had met Piers properly at last even if he was a bit of a cliché with his big house and his Ferrari and, now she had looked at him properly, a very handsome face and a figure that made a tatty old coat and jeans look good. But he hadn't made a play for her. Like her he had been somehow defensive and a bit cold as though he didn't want any romantic involvements either. But he had had the compassion to take in a cat. The thought of it made her smile. Piers and Audrey. Her posh elderly neighbours from the Home Counties. Except they weren't. Nothing was ever what it seemed. Something stirring in her soul told her that with Jean-Guy and Piers now in her life things were about to get disrupted in a way she couldn't imagine. Two chance encounters made her think, for the first time, that maybe her life was about to change for ever.

Jean-Guy Dechaume arrived in Earl's Court on Wednesday morning with his cold almost gone, his tatty bag over one shoulder and Kathy's violin case in his hand.

There was only sincerity behind Kathy's smile as she flung open her front door, plus a huge relief that her violin had turned up safely.

"Hullo!" she cried in greeting. "Glad you made it. Any problems on the way?"

"No, nothing. Nobody bothered me at all. I am glad to be here too." He kissed both her cheeks in greeting and handed across the case. "Here is your violin. I think I should play that instead, it is much easier to carry." Neither of them mentioned the man at Liverpool Street station. Kathy had rung the Professor the day it happened to let him know and he had told her not to worry, it was most likely just someone looking for a session musician as he had said.

The flush cooled on Kathy's face although she knew his greeting was from habit and not from affection. "We'll have to buy your cello a tougher case. Come on in and I'll show you around then you'll have to look after yourself as I've got a rehearsal to go to." Kathy put her violin in an armchair and began her conducted tour.

"Sitting room where we spend most of the evenings when we're not working. Very good Broadwood baby grand that is technically Emma's but as she's moved into a very small flat she's said it can stay here. The television and record player are mine." She led Jean-Guy through into the kitchen. "Eating room. Emma and I rarely ate together so we each used to buy our own food. It was quite an event if we ever managed to share a meal. But I've stocked up so there's plenty for you to eat." Back through the sitting room into the hall and Kathy pushed open the bathroom door. "Washing

41

room. We took it in turns to clean it unless one or other was away on tour in which case it rather went by the board." Two steps down the hall and Kathy opened the door to the smaller bedroom at the front of the flat. "And this is for you. Make yourself at home. I'll go and make some coffee so come into the kitchen when you're ready."

Jean-Guy noticed his cello in one corner of the room, flung his bag onto the bed which he saw an efficient Kathy had made up for him, and announced: "I am ready."

"Yes," Kathy agreed ruefully. "You don't have much to unpack."

"I have letter for you," Jean-Guy remembered. He took an envelope from the pocket of his baggy tweed coat and handed it to her before throwing his coat over his bag and she saw he was still in the same clothes he had been wearing last time she had seen him. "I also have some money which Professor Mihaly has given me. No, which Professor Mihaly has <u>lent</u> me. But I think it is all in the letter."

Kathy opened the envelope as the two went in to the kitchen.

Dear Kathy

I am sending you one refugee with £100 in his pocket. Please, please buy him some new clothes as he only has what you can see him wearing! I am also putting in with this note a cheque to cover the first two months of his rent, with a little extra to meet the bills as Emma told me you share the living costs.

Take care of yourself, and ring me if you think I can help.

Petr Mihaly

42

Kathy pocketed the note and the cheque and collected mugs and coffee from the cupboard while the kettle came to the boil. She looked out of the large rear-facing window with its view of the District Line and wondered how Audrey was getting on in her cosy kitchen. In spite of Piers' offer she hadn't been back to see the cat as her concert tonight had kept her practising at home during the day while the neighbours were out, and as she didn't know what kind of hours a pilot worked she hadn't wanted to disturb him in the evenings.

"We have to go shopping," she said abruptly trying not to think of Piers and feeling a bit guilty she hadn't taken him up on his offer to visit the cat.

"Yes, Professor Mihaly begged me to get clothes. All I have is what you see and set of full concert clothes in the bag. And your sweater, of course, which I will give back when I have washed it." He located the milk in the fridge and put it on the kitchen table.

"Please keep the sweater. It's an old one and I have plenty more. Do you take sugar?"

Jean-Guy shook his head. "I am nuisance to you," he said miserably. "I wear your clothes, I have no money and I have no job."

"I've found you a job," Kathy announced, unable to keep all the smugness out of her voice. "There's a small restaurant down the road that wants someone to wash up. I saw a note in their window yesterday so called in and asked. Cash in hand and nobody tells the tax man as you're not legally allowed to work yet, but they were refugees themselves once so they're happy to help you. They'll pay you each day according to how much gets done and it's from seven in the evening until midnight, days as you want them, just arrange the evening before."

The look on Jean-Guy's face was indescribable and Kathy was afraid she had offended him. Why on earth would a famous concert cellist want to spoil his hands by washing up in a restaurant? "I'll keep looking for you but it was all I could find."

His reply consoled her. "Kathy, you really are an angel from heaven. I shall wash up with no problems and not telling the tax man."

"You don't mind that it might ruin your hands for playing?"

Jean-Guy shrugged. "My hands have done hard work before and they will cope."

The kettle boiled then so Kathy was able to busy herself making coffee as she continued, "You can start tonight if you want to. I'll give you a set of keys in a minute. I've got a concert tonight so I'm glad you brought my fiddle. I'll be away this weekend but then I've got just rehearsals and recordings with an orchestra until April when I'm away for a month on tour with them."

Jean-Guy seemed only to be half listening as he looked out of the window and watched a train in the District Line cutting at the foot of the garden. "How can I ever thank you enough? You have shown me nothing but kindness and I am total stranger to you."

Kathy fought down her feelings of pity for this lost and confused man. "Let's just say I have a sympathy for victims. When do you want to go shopping? Only I have to be at my rehearsal at two o'clock."

"May we go after coffee?"

"Of course. Drink up." Kathy tried to forget the illustrations of Moly in his black smoking jacket. "What sort of clothes are you looking for?"

Jean-Guy shrugged. "Casual, I suppose. I have full concert clothes. White tie, tails and everything."

"Couldn't you have managed to bring a bit more with you?"

"No, because it was hot weather. I had enough trouble just to bring coat. I could not bring case as well."

Kathy didn't take Jean-Guy up to the expensive shops in Kensington but kept it more local and affordable in Earl's Court, including some of the cleaner charity shops. She noticed he spent his money wisely and the only thing he bought new was some stronger shoes to replace the tatty sneakers that seemed to have walked many miles.

Kathy's next concert was with a small ensemble which specialised in contemporary music. She had played with them before and ordinarily she would have been looking forward to the festival that weekend in which they were playing. Shoenberg, Carter, Davies, all flowed from her violin as if by instinct throughout that afternoon's rehearsal. Kathy Fairbanks was not known for being noisy and vivacious so nobody thought too much of it when she sat there and played the notes faultlessly. Her fellow musicians would have been surprised, almost shocked, if they had had any idea of the thoughts occupying her mind as she kept going over and over again how her life had changed since Emma's wedding day.

Not so long ago she could never have called two men her friends. She hadn't had any close friends except for the faithful Emma who wouldn't leave her. Even now that awful shadow was still in her life. Still holding her back no matter how much she tried to break away from it.

But now it was as though someone had torn a tiny split in a dark cloth and if she looked through that split she could see a brighter life ahead with Jean-Guy and Piers as part of it. She liked both men but differently. Piers was the cool, independent one earning his living flying among the clouds. He would offer her a life of adventure and mad excitement but somehow she sensed he had a darker side to his life. Why had he so completely schooled the Irish from his voice? Jean-Guy had done perhaps the bravest, or most foolish, thing he could have done with his life. He had taken his one leap of faith and needed to get over it. He wouldn't offer her excitement and adventure. He was the timid, nervous Moly, lost in a strange world, who needed her to look after him.

She declined the offer to join the others in the pub over the road from the rehearsal room but didn't tell them she was anxious to get home to make sure her new flatmate was still safe. Kathy didn't often drive to her various jobs as it was in so many ways easier to get around London on the Tube but this particular rehearsal had been almost out in the suburbs and parking had been easy but as she drove back to Earl's Court after the rehearsal it was stop-start at all the lights and junctions and she was glad she wasn't fighting a Ferrari in all that traffic. Her elderly car stalled at some lights and within two seconds the driver behind her had given her a blast on the horn. Must be nice flying planes, she thought, with no traffic up in the sky. Jean-Guy hadn't given any indications of whether he could drive or not but it wasn't so long ago she had been expressly forbidden to learn. So it had been one of the first things she had done after she had run away. Which had unexpectedly resulted in a brief but very intense relationship with her driving instructor and Emma had been quite proud of her. Kathy didn't often think of that relationship. It hadn't ended badly, the driving lessons had continued until she had passed her test but it had taught her sex wasn't the answer to her problems.

Jean-Guy was playing scales on the cello when she went into the flat but he stopped on hearing her call, "Anyone home?"

He replied from his room as the door was open. "Why do you ask when you know the answer?"

"It's what Emma and I always did. Any news from the Home Office?" Kathy asked as she stopped in the doorway.

"It is much too early." Jean-Guy got to his feet rather stiffly for one of his age and stretched upwards and sideways a bit as though easing an ache.

"Back trouble?" she asked lightly. "Too much spring-cleaning."

Jean-Guy looked at her through his Moly spectacles. "Pardon?"

Kathy was annoyed with herself for speaking out loud. "Sorry, you just remind me of a character in a book."

"Ah, someone who spring-cleans?"

"Um. Yes, sort of." However she put it, it wasn't going to sound good.

"I'm afraid I don't read too well in English. What is the book?"

Thankful he wouldn't know it, Kathy admitted "*Wind in the Willows*."

"*Le Vent dans les Saules*. I have read it in French and there is only one character who spring-cleans. Am I then your Mole?"

She looked at him and then they both laughed. "Sorry, I just can't get it out of my mind."

"I like Mole. He is also the one who ran away."

"Yes, I suppose he did," Kathy agreed.

Jean-Guy was still smiling gently to himself. "Do you think I should eat before I go to work?"

"Are you hungry?" Kathy asked, surprised by the question.

"No, not really. I just eat whenever there is food these days."

"You mean those days. These days you eat when you want."

"Very true. In that case I shall not eat yet. But maybe a cup of tea."

"Well I'll eat now as I'm playing tonight. I'll make a cup for you too as I'll be having one anyway."

The two went into the kitchen where Kathy set about preparing her meal. Jean-Guy sat at the table and watched her without speaking. She found such scrutiny unnerving which made her clumsy and she dropped the metal lid of the butter dish taking it from the fridge to the table. It hadn't helped that she had let that awful black shadow drift across her mind during the rehearsal. She handed Jean-Guy a cup of tea and it seemed to rouse him from his thoughts.

"Thank you. May I have a key or will you let me in tonight?"

Kathy was grateful to have practicalities to think about as she was almost getting scared now as she could feel the blackness building up in the room with her. A dark shadow in the corner. "Oh. Um, I'll let you in tonight. Sorry, I'm all a bit muddled today what with the concert tonight and everything." There was no way she was going to admit anything more than that. "I haven't been able to find Emma's keys so she must still have them and I can't remember where we put the spares. I'm sure we do have spares. My concert's due to end at ten and you won't finish before midnight."

Jean-Guy made no attempt to touch her but waited until she had sat at the table and was clearly having problems eating a cheese sandwich. "Kathy," he said softly and she jumped. "Sorry, I don't mean to scare you. Can you not talk to me about what it is that frightens you so much? I know I'm not very big and strong but I will do my best to look after you if you would like me to?"

Kathy put down the sandwich which tasted like dry cardboard. "I'm sorry. It's nothing you've said or done. I just had some unhappy thoughts this afternoon." She looked towards the window to see night was falling and the reflection in the glass showed her two people sharing the table in the kitchen as though they were old friends. But this was London and she saw the flashes of blue light from the Tube and way up in the sky where the street lights scared away the stars she saw the winking lights of an aeroplane. The shadow of a bird crossed the window and made her jump.

"You can talk to me," came the soft reassurance from the man at the table with her. "I can keep secrets."

She looked into his worried face and knew he could see the shadows in her eyes. "About four years ago," she started then stopped. It was too hard to tell, even now. Even to this kind and sympathetic man who had probably experienced things far worse. Why else would he have run from his home? "No, it's a story for another time. I have a concert to play in and you have to go and wash up."

"Tomorrow," he suggested kindly. "You have no concert and I will have all day to listen to you."

The practicality of his voice helped her a lot. "Tomorrow. Thursday. OK, I'm not leaving until Friday morning." She had an idea and thought it would work. "If you like we can go and see if a cat called Audrey is at home."

Jean-Guy looked at her slightly quizzically. "And does this cat called Audrey come with a human?"

"Yes." Kathy stopped and changed her mind. She didn't want to make him feel even more lost by telling him that the cat's human was an enigmatic and beautiful man with hair like the wing of a raven and who earned his living flying the rich and elite in Concorde. "Yes, she does but I have a feeling he said he was going to be working away tomorrow," she said to get herself out of any explanations.

"Another day for the cat, then?" he asked lightly but she could feel he was watching her very intently.

"Another day. And, to save you asking, Audrey's human is not my boyfriend. I don't have a boyfriend. And, to save you thinking about it, right now I don't want one."

She looked at him then and to her vast relief he smiled hugely and clutched his chest. "Ah, now you break my heart. It is true what they say about you English women."

"Oh? And what is that?"

He just laughed. "Maybe you should cook your sandwich? It may taste better?"

"Yes, maybe it will," Kathy agreed and began to think that perhaps this well-known and talented cellist, like a Concorde pilot, wouldn't be interested in a dull little violinist as a potential girlfriend. Funnily enough she was more sad about Jean-Guy feeling like that than if it had been Piers.

Kathy had to leave the flat first that evening, carrying her violin and her viola on the Tube as the concert was on the South Bank and she hated trying to park her car round Waterloo. It was a routine, rather dull concert with a small audience who applauded politely at the end but clearly hadn't enjoyed the music. She was glad to get back to the solitude of her flat where she had a shower then put on a late-night film to cheer herself up before Jean-Guy came in. Annoyingly, she had found the spare set of keys almost as soon as she had got in after the concert and realised Emma must still have hers. She was just beginning to wish she had left the doors on the latch, even though she wasn't supposed to, when the street door bell buzzed. Thankfully she admitted Jean-Guy to the flat and held out a pair of keys.

"Silver one is the street door, the other one is the flat door. Found them about five minutes after I'd got in and in just the place I should have looked for them first."

She caught a scent of the hot water and detergent on his hands as he took the keys from her and noticed that he had borrowed an old coat that Emma had left behind and asked Kathy to take to the charity shop. The coat was long and dark and had a hood and from the state of his hair, Jean-Guy had kept the hood up while he was walking outside. It occurred to her that perhaps the new defector hadn't wanted to be seen out and about on the streets of London. Such subterfuge hadn't crossed her mind and she consciously tried not to think of it

"Thank you. Very annoying for you," he sympathised and paused, obviously trying to judge her mood. "You look very tired. I'm sorry if it was my fault. Was it a good concert?"

"No, not really. Good night. Help yourself to some more food if you want it."

He could tell from her face that she didn't want to chat and he knew what a less-successful concert felt like. "No, I will go to bed too. It has been a long day and they gave me food at the restaurant. I have never eaten Lebanese before but it was good. I told them I have been a waiter in the past so they said I could maybe try out with them which would be a pay rise. But, go to bed. We can talk tomorrow."

Kathy let him give her a slight hug and a soft kiss on the cheek. "Yes, tomorrow. Good night," she agreed and went to her bed lonely, confused, and very sad. Lying awake until nearly dawn looking at the shadows moving round her room.

The next morning began for Kathy with a loud knock at her bedroom door. She modestly pulled on her dressing gown over her nightdress before telling Jean-Guy he could come in. She felt as though she hadn't slept at all but managed a weary smile for the man who handed across her pink mug with the daisy on it.

"I'm sorry," he said apologetically. "Did I wake you? It is already late and I didn't think you would still be asleep."

"Bad night," she said vaguely and took the mug from him. The coffee was hot so she put the mug on her bedside table and saw he was holding out her post.

"You have a letter," Jean-Guy told her and handed it over. He was about to turn away when Kathy looked at the envelope he had given her, shrieked once and hid under the bedclothes.

"Kathy?" he asked anxiously, but thinking maybe he would learn why this beautiful woman was so scared of, if not him, then of something in her life. "Whatever is the matter?" He cautiously peeped under the blankets and two enormous blue eyes looked back at him. It had been a long time since he had seen such terror and he had thought never to see it again. He reached out towards her but she just retreated even further. "What is it? Is it what you couldn't tell me yesterday?"

She stuffed the letter into his hand from under the covers and knew she had to tell him now. "This. Oh, I don't know where to start."

Jean-Guy folded back the blankets a bit so at least she could breathe. The envelope seemed innocuous enough. Handwritten in a rather over-large but clearly masculine hand. Proper ink, not a ball point. First class stamp, posted in High Barnet yesterday. "Start where you like. I have all day to listen to you," he said kindly and sat on the side of the bed, close enough for comfort but not so close as to be threatening.

"My ex," she half gulped, half wailed. "I couldn't see it at the time but he was… he was abusing me. He told me which concerts to play in. His friends had to be my friends but mine couldn't be any longer. I was so stupid I couldn't see it. He told me that he was helping me and I believed him. We got engaged but I knew it was

53

the wrong thing to do. If I said anything he... he hurt me. And then, the day before our wedding, he thought I was going to run away so he... he..."

"He what?" came the gentle encouragement.

"He raped me," Kathy whispered hoarsely, telling her secret at last.

Jean-Guy said nothing but offered her his hands and let her pull herself into his arms so he could hold her while the tears poured down her face and her breath came in huge gulping sobs.

Kathy couldn't have expressed the relief she felt that this most sympathetic of men finally knew what it was that haunted her life. She was safe now as he held her gently, not so tightly she didn't feel she could break away, but not so uncertainly it felt as though he didn't mean it. She sniffed rather inelegantly and continued, believing he would understand. "And that," she told him, "was when I saw the raven."

It made no sense to him so he waited for a moment, just holding her and remembering how his sister had been like this when she had come home that time after she and her friends had met the same fate at the hands of a regiment of Soviet soldiers. He had to remind himself this wasn't Marianne.

"It was on my balcony," she tried to explain. "It told me to run away. So I did. And I carried on running. For years."

Jean-Guy wasn't quite sure how a large bird fitted in to the story so he kept his tone quietly practical. "Have you told anyone?" he asked softly.

"Only Emma. I was too ashamed. We were engaged. Who would have believed me?"

"I believe you. Your true friends would have believed you."

"Emma could see what was happening but I just couldn't. She wouldn't let him drive her away. We used to meet in secret and try to share concert bookings if we could just so we could talk. She let me stay with her dad for a few months to get over the worst. It was four years ago now. And now he just won't leave me alone. Everywhere I go, first he gets my address, I don't know how, I don't even register to vote any more. So he writes to me. Then he gets my telephone number. Again, I don't know how as I'm ex-directory and all my bookings are done through my agent. So he starts phoning me. Then he starts following me home. He's chased me through the streets before now but he can't run very fast and I can. I used to lose him on the Underground and then go home. I've been safe here because I was sharing with Emma, I should have done that years ago. But now she's left and he's found me again. How did he know she'd left?"

Jean-Guy felt there was probably a perfectly simple explanation, but he couldn't think of it right now. "I know very little of your laws but surely this cannot be allowed in England?"

"I just can't bear the thought of having to tell it all to the police. What good would it do anyway? I think he's mad. The best I could hope for is a court injunction telling him to stay away. If he breaks that he goes to jail and then he comes out again and it starts all over again. They can't send him to prison for life for stalking me."

"If we only lived in Czechoslovakia I could find someone to kill him for you. I could kill him for you if you like?"

The offer was so serious, Kathy was shocked. "You can't just kill someone."

"Yes I can. Anyone can if they really have to."

"But then you'd go to prison or get sent back to Czechoslovakia. Why are we even talking about it? The whole idea is ridiculous."

"Maybe now, at this time, yes. Would you like me to read his letter to you?"

"No. Just throw it away."

"That is another way of hiding on the Underground. Listen. I will read to you."

Kathy closed her eyes. Somehow hearing the words in Jean-Guy's accented English was not as bad as reading them herself. And he clearly struggled to read anything at all in English.

Dearest Kathy

I heard that Emma has married, taken her vow to honour and obey a man.

I'll call at your flat at 8 on Monday evening so you can honour and obey me too. You know it is what you want. What you need from me. Without me you are nothing.

All my love, Ricci

Jean-Guy thought that was in so many ways the most threatening letter he had ever read. "What usually happens now?" he asked simply.

"I don't read them. I just see the envelope and then I run."

"Then I think perhaps on Monday night you will be at home."

Kathy panicked. "I can't. He's going to rape me again, or kill me."

"He won't kill you," Jean-Guy assured her quietly. "Because I will kill him first if he so much as speaks loudly to you. Did he hit you much?"

After he had learned so much, it wasn't difficult to tell him. "Not at first. And he was always careful. Never anywhere that would show. And after every time he told me he was sorry, said he'd never do it again and then we'd go to bed. I was too scared to refuse. But that last day. That last morning, it was the day before our wedding and I knew I needed time to think, away from him and his bullying. So I asked if I could go home to Mum and Dad; to spend my last single night in my old home. In some ways that was true, but he wouldn't believe me. He just threw me against the wall and I couldn't breathe properly but I was trying to push him off me…"

Jean-Guy gathered her back into his arms and rocked her like a child. "Hush," he said softly. "He won't hurt you any more. Ever again." She began to calm down a bit and he gently brushed the tear-sodden hair back from her face and an idea came to him. It sounded a bit desperate but it was the best he could think of. "Now drink your coffee then you and I are going to go shopping for wedding rings."

"Do what?" she asked incredulously, thinking she hadn't expected that as a response at all.

"When he turns up we tell him I've married you just so I can stay in the country."

"He'll kill you too."

"No he won't because we will have witnesses. And if we say we have married then he has lost control. And what he did to you was all about control. That has to be taken away from him for him to let you go."

"I can see your point, but I'm not convinced it'll work."

"I have learned a lot about control and pain. And trust. You must trust your Moly on this one."

Kathy had to smile. "Sorry."

"Don't be, I think it is rather fun. So if I am Moly then he is King Weasel."

"There aren't any women in the book except the jail keeper's daughter. Which I suppose is appropriate for me as I feel as though he still keeps me in a prison."

"Did he stop you from seeing your friends?"

Kathy nodded. "Except Emma. And he would have stopped that too if he'd known. There are people I'm in groups and orchestras with but they're not really going-down-the-pub type friends."

"Are there any you could invite round on Monday evening?"

"I've never invited anyone round before."

"Can you ask a violinist and a viola player? I will tell café I need Monday as my night off. Then we can say we are practising quartets."

"But you said you wouldn't play again until you are free."

"True, but I have a job and home now so I am nearly there. Also if he sees you as part of a group he has lost control over your friends."

"I know a viola player who lives in Fulham but he doesn't play much as he has an injured hand." Kathy paused as a thought occurred to her that maybe he was breaking his promise to himself so he could help her. It seemed unlikely somehow.

"Is he good?"

"For short periods of time he is the best viola player you could imagine. Probably because he's never played a violin. He'll be OK for one evening."

Jean-Guy got the impression there had maybe been a bit more than music between Kathy and the viola player, but this wasn't the time to ask. "And for violin?"

"Well, Emma will still be away. There's Philippa, she's quite local in South Ken but she's, well, slightly eccentric. And can be a bit of a diva. She'll only come if she can play first. We both play in a chamber group so we've often worked together, but not really socialised and she knows Danny as I managed to persuade him to play a couple of gigs when we were desperate for viola players. She doesn't play so much now she and her boyfriend have got a baby on the way so she'll probably be glad to get out for an evening."

"Shall we see if they are available? If there's one thing you mustn't be on Monday it's alone and I would be happier if it was more than just me with you. He only told you to be at home so you are not disobeying him."

"He won't like to see me play second."

"Even better. But we will have to tell other two what we are doing. Are you OK with that?"

Panic grabbed at Kathy again and she physically looked round for the shadow in her life.

"It's OK, he's not here," came the soft tones beside her.

Kathy blinked as she realised for the first time in four years that there were no shadows in the flat. Just lots of winter sunlight coming in through the thin curtains and spotlighting the dust motes' dance.

"No, he isn't, is he? And I'm going to start knitting again. He hated to see me knitting. He said it made me look like his granny."

"Perfect. You can knit me a sweater," Jean-Guy said hopefully.

Kathy smiled back at him and nearly kissed his cheek. "It will be my pleasure. We can go and buy some wool while we're getting wedding rings. Not proper wedding rings though, they're way too expensive. Or are we not doing that any more?"

"Will the other two gossip?"

"Danny won't. He doesn't say much at all really. Doubt if Philippa will, we're more co-workers than best friends."

"Then we shall tell him we are married. It's what he never expects for you." Jean-Guy had a sudden thought. "Does either of them have a cat called Audrey by any chance?"

"Oh, no," Kathy smiled. "Audrey's owner isn't a musician, he flies aeroplanes. And eats noodles. Now be a sweetheart and put me on some toast please while I get myself decent."

Jean-Guy went off to the kitchen to try and work out how to make toast, silently hoping he wouldn't burn the house down.

Fool's Fanfare

Kathy felt almost nervous as she opened the door of her flat at 7.30 on Monday evening. "Hi, Danny, thanks for coming."

He just smiled and vaguely kissed her on the cheek before he passed her in an appalling stink of cigarette smoke. "Pleasure," he said absently as he wandered down the hall.

Jean-Guy was in the sitting room, rearranging the furniture to make room for a string quartet and he looked up as a man in his thirties ambled in looking a bit lost. Kathy certainly knew some waifs and strays, Jean-Guy thought to himself but he could see that she would find this man attractive in a scruffy kind of way and guessed maybe his original supposition about the viola player had been true. Kathy followed the new arrival into the room.

"Jean-Guy Dechaume, please meet Danny Tarling."

There was a bit of a pause between the two men before they shook hands.

"Bloody hell, have you defected?" Danny asked and hooked his long hair behind his ears.

"In a word, yes. And are you a relative of David Tarling?"

"Nephew. Ninth generation in the family to play the viola."

"Related to Donald?"

"Half-brother. I'm the elder but he's the professional viola player."

"That is one hell of a legacy."

"Yeah. Pity I can't live up to it," was the wry comment with a glance at a badly scarred left hand but no explanation was offered.

A manic rhythm played on the street door buzzer.

Danny and Kathy looked at each other. "Phil," they said in unison.

Kathy went to answer the door and Jean-Guy wondered why Danny had moved to one side of the room. He got his answer a few moments later when an impressively tall and buxom young woman barrelled into the room and made a beeline for the two men. She hugged them both and kissed them on the cheek, enveloping them in clouds of perfume and green sari fabric.

"Danny, darling, how are you?" She didn't expect a reply from the notoriously shy young man. "Well, hello, stranger. Philippa Williamson-Brown. Do call me Pippa. And who are you?"

"Jean-Guy Dechaume."

"Oh good God. Have you defected at last? Saw you in Oslo in 76. Totally brilliant. Well, glad you're here. So looking forward to playing with you."

Jean-Guy was convinced he heard Danny and Kathy snort quietly with laughter in the background.

Pippa went round the room like a bright green whirlwind and shed sari fabric scarf, green faux-fur coat and a pair of neon green mittens with matching beanie hat. Underneath it all she wore a loose kaftan in every colour of the rainbow which did nothing to disguise the fact she was heavily pregnant. White cowboy boots somehow managed to thud even on the carpeted floor and the other three just looked on as she twirled herself neatly into the first violin chair with a triumphant grin on her face.

"Crack open the gin, darling," she said to Kathy. "I don't suppose you've got any Campari?" She pretended to raise a glass. "Here's to playing quartets with Dechaume and Tarling, two of the heavyweights of our world. Even if you are a pair of skinny wretches."

"Tea," Kathy said firmly.

"Oh, darling. How sordid."

"I'll help you," Danny offered and the two went off to the kitchen.

"So, Jean-Guy, what have you got lined up for us to play?"

Her pronunciation of his name was excruciating but Jean-Guy couldn't help but like this outspoken diva of a woman, even if she was taller than him. "I'd thought maybe Borodin's Second?"

"Oh, good choice. Most people want to play Haydn and I find him sooo boring. Don't you, darling? I suppose he's OK for amateurs and you do have a very dodgy viola player."

Before Jean-Guy could defend one of his favourite composers as well as the luckless violist, the other two came back with a tray of mugs of tea and the biscuit tin.

"Digestives?" Phil asked hopefully.

"With chocolate on," Kathy assured her.

The other three took their seats in the quartet formation but held mugs of tea rather than instruments. There was a short pause while nobody was quite sure what to say.

Jean-Guy caught Kathy's eye and cleared his throat. "OK, Pippa and Danny, we have to ask you to take part in a bit of a plot."

Jean-Guy Dechaume, celebrated cellist and defector, had never thought he would laugh as much as he did that evening. At one point he had to excuse himself and go to the toilet just to give his aching ribs a chance to recover. He had heard Kathy play and knew she was perfectly capable of playing the second violin part but Philippa had the attention span of a flea and was inclined to chat, while Danny kept swearing every time his hand hurt and he played a wrong note. Sitting next to the viola player, Jean-Guy could clearly see that Danny's left hand had at some point met with an accident. The back of the hand was badly scarred as though it had been burned and the middle two fingers looked as though they had been broken and left to mend themselves. Creepily the thumb seemed to have one joint too many in it and Jean-Guy's musician's eye could see the other man was barely using the thumb at all as he played which made his technique peculiar to say the least but didn't stop him flying through the most difficult passages of the music.

At nearly nine o'clock the viola player pleaded for a break as his playing was getting worse and worse. He and Philippa leaned out of the kitchen window smoking cigarettes while discussing the music with the two still in the living room when the street door bell buzzed.

"Thought he wasn't coming," Kathy muttered to Jean-Guy.

"This is his mind game. He thinks you have been waiting alone and thinking of him."

Kathy went to the intercom. "Hullo?" she asked and hoped the two in the kitchen wouldn't start giggling again and spoil the effect.

"Kathy, love, how are you?"

"Oh, OK." She pressed the buzzer to let the arrival in and Jean-Guy went to get the other two from the kitchen feeling as though he was rounding up a couple of naughty children.

Kathy let Richard into the flat and dodged away from the kiss he tried to land on her lips. She could hear the other three in the living room and it gave her the confidence she needed. From the way he didn't react, she guessed the man confronting her thought he could hear something on the TV, he had that smile of certainty on his face that once she had found endearing, then frightening and now it just made her feel sick. She began backing away along the hall towards the others.

"Beautiful as ever," he told her and tried to catch her to him but she, familiar with every lump and bump in the floor from creeping home in the dark, could reverse down that hall faster than he could walk it forwards. She held up defensive hands and as they had hoped, he caught a glimpse of the silver ring she was wearing. "What's that?" he asked and made to grab her hand but missed as she was too quick for him.

Kathy was already in the sitting room. "Sorry, we're just in the middle of a quartet practice."

The other three were back in their quartet places and looked faintly astonished. Kathy thought they looked like a trio of fools and then realised they wouldn't have known her ex was more than a foot taller than her and weighed over twice as much. She saw the mixed look of fury and apprehension on Jean-Guy's face when he saw the physical size of her torturer.

"I don't think you ever met Philippa and Danny and this is Jean-Guy. I, um…" she said pleasantly then stopped, unable to go on with the charade.

The magnificent Philippa physically rose to the occasion as she was the tallest and widest of the four of them. "He's her husband, darling. Married just this morning. And still they insisted we come to rehearse our little group even though this is their wedding night. Isn't that sweet? Mind you, they made us celebrate with tea and didn't crack open the Bolly."

Danny took his cue and regarded her solemnly. "Personally I prefer Moët."

"Snob," Philippa challenged.

"Man of discernment," he corrected without a smile on his face.

Richard was looking at the four of them as though he didn't know what had happened. Before he could speak, the street door buzzer sounded again.

Philippa crossed the room in five paces and looked out of the living room window which overlooked the street. "Know anyone who drives a black sports car? If my dreams have come true it's a Ferrari?"

"Yes actually. He's a Concorde pilot." Kathy didn't dare look at Pippa, obviously protecting her like a mother hen, but fled to the intercom. "Hullo? Piers?"

"Hi, Catwoman. Thank God I've got the right flat at last. Can you take Audrey for a couple of days please? I've been called in as the only available who knows O'Hare and she's too little to leave for so long."

"Bring her up. First floor," Kathy invited and opened the street door.

A few moments later a breathless Piers strode into the flat with the cardboard box in his arms with Audrey howling her protests from inside it. He wasn't trying to hide anything today and looked extremely handsome in his pilot's uniform. "Sorry, I'm double parked as it is. I'm only doing one on-call shift this month and the bastards paged me just when I was starting to think I'd got away with it. Thank you." He put the box on the dining table and dumped a Sainsbury's carrier bag next to it. "I'll be back Wednesday latest as I'm holding a line to JFK on Thursday. Want to give me your number or will it be OK just to call by?"

"I'll give you the number, I may be out at a rehearsal or something." Rather than give her number out loud so Richard could hear it, Kathy quickly wrote it on the pad next to the phone and handed the page over, and the human tornado dashed out of the house again. A few seconds later there was a cacophony of car horns, Piers' voice yelling abuse and the roar of the Ferrari's engine as he set off.

"Oh, my, God," Pippa intoned. "What, or rather who, the hell was that? Captain's uniform I do believe and, honestly, a Ferrari?" She sat in her chair and fanned herself with her hands. "Darling, I think I am overheating like a Morris Minor in August. And don't you dare give him that kitten back without introducing me to him first."

Kathy didn't know whether to laugh or cry. They needn't have worried about the sham wedding idea. Richard just turned on his heel and slammed out of the flat without saying a word.

Jean-Guy looked at the tiny tortoiseshell cat who stepped so elegantly out of the box and sat on the dining table as if wondering what all the fuss was about. "Let me guess," he said to Kathy, who had decided to laugh about it after all. "This is Audrey."

"You know he's just left you with the cat, don't you?" Emma asked when she rang for a chat on Wednesday morning. Kathy got the impression it was a guilt call because of landing her with Jean-Guy and also a bit of not very subtle fishing to see whether things were progressing on a personal level to her satisfaction. She seemed quite disappointed there was nothing exciting to report there, but profoundly relieved to learn they had almost certainly seen the last of Richard.

Kathy had thought her friend would like to hear the story of the chaotic evening but she hadn't laughed at all. She seemed more concerned that Kathy had been chatting with an unknown man in Sainsbury's and had focussed on Piers instead.

"Is he really a Concorde pilot?"

She was so positive Kathy started to have doubts. "Why would he lie about it?"

"Well you must admit it's pretty unlikely. And why make such a point of it if he wasn't after something?"

Kathy thought of the way Piers had mentioned how he earned his living and hadn't been the slightest bit boastful. "I just thought he was a policeman when I met him in the corner shop."

There was a short pause. "Oh, that one," Emma said, sounding far from pleased. "Yes, I remember you telling me about the nice policeman who let you have the last packet of custard creams one evening. I bet you anything you like you've still got that cat when I'm back from honeymoon next week. Did he leave you any money for cat food?"

"Um, he left a couple of tins of food, I must admit he didn't leave any litter but it was all such a rush. But you've never met him, so don't be so judgemental." She guessed it wouldn't be a good idea to let Emma know that the suspected conman had admitted his car was on finance and his house heavily mortgaged. Although, to her mind, if you were a conman, you just showed off the Ferrari and the large town house borderline Kensington and didn't let on you hadn't actually paid for them yet. But then again, she didn't know much about conmen and the starving kitten routine had certainly got her round there.

"He'll have worked out in the first five minutes you haven't got any money so of course you're safe from him. Anyway, got to go, we're booked on an evening cruise to see the Northern Lights."

"Come round next week and tell me all about it."

Kathy looked round the living room as Audrey raced out of the kitchen like a mad thing, leaped on and off the dining table then shot up the curtains just as the street door buzzer went and she heard Jean-Guy go to answer it.

"Oh I will. And I look forward to meeting the cat."

"Audrey. Her name is Audrey. And she will have gone home by next week."

"'Bye, Kath!"

Kathy put the phone down and turned to see who had come into the flat. She couldn't believe the timing when Piers came in behind Jean-Guy and from the way the two were chatting she guessed they had introduced themselves. Piers wasn't looking so smart this time in jeans and the shabby green sweater that was about four sizes too big for him and with a moth hole in one elbow. To her disbelief Audrey launched herself in one spectacular leap from on top of the curtains and landed neatly on Piers' shoulder. He didn't seem the slightest bit bothered although it must have given him quite a shock but calmly plucked the cat off and gave her a cuddle before putting her gently down on the floor.

"How was the trip to O'Hare?" Kathy asked.

"Boring. Sorry, but I thought I'd got away with that on-call shift. At least this time I was only heavy crew on a 747." He saw her looking at him and probably trying to work out how much he weighed. "Think of it as a spare pilot on a long-haul in case something happens to one of the operational crew. Sorry, we have our own terminology. Just like you violinists no doubt."

"True," she agreed. "I do have to know my up-bows from my pizzicato. And what is holding a line?"

"A line is the shifts I bid to do when the rotas come out. And my regular crew pick the same ones so we stick together. Kind of unusual but we're used to each other now. On-call work is mainly only for the newest pilots but it breaks the monotony in what would otherwise be a routine kind of job as I usually only fly the JFK route, and it keeps the bosses happy." He smiled in that self-effacing way he had. "Plus I'm still type-rated for a few aeroplanes in the fleet, which is even more unusual, but I'm useful as I live only half an hour away. So my bosses love me, most of the time, and we work out a few deals between us. How's Audrey been behaving? I hope she hasn't been any trouble?"

"We're thinking of abducting her," Kathy told him while still trying to process all the information. It sounded a bit too much like rule-bending and she was veering towards Emma's point of view now. But he made it sound so believable. She stuck with talking about the cat. "She's just a total sweetheart and I'm glad you weren't half way to Caracas when she chose your doorstep to collapse on."

He gave her one of his lovely smiles. "How much do I owe you? Sorry it was all such a rush."

And now she believed him again and thought Emma was way off the mark. "One pound eighty five for some food and a bag of cat litter."

Piers cheerfully handed over a five pound note. "That's a bit extra for the claw marks in your furniture. Hope she didn't go for the piano."

"She's been sitting on it a lot," Jean-Guy told him truthfully. "Looking as though she's waiting for one of us to play it to her, but neither of us can. Do you play?" he finished politely.

Kathy noticed there was just the tiniest pause.

"No," Piers said almost curtly and looked away from the Broadwood. He gave the carrier bag he was holding to Jean-Guy. "Here you go, souvenirs of Chicago for you both. Nice city, cow of an airport."

Jean-Guy looked inside. "Peanut butter and grape jelly. Do we eat them together?"

"I do."

"Have you time for coffee?" Kathy asked, wondering if they had somehow offended him. "It's only instant but you always seem to be in a hurry so won't take long to make."

Piers gave a little shrug. "Why not. Thank you. Be nice to have a chat without engine noise in the background."

Audrey returned to the top of the curtains watching very carefully as the three people in her life settled at the dining table with coffees and the few chocolate digestive biscuits Philippa had left them.

"How did you get into flying?" Jean-Guy asked curiously after a few moments of silent drinking.

Piers didn't seem to want to talk about it. "Usual way. RAF after school, learned to fly, finished my commission then went freelance for a few years. Finished up in commercial. Nothing remarkable." He suddenly smiled and his blue eyes twinkled again. "Mind you, when I say freelance, I was out island-hopping in the Caribbean carrying anything from presidents to pineapples."

Kathy doubted Emma again now and a ridiculous thought occurred to her that she had found the Ratty to Jean-Guy's Moly.

"Sounds interesting," Jean-Guy said to Piers. "I sometimes wish I'd done something useful like that. I think my parents wanted me to go into the civil service and get a steady office job rather than be an irresponsible cellist. But I am like you and your on-call, I like not knowing what will happen next."

Kathy felt an odd atmosphere in the flat now Piers had slowed down; it was as though the three of them had established some kind of connection and they each understood the other even though they were so different. There was some kind of bond between them and it wasn't going to be broken. She was safe at last with these two to watch over her and she wouldn't need to run any more.

Piers sucked chocolate off his fingers. "What made you want to come and live in the UK? I'm guessing you're French?"

"Ah." Jean-Guy hesitated, not knowing how much he should say. Clearly this man who flew aeroplanes for a living had no idea what went on in the classical music world and was blissfully unaware he was sharing a biscuit tin with a defector. "Well, it wasn't the climate."

They were all distracted by the phone ringing and Audrey scrambled down from her perch to sit on top of the piano again. Kathy answered the phone feeling certain it wouldn't be Richard after the way he had slammed out of the house on Monday night. She realised the two men were talking about something rather than listening in on her conversation. Whatever it was they were talking about was forgotten completely when a cheerful voice greeted her.

"Hi, Kathy, how are you?"

"Oh, hi, Jane." Kathy was always pleased to hear from her agent as it invariably meant there was a new booking for her diary. She had been hoping some more work would come her way as she needed some more hours to fill the next few weeks although she had learned that the beginning of the year was often a lean time. She was reaching for her diary which she always kept in her bag by the phone but Jane's next words stopped her in her tracks.

"Sorry, Kath, it's all a bit odd, but the orchestra who had booked you have just dropped you. I got the message a few minutes ago."

"Oh. Did they give a reason?" Kathy asked feeling the first tinges of panic as she had now lost her only booking until April.

"Not really. But I'm sure something else will turn up," Jane finished, knowing full well that if Kathy didn't work neither of them got paid.

"Well, I hope so. I've got a bit put by to cover my rent for a month or so but I can't go any longer without work."

"Kath, once I put word out that you're available they'll be biting my hand off to offer you work. So don't worry about it and I'll get back to you when I've got some offers for you."

"Oh, OK, thanks, Jane," Kathy was going to ask more but Jane had already hung up. She put the phone down and looked at the others. "That was the weirdest phone call I have ever had from my agent. I've now got no work until April and she wasn't promising me any more. I know this is a bad time of year but that was pretty harsh."

"Do you have any kind of insurance against such things?" Piers asked quite practically.

Kathy shook her head. "Technically I count as self-employed so if I don't get work it's my fault I'm not getting paid. Perils of being a freelancer as you probably remember from your pineapple days." She suddenly smiled. "But I do still have my busker's licence if all else fails."

She saw from his smile he understood perfectly. "Didn't realise you had to be licenced."

"Oh, yes. It's actually quite strictly regulated. Something else my ex didn't like me doing."

"That bloke standing in the middle of the room on Monday night? Built like a brick shit house and a face like a slapped arse?"

Kathy realised what they had been talking about while Jane ripped the rug out from under her. She was surprised Piers had apparently noticed so much and could have hugged him for that description of the ex. "That was him. And I hope I never see him again."

"Can sympathise with that. I hope I never see my ex again. Thank Christ there weren't any kids to complicate things in the divorce settlement. Nearly twenty years of marriage and damn all to show for it."

Kathy looked at him and realised that when he smiled there were slight crow's feet at the corners of his eyes and there were a few grey hairs sprinkled among the dark. "You don't look old enough," she fished.

"Flattery," he laughed. "They don't let kids loose on Concorde. But I'd flown supersonic in the military and racked up the hours in my career so they got me to help out with their new aeroplane before it went into service." He decided to satisfy her obvious curiosity. "I've just turned forty five, OK?"

Kathy privately thought he could have knocked fifteen years off that and she would have believed him.

Piers got to his feet. "Anyway, sorry to hear about your job. But I'll definitely put some money in your pot if I see you busking on the street corner."

"I've got a pitch up at South Ken. That's how I first met Phil, pregnant first violin lady you saw, as she works the same patch. We used to play duets if we met up until we heard someone call us Winne-the-Pooh and Piglet."

He laughed again and shook his head. "You kill me," he told her. "Don't eat too many haycorns. Right, come on, Audrey, get off the Broadwood, it's home time."

"Not flying today?" Jean-Guy asked, clearly a bit confused by this rapid English backchat.

"Back to Concorde tomorrow but it's a same day turnaround for me to cover sick leave so New York and back in not a lot more than twelve hours. Do you think puss will be OK?" He saw the look on Kathy's face. "Oh, for pity's sake. I'll try to drop you off a spare key this evening if I can find one, and you can go and check on her. I can't keep bringing her round here."

Kathy tickled the tortoiseshell under her chin and Audrey purred fondly at her. "Well, you could…."

"No. Get your own cat."

The flat seemed oddly quiet after Piers and Audrey had gone.

"He's a bit of a live-wire, as I believe you say," Jean-Guy remarked. "Known him long?"

"Not really, we sometimes see each other in the grocery store if I'm doing some shopping after a concert. I used to think he was a policeman getting himself something to eat after a shift."

Jean-Guy looked at her but she didn't seem to be particularly love-struck. "He's a very good-looking man," he offered, trying to find out if, perhaps, one day he may be able to get closer to this woman or whether there was already a suitor in her life.

"You can have him if you want him," she said laughingly. "Emma thinks he's a conman and not really an airline pilot at all."

"Well, if he is, he's a bloody good one."

"Isn't that the point?"

Jean-Guy realised something and looked at the piano. "When he got up to go, exactly what did he say to his cat?"

Kathy smiled to remember. "He told her to get off the Broadwood."

"He did. But the lid is closed so the name doesn't show. How the hell did he know it's a Broadwood? Anyone who is not a pianist would just have told her to get off the piano."

Kathy caught her breath. "And when you asked him if he played, he kind of hesitated a bit. Did you notice?"

"I did. What do you make of that?"

"I think he works in a really blokey place like an airline and if he told anyone there he knew how to play a piano they'd laugh themselves silly at him."

"Good idea, but he knows you play a violin and I play a cello. So we are two people who would not laugh at him."

"In that case," Kathy said decisively, "he does know how to play and was simply trying to stop us recruiting him into a piano trio."

"Now that I am willing to believe. Or perhaps he has heard of my reputation with accompanists."

Kathy looked at him. "He didn't even seem to know who you are." She paused. "What reputation?"

"I am not very nice to them. Either they try to outplay me or they are useless. I have yet to find one I can respect and work with for more than maybe three recitals."

"Don't believe you."

"Ah, you have not seen me when I am properly at work. Not yet."

They had barely taken their mugs out to the kitchen and had moved on to discussing what to eat for supper when the phone rang again. Jean-Guy answered it this time.

"Oh, hullo, Piers, did you forget something?" He was going to ask about the piano thing but didn't get a chance.

"No," was the clearly furious reply. "You know that phone call Kathy had from her agent? Well, I've just had the strangest equivalent of it from the Personnel department. I'm to do tomorrow's Concorde run but then I'm suspended until further notice. Apparently some irregularity with my other ratings which is a load of bollocks. Add to that there was a letter on my mat when I got home from your place just now summoning me to a meeting at the Home Office. What the hell is going on?"

"Oh my God," Jean-Guy said dully which brought Kathy within earshot. "When is your meeting?"

"Friday morning, ten o'clock."

"Kathy," Jean-Guy requested, "can you go and check your post, please?"

"OK. Anything in particular?"

"A letter from the Home Office."

"The what?"

"Just go and look. Please." He turned back to the phone. "Can you hang on just a minute?"

"Sure. Not like I'll be going anywhere is it," was the grumpy reply.

"This has to be my fault. I am not French as you thought. I am from Czechoslovakia and I defected while giving a concert with a French orchestra. But I don't know why you two are being targeted. That makes no sense."

Kathy came back into the flat, puffing slightly from running up the stairs from the hall. "I have a meeting at the Home Office at ten o'clock Friday morning. What the hell is going on?"

Dark Angels

Kathy felt like the heroine of a corny movie on Friday morning as she ran down the front steps of the elegant London townhouse to the snarling Ferrari waiting for her at the kerb. If it had been a movie, she told herself, she would no doubt have exchanged an extremely passionate embrace with the drop-dead gorgeous driver but something told her he was in a foul mood so she made do with a cheerful, "Good morning. How was New York?"

"Still there," he said snappily and roared away, cutting up a Royal Mail van making its innocent way along Hogarth Road.

Kathy didn't like to chat too much with him in that mood but as he turned into the Earl's Court Road at the speed of a rocket he suddenly smiled.

"Sorry I didn't get round to dropping off the key Wednesday night. Spent the whole bloody evening looking for all the sodding paperwork these miserable gits asked me to bring as I knew I wouldn't have time last night. You got any ideas what the hell this is all about? Surely they wouldn't call us in just because we've eaten biscuits with a Czech defector?"

Kathy knew it wasn't going to be good news. Jean-Guy had spoken to the Professor and she had been advised not to say anything to Piers in the hope that it would just be a quick check by the authorities and then the two of them would be cleared to go back to their lives.

"Not really," she replied a bit less than truthfully. "But Jean-Guy says the less you know the easier it'll be."

"That is probably true. So tell me nothing at all."

Kathy looked at the pile of papers she was now holding as she had had to move them off the passenger seat so she didn't sit on them. She just wished Emma could have been there to see it all. All she had to bring were her passport and birth certificate but he had what to her uninitiated eyes looked like two passports, birth, marriage and divorce papers, pilot's licences, log book and all sorts of other documentation which made no sense to her but finally convinced her he wasn't a conman. That was too much paperwork to forge just to trick an itinerant violinist.

"How's Audrey?" she asked in an attempt to change the topic of conversation. Part of her really wanted to hang on to the dashboard as he was driving so nippily in and out of the traffic, but a much larger part of her was enjoying the ride.

"Oh, she's fine. Brought her back some American cat food so she forgave me for leaving her yesterday." Piers zipped round a cyclist who wasn't looking where he was going. "Daft cat insists on sleeping on my bed though. If I shut her out of the room she just howls the house down until I let her in. So if I want to sleep, I have to share."

Kathy looked out of the side window and heard herself say, "She's looking after you, that's all." As soon as she had spoken she was waiting for the snide answer and the laugh.

Piers pulled into a car park Kathy didn't even know existed. "I know," came the quiet reply. "I'm just not used to it. OK, out you get. Let's get this over and done with."

There were three men clearly waiting for them in the impressive entrance hall. Piers took one look and muttered softly to her, "Oh, shit. That's not good."

"What isn't?"

"Bloke in the middle. Had dealings with him in my RAF days."

Kathy didn't see Piers again until nearly half past two in the afternoon. He was quietly waiting for her in the entrance hall and looked exhausted but gave her a weary smile. "Cleared to go?"

"I've been told to get out of London," Kathy told him and her voice wobbled. "They said it wasn't safe for me to be here for a while." She couldn't remember the last time she had been so scared. This was in so many ways worse than Richard as she didn't know who the enemy was any more.

Piers still seemed more annoyed than anything which, in an odd sort of way, made her feel better, and he gave her a lovely smile. "They said exactly the same to me too."

"They told me I'm to stay with my friend Emma's father in Suffolk. I'm sure he won't mind if you and Audrey come too as he's already got loads of cats. Did they tell you not to take your car?"

"Yes. I'm to leave it at my house." Piers took a long breath and suddenly his temper disappeared and he was calmly back in control. "They told me I'm to go with you and we have to take Jean-Guy with us. Are you allowed to take your car?"

Kathy shook her head and remembered what Emma had said to her on her wedding day about people passing through the old farmhouse. It was another glimpse into that frightening world but now she had an awful feeling she was getting too close to it. "When was the last time you went on a train?"

Piers almost laughed. "Christ knows. I haven't seen the inside of the Underground for years."

Jean-Guy was pacing the flat like a caged tiger when Kathy got home. In a show of relief he gave her a hug and she was convinced he had been crying.

"Petr Mihaly has rung. We all three have to go and stay with him. Where's Piers?"

"Gone to pack a case and get Audrey. I don't understand. What is going on?"

"I think the Professor will explain it better than I can. Are you happy for Piers to come with us? I got the impression Petr wasn't keen."

"Oh, no, he'll be fine. I think he's as confused about all this as I am. And he's definitely not a conman."

Jean-Guy didn't answer the first part of that. "Might have been easier if he were."

"What do you mean?"

"He has a bad family history out in Ireland. Did you see he has two passports? Dual nationality as his mother was born in the Republic so he has had Irish passport since he was a child. Born in Northern Ireland though so he has British passport too."

Kathy was starting to feel very afraid. "Is he dangerous? No, he can't be, or they'd never have told us to take him with us. Oh, I'm so confused now. He always seems so nice and he has twinkly eyes like Ratty in the book."

"So he is Ratty to my Moly? No, it is just the opposite. He is fugitive like me."

"But he's British. Like me. Why are we running away in our own country?"

"He's Irish. I don't understand your country's history but there are people he doesn't want to find him. That is why he changed his name and went into armed forces. Don't ask anything. Go and pack some clothes and we must hope that man at the station isn't still looking for me."

With a jolt, Kathy remembered the man at Liverpool Street Station the day she had passed through there with a cello. "So it's you they're after and he wasn't just looking for a random cellist then?"

"Please, just go and pack. Is Piers coming here when he is ready?"

"Yes, although I don't know how we'll manage Audrey on the train as he hasn't got a basket for her."

"He will have to leave her behind."

"But she's so tiny, she'll never survive."

"If he has any compassion he will drown her before he comes here. And he will know that."

Overwrought with emotion, Kathy burst into tears and fled into her room so she could pack a case. She had no idea how long she would be away, but at least there was a washing machine in the Prof's house. She was sniffing rather than crying but had packed what she would normally take for a fortnight when she heard the street door buzzer and wasn't surprised to hear Jean-Guy call out to tell her Piers had arrived.

It was quite awkward getting down the stairs with cases, a violin and a cello but Piers was waiting for them on the pavement with apparently no luggage whatsoever. Kathy noticed he had changed out of the smart suit and tie he had worn to the Home Office but didn't look any more relaxed in spite of the scruffy clothes.

"Hop in," he invited and opened the doors of a large and ramshackle khaki Land Rover that looked as though it had been round the world at least twice in its life. "Chuck your stuff in the boot, but you might rather keep the cello on the back seat as that case looks worse than useless."

"What the hell?" Jean-Guy asked, a bit surprised that the other man had so effortlessly taken control but he guessed that was what airline captains did without thinking.

"Borrowed it. They'll be watching the railway stations so this will be safer."

Kathy climbed into the front seat and Jean-Guy loaded the luggage into the back then got into the rear seat next to Audrey, quietly sleeping in her box.

"You kept the cat," Jean-Guy remarked.

"It's her fault I'm in this mess. I've fed her so she'll sleep for a while now. Then it's up to you to stop her wrecking the car. OK, I know how to get to the A12 but after that you'll have to tell me the way. Sorry it's a bit basic."

"It smells of fish," Kathy commented, trying to think of something ordinary to say.

"I've done a car swap with my neighbour and he got married just after New Year so that'll be something to do with the kipper it had on its engine block."

The London traffic was bad and roadworks on the North Circular didn't help so it was long dark by the time they got to Suffolk. The Professor had heard the car coming down the track and was at the front door to meet them when they got out of the vehicle.

"Any problems?" he asked anxiously.

Jean-Guy shook his head.

"Just roadworks," Kathy yawned. It seemed ages ago that she had last been here, yet it was only two weeks.

The Professor seemed not to hear her. "And you must be Ciaran Maloney."

"Not for a long time," came the quick correction. "Didn't they tell you that?"

"I think they told me everything, those dark angels who guard us. Come in, come in. I have made soup for you all as I didn't know what time you'd get here. Kathy, you are in Emma's old room again, Jean-Guy you are in the small room at the front where you were last time and, Piers I have made up the room at the back for you. Kathy will show you the way as she has been here many times before."

To Kathy that simple meal of leek and potato soup was one of the strangest she had ever had in that house. The three travellers were too tired and shocked to speak much and they were all in their rooms by ten o'clock each with their own thoughts. Audrey, Kathy noticed, was not going to be parted from Piers for an instant and followed him devotedly up the stairs.

Kathy woke in the morning and looked round Emma's old room. Just for a moment she wondered if it was the day after the wedding and she had dreamed the whole thing. She had had a crazy dream about the policeman in the grocery shop and all she had to do was take a cello to London and her life would carry on as it had before. It was also freezing cold as the eccentric heating system wasn't working again although she could see from the gap in her curtains that it was daylight. Dressed in several layers of clothing and realising from the fact she had a suitcase with her that it hadn't all been a dream, she went downstairs where all was reassuringly normal and the Prof was making porridge. He always made the best porridge she had ever tasted.

"Morning," she said sleepily and gratefully wrapped her fingers round the mug of tea he gave her. "What time is it?"

He looked at the clock on the kitchen wall. "About eight thirty. Any signs of the other two?"

"Nothing. I was just about to ask you the same. Mind you, Jean-Guy doesn't usually appear until about ten."

"And have you managed not to get fond of him?"

"I like him as a friend," Kathy hedged. "And he now knows all about the mess with my ex. So, yes, I got fond of him but not like you're thinking."

"And your handsome young pilot?"

Kathy laughed. "He's nearly twenty years older than me, seems to have been through a very bitter divorce and he flies Concorde for a living. I think he's way out of my league, don't you? He's kind of like a big brother and I never had one of those."

"He's also very useful and I'm glad you have finally managed to bring him in. Here, sit and eat before it gets cold."

Kathy sat at the table, a bit puzzled by the Prof's odd turn of phrase, but soon forgotten as she spooned her habitual honey onto her steaming bowl of porridge. "You mean in case we have to make a quick getaway in a jet fighter?"

"Silly child," the Prof said kindly but didn't explain.

Kathy was on her second bowl of porridge before they were interrupted. Next into the kitchen was Piers, looking cold in at least two sweaters, jeans and thick woolly socks. Audrey trotted behind him and jumped on top of the Aga. She looked totally disgusted and miaowed at Piers.

"Sorry, Audrey, the Aga is cold," the Professor apologised to her. "I have no idea what's wrong with it."

"What fuel does it burn?" Piers asked as he too sat at the table and was given tea and porridge without being asked if he wanted it.

"It has been adapted to wood. I have a whole pile of wood but I can't make it stay lit. Or if it does light then it doesn't heat the water. Or if it heats the water then the radiators are cold. I have no idea what is the matter with it. I had the chimneys swept in the autumn so I know it's not the flue."

Piers looked at the huge six-oven monster in the inglenook. "I'll have a look at it for you if you like. It's got to be better than dying of hypothermia."

The Professor watched as this new visitor to the house got through porridge and tea as though afraid someone would take it away from him. "Would you like some more?" he asked amusedly.

"Oh, no, thanks. I don't normally eat breakfast. But it was good. Made a change."

The Professor gave him a stern look. "While you are in my care you eat properly and sensibly. You're not on shifts now so you eat three meals a day and you sleep at night. Understand?" He cut off the rising protest with a raised hand. "They have told me about you."

There was a grudging smile on Piers' face but he didn't say anything.

By the time Jean-Guy came into the kitchen only a very hot and grubby Piers was in there, sitting on the floor with the Aga partially dismantled and a lot of greasy soot on a newspaper next to him. He was surrounded by at least six curious cats watching critically as he cleaned and de-gunged the Aga's parts. Jean-Guy could hear Kathy was practising her violin in the sitting room and he could see the Professor at his desk in the study with his head bent industriously over some papers.

"Bit different from Concorde?" Jean-Guy greeted the man on the floor.

"Yup. There's some porridge around here somewhere if the cats haven't eaten it."

"What the hell is porridge?"

"Sloppy white stuff in a saucepan."

"Found it." Jean-Guy watched as Piers finished cleaning and reassembling the Aga before lighting the fire in it.

"OK, give it an hour or so and things should warm up a bit with any luck."

"Thank God for that, I've never known such a cold place. What the hell do you do with this?"

Piers tipped some hot water from the electric kettle into the sink so he could at least make a start on cleaning up. "Up to you. I usually just put some sugar on it. Give it here and I'll warm it up again for you. Thank Christ the old boy's got a proper cooker as well as that monstrosity. Tea?"

"Yes please."

Kathy was still practising when the Professor joined the other men who were still in the kitchen both looking at the Aga as though they could wish it into life more quickly. He closed the door and sat with them at the table.

"It is time we talked straight," he began. "You are not stupid men, you both know the risks and I am trusting you to look after Kathy. She is the innocent in this," he raised a finger seeing a protest was imminent. "Yes, Piers, you didn't ask to get caught up in this mess either but you have been trained, unlike the other two, how to cope. In the meantime I can only suggest that you all try to fit into life round here. You can walk into the village if you like, it's only a mile or so if you take the coast path and it's easier than driving all round the marsh road. Other than that, unless you're into birdwatching, there isn't a lot to do. I don't have a television but there are at least two record players and lots of radios. And books to keep you reading until Doomsday. All I ask is that you don't touch anything in my study without asking first as I need nearly everything in there for my work."

"How long might we be here?" Piers asked thinking life was going to be pretty dull until they could get away again.

"Truthfully, I don't know. There are people out looking for Jean-Guy and until they are found then you can't really be safe as you and Kathy have already been identified as associates. We think the cello case attracted some interest at Liverpool Street, and then you and Kathy have had contact several times over the last few days." He turned to Jean-Guy, "I'm afraid your defection has upset the Russians and they want you back. It is almost certain now they are pretty sure you are in London as they are certain they identified the cello, We are certain they would have followed Kathy to her flats, they would have followed her and seen her meet with you, Piers. I know they told you to change cars and make sure you weren't followed but those trying to find you all, we hope may think you, Kathy and the cello were a ruse as we believe they are also still looking for you in Paris and also in Bonn." He half smiled. "That is why I am out here. Nobody comes out to this part of England especially now there is no railway any more and the main road is too far west. So go out, find things to do, but always keep one eye behind you."

By lunchtime, the house was definitely getting warmer and Piers had shed one of his sweaters. It was Kathy's idea that they should go for a walk to visit the village but Jean-Guy wanted to do some cello practice and the Professor had work to do so Kathy and Piers set out after lunch. The Prof told them to be back before dark and made sure they had a torch with them anyway.

The North Sea was dark grey and hissing on the shingle as they set out in the bitter cold of February on the east coast. The wind whipped across the sand dunes and cut through their layers of clothing, making their eyes stream and their noses run.

"No wonder the old boy moved out here," Piers remarked his voice muffled by the scarf that covered half his face. "Shouldn't think anyone ever comes out here."

"Used to be popular with smugglers last century."

"Can see why, the excise men wouldn't want to come out here either."

The village main street was set back enough from the beach for the wind not to be quite so biting, but it was in its winter sleep with the holiday homes in darkness and the village shop running on reduced hours. It was still open, hoping to catch some trade from the passengers off the last Ipswich bus of the day, and Kathy and Piers thankfully stepped into the warmth and unwrapped themselves a bit.

"Shall we buy a cake to take back for supper?" Kathy asked. "They're made by a lady in the village and they're really good."

They chose the lemon drizzle, although the chocolate fudge was a close-run second, and Kathy said she would pay for it. She smiled at the young woman at the till, her face familiar from frequent visits to the Professor over the years.

"Hullo, love," the young woman greeted her. "How's married life suiting Emma?"

"Fine so far as I know. She rang me a few days ago. Do you still sell knitting wool? I totally forgot to bring my knitting with me."

"Not much left. We're running the stock down now as nobody knits any more. Over there in the corner. Been a while since you brought a boyfriend in here."

Kathy had a feeling that Sarah was getting rather curious about Piers which was odd as she'd never shown any interest in a visiting man before. She'd never taken any of her boyfriends to Suffolk over the years which made Sarah's comment even more odd. "He's not my boyfriend," she offered.

"Is he married?" Sarah cut in rather rudely and then blushed as though she had said something she shouldn't.

This surprised Kathy even more but her first instinct was to protect the innocent. "Divorced. Very messily." Not sure how to explain Piers' arrival in the village, Kathy didn't elaborate. She looked at the man scanning the racks of local history books and guessed he was tough enough to cope with Sarah who had a reputation for being rather sharp. "Piers, come and say hello to Sarah."

He had the manners to take off both gloves from his right hand to shake hands with Sarah. "Hi, Sarah. Is this your shop?"

Kathy watched as an odd look passed between the two as their hands touched. It was as though they had met before but neither could remember when, and the notoriously unromantic Sarah blushed scarlet. "Well, family shop. Technically my mother owns it."

His blue eyes were more twinkly than ever. "Got any chocolate?"

"Over there." Sarah couldn't take her eyes off him as he went to see if any of the stock appealed to him. "What does he do for a living?" she muttered to Kathy. "Is he an actor? Or a model with those looks?"

Kathy almost felt sorry for her. "He's a Concorde pilot."

She got the impression that if it had been possible, Sarah would have melted into a gooey mush behind the counter of the shop.

It was quite hard to share a bar of fruit and nut walking back along the coast path, but Kathy was mindful of the Professor's caution to get back before it was dark. The walk back was very dramatic as thick, dark clouds were rolling in from the east and the wind was more biting than ever. Everything was a shade of iron grey around them from the scruffy grass on the dunes to the hissing sea and the clouds in the sky. The air had that metallic taste to it that comes before a snowfall

"Going to be a storm tonight," Piers mused, looking at the sky as he tried again to break the chocolate while wearing two pairs of gloves. He triumphantly handed a chunk to Kathy. "Don't let it spoil your supper."

"No chance," she laughed.

By taking the coast path, they approached the Professor's house from the back and already lights were on in several of the windows, casting a welcoming glow across the bleak and desolate garden. Kathy opened the door and the two walked into a warmth she had never known in the house before. The Prof was humming an unidentifiable tune as he prepared the evening meal but he heard them arrive and beamed a welcome at them.

"Kathy, why did you not bring Piers down before? I have never known the Aga to work so well, I can cook on it at last. We have heat, we have hot water and I only need one sweater."

There was a line of very happy cats in front of the Aga and Audrey had muscled her way in there between the old tabby Brno and a sleek grey whose name Kathy could never remember.

"Brought you some cake," she told the Prof and handed across the lemon drizzle.

"Ah, you have been to the shop," he remarked unnecessarily. "How is Sarah?"

Kathy looked round but Piers wasn't in the room. "Smitten," she smiled and unwrapped herself from her scarf, hat, mittens and coat.

"He is a very good-looking man. Quite a heart-breaker in his day I would imagine."

The snow fell overnight and the residents of the house had never been more grateful for a working Aga than they were that morning when the drifts were over the back door sill and the window of the pantry had ice on the inside.

Kathy, Jean-Guy and the Prof played piano trios for most of the morning but Piers decided he would go out for a walk. The other three were perfectly aware that the non-musical among them was very bored but weren't quite sure what to suggest he did. Jean-Guy had asked him again whether he played the piano but again the reply had been a slightly regretful 'no'.

Piers turned up for lunch looking much happier. "What's the history behind the little house on the drive?" he asked as they all sat down to eat.

"A couple of labourers' cottages for farm workers," the Prof explained. "They were just about habitable when I moved here but have been falling down for the last twenty odd years. I know this house dates back about five hundred years in parts but I don't think the cottages are that old. Maybe eighteenth century. I have seen an old photo in a local history book and they used to be thatched."

Kathy thought those two little cottages would have looked lovely back in the day when the stonework was new, there had been curtains at the windows and a cosy thatched roof just to complete their perfect Englishness. "You should mend them and then let them out as holiday cottages."

"Hm. What you are forgetting is that I have no money to make holiday cottages."

Kathy walked out along the track with Piers that afternoon to have a proper look at the derelict cottages huddled in the curve of the track behind some trees so not visible from either the road or the farmhouse. She had never paid much attention to the building before but, standing ankle deep in the snow that bitter afternoon she felt quite sorry for it. There was still glass in some of the windows and one of them did have quite a good front door on it hanging open on one hinge and most of the tiles were still on the roof. They had once had brick floors but these were uneven as the encroaching weeds had pushed up from the earth below and there was ivy climbing up the walls which smelled strongly of damp and mildew. Going into the one without a front door they could see it had an old box staircase but the stairs themselves looked so rickety neither of them even suggested going to see what was upstairs.

"Seems such a waste," Kathy said sadly, "but I don't think the Prof would like to have neighbours no matter how temporary. I didn't realise until quite recently that Jean-Guy isn't the first defector to come through here. When Emma told me I just thought it was all quite glamorous and wished my dad did such exciting things. But I think the Prof was a bit cross she'd told me."

"Excitement isn't always all that it's cracked up to be."

"So I'm beginning to realise. This still doesn't feel quite real."

Piers pulled his woolly hat down over his ears a bit more. "I'm going back inside, at least it's warm in there now and unless I'm much mistaken there's a lot more snow in that sky."

Early morning echoes

For nearly a week it snowed relentlessly and the temperature stayed below freezing along most of the east coast while the weather battered it all the way from Siberia and four people in an old farmhouse were grateful for a working Aga and a well-stocked kitchen.

Kathy could never quite get up early enough to beat the Professor into the kitchen in the mornings, but she went down one morning to realise the sun was shining and the light levels in the house were extraordinarily high as the sunlight reflected off the snow.

"Postman got through this morning," the Prof greeted her. "I've had a letter from Emma wanting to know why you aren't answering your phone. She's back from honeymoon and wants to meet your cat."

Kathy smiled. "And I bet there are about thirty messages from her on the answering machine at the flat and a snotty letter for me in the hall. Wonder if any of the neighbours will think to put it through my letterbox. It's going to look a bit obvious I'm not there."

"What happens when you are away touring?"

"Emma used to pick them up if she was there. Otherwise our post would just stack up until one of us got round to collecting it. We don't see the neighbours much."

"Does Emma still have her keys?"

"Think so. I couldn't find them to give them to Jean-Guy anyway so I gave him the spares."

"Good. I suggest you ring her after breakfast, ask her to go to the flat and collect your post and anything else you want and to bring it here."

"Is it safe for her to come? Because if the people looking for Jean-Guy knew she'd been to our flat and then here they could kidnap her and ask her what's going on."

The Professor had to acknowledge that Kathy was learning about his lifestyle. "Anyone watching your house won't know which flat she is visiting," he pointed out. "Yes, they may see her but as you and Piers have now both disappeared from Earl's Court it is unlikely the area is still of interest. Sit and have some toast and I will explain to you." The Professor couldn't be unaware that Piers had just arrived in the kitchen so he started making some more toast. "As my daughter, Emma knows what may happen. I sent her away to school to shield her from some of it which is how you met her. I have mentioned the dark angels who guard us, and they always guard her. Her husband is one of them."

"What? Derek? But he's a minor civil servant. She met him in the Prom queue a couple of years ago. Both wanting tickets for the arena. He works for the DHSS at one of the local job centres. Or he did. I think she said he's changed jobs."

Piers poured himself a mug of tea from the pot. "Bet your bottom dollar he's a spook. And anyone looking out for us probably won't make the connection between an apparently random visitor to your flats and us. They would almost certainly have seen us leave your house, but we weren't followed out of London. You could spot a tail on the A12 a mile off as there's so little traffic on it this far east."

"You see," the Professor told her, "I told you Piers would be useful to us."

Kathy could feel a headache coming on. "What?"

Piers offered her the toast rack, now full of hot toast. "Tell you what, we'll have a freezing cold walk along to the shop now it's stopped snowing, and I'll explain about spooks." He dithered between strawberry jam and marmalade. "I may even tell Sarah stories of my latest photo shoot for *Vogue*."

Kathy gasped and had to laugh. "You weren't supposed to hear that."

He smiled and tapped his left ear. "Got to have good hearing in my job. Helps you to know if the wheels are about to fall off."

Kathy triumphantly snatched the marmalade from his hand. "Idiot," she said fondly.

Kathy decided she would ring Emma in the afternoon as she was more likely to be in about lunch time even if she had a concert in the evening. Jean-Guy still hadn't come down for his breakfast when Kathy and Piers bundled themselves up against the wind and set out along the coast path again. The wind had died down a lot overnight and they both scuffed along quite happily in their borrowed wellies.

"So, spooks," Kathy prompted.

"Boring. Tell me instead why you are reading *Wind in the Willows* at your age?"

"How did you know that?"

"Saw it on your bedroom floor as I was passing your door."

So she told him about seeing Jean-Guy as Moly and somehow let slip that he reminded her of Ratty. He didn't seem the slightest bit offended, more amused than anything.

"Oh well, at least nobody ever called me Piglet," he told her and offered her his arm in the old-fashioned way.

Kathy tucked her hand through his arm and found it comforting somehow. "Spooks," she reminded him firmly.

"I'm guessing you don't read many spy stories."

"You mean James Bond and all that stuff with macho men and useless long-haired women with no brains? Can't stand them."

"Well, you've got the hair," he teased.

She nudged his ribs. "Oi, Ratty, stop avoiding the issue."

"Piglet, I'll tell you stories that'll put you off your lunch and I've seen how you can pack it away."

Sarah looked round from her shelf-stacking when the shop doorbell pinged and she watched as Kathy disentangled her hand from the arm of the handsome pilot and he let her step into the shop first. It was odd, but she had believed Kathy when she had said Piers wasn't her boyfriend. Looking at them now, she still believed it. A tiny flame of hope began to burn in her heart.

"Hi, Kathy. Not snowed in then?"

"Not quite, but hasn't it been bad?"

"Seen it worse," Sarah said grudgingly, resenting the other's bright-eyed happiness. She saw Piers looking at the papers. "More terrorists in London," she told him. "Glad I live out here."

"Don't you get bored?" he asked curiously and selected a paper to buy. "I can imagine you're busy in summer but what is there to do this time of year?"

"Not much trade," she had to admit. "But the holiday homes and caravans will open next month so not long now until the season starts."

He tucked the paper under one arm and started sorting out some change. "You've got grape jelly," he remarked seeing the half dozen jars on the counter. "Never seen it outside the States before."

"Lads from the air base go mad for it. Of course they have their own shops on the base but occasionally they bring their families down to the beach for the day."

"What air base?" he asked and there was a certain sharpness to his tone.

"Oh, there are loads round here. Nearest is the US Air Force up at Bentwaters. If the weather hadn't been so bad you'd have seen their aeroplanes flying over by now. They're at Hollesley as well, although we should really call it Woodbridge, then there's their bases at Mildenhall and Lakenheath. And we've got the RAF at Wattisham and Honnington not too far away and Coltishall but that's a bit further up north, more Norwich way."

"Christ never realised it was still so busy round here, I was at Honnington for a while, years ago now," he remarked and added a jar of grape jelly to his shopping. "Don't suppose you've got any peanut butter?"

"Smooth or chunky?" Sarah asked.

Kathy knew what Piers was going to say. Before he could get his words in order, she plonked a jar on the counter. "Smooth," she told him. "You're definitely not chunky."

The proverbial penny dropped and Sarah shrieked with laughter. "Nearly missed that," she howled in her broad Suffolk brogue. "At least you didn't say you'd be smooth and I can be chunky." She looked up and just wanted to stare into his blue eyes for ever. A perfect deep cornflower blue. With what looked like an enchanting gold speckle in the left one.

"I wouldn't be so rude," he assured her and finally looked away. "Piglet, you going for the chocolate cake today?"

Kathy saw the way those two had looked at each other. She would never have believed it and thought it was rather sweet. "Now who are you calling chunky?"

"Do you know what?" Piers said. "I wish I'd never started this now. Hen-pecked, that's what I am."

Kathy and Sarah looked at each other and grinned in solidarity.

Sarah watched her two early-morning customers leave the shop, bantering about something again and was convinced there was still laughter echoing in the shop. She was consoled. Kathy certainly loved her handsome pilot but not in that way. And for a man getting over a very messy divorce he certainly had a wicked sense of humour. She looked down at the counter where a new poster was waiting for her to pin it up on the local noticeboard. She hoped there might be help from the old farmhouse for the pub team in the Smugglers' Race this year. She looked at the closed shop door and knew there would be some help for her too.

Kathy settled in the kitchen to ring Emma after lunch. There were two phones in the house, one in the hall where it was always cold and one in the kitchen where these days it was always nice and warm. Jean-Guy carted his cello up to his room to do some practice and the Professor took Piers off to the sitting room threatening to give him a piano lesson just to stop him getting bored. He didn't say anything, just went quietly to his fate.

Kathy listened to Emma's phone ringing with one ear while the other listened to some very basic Mozart being played. She realised they had been right and Piers knew his way round a keyboard. She winced at a wrong note.

"2519," said Emma's voice very cheerily.

"Hi, Emma. It's me."

"Kath! Where the hell are you? Your tour doesn't start until April the second."

"I'm with your dad."

"Is he all right? He only rang me a couple of days ago."

"He's fine. But can you do me a favour and bring me some stuff from the flat next time you come down, please? And my post?"

"I picked up your post today as I was round there looking for you. You must have been away for days. And there was no sign of Jean-Guy either. What's happened? Are you OK?"

"I'll explain when you get here. Don't worry about us. But please bring my knitting. I spent half a month's wages on some really expensive wool to knit a sweater for Jean-Guy then forgot to bring it with me."

There was a short silence. "Knitting? Since when have you gone back to your knitting? You said it made you look like your granny."

"No, Richard said it made me look like his granny. Now I don't care any more."

Both women realised that was the first time Kathy had said his name out loud for a very long time.

"I will bring your knitting. Anything else?"

Kathy had missed female company. Being stuck in a house full of men had been a very odd experience as she had had only a younger sister growing up. "Just chuck me some more clothes in a bag and bring you with your gossip and chat and I really wish you could bring me a cappuccino. With a dusting of chocolate on top. And an all-night grocery shop and a bunch of mad Australians from one of the cafés in Earl's Court."

"So why are you out there if you're miserable and cold and nobody's ill?"

"It's not cold out here now Piers has mended the Aga." Kathy had a sudden thought that she probably shouldn't have mentioned him.

Emma sounded furious. "You have taken that conman out to meet Dad? Why the hell did you do that?"

Kathy didn't know what to say without digging an even deeper hole. "When can you get here?" she asked instead.

"Oh, I'll be there tomorrow and I'll send him on his way with a flea in his ear if he's tried any of his dirty tricks on my dad. In fact I'll probably have him arrested." She slammed the phone down and left Kathy feeling guilty.

She slunk into the sitting room where the Prof and Piers were still sitting at the piano with the latter being given some very monotonous exercises to do.

"That was quick," the Prof remarked while still paying attention to his pupil. "You and Emma usually chat for hours."

"Um, I'm afraid I let slip Piers is in the house and now she's hopping mad as she still thinks he's a conman. But the good news is she'll be here tomorrow. Probably with a couple of police constables to arrest you and cart you off to jail."

Piers triumphantly modulated to the last key in the sequence. "At least I won't get made to play the piano in prison."

"I'm guessing that when you were younger you played quite well," the Prof told him. "Although I'm not sure why you have taken your shoes off, I'm not so concerned about the piano I think you will damage the pedals."

He stared at the keys for a while then began a beautiful rendition of the opening of Schubert's *An die Nachtingall*. "Old habits. My sister is a singer, total child prodigy back in the day. I was trained to be her accompanist. Another reason I couldn't wait to join the forces as soon as I could. Hated it."

"Never in the limelight," the Prof mused. "What name does she sing under?"

"Roisin Thompson. We haven't been in touch for nearly thirty years."

"But I went to her Mahler recital last year…" Kathy began but the Prof shot her a look that silenced her.

"Then I'm sorry I brought back memories," the Prof said kindly and laid a gentle hand on Piers' arm. "You don't have to play any more if you don't want to. I didn't make the connection at first. I should have done. You look so much like her."

Piers just shut the lid of the piano and put his hands in his lap with his head bowed. The Professor got up and steered Kathy out of the room before she could ask any questions. He closed the sitting room door behind them and took her into his study where he looked along the many shelves of LPs until he found the one he wanted.

"I am an idiot," he told her and sounded strangely excited. She just looked at him. "Why did I not make the connection?"

"Nope, sorry, you've lost me."

He showed her the LP he had taken down. It was an old recording of Schubert's song cycle *Die schöne Müllerin* by Roisin Thompson, she had long dark hair, wore a red evening gown that was too old for her and looked about fourteen. Her accompanist wasn't mentioned by name but he was in the background of the black and white photo on the back. A skinny, unassuming child in formal evening wear that was too big for him, he looked about ten. "Roisin Thompson's childhood accompanist was never named at the time but she later said it was her brother. When he is not around you must listen to this. You have no idea, have you, just what you have brought into this house?"

"None whatsoever. I mean I've heard her sing recently but that LP is before my time."

"She had the most extraordinary talent as a child. And the boy who played the piano for her, I have never heard playing like it. If he has kept half that gift he will be the best accompanist for Jean-Guy we could ever find. But we have to be careful of disturbing the ghosts." He put the record back on the shelf. "Now go and fetch Jean-Guy for me and I will make us some tea. We'll leave Piers alone with his memories for a while. It's best if he doesn't know I've got this."

Kathy found Jean-Guy stretched out on his bed with the cello on its side on the floor and three cats keeping him company. His eyes were closed and she thought he was asleep.

"Great Schubert," he said without opening his eyes. "Didn't think you played."

"That wasn't me, that was Piers."

Jean-Guy sat upright with a suddenness that startled Kathy and made the cats scatter. "So he mends Agas, can play Schubert like a pro and then what does he do on his day off? Oh yes, he flies bloody Concorde."

Kathy suddenly got it. "Are you jealous of him?"

"You must admit, he is too good to be true."

"Emma thinks he's a conman. But I saw all the papers and things he had to take to the Home Office and, well, I like him."

"You liked Richard once."

Kathy almost physically reeled, doubly stung by his scathing tone and the words. "How dare you!"

Jean-Guy sat on the side of his bed and looked at her pleadingly. "You were duped once by a conman who finished up doing to you the worst thing a man can do to a woman. Please don't let it happen again."

Kathy realised that he genuinely cared about her and sat next to him on the bed. "Piers will never hurt me," she assured him and believed it. "Ever since I thought he was a policeman I've felt as though he looks after me. Which I know sounds silly." She didn't flinch as Jean-Guy put his hand over hers.

"Take care of yourself, that's all I ask."

His obvious concern touched her. "Please don't worry about Piers. We are just friends, really. He treats me like an annoying little sister."

"I don't understand half the things you and he talk about."

"It's just silly chat. I'm sorry, I didn't realise you felt left out." She squeezed his hand. "But if he can play Schubert like that, just think what an accompanist he'd make for you. We'll have to work on him."

His lips smiled at her but his eyes were worried. "He told us he didn't play and we believed him. What other lies has he told us? Don't let him beguile you."

"But when we asked him, he probably hadn't played for years so I suppose it was more natural for him to say he didn't play at all."

Jean-Guy thought it was touching the way she defended the man she claimed she had come to think of as a brother. "And now he calls you Piglet. I don't understand that at all."

"Ah. Then you need to meet Winnie-the-Pooh. Anyway, come and have your tea. But don't talk about accompanists just yet. I'll get the Prof to explain."

One star at last

It was quiet in the old farmhouse the next morning. Outside the snow and sun had been replaced by cold sleet that washed the snow away but didn't do anything to warm up the air temperature. The Professor wondered where his house guests had all gone and went out of his study to look for them. There was no music practice to be heard in any of the rooms and all the coats and boots were in the hall so nobody had gone out.

He found them in the sitting room. The fire was blazing in the hearth so the room was pleasantly warm, the old longcase clock in the corner resonantly ticked the time away and at least one of the cats was purring. Jean-Guy and Piers were sprawled in the two armchairs in front of the fire, one of them slowly working his way through *The House at Pooh Corner* and the other smiling over *The Wind in the Willows* with Audrey curled round on his chest. Kathy was lounging on her front on the hearth rug, totally absorbed in Emma's dog-eared copy of *Heidi*.

"Here's where you all are," he said in surprise and all three looked at him with the slightly out-of-focus look of those who had been reading too long. "It is nearly lunchtime and nobody has been out. Do you want to eat early before Emma gets here or wait for her so we may all eat together?"

"Oh, wait I think don't you?" Kathy said, itching to get back to the book.

The phone rang just then and the Prof, as the nearest to the door, went into the hall to answer it. By the time he got back to the sitting room they were all engrossed in their books again.

"That was Emma," he told them rather too loudly. "She says she can't come today but will be down first thing tomorrow."

"Nothing wrong, I hope?" Kathy asked.

"My daughter now has a doctor's appointment this afternoon. It seems that after less than a month of married life she has found herself sixteen weeks pregnant."

Kathy shot to her feet and gave the Prof a hug. "But that's wonderful! Can I ring her?"

"She's still on the phone, waiting for you."

"Emma!" Kathy tried hard not to shriek. "You total dark horse! Congratulations to you and Derek. How come you didn't tell me?"

"I really wanted to, but everyone says you shouldn't say anything for the first twelve weeks as it's unlucky, then there was the wedding and then everything just went all peculiar with you."

"How's Derek taken it?"

"If I said he was happy then I'd be understating. He's told me not to take on too many gigs and I think he's hoping I'll give up playing altogether after the baby's born and just stay at home with it."

"Is that what you want?" Kathy couldn't imagine Emma not playing her violin. She had always adored the audience appreciation and had been determined that one day she would play the Mendelssohn Concerto in the Albert Hall with something like the London Symphony Orchestra behind her.

"I don't know. I hadn't planned on having babies so soon but maybe I could take a bit of time off then go back to my career when it's a bit older. We could probably get a nanny or something."

"Do you want a boy or a girl?"

"I really don't mind," Emma laughed. "But I think Derek is secretly hoping for a boy. And how are things between you and Jean-Guy?"

Kathy dodged the issue. "Well, I've got him reading Winnie-the-Pooh. Except all I could find was *House at Pooh Corner*, have you got the other one?"

Emma was long used to her friend's dodging tactics. "Have you at least kissed him yet?"

"No I haven't!" Kathy wasn't going to mention the gentle hand-holding of the previous day. "I hadn't yesterday when you asked me, and I still haven't today."

"Oh God, please tell me you haven't been snogging the conman?"

Kathy saw the perfect diversion. "No, but I think Sarah in the shop would like to."

"What? That fat old lump? He's not going to go for her."

"Well, if he's a conman as you say, he's already found out her mother owns the shop..." Kathy really wished Emma wouldn't put these doubts in her mind. She had thought Piers was just being polite.

"Ah-ha! Told you so."

"And she's not that fat or even all that old."

"Oh, come off it. I remember her thirtieth birthday. Real old maid material if ever I saw it. But, if she's got money, then maybe she's in with a chance." There was a bit of a pause. "I've just thought of the best idea ever that'll rumble his little plot." Emma half-laughed to herself. "Just got to make a couple of phone calls. Oh, by the way, have you heard about Prince Charles and Lady Di?"

"What about them?"

"They've announced their engagement. There's talk of a summer wedding and a bank holiday for everyone."

"You are just obsessed with babies and weddings. I wish them luck, don't think I'd like to marry into the royal family."

"Oh, I don't know. I think you'd quite suit a tiara. Now buzz off while I hatch my plot."

Three people all braved the coast path walk that afternoon. Six cats accompanied them as far as the garden hedge but then decided it was much more pleasant in the house and all melted back through the cat flap into the kitchen.

The shop was busy that afternoon and they had to wait for one of the village ladies to finish her gossip with Sarah as she was totally blocking the doorway while she chatted. It was Kathy who saw the poster in the window and she nudged Jean-Guy's arm and pointed it out.

"Now there's a crazy English tradition for you. Or maybe just a crazy Suffolk one."

His reading of English was getting much better. "What is a Smugglers' Race?"

"They do it here really to get the tourist season going, I'm not usually around for it although I did catch it once many years ago. They have local teams who have to haul a barrel of rum from the edge of the sea to the pub and traditionally the one who got there first gets to drink the contents, but they don't do that any more, they drink beer out of the trophy instead. And these days it's a barrel of water because a lot of them get damaged on the way and rum's too expensive to waste. Teams of up to six people and all you have to help you is about five yards of rope. Oh, and you're not allowed to roll it."

"Totally mad," Jean-Guy decided. He looked at Piers. "We should have a go."

"We'd need more than the two of us."

"Well, I'd make three," Kathy offered. "They do allow women to join in these days you know. We can't use Emma now but maybe Derek would join in."

The local woman came out of the shop at last. "Hullo, love," she greeted Kathy. "Good news about Prince Charles isn't it?" she said as she passed them.

"What is it with you English and the royal family?" Jean-Guy asked when the lady was safely out of hearing range.

Piers held up his hands. "Times like these I remember I'm Irish."

Jean-Guy hadn't been in the shop before so he went to explore the stock while the other two looked at the photos in all the newspapers.

"I love her sweater," Kathy remarked looking at the picture of Lady Diana perched on the back of a painted bench while her fiancé stood next to her.

"One of the greatest moments in the recent history of the monarchy and all you can say is 'I love her sweater'?"

"You going to buy a paper?"

"Nah, I'm not that interested."

"And you a former member of Her Majesty's armed forces."

"Yup," was the unrepentant reply. "Tell you something to amuse you, it was His Majesty when I first signed up. I'm so old I had to swear my original allegiance to the King. But then the silly sod died a few days later."

"And how are you all today?" Sarah asked, joining her latest customers by the newspapers, apparently not caring she was interrupting their conversation. "Have you seen the Smugglers' Race poster? I hope you'll all be entering it this year?"

"I don't think three of us qualify as a team," Kathy told her.

"Oh, no, but the village lads could do with some help. We've got my cousins Ian and Trevor, the brothers from the pig farm who are up for it, but their dad and uncle say they've done it for forty years and it's time to hand over to the young ones. Minimum of four per team." She looked across at Jean-Guy who was standing with his head on one side, puzzling over the selection of local history books. "And who's he?"

Kathy wasn't about to let Sarah anywhere near the more vulnerable Jean-Guy. "That's Jean-Guy. He doesn't read English all that well. 'Scuse me." Kathy left Piers with Sarah and went over to join Jean-Guy. "Found anything interesting?"

"I wouldn't know. The titles all look very strange."

"That's because a lot of them are Suffolk names and words. They're all about local history. Are you interested in history?"

"Not really." Jean-Guy's gaze dropped to the children's books below. "But there is your Winnie-the-Pooh. I shall buy that one."

Kathy looked round and realised the chatty Sarah had got herself very close to Piers without actually touching him but he hadn't made any attempt to move away. "I think Sarah has designs on our Concorde pilot."

It wasn't a phrase Jean-Guy knew but he looked across and guessed the meaning. "He seems to like it. Shall we rescue him?"

"Probably should. But it's quite fun watching them. I guess he's just being polite, there'll never be anything between them."

Jean-Guy saw it from a different perspective. "He is letting her stand close. I think maybe he has designs too."

Before Kathy could disagree, two young village women came into the shop bringing a blast of cold air and lively gossip about something they had heard in the pub last night. They both frankly appraised the man with Sarah and one of them whistled and said,

"Well, things are hotting up round here. You can warm up my bed any time you like."

To Kathy's admiration this didn't bother Piers in the slightest, she guessed with his looks he was used to it, but a furious Sarah stood defensively between the women and Piers. "Leave him alone. He's a friend of the Professor's."

"Out of your league then, Porky," came the vicious jibe. "I'll take my usual ciggies."

Sarah's face flushed scarlet and she looked as though she was about to cry. Kathy and Jean-Guy knew Piers was plotting something and to their relief, he gently gathered Sarah in his arms and gave her a slow and intense kiss. "See you at seven tonight in the pub then?" he said to her just loud enough for the dumbstruck onlookers to hear. "And please don't turn up wearing that pinny, you know I can't get it untied." He looked across to his companions and asked, "You two buying anything or just enjoying the floor show?"

"Floor show, definitely," Kathy laughed. "Just the book for Jean-Guy."

"Go on then, hurry up. I've got me a hot date for tonight now. Haven't I, Sarah?"

Her face was no less red but she was smiling now. "Seven o'clock," she confirmed.

The Prof roared with laughter when he heard what had happened, then he said to Piers, "That was a kind thing you did even if it was just you having fun. The village women are cruel to her and I wouldn't like to think you will be the same. Let her down gently and show her some respect, she's never even had a boyfriend so far as I know. Which is a shame as her heart is all gold."

Rather than walk the coast path in the dark, they took the Land Rover to the pub and Kathy realised how glad she was to get out of the house for an evening. The pub was busy but Sarah was already at the bar, looking no slimmer but a lot more fashionable in a pair of jeans and trendy picture sweater. She had taken her fluffy, dark blonde hair out of its work-hours ponytail and it hung to her shoulders in a style that was too old for her. She wore no make-up but at least she wasn't wearing her shop tabard and her smile of welcome lit up her face. There was a slight hush as the three came into the bar and Kathy was glad she was bunched between the two men.

"I'll get the first round," Piers told them. "You two go and find a table. What do you want?"

Kathy and Jean-Guy sat themselves at a vacant table at the back of the room as most people were crowded round the bar and watched as Piers greeted the madly blushing Sarah with a casual arm round the waist and a kiss behind the ear as though he had been dating her for years.

"You see," Kathy muttered to Jean-Guy, "when he acts like that I believe Emma about him being a conman. Then he sits and cries over a piano keyboard and I don't."

"Why was he crying over a keyboard? What did you find out about his piano playing history?"

Kathy felt a bit of a traitor. "Ah. What do you know about the mezzo Roisin Thompson?"

"Saw her in Leningrad a couple of years ago. We were both there at the same time and happened to go to each other's concerts so we met backstage twice. Her Mahler technique is just incomparable. And she can sing Prokofiev like a native as her spoken Russian is totally fluent. We had to speak in Russian as we had people in the same room who wouldn't have liked it if we had spoken English."

"Well that guy over there is her baby brother but we mustn't ever tell anyone. It brought back some bad memories when he played yesterday."

"Shit," was Jean-Guy's immediate reaction. "I have heard some of her very early recordings. If that was him playing as a child I must get him to play for me." He caught her look. "And, yes, I will tread carefully so I don't wake the ghosts."

Piers and Sarah came to join them, carrying four drinks between them, bringing with them two strapping young men who were confusingly identical and who made it quite a squash round the table.

"These are my cousins Ian and Trevor," Sarah introduced the men. "The pub's Race team so far."

117

A confusing round of handshakes and introductions took place then Trevor raised his glass and roared across the bar, "Set them up, Barry! The pub's got itself a proper Race team this year!"

The whole crowd in the pub started yelling and cheering and Kathy wondered just what the heck she had let herself in for.

It was a cold frosty night when they left the pub when it closed at just gone eleven and as Kathy lurched against Jean-Guy she realised that for the first time in years she had drunk way too much alcohol. She couldn't remember the last time she had had such a riotous evening and she couldn't quite stop giggling.

Ian and Trevor said they would see Sarah safely back to her home next to the shop and the three reeled off drunkenly into the night, somehow knowing where they were going although the only illumination was a faint distant glow from the power station lights.

"Oh God," Jean-Guy groaned and staggered back against Kathy. "I think I have drunk too much."

"Me too," Kathy giggled in a silly high-pitched voice and nearly fell over her own feet. Jean-Guy put out his arms to steady her and suddenly she found herself held close against him and the two of them were snogging the tonsils out of each other.

"Oh, for pity's sake!" came Piers' voice and he grabbed them each by the coat collar. "Just pour yourselves into the car and get a room."

"Just because your girl's gone home with the pig farmers," Kathy told him and kissed him too.

Piers almost gagged at the taste of alcohol Kathy left in his mouth. He unceremoniously tipped the two of them into the back of the Land Rover and shut the door on them. He heard some grunting and giggling from both of them as they got settled and he hoped they wouldn't have sex in the car while he was driving it. He looked up to the sky and saw one star hanging low that had at last breached the incessant cloud and he smelled the frost in the air. He climbed into the driving seat and shut the door before starting the engine.

"Next time," he said to the two who weren't listening to him in the slightest, "one of you can drive."

Kathy woke face down in the morning to realise she had a pounding headache, her mouth was dry and her lolling tongue had somehow got stuck to the pillow. She peeled herself off the pillow and just knew something wasn't right. Turning her head more quickly than she should have done, she saw Jean-Guy was sleeping in the bed next to her, lying on his side facing her and looking very sweet and Moly-ish.

"Oh God," she said quietly and started shaking. "What have I done?" It was only as she slid out of the bed without waking him she realised she still had her T shirt and floral trousers on from last night. She had one sock on, her hair was all over the place and she was really craving a cup of tea and the loo. "Tea," she said more firmly as she crept across to the door and peeped out to see who else might be stirring. There was no sign of anyone so she guessed she could sneak about without being seen.

The stairs didn't squeak, Emma had always said, because they were so old they were made out of one piece of wood so there weren't any joins to rub, and Kathy cautiously approached the kitchen, hoping only the sympathetic Professor would be up and about. She couldn't hear any voices so she went into the room to find both the Professor and Piers at the table but it was too late to creep out again.

"It's alive," Piers remarked and sounded annoyingly cheerful.

The Professor understandingly handed her a mug of tea. "I gather you and Jean-Guy met the local real ale last night."

Kathy gulped down tea with more gratitude than dignity. "I don't know what it was but I can't remember the last time I got so drunk." She sat at the table and looked at Piers with huge blue eyes. "Tell me, what did I do?"

"Nothing. You gave me a hell of a kiss in the pub car park but otherwise you were totally engrossed with Jean-Guy. Is he still in your bed, by the way? I gave up trying to get the two of you apart last night and he was way too pissed to misbehave with you."

"Um, yes," she admitted and was sure her face had gone scarlet. The tea began to clear the fog in her brain. "Oh, God, was that you?" she groaned. "You had a sweet under your tongue or something. Felt really weird but kind of hot." She sank a second mug of tea the Prof gave her and the fog cleared a bit more. "Wow. Sorry, didn't mean to say that. Or kiss you last night. I'm so sorry."

"Don't be, I quite enjoyed it. Then I got one almost as good off Jean-Guy when we got back. No idea why, I think he was aiming for you and missed, so I won't take it personally. Anyway, get some breakfast down your neck as we've got to be at the beach in an hour."

"What on earth for?"

"Smugglers' Race practice. The lads can take a break from work and Sarah said her parents will mind the shop for an hour."

Six people stood in a bunch on the windswept beach and realised they had a problem. Ian and Trevor had told the novices that you had to start by getting the big wooden barrel out of the sea. The barrels would be on a raft anchored several feet from the shoreline so the first thing you had to do was get very wet going out to the raft to bring the barrel to the beach. The second thing was that the barrel itself was soaking wet, full of slopping liquid and very, very slippery. Barry from the pub had given each team an old barrel to practise with and they could see another group involved in a similar exercise a bit further along towards the power station.

"Team from the power station," Trevor told them gloomily. "They've won it the last five years."

"Who else puts up a team?" Kathy asked him and looked as the group along the beach started hauling with the synchronisation of a team of well-trained shire horses.

"Well, our village pub, there'll be teams from at least two other local pubs, teachers from the village school always have a go just so the kids can laugh at them. Then there's the lot from the power station and usually the air base sends along at least one team too just as a community thing."

"Why did I let you talk me in to this?" Kathy asked Sarah.

"Oh, and you have to dress up as a smuggler and do it barefoot," Ian added

The three who had never done it before just gawped at him.

"Are you for real?" Jean-Guy asked. He had hardly dared look at Kathy since he had woken alone in her bed and all he could hope was that she had slept in his room last night. He really couldn't remember a thing about it.

"True," Sarah told him. "I've got some photos of previous years I can show you."

"Oh God," Piers groaned quietly. He pointed a stern finger at Sarah. "You so owe me big time for this."

Ian and Trevor stared at the shop girl who had been the butt of village jokes for years and they had never seen her smile like that before.

Unbroken circle

Three very wet and tired people trudged back to the farmhouse going in through the back door to find Emma seated at the kitchen table looking very calm and elegant in her fur coat and with her husband and father keeping her company.

"Oh my God!" she shrieked when she saw them. "Kath, have you got seaweed in your hair?"

"Probably," she admitted. "I think I've drunk ten pints of sea water. Lovely to see you too, by the way."

"What the hell have you been doing?" Emma wouldn't look at the two men who were with her friend. She remembered Jean-Guy well enough but she hadn't seen Piers before and had to admit to herself he was breathtakingly handsome, so she could understand why Kath would fall for him.

"Smugglers' Race practice," Kathy told her. "We weren't very good at it. OK, I'm for the bath."

"Not if I get there first," Jean-Guy told her and somehow there was a scrum of laughing, soggy people and a small tortoiseshell cat all dashing along the hall and up the stairs in one mob and a succession of slamming doors from upstairs.

Emma looked at her father and raised questioning eyebrows. "What has happened to Kath? She was always such a mouse."

"She has made two good friends who care for her."

"Do you mean I don't?"

"In your own way. But I think you liked her better as a mouse."

123

Emma checked her watch. "I'd better go and tell her Derek and I want my room tonight. She can go back in her old room at the front."

"Jean-Guy is in there at the moment."

Emma tutted. "Well, he can bunk up with the conman. This is my house and I want my room for the night."

Kathy came down from the bathroom first, dressed in jeans and her favourite bright pink sweatshirt. Her long blonde hair was loose down her back and still wet from having the sea water washed out of it and there was a glow to her face and a sparkle in her eye that Emma hadn't seen for a long time. She gave her friend a hug now she was clean and mostly dry.

"You're settling in here then?" she asked. "Dad's given me as much information as I need to know but I'm still not convinced about the conman."

"Please don't call him that," Kathy said. "I don't know how he can prove it to you."

"I do," Emma told her but wouldn't say any more.

Jean-Guy was down next and Emma was sure he had put on weight. He certainly looked a lot different from the pale, snuffling young man she remembered from her wedding day. She and Jean-Guy shook hands very formally and exchanged some chat about living in Suffolk; she wasn't quite sure what to say when he told her he was reading Winnie-the-Pooh.

Piers wandered into the kitchen last in his scruffiest old jeans, the green sweater still with a moth-hole in it and only socks on his feet. His smile was at its most charming but his eyes were cautious as he introduced himself to Emma and she couldn't help but accept his handshake. Even Derek looked impressed as he was introduced too.

"So now we are all here, we will have lunch," the Professor decided. "It is only a stew."

Emma sat and watched as the others, with the skill of practice, got the table laid and the stew ladled out into bowls. A loaf of bread came out of the Aga, which she couldn't ever remember working properly and Kathy put the kettle on to one of the hotplates so it would be ready for them to make tea afterwards.

"So," Emma said to Piers as she picked at her stew, "How did you learn to mend Agas?"

"It was a case of having to," he told her. "The ex and the solicitors had pretty much bankrupted me between them, but I just about afforded my house by mortgaging it to the hilt and the Aga was already there when I moved in after the divorce. When it broke down I couldn't afford to get it mended so I went into Foyle's, bought a book and just got on with it."

"Kath says you're a pilot?"

"When I'm not mending Agas, yes. Want to see my licences?"

"I want to see you fly. Anyone can forge a licence."

There was a silence at the table and everyone looked at her. Petr Mihaly was starting to feel ashamed of his daughter. "Emma," he began to remonstrate gently. "I think Piers will need an aeroplane if he is going to fly."

She took some papers from her bag and triumphantly slapped them onto the table. "I've booked you a training session at Ipswich Airfield. Thought it would make a nice day out for us all tomorrow."

There was just a brief flash of something that could have been annoyance or amusement in his eyes, but Piers spoke quite calmly. "I've been flying aeroplanes, military and civilian for nearly thirty years, why would I want a training session?"

"Are you refusing to go?" Emma challenged.

The spark in his eyes became the anger Kathy had seen that morning at the Home Office. "I'll go if it's that what it takes, but I'll be wasting their time." He shrugged and the spark disappeared, "Still, I suppose a few more hours in the log book won't do any harm. What sort of aeroplanes do they fly?"

"I have no idea. Why do you ask?"

"It's just that I haven't flown a prop for years but I'm guessing they won't have any jets on offer."

"I'll give you one thing," Emma told him, "you're bloody convincing."

He just smiled and went back to his lunch.

Kathy didn't sleep very well in the narrow bed in the room that Jean-Guy had been using. She had got used to the double in Emma's room and missed the space. As was usual, she went down in the morning to find the Prof and Piers at the kitchen table.

"Looking forward to your flying lesson?" she asked brightly.

"More if I wasn't so darned tired. You could have told me Jean-Guy kicks like a donkey when he's asleep."

"Get him drunk. He was no trouble when he shared with me."

"Want him back?"

"Nah, you can keep him."

The Professor smiled and thought how he was going to miss the company of these young people when they left.

Derek had a brand new Ford Capri to drive and Emma insisted her father and Kathy came with them which left Jean-Guy and Piers to follow along behind in the disreputable old Land Rover. Kathy would far rather have travelled with them but she sat squashed meekly in the back seat of the Capri while Emma regaled her with early pregnancy stories which made Kathy glad Jean-Guy had been too drunk to do anything with her the other night.

"If you think Piers is a conman, why are you making him fly?" she suddenly asked, cutting across Emma's chat.

"But that's exactly why. If he's as qualified as he says then the instructor will know and can tell us. Then we can go to The Horseshoes afterwards for lunch."

The flying school was easy to find at Ipswich airfield as its name was prominently displayed on one of the hangars and they presently met the designated instructor for the session who introduced himself as Pete Finch.

"OK, so which one of you wants to join the Red Arrows?" he quipped.

"That would be me," Piers admitted. "Sorry, but I think you've been got here under false pretences. I am a qualified pilot already but Emma here thought she was treating me to something."

Pete raised a cynical eyebrow. "Well, come along to the briefing room anyway. Got your licence and log book with you?"

"Of course."

Pete smiled at the rest of the group. "Well, it's an hour session so I suggest you all go and have a coffee in the club lounge and we'll join you when we're done."

To Kathy's unspoken joy there was a coffee machine in the club lounge and she finally got the cappuccino she had been craving. The club lounge had floor to ceiling windows facing the runway and there were a few aeroplanes taking off and landing for them to watch.

Emma was very quiet as she sat next to Kathy and stirred sugar into her coffee. "Please tell me you haven't fallen in love with him," she said softly.

Kathy was startled. "I like him," she said and hoped Emma wouldn't respond in the same way Jean-Guy had.

"The three of you seem very close."

"I suppose we are in a way. But we're all living in an unreal state so we're kind of clinging together to try and make sense of it. Piers and I have been slung out of our jobs, Jean-Guy still hasn't got his asylum. We just don't know what's going on."

"Can see your point," Emma conceded. "But I don't know how you can share a house with him and keep your knickers on."

Kathy felt herself go cold and wondered what had happened to the sympathetic friend who had helped her so much when her relationship had ended in such violence. She jumped as she felt Jean-Guy put his arm across her shoulders.

"How do you know she has?" he asked sounding quite amused at the idea of Kathy and Piers ever getting up to anything. "Isn't that the instructor walking towards us? What has he done with Piers?"

"Locked him up and called the constables I would hope," Emma snapped.

Jean-Guy tightened his grip on Kathy and she leaned into him, wondering if one of her dreams was about to be shattered.

"What have you done with Biggles?" Emma asked Pete cheerily when he joined them at their table.

He smiled broadly. "You remember my crack about the Red Arrows? Well he really has flown with them. Just for a few months. Nearly thirty thousand flying hours in his log and I'd pay him to teach me half of what he knows."

"You're joking," Emma tried bravely while the others all tried not to look smug.

Pete nodded towards the window. "That's him now in the blue and white just taxiing for take-off. Not often that one gets to go out as it's a twin engine and we haven't got many qualified to fly it."

Emma got abruptly to her feet. "Kath," she requested, "Come and help me find the ladies' room."

"Just to the left of the bar," Pete told them with a wave of his hand.

There was nobody else in the ladies' toilets and Emma sat on one of the toilet lids with the cubicle door open while Kathy waited next to her and missed her cappuccino which would be getting cold by now.

"What have I done?" Emma whispered sounding mortified. "What the hell am I going to say to him when he gets back?"

"If I were you I'd just be nice and smile. Odds are he's going to have a whale of a time buzzing about in the plane and he'll love you for ever just for letting him fly for an hour or so."

"Derek's going to kill me, he paid for it." Emma finally remembered the other woman had been in a relationship that had so nearly become fatal. "Sorry. Tactless of me. Oh God, I'm such an idiot."

"No you're not," Kathy said loyally. "You were just looking out for me and your dad. Quite understandable. No, don't cry. Emma, please don't cry."

"It's my hormones," Emma sobbed. "They're all over the place at the moment. Now go away, I'm sixteen weeks pregnant and I really do need to pee."

Kathy went back to her coffee which was still at a bearable temperature.

"Is she OK?" Derek asked sounding quite worried.

"She'll be fine. Just being Emma and going off half-cock as always. Has Piers taken off yet?"

"Just going now. There was a beginner in the red Piper in front of him," Pete explained. "Having a bit of trouble. Now it's his turn."

They all watched the little blue and white aeroplane line up at the runway and then obviously given clearance by the control tower it shot down the runway and was off, up and away with a quite remarkable speed.

"Someone had better tell him he's not flying a bloody Lightning at Mach 2 any more," Pete muttered. "He'll have the wings off that thing."

"How long will he be gone?" Kathy asked.

"Well, he's paid for an hour, got a top of the range Omega pilot's watch slapped on his wrist to keep track of everything, and enough fuel to get him to Holland and back. Not that his flight plan takes him that way. Should go north up to the Wash and then loop back

130

across Cambridge. Avoiding the military bases. Don't want them scrambling the jets after him, do we?"

"Do you think he'll behave himself?" Kathy asked, having visions of the little plane being chased and shot down.

"Every confidence. Flown fighter jets for years and now Concorde. He's not a risk taker. They wouldn't put him in charge of a supersonic jet if there was the slightest doubt. Have you any idea the mental and physical checks they run on men like him?"

Kathy was just glad Emma wasn't there to hear such commendation. "In which case, I'm going to have another coffee. I've missed my posh coffee."

"Leave you to it," Pete said and went back to the hangar.

Emma joined them a few minutes later, looking tired and tearful and Derek asked her if she wanted to go home.

"Not just yet," she sniffed and blew her nose on a well-used tissue. "I owe Piers one heck of an apology."

So they watched the planes for a while and when the blue and white one came back right on time they had seen enough take offs and landings to recognise the skill with which that little plane touched the runway and was gently brought back to the hangar.

A bright-eyed Piers joined them about twenty minutes later with a broad grin on his face and lights in his eyes none of them had seen before. Emma had got to her feet to make her apologies but he just picked her up and swung her round before landing a kiss on her cheek.

"You have no idea how grateful I am for that," he told her. "Got my head sorted out at last. I'll pay for lunch just to say thank you."

Emma looked slightly dizzy. "I owe you an apology," she began hesitantly.

"None needed. Really. Best hour I've spent for weeks."

"Well, you're very welcome," Emma said, sounding faintly bewildered.

Jean-Guy leaned close to Kathy and whispered in her ear, "Ratty has been messing about on boats."

They had forgotten Piers' hearing. "'And there is nothing – absolutely nothing – half so much worth doing'," he assured them. "Come on, lunch. My treat."

With peace restored, Emma decided she would like to stay at the farmhouse for a bit longer, especially now it was a lot warmer and having three younger people living there had put an energy into the place that had been missing for so long. She wondered how her father would cope when he was on his own again. But he had never said he was lonely. He had his articles and reviews to write and the occasional defector passing through his hands.

"Who's been playing trios?" she asked, seeing the music on the piano. "Have you made Dad come out of retirement?"

There was a bit of a pause. "Yes," Kathy said quickly not liking to mention Piers' piano playing as he wasn't in the room at the time.

"Wow. He hasn't played for years." She went off to find her father who was hard at work at the typewriter in his study. "Hi, Dad. Kath says you've been playing trios with them."

He knew his daughter of old. "No, I'm not playing today. I am on deadline for this record review and you took me away from my desk most of the day with our little trip to the airport. Not that I didn't enjoy it," he added, seeing her face fall. "Go and ask Piers," he suggested kindly. "After the treat you and Derek gave him this morning I can't see him refusing you anything."

"Oh, OK." Emma wandered back into the sitting room thinking life in the farmhouse was very odd these days. Piers had turned up and was sitting in one of the armchairs in front of the fire. He was reading *The Wind in the Willows* and had a young tortoiseshell cat draped over one shoulder. "Dad says you three have been playing trios," she said more to Kathy than anyone.

"Not really," she hedged with a furtive glance at the reader by the fire. "I mean Piers can play the piano a bit but we haven't played together."

Emma hung on her most beseeching face. "Pleeeease?"

"Well, I'm up for it," Jean-Guy announced as he hadn't done any playing that day and had been about to excuse himself and go to his room to practise. "Hey, Ratty, time to leave the river bank and earn your keep."

"What?"

"Piano. Beethoven. Now. The pregnant lady wants a concert."

To Kathy's surprise, Piers didn't even hesitate but got to his feet and gently put his cat on the chair. "For the lady who pays for my flying lesson, anything, But don't expect miracles."

"I'll fetch my cello," Jean-Guy announced feeling stupidly excited at the thought of playing with Roisin Thompson's accompanist and hoping this could be the start of something good.

The three got themselves sorted out and all felt oddly nervous but didn't know why.

"Tuning from you please, Piers," Jean-Guy requested. "I'll set the tempo."

A few words of advice from Derek who had been appointed page-turner by his wife, and Piers knew the notes to play for them to tune to. "Do you always get so bossy when you've got a cello between your legs?"

Jean-Guy never took any nonsense from his accompanists. "Always. This is my work as flying Concorde is yours. Please respect that." He looked across and caught the pianist's eye and was thankful to realise the other man wasn't the slightest bit offended.

Petr Mihaly looked at the blank sheet of paper in his typewriter and didn't know where to start. He had listened to the LP a few times now and had tried to pick over the bones of it to find a positive thing to say about the performance. The players were all very young, about the same age as Kathy and Jean-Guy but nowhere near as experienced and it showed. He turned his head slightly to listen as the very piece he had been trying to review came out of his sitting room and it wasn't until the pianist missed an entry that he realised it wasn't another recording he was listening to. There was some mild-mannered abuse to be heard from the sitting room, then the *Archduke* started again a few bars back from where it had left off and the pianist didn't miss his entry a second time.

The slow movement of the trio finished in grand style then Piers looked at the clock as he had taken his watch off again. "Right, that's it. Everyone down the pub. Team talk tonight."

The other two groaned. "You must be joking. My liver hasn't recovered from the last time," Jean-Guy complained.

"But Sarah said she'd bring the photos of the old races," Piers tried. "Come on, you lightweights."

"Ring the pub and tell her we'll come tomorrow," Kathy tried.

"I'm not standing her up."

"I wouldn't mind a trip to the pub," Derek offered.

"Well I'm not drinking at the moment," Emma remarked. "Makes me feel sick. Why don't you two go?"

Piers and Derek looked at each other, and went.

"Shall I make tea?" Kathy offered.

"Good idea, I'll help," Emma replied.

On the kitchen table was what looked like a copy of the Professor's record review.

"Odd," Emma remarked. "He doesn't usually leave these lying around." She picked up the sheet of paper and had to smile. "He's reviewed your playing. Listen:

"There are three friends playing this piece in my sitting room and only one of them is currently a professional musician. They are making a much better job of it than the three on this LP so here is my review of their version instead.

"I could not say there is a leader to the group, they are one soloist playing three parts which gives a perfect balance to the sound. The cello playing is phenomenal with a light, lyrical touch and superb tone quality. For the violin there is a freshness to the sound which is so delightful to find in such a well-known work. It is like hearing it for the first time. The pianist has that

rare ability to blend with the others and unlike the version on the record has perfect control of the left hand, the lack of which is so often the mark of an amateur.

"Altogether it is a beautiful performance. It is an honour and a privilege to hear them.

"But I wish the pianist would pay attention and stop flying aeroplanes in his head. That is the second time he has missed an entry!"

"He's so getting a biscuit with his tea," Kathy laughed.

It was his own nightmare that woke Jean-Guy before it was daylight. Vivid, violent images where Kathy was tortured and killed by a nameless and faceless boyfriend while he, restrained by no means he could see, was forced to watch. In his dream he eventually broke free and it was the physical sensation of his arm hitting the bed that woke him.

Thankful to have woken from the nightmare, he looked across but the other half of the bed was empty and his first thought was relief that he hadn't whacked a sleeping Piers. The bedside clock told him it was 4:43am and relief turned into something less pleasant. Trying to quell the rising panic, he got from the bed, opened his door and listened but the house was silent and there wasn't anyone in the bathroom. Maybe Piers had come home so drunk he had crashed out on the sofa downstairs. That had to be better than the alternatives that were starting to play in his mind. He tried to think back over the previous evening. After the trio, Derek and Piers had gone off to the pub in Derek's car. After cups of tea he, Kathy and Emma had gone to their rooms leaving the

Prof still trying to write nice things about a bad recording.

The car. If the car was back then so were Piers and Derek. Jean-Guy set off along the landing, groping his way in the darkness and feeling for the stairs with his toes. He was reaching out for the front door when a hand grabbed his shoulder with a strength and suddenness that made him gasp.

"What the hell are you doing?" the Professor hissed at him in Czech.

"Piers isn't in bed. I was going to see if the car was here."

"Come into the kitchen."

In the kitchen, the Professor put the kettle on and parked Jean-Guy at the table. The two still spoke in Czech.

"Piers is with Sarah. Fortunately Derek got back before I went to bed and told me. He wasn't happy about it and I am going to have words with that young man when he gets back."

"Is he in danger?"

"Not directly but I don't know what story he will tell her. I would have briefed him on his cover story if I had known he was going to get involved with her. This is the safe house with the radio equipment and the hotline telephone. Physically it is hidden from view by the hedges. He must not put us at risk."

Jean-Guy could sense the controlled anger in the other man and began to realise that maybe there was more going on here than he had assumed.

The Professor hadn't quite finished. "He has to understand it is not some funny adventure. Not even

Emma really knows what I do but it is much more than temporary shelter for defectors."

The kitchen door opened and Kathy peeped in, her eyes huge in a worried face. "Is everything all right? I heard voices downstairs speaking Czech and didn't realise it was you two at first."

"Piers has gone to spend the night with Sarah," Jean-Guy informed her.

Kathy's immediate reaction was to wonder why that was such a big deal. Then she thought about it. "That doesn't sound very sensible. But he was so wound up with excitement after his flight in the morning I'm not really surprised. I wonder what he'll tell her about being here. I've never said anything."

The Professor turned to Jean-Guy and shrugged. "You see, she understands and she is not some smartarse Concorde pilot. I will sit and wait for him now. He will sneak in at first light thinking to be here before I am awake."

"Shall I make us some coffee?" Kathy asked. "How will he get in?"

"He asked Derek to leave the kitchen door unlocked, saying he would be back before midnight and would lock up. Kathy, if you look in the pantry you will find some packets of stuff that are supposed to make cappuccinos. I have no idea what they will taste like but they were free with the usual coffee when I last went shopping."

"Frothy coffee at five in the morning," she remarked. "I can't remember the last time I did such a thing."

The packet cappuccino wasn't that good, but it was a hot drink and Kathy tried to get the Prof to talk to her about the record he had been reviewing.

"I know what you're doing," he told her. "You are trying to make me less angry for when Piers gets in. I am glad you are trying to protect him, but please stop."

"Do you want us to go?" Jean-Guy asked.

"Up to you. I don't mind the company and now we all have drinks. We can talk for a while but as soon as it starts to get light we must sit in absolute silence or with those rabbit-ears of his he will hear us."

That put such an image into Kathy's head she wanted to laugh. "Well, if we're going to sit up chatting I'm going to pop upstairs and put some clothes on. Don't really want to sit round in my nightie for the next hour or so."

"Good idea," the Professor agreed. "I think I will do the same. I'll leave the light on so we can find our way back then I will turn it out. I'm only thankful Emma sleeps so deeply she won't get woken up too."

The sky was quite light by the time the back door opened and Piers stepped into the kitchen. He saw the three at the table and physically jumped.

"Oh, shit," was all he said.

The Professor got to his feet. "Yes, and it has hit something. You go into my study. And you two go outside where you can't hear. This is not going to be pleasant."

Kathy and Jean-Guy just stopped long enough to grab coats and boots then walked down the drive in the sunrise where they went into the old cottages and looked out through what had once been a side window and which would have had a commanding view of the sea except the rhododendrons had grown up and totally blocked not just the view but most of the light as well. The encroaching shrubbery bathed the abandoned cottages in a peculiar green light but there was an atmosphere of serenity there which was a total contrast to the tension that had been building up in the farmhouse kitchen.

"I have never, ever seen him like that before," Kathy whispered and sounded as scared as she felt.

Jean-Guy took her hand. "It's how he has survived out here, doing what he does for over twenty years."

Kathy turned into his coat and put her arms round him. To her relief, he guessed what she wanted and enfolded her in a gentle hug.

"It reminded me….." she began.

"Hush," he said softly and kissed the top of her head.

She clenched her fists round the lapels of his old tweed coat. "No, I have to tell you. You need to understand. I've told you how my story ended so now I need to tell you how it began."

Jean-Guy didn't speak for a moment but held her a little more securely. He knew just how hard it was for her to tell him this story of what had turned her into the mistrustful woman who hid under the blankets when she saw the handwriting of a man from her past. He had heard and seen many bad things during his time in Czechoslovakia. The Soviets hadn't always been kind. "Just tell me," he whispered to her. "You have told me a little and so far as I can understand you have done nothing wrong. We all do wrong things."

"Everyone tells me it wasn't my fault," Kathy began hesitantly. "But he made me feel as though it was and that's what I can't get rid of."

"Tell me your story. Do you want to stand here or would you rather walk?"

"No, let's stay here. I don't know why but I feel safe here. These were happy houses once and I like to think they will be again. They're like me." She could feel the tears starting at the back of her eyes. "Maybe I need the help of a builder too. But a builder of people not of houses."

Jean-Guy waited for her to continue. He knew that she needed to speak now. She needed to tell her story because as long as she held the secret she couldn't move forward with her life. And he wanted her to move on, taking him with her.

Kathy didn't try to stop the tears from falling. The atmosphere of the houses and the security of Jean-Guy's embrace made her feel safe at last. This man who had been through so much himself wasn't going to judge her or criticise her. This was the man who would hold her hand and lead her to a brighter future.

Petr Mihaly found them still in the derelict cottage, still standing in each other's arms and looking totally at peace. Somehow innocent like two small children and it warmed his cynical heart.

"You can come back now," he told them. "I have even made porridge."

Kathy wiped her nose on the cuff of her coat, exhausted but happy after her talk with Jean-Guy. "You do make the best porridge," she told the Prof and managed a weak and wobbly smile.

141

The Prof misconstrued her feelings. "It's OK, he's still in one piece. Just about. I put him through a bit of a mangle but that is all."

"Did you hit him?" Kathy asked.

The Prof didn't seem surprised by her question. "No. He is an intelligent man and thankfully has given himself a good cover story."

Kathy gulped and sniffed a bit more. "Sorry, I don't seem to have any tissues."

"That is what coat sleeves are for," Jean-Guy told her. "Want to borrow mine?"

"Silly," Kathy said gratefully and cuddled against him. She was glad she had decided to trust this quiet, flawed man with her own story. He had understood her fears and her anxieties and she knew he understood that maybe sometimes she would be afraid still. There may even be times when she would feel she couldn't trust him although deep inside she knew she could. He had offered her a guiding hand and she had accepted it, trusting him to walk beside her for a long time to come. As steady and constant as the old stone walls that still stood around them even if the roof was falling in.

The Professor looked at them but didn't ask.

"Kathy has told me of her engagement," Jean-Guy explained quietly. "I mean really told me. I think she was afraid you may show Piers some violence too. Or he may have hit you."

"Ah," said the Professor, who had heard the story at the time from Emma as Kathy had been too terrified to tell him. "No he stayed quite calm and understood me perfectly, although I would believe him capable of violence. I'm afraid our conversation has upset him more than I had thought it would as it has opened up some old memories and wounds. But he understood why I had to do it even if he did resent what he saw as my intrusion into his life, but he and I are still friends so come and have your porridge."

Kathy thought she would find a subdued and repentant Piers at the table. She did not expect to see Emma and Derek making inroads into the pan of porridge that was keeping hot on the Aga. The door to the study was closed and Kathy could feel a tangible silence coming from the room.

"Is Piers not eating?" she asked.

"Not yet," Emma told her. "Dad's left him in the study for a while. He'll be out for his breakfast when he's good and hungry."

The rippling notes on the piano made them all jump. They knew it was the upright piano in the study being played as the bass strings would never stay in tune and the D below middle C had a stuck hammer that no amount of persuasion would release for more than five minutes at the time.

"I left him with some Liszt," the Professor explained. "Nothing like a bit of *La Campanella* to get it all out of your system."

Emma looked at her father and her face had paled. "But, Dad…"

He silenced her with a warning smile. "Not this time."

Those in the kitchen listened to the piano being played. It was nowhere near a perfect performance but it was good enough to impress them. Run-though over, the pianist in the study seemed to be settling down to some serious work on the trills and jumps of the piece which was just as fascinating to the listeners in the kitchen.

Sometimes the jumps worked, sometimes they missed. After a series of successful jumps there came the sound of the piano lid being closed with an unmistakeably triumphant bang and then Piers joined them in the kitchen.

"Any breakfast left?" he asked and walked rather stiffly across to the Aga to see what was in the saucepan.

Kathy looked at the clock. "I think it's nearer lunch time than breakfast."

The Professor gratefully retired to his study now it was free again and Emma and Derek discreetly left the other three in the kitchen.

"You OK?" Kathy asked. "You look as though you've hurt your back."

He smiled a bit sheepishly. "Turned my ankle on a stone walking home and jarred it. Nothing to worry about."

"You're sure the Prof didn't give you a walloping?" Kathy checked.

"Quite sure. I haven't had such a bollocking since I left the forces but I guess I deserved it."

"Was she worth it?" Jean-Guy wanted to know. He and Piers exchanged a look that Kathy was amused to realise they assumed she wouldn't understand.

There was a quiet smile on Piers' face as he replied cheerfully. "Definitely. Can't say too much as there's a lady present. I meant to be back by midnight but we both fell asleep. Christ but I panicked when I saw the time."

"Oh, don't think of me as a lady," Kathy insisted, still amused to be part of this masculine conversation. "Do tell."

Piers looked slightly startled. "No. It's personal."

"Uh-huh? Think I won't understand?" she teased him.

Jean-Guy watched as the two of them got going again and was relieved to see that Piers' smile was definitely of charmed fondness, as a big brother would give a slightly annoying little sister and he no longer felt the other man was quite the threat he had once thought he was.

"No, I think you probably will and that's worse."

"Oh my God. You didn't hurt your back on the path, did you? What the hell did you two get up to last night?"

"Don't be so bloody nosy."

"Fine. I'll just ask Sarah." Kathy grinned hugely. "Did it involve chandeliers?"

Defence turned to attack. "Chandeliers, huh? Always knew you were posh."

"I'm not. I'm the least posh person I know."

"You're from bloody Wimbledon."

"I'm not the one with the pilot's wings and the elocution lessons."

Jean-Guy decided it was time to intervene or those two would still be going at midnight. "Seeing her again?"

Piers stood up, then to the fascination of the other two, calmly bent forwards until his hands were on the floor, his head was on his knees and there was a loud crack from his spine. "Yes," he replied and carefully pulled himself upright again. "Another race practice for all of us this afternoon as the other three can get time off."

"How did you do that?" Kathy asked.

He gave her one of his smiles. "A misspent youth and a very bendy back."

They did a bit better that afternoon. They were the only team on the beach and got hot and wet in the winter sunshine but they worked out an efficient way of hauling the barrel out of the sea although they then had no energy left to try and get it all the way up the dunes to the pub.

Six puffing people stood on the beach and watched the water leaking out of the barrel that had had quite a bash on a rock. Something that would have had them disqualified from the race as barrels had to arrive at the pub intact.

Trevor looked up at the sky. "Time to call it a day. More rain coming in if I'm not mistaken."

"Getting dark too," Sarah remarked. "But it's not that late."

Kathy was puzzled by Sarah and Piers. They were certainly friendly and relaxed towards each other and had got extremely close and personal when hauling on the same bit of rope, but there was no cuddling or hand-holding or even any signs that they had spent the night together. She didn't hear them making any plans to meet again, not even a mention of a trip to the pub and she was getting very curious, even though she knew it was really none of her business.

They had walked along the path to the beach practice and automatically turned to go back that way as the other three started towards the village.

"Will you be alright on the path?" Ian asked. "Light's going with that storm coming and I can always give you a lift back in the pig van."

"We'll be fine," Jean-Guy said firmly. "It's not far."

The coast path was getting very gloomy as they set off back to the farmhouse. Heavy black clouds were rolling in from the east and there was a flash of lightning out to sea. Unconsciously the three all quickened their pace as the first heavy drops of rain fell. The wind got up and was beginning to howl in the fir trees on the land side of the path and the hard grass on the dunes whipped their legs as they walked. A loud clap of thunder took their breaths away and then the rain lashed down and soaked them through in minutes.

"I've never got so wet so often," Kathy shouted into the wind but the other two didn't seem to hear her. She couldn't quite believe it when Piers stopped and turned to look back the way they had come. The rain had plastered his hair down as he wasn't wearing a hat and was dripping off his nose and chin.

"What?" Jean-Guy asked, clearly not wanting to stop.

"Heard something."

"All I can hear is rain and thunder."

"Something out there. I'm sure I heard it."

"Wind in the trees," Jean-Guy replied shortly seeing that Kathy was starting to look spooked. "Let's keep walking."

They walked on for a few minutes but Piers stopped again and looked back into the gathering darkness. He turned back abruptly, put himself between the other two and grabbed them by the arms. "Walk," he said shortly, "Walk past the house as though we're going to the caravan park."

"But it's closed," Kathy remarked and wished the two men didn't walk so fast.

"Just hope who or what ever it is behind us doesn't know that."

They had just passed the gap in the hedge that would have taken them to the back garden when the darkness was split by a powerful torch beam and they distinctly heard Emma's voice calling:

"Boysie! Boysie! Where are you, you stupid dog?"

The torch beam shone down the coast path but the three soaked walkers were behind it. Emma swung the torch from side to side picking up an empty path from the fir trees to the beach.

"Stay behind the torch," Piers whispered and shoved Kathy and Jean-Guy towards the gap in the hedge.

"Boysie!" Emma yelled again as she felt three people enter the garden behind her. "Oh, you idiot animal. I bet you're back in the caravan. Boysie!"

She snapped the torch off and all four bundled into the farmhouse kitchen where the Professor and Derek were sharing a pot of tea.

"Sorry," Kathy said. "Didn't think it was going to get so dark so quickly. Maybe we should have had the lift in the pig van."

"What made you suspicious?" Jean-Guy asked.

"We weren't," Emma told him. "Standard practice when someone's out in the dark and we want to get them in. Call the dog and see who turns up. What happened?"

"Rabbit-ears here thought he heard something," Jean-Guy replied.

"What sort of something?" the Professor asked as he watched Piers and Kathy collect three mugs from the dresser.

"Dunno," Piers replied vaguely. "Just something that wasn't storm or sea sounds. Maybe there really is a lost dog out there."

"There's a ghost dog that haunts the path," Emma told him. "Maybe that's what you heard. Supposed to be the soul of a hound that got washed out to sea and is forever trying to find its way home."

Kathy had heard the story before. "More likely a story put out by the smugglers to keep the customs men away from the beach," she said cynically and saw the smile Jean-Guy gave her. "Oi!" she exclaimed as Piers snatched the towel from her so he could dry his hair. "I was still using that!" She grabbed it back and a minor tussle ensued.

"Children, behave!" the Prof told them even though it was amusing to watch. They all meekly sat round the table, drinking mugs of tea and dipping into the biscuit tin. Petr Mihaly looked round at the others at the table and raised his mug of tea. "Here is to the circle," he told them. "May it stay unbroken. You are each only as strong as the man next to you and today you have proved to me that this unbroken circle is strong."

House of Winter

Emma and Derek left the next morning, heading back to their flat in Southfields and full of plans for buying a house out in the suburbs or even moving right out into the country to give their child the best possible life. Emma was half way out of the door before she remembered she had had Kathy's letters in her bag the whole time and finally handed them over.

Kathy took her post into the sitting room where Jean-Guy was stretched out on the sofa still reading *Winnie-the-Pooh* and Piers was at the piano working on the more difficult sections of the *Ghost* while Audrey crouched on the closed top and watched his fingers very carefully.

Just for a moment, Kathy wondered what had made him decide to go back to his piano playing but she didn't like to interrupt his concentration by asking. "You'll wear that keyboard out," she told him instead and flopped into one of the armchairs. "Oh, a card from Danny, wasn't expecting that." She turned over the picture of Ben Nevis and laughed. "What sane, rational human being goes on a music course in Scotland in February?"

"Ow! Sodding cat! Get off."

Kathy looked round to see Piers was sucking the fingers Audrey had just pounced on.

"Why would any professional musician go on a course anywhere?" Jean-Guy asked lazily from his comfortable sofa.

"Oh, he's not a professional. He taught me to drive, that's how we met."

"He is one of the Tarling dynasty and he teaches people to drive?"

"Told you he couldn't play much with his injured hand."

"What happened to it?"

"Don't know. He's never said."

Piers tried to go back to his piano playing but it didn't sound much like Beethoven with Audrey stalking his fingers. "I met a David Tarling once, is he a relative?"

Jean-Guy paid him strict attention. "He was Danny's uncle. How did you meet him? He was famous for never meeting people."

Piers stopped playing before Audrey scratched his hands again. "Donkey's years ago. I must have been about fourteen and he tried to recruit me as his accompanist. My father just told him to piss off."

"Why? Surely that would have earned money for you?"

"For them you mean," Piers snorted. "Roisin and I never saw a penny of what we earned them. No, apparently I was exclusive to my sister. There were a few soloists who came sniffing round for me in those days."

"And you didn't want to play for them?" Jean-Guy persisted.

"Never given a choice. Parents always told me I wasn't good enough."

Jean-Guy leaned on the back of the sofa and looked at him hard. "I heard one of your recordings once, a long time ago. You were better than good. It wasn't until Kathy told me who you are that I learned Roisin Thompson's early accompanist was a child like her. Why did you stop playing and join the Air Force?"

Piers closed his eyes for a second and was clearly fighting some very unpleasant memories. "Because I had had enough. OK, here's the potted autobiography then you drop it. Right?"

The other two nodded and physically leaned towards him to hear better.

"Roisin and I spent the war in County Donegal with our grandmother. Our father had sent us there with our mother as the Republic was a neutral country and he thought we'd be safer. My mother used training techniques on me that were questionable even then and would be downright illegal now. My father and his twin brother were notorious hellraisers for the Irish cause and they brought us back to the Province after the war so they could train me to join their fight. Their training made my mother look like bloody Mary Poppins. So as soon as I could I signed my life over to the military as I couldn't see any other way out. No matter what civilian occupation I had tried they would have found me, in the Province or on the Mainland. The military was the one place I could hide as it probably wouldn't ever occur to them that was where I would go. Chose the RAF as the Army seemed to have to do all the unpleasant things and the Navy is too wet. No greater reason than that and signed on as a trainee mechanic Aircraftman with no ambitions to fly. My father was shot dead a few years later and last I heard my uncle was serving life for murder. If my Irish family ever found me the least I could expect would be to lose my kneecaps for siding with the enemy. The RAF was my way out of that bloody life my family were giving me but I wrote and told Roisin I'd joined the military as she was the only one who ever showed me any compassion. But I never even told her which service I'd gone into and never gave her any address to write back to and asked her not to try to find me. So far as I know she never did. Now you know."

"I met your sister a few years ago. I don't suppose you know how come she speaks fluent Russian?" Jean-Guy asked while Kathy's mind was still reeling at the thought of the childhood Piers must have had, although she did think Jean-Guy was being a bit heartless considering what they had just been told. It suddenly occurred to her that maybe Piers' life-story wasn't that shocking to a man raised under the thumb of the Soviet authorities.

"No I bloody don't," Piers snapped. "Now, just forget it. Not going to talk about it again."

"Please, just one thing," Kathy asked gently, afraid of upsetting him even more but needing to know. "If it was so bad, why have you gone back to the piano? We'll understand if you don't want to. Please don't be unhappy for our sakes."

Piers got his emotions under control. "I'm fine. Really. If I didn't want to play then I wouldn't."

The Prof came into the room and Piers went back to his playing. "Coffee, anyone?" the Prof asked but nobody answered and he looked from one to the other. "Is there a musical problem I can help with or is something else bothering you all?"

Kathy saw the way the Prof looked so sharply at the man at the piano but he kept his eyes on the keyboard and was sitting so still he barely seemed to be breathing.

"Jean-Guy was asking Piers how his sister learned Russian," Kathy offered as the most diplomatic way out and she caught the grateful smile from the man at the piano as he slowly raised his head.

"You should have asked me," the Prof told them still watching Piers very intently, obviously aware the younger man was either upset or troubled. "It's in her book. She went to the Soviet Embassy in Dublin to get a visa for a tour back in the fifties and met a young Cultural Attaché there. They married in Dublin in 1958. They have three children: Siobhan, then twins Ciaran and Ruairi, and the family split their time between Moscow and London. Any of you want to borrow the book? It's in my study. I gave it a mostly favourable review."

"Am I in it?" Piers asked, obviously struggling to get his head round the idea he had been an uncle for twenty years and had never known. Kathy wondered if, perhaps for the first time in his life, he realised that by running away he had avoided many things but missed out on so much more.

Petr Mihaly now had an inkling of what had upset Piers and he admired the other's courage in even speaking of his past. "She mentions you briefly under your birth name. She couldn't really leave out her childhood talent but in my review I did say I would have liked more about that part of her life. The book really starts when she went to music college in Dublin. She dedicated it to her husband Nikita Fyodorovich and her late brother Ciaran."

"So she believes I'm dead?" Piers didn't sound surprised. "Suits me."

"How can you say that?" Jean-Guy wanted to know. "I miss my family so much."

"You've only just left them. I've got thirty years head start on you. And if you miss them so much why the hell did you run?"

154

Jean-Guy slapped down the book he had been reading. "I ran, as you put it, because my parents are faithful communists and I don't hold with their ideals. I don't like the repression, the state involvement or what they stand for. But as human beings they are my parents and I presume I am allowed to miss them? Not forgetting my little sister Marianne who got gang raped by half a regiment of Soviet soldiers who happened to fancy a bit of fun with the Czech girls when she and some friends were going home from school one day."

Kathy moved to offer consolation but Jean-Guy got to his feet and just avoided knocking her to the floor.

"So now that's my story too," he snarled and brushed past the Professor before they heard him pounding up the stairs.

"Did you have to speak to him like that?" the Prof asked Piers curtly.

"No. Sorry. It's not his fault and I didn't need to bite his head off. I'll take his coffee up to him and apologise. It's the least I owe him."

Petr Mihaly had been told about this surprisingly compassionate and understanding RAF officer who always had time for the lower ranks but could also be as unfeeling and ruthless as needs demanded. "I mustn't forget you've had men under your command, and know how to handle them," the Prof acknowledged. "OK, I'll leave him to you."

"What was all that about?" Kathy asked the Prof after Piers had gone upstairs with two mugs of coffee and a packet of Penguin biscuits, and a tortoiseshell cat chased after him.

"I think our Concorde pilot could prove to be even more useful than we first suspected. He told Sarah he got to know Emma through mutual friends in London and she invited him down for a while as his employer had signed him off with mental exhaustion. Neatly done and didn't invite questions as people are too scared to want to talk about mental health matters."

"What did he say when you offered him a piano lesson?" Kathy asked curiously. "He didn't tell us much but it sounded as though his early lessons were, well, barbaric I suppose would be a good word."

Kathy saw the brief shadow that passed across the Prof's face and knew there were dark secrets that weren't being told. "I was given some information on him before he was sent here, that is the way of those I work for and they thought I needed to know. What happened to him before he joined the RAF is a closed secret but they gave enough clues for me to realise it was far from a happy childhood although they never mentioned his musical past to me. But he just smiled in that way he has and said he guessed he didn't have a choice any more. Then some things began to make sense like a very complicated puzzle."

Kathy thought about that for a while. "Do you think he should get in touch with his sister? It sounds as though she was the only one who was ever nice to him and it seems a bit mean to let her think he's dead."

She was not expecting her question to be met with another. "Do you remember I warned you against getting involved with Jean-Guy when you first met?"

"Yes," she admitted cautiously, not wanting to encourage that particular conversation as she wasn't sure what her feelings were herself.

"Well, even more don't get involved with the other one. That is not a kind word as a father figure; that is an official warning. Keep it as you are now, a bit of brotherly fun between you but no more." He knew what that look on her face meant. "Kathy, I am being very serious now. Back away from him and keep away."

"And have you said the same to Sarah?" Kathy asked waspishly. She hadn't even been thinking about Piers in that way and didn't like being told what to do.

"I am monitoring the Sarah situation but it is hard as he knows what I am up to and he is too devious for me. I think we will just have to let that one ride and see where it goes for now. Anyway, you asked me about getting in touch with Roisin. My answer has to be 'yes and no'. I think we all need family, which is why I'm so pleased Emma and Derek are starting theirs. But I don't think it would be a good idea for his old identity to be known until there is peace in Ireland, maybe not even then, and by getting in touch with her he runs that risk."

Kathy acknowledged the conversation had moved on but somehow knew it wasn't over. "I'd love to know what she thinks."

"Want to read her book?"

"Yes please."

Kathy settled on the sofa to read Roisin Thompson's autobiography as soon as she had had her coffee. Roisin made just enough mention of primary school choirs and then teenage recitals to satisfy the reader. She wrote lovingly of the grandmother in County Donegal and the sight of the setting sun on Gweebarra Bay. She glossed over her father as *a distant figure as was so often the case in Ireland in those days* and then Kathy came to the last paragraph in the chapter on Roisin's early years.

I cannot leave my childhood without writing all too briefly of my younger brother Ciaran. Trained to be my accompanist from a ridiculously early age and a superbly gifted pianist, he was never credited in programmes or on recordings. I didn't think anything of it at the time as accompanists usually went uncredited in those days. After I had gone to Dublin, I begged him to join me at college and as my tutors were familiar with his talent through my early recordings and recitals, he was offered a place at the age of fifteen to train as an accompanist. He accepted the offer but he never joined me in Dublin as at the age of sixteen he made use of the dual nationality we had both had since infancy by joining the British armed forces. I never heard from him again, but the day before my 25th birthday I received a letter from a family friend telling me Ciaran had been killed on a training exercise on December 13th, 1956. He never even made it to his 21st birthday and I felt at the time that somehow it was my fault he had died. I wished then, and I still wish now, that I had tried harder to get him to join me in what would have been an outstanding career. If I have one last wish in my heart it is to have the chance to tell Ciaran how much I love him, how much I miss him, and how much I would give to sing Schubert's Ave Maria *with him just one more time.*

"What the hell's up with you?" came a voice in her ear and Kathy realised she was in silent floods of tears and that the subject of the paragraph she had just been reading was sitting next to her and looking quite concerned.

Kathy had never noticed before that Piers had really very attractive dark blue eyes with a distinctive gold fleck in the left one. She just squeaked a bit and jabbed her finger on the page in the book. He leaned against her to read the few lines which he did very quickly, then he snatched the book from her and slammed it shut.

"Yes," he said sharply, "Ciaran Maloney is dead. He was a Private in the Royal Artillery, inquest brought in a verdict of accidental death. By that time I'd been Piers Buchanan for nearly four years but I guessed news would get back to Ireland even though the papers didn't make a big fuss about it. So I can't ever tell Roisin the truth, especially now with her Soviet connections and my military background."

"Did you read her book?"

"Yes."

"Did it make you want to get in touch with her?"

"I can't," was the desolate reply. "Yes, it made me feel bad knowing how much my supposed death has affected her. But, and I know this sounds hard, I can't be sure she'd keep my secrets."

Kathy remembered the Professor's warning to her and consciously backed away. "I just thought you were a policeman who was buying cat food in Sainsbury's."

There was a slight smile on his lips as though he knew what was in her mind. "Why on earth would you think that? About me being a policeman I mean?"

"I don't know. You just looked like one with your short hair and your shiny black shoes. And you're tall enough."

"I can't think of a job I'd hate more."

Kathy raised her eyes to his face and knew she had to keep the conversation light. "You have a speckle in your eye."

"I know. And Roisin has the exact same flaw but in the other eye. Our grandmother told us it was because the Little People had blessed us and put a spot of Irish gold in our eyes." He gave her a hard look. "The Prof's warned you off me, hasn't he?"

Kathy unsubtly dodged the question. "So you believe in the Little People but not ghost dogs?"

He silently accepted the rules of her game. "Piglet, I would never get involved with you. You're too short. And I'm very choosy about my superstitions."

"Black cats?" Kathy asked, pointing to Sooty who had just walked in the room. "And I'm not that short."

"I've known leprechauns taller than you. Any cat is good."

"Magpies? And don't you call me a leprechaun."

"I'll call you a bloody fairy then if you prefer. Don't like birds."

"Oh, are you scared of them? I'd rather be a naiad."

"It's not that. Did you know a single crow can bring down an aeroplane? And what the bloody hell is one of them?"

Kathy looked him straight in the eye, laughing now at the absurdity of their double conversation. "A water nymph to you, don't they teach you anything in Irish school? So, my Aga-mending, Concorde-flying accompanist, what are you scared of?"

He was laughing now too. "Solicitors. Go on, get back to your book."

Kathy picked up the book and found her page. "When do you see your sweetheart again?"

"No idea. Her parents have decided to clean and reorganise the shop for the new season so she's not getting any time out right now. Which reminds me; her mother says if you want the rest of the knitting stock you can have the whole lot for a tenner, or it all goes to the Scouts' jumble sale. Patterns and wool I think she said. They'll keep a few needles and things for holidaymakers who've forgotten or broken theirs."

Kathy put the book down again. "Can we go now?"

"Did you just say 'we' and 'now'?"

"Go on, you know you want to see her any way you can."

With a mock sigh of resignation, Piers got up from the sofa. "I'll get the car keys."

"Really? Why?"

"You'll see."

They were just about to set off when Jean-Guy came tearing out of the house and hurled himself into the back seat. "The Prof says can we bring home some ham for lunch, please," was all he said.

Piers caught his eye in the mirror. "Feeling better?"

"Fine now. Don't want to talk about it."

The village shop was in a state of minor chaos when they arrived. Sarah's mother was behind the till serving customers as best she could while Sarah and her father were clearing shelves and putting stock in boxes.

"Sarah!" her mother called across the shop. "They've come for the wool."

Sarah looked round and her already hot and flushed face went an even brighter shade of red. "Hullo," she said sounding nervous. "Can I take them round the back?"

Her parents smiled benevolently at their flustered daughter. "Just be careful, there are boxes all over the place," her mother cautioned.

"I'll stay here," Jean-Guy offered. "One of us needs to remember the ham."

Sarah led the way through a strip curtain at the back of the shop and into a stock room stuffed full of boxes either on shelves or on the floor. To Kathy's vast amusement, it was Sarah who put her arms round Piers and took a gentle kiss from his lips.

"Shall I go and look through the knitting stuff?" she asked diplomatically.

Sarah disengaged herself from Piers just long enough to say, "It's over behind the racking." She waved her hand vaguely towards the back of the stockroom. "Take what you want in the way of wool and patterns. We can't sell them any more."

Kathy went round to the back of a set of shelves and was completely out of sight of the other two. She sat on the floor and started looking through several plastic bags of knitting yarn and boxes of patterns. Totally engrossed in her search she wasn't even thinking about what might be going on behind the shelving and was quite surprised when Piers crouched down beside her.

"Found anything?"

"Loads. No wonder you brought the car. Where's Sarah?"

"Just getting her clothes straight."

"Do you mean to tell me…."

He tapped the side of his nose. "Come on then, let's start hauling sacks of wool."

Six bags of yarn, a bag of patterns, a pound of sliced ham and a bunch of bananas were put into the back

162

of the Land Rover and Kathy stood with Jean-Guy waiting while Piers and Sarah said their goodbyes just inside the shop door.

"Go on," Sarah told him softly. "We're closed all day Sunday so I'll see you then." They exchanged one last, lingering kiss. "I'll probably be covered in paint."

What he said in reply the other two didn't hear but Sarah went bright red and giggled. "You would too, wouldn't you? Go home. I'll see you on Sunday."

The ham was eaten but the table hadn't been cleared when the Prof took a pile of music off the dresser and put it in the middle of the table and announced. "I've come to realise over the last few weeks that you are all getting quite bored. So I propose you stage a small concert which will focus your practice time. You can each choose a charity and stage it in the village hall. I have been through my library and would like to suggest these works for you to play. First, your Beethoven was so good, you can open the programme with *The Ghost*. Kathy, I have chosen the Franck for you and the Grieg for you, Jean-Guy. Piers, you should stick with *La Campanella* as you are managing the technicalities so much better now. And I would suggest you close with another trio."

Jean-Guy and Kathy were quite excited by the idea but Piers was far from impressed. "I'll have long gone from here before I've got that lot up to standard."

"Maybe," the Prof agreed. "But don't underestimate your ability. Anyway, listen as this concerns you a lot. Although I don't believe in fate or coincidence I had a phone call today from the publishers of Roisin's autobiography. They want to bring out a second edition with more emphasis on her early years as well as bringing it up to date. and have asked me if I will be the editor. It will mean that I will be meeting with her at least once and I propose to invite her here. This will very likely happen before you go so you will need to decide what you want to do about it. Now, did you three think to bring back cake or shall I open a tin of fruit?"

"We brought back mince pies but Piers says he doesn't eat them, so more for us," Kathy told him. "Sarah's mum found them down the back of some shelves and they were too squashed to sell so she gave them to us."

Piers just sighed quietly and then, as the Professor had guessed, years of indoctrination and training took over from raw emotion and he went to help Kathy find bowls and spoons for the pies. "Even got you some cream to go with them," was all he said and helped himself to an apple from the fruit bowl.

Kathy had thought to put the pies in the warming oven so they were pleasantly hot to eat and she looked at the man who had said he didn't eat them. "Please do the concert with us?" she asked. "Come on, grumpy bunny. Just the three of us in the village hall as a charity gig. It'll be fun."

He crunched up the core of the apple. "Since when were concerts fun?"

She put her head on one side and gave him the wickedest grin she dared. "Since you started playing with me?"

Audrey's delight knew no bounds when her chosen human started spending hours of time with his out-of-practice fingers dancing across the keyboard of the piano in the sitting room and she spent an equal amount of time pouncing on them. Piers refused to play with the other two until he had practised although they were often in the room and got used to the periodic yelps as Audrey managed a better aimed swipe and Piers got yet another scratch on the back of his hands. They never said anything to him or even to each other, but both were secretly fascinated as a brilliant former talent was painstakingly rekindled.

February had gone out as it had begun with iron hard frosts and bitter winds and as the three in the house had music to work on, they went out on the coast walk less often. Piers took the Land Rover into the village a few times to meet up with Sarah but he was always careful to be back well before midnight. Kathy was aware that the Professor was watching Piers, not quite suspiciously but certainly with curiosity and Kathy thought the older man seemed to spend a lot of time on the phone in his study these days. But she didn't have time to think about it too much with her own practice to do and so much knitting she was spoilt for choice. Jean-Guy was glad he had his music to distract him as the days went by and still there was no news from the Home Office. They chose their charities for the event: Kathy opted for the Cats Protection League, Jean-Guy chose Amnesty International and Piers went for the NSPCC. Jean-Guy even designed a poster for it which waited in the kitchen, just needing a date for the concert which the Prof said he would organise when he felt they were all ready.

March was barely two weeks old when the Prof received a phone call in his study and took the unknown step of calling Piers in to speak to whoever it was on the phone. The Prof went to join Kathy and Jean-Guy in the sitting room where they had carried on with their trio practice.

"That was a call for Piers as the airline want him for some flying practice so he doesn't lose his licences. It is very complicated but I can see why they would."

"So he can leave?" Kathy asked and part of her wished she could go too.

"No. Someone from those I work for will come and pick him up and it has been arranged that he can do his work out in Ireland. It is little more than a formality and they just want to keep him current on Concorde." He knew what she was thinking. "I'm sorry, but the two of you must stay here. He will only be gone for a couple of days and he will be very closely guarded the whole time." He allowed himself a little smile. "Which I have no doubt he will hate, but he will also know why it has to be done."

Piers left the same day, he was back as the Prof had said within forty eight hours, and as if in celebration the wind changed from the east to the south and the frosts and snow were replaced with sunny days and the lightest of breezes that was even more tempting to Kathy who still felt trapped inside the old farmhouse that had seen her through the worst of winter.

"Ow! Audrey! Sodding cat, your aim's getting too good. Get off the piano. Off. No, don't just look at me like that. I'm not playing another note until you get off."

Jean-Guy and Kathy had been in the sitting room, trying not to be too distracted by the spring sunshine that was showing how dirty the windows were, and both thinking how much Piers' playing had improved. His hands were in a mess but Kathy triumphantly sewed in the last few ends of her latest knitting project and went across to the piano where man and cat were at a stand-off.

"Present for you," she told Piers and felt so sorry for him as Audrey's loving swipes meant his hands were quite scratched now.

He took the soft bundle from her and had to laugh. "OK, Audrey. You lose." He put on the fingerless gloves Kathy had made and admired them. "Thank you, Piglet. I could have done with these last month when we all had hypothermia. Shall we have a go at *The Ghost* now I have my armour on?"

Kathy and Jean-Guy didn't wait for a second invitation but rushed to fetch their instruments.

Petr Mihaly was in his study, one ear listening for the doorbell and the other listening to the sounds from the sitting room. He had heard so many trios over the years but this one was like none he had ever heard before. There was only one yelp from the pianist once the full trio got underway so he guessed Audrey wasn't able to keep up with the rapidly flying fingers but the music didn't falter any more. He almost didn't hear the doorbell as it rang during one of the more tempestuous passages.

His visitor clearly didn't find it at all unusual there should be a performance of *The Ghos*t thundering out of her host's living room and she wasn't offended when he asked her if she would mind sitting in the kitchen for a while as the sitting room was occupied.

The Ghost went into one of its more lyrical passages and the visitor sat listening intently as her host made coffee for them both. "That has to be the best piano trio I think I have ever heard," she mused in her gentle Irish tones. "Is it a recording?"

"No, it's some friends of my daughter who asked if they could use the house to rehearse as I have a full concert grand. They're hoping to do a charity concert fairly soon." The Professor hadn't asked for this meeting, but the publisher had set it up at very short notice as it was the only space in the visitor's diary for nearly a year. His only hope was that it wouldn't last as long as the trio rehearsal as he hadn't wanted to mention it to them.

There came a loud yelp from the sitting room and the music broke down in disarray.

Host and visitor exchanged a glance but before either said anything a laughing young woman with long, fair hair carried a yowling and wriggling tortoiseshell cat out to the kitchen. "Oh, sorry," she said. "Didn't realise you had a visitor."

"Didn't the gloves work?" the Prof asked, trying to think of a way round this discovery.

"The gloves work just fine. Audrey changed her target and went for his feet instead."

"Well if he will play the piano in his socks what does he expect? Just leave Audrey here, we'll keep an eye on her for you."

"Lovely trio playing," the visitor said and got up to greet the blonde woman properly. "Hullo, I'm Roisin."

Kathy wondered why they hadn't been forewarned. "Oh, hullo. I'm Kathy and this is Audrey."

"Pleased to meet you both." Roisin shook hands with Kathy then solemnly took hold of Audrey's front paws. "Now, Audrey, be nice to the pianist. I knew another one once who used to play in his socks."

Audrey looked at Roisin, mewed quietly and reached out for her. She got her front claws in Roisin's smart blue cardigan and refused to let go.

Roisin just laughed and gently took charge of the cat who promptly put soft paws round her neck. "Well, you're a friendly little thing, aren't you?"

Kathy really had no idea what was supposed to happen now. She privately thought Roisin Thompson was as beautiful as her brother was handsome. Her dark hair was cut short and it curled becomingly framing a gentle, pale face that looked younger than she could possibly have been.

"Piglet, what are the hell you doing in there?" came an exasperated voice. "You only had to get rid of the damned cat."

Kathy started towards the door with the idea of keeping Piers out until he had been told about the visitor but the kitchen door crashed open and he arrived in the doorway. There was a short, terrible pause as the visitor turned to greet the arrival and two pairs of speckled cornflower blue eyes met across a loudly purring cat.

Roisin's pale face went a deathly pallor somewhere between white and grey and her hand physically shook as she extended it towards the man who seemed to be frozen in the doorway. "Ciaran?" she whispered. "Is that really you?"

Into the Labyrinth

Kathy thought she had never seen anything as emotional as that reunion between brother and sister. At first all Roisin could do was cling to her brother as though he might run away from her at any moment and she had cried. Then she had got angry with him and shouted at him for letting her believe he was dead.

"I had to," he told her. "You must understand that."

"I can understand you didn't want our family to know where you'd gone, but you didn't have to cut me out too. I couldn't answer that letter you sent and I even tried contacting the Ministry of Defence as I was so frantic for news about you but they wouldn't tell me anything. I would never, ever do anything to put my baby brother in danger. Why did you do it, Ciaran?"

"You of all people know why. I started my planning the day you went off to college as I knew I was on borrowed time after Coleraine. What the hell did you think they were going to do with me?"

She slumped at the table with her head in her hands. "I suppose I had had a rather naïve idea that maybe it would stop. That maybe they'd let you join me in Dublin. But they were never going to do that, were they?" The tears started again. "I was so happy to get your letter saying you'd joined the army. I've still got it. At least it meant you'd survived. And then I learned you'd died. And in a way, in a horrible, horrible way, I was glad it was all over for you." She took his hands in hers and didn't even try to stop crying. "Ciaran, I left you to die. Can you ever forgive me?"

He sat beside her at the table. "You left home believing there was an outside chance they'd let me live if only to serve their cause. I don't blame you for anything."

Kathy looked across at the Professor and tilted her head towards the door, suggesting maybe they should leave the room and was surprised when he shook his head in reply.

"And you're still playing the piano," she said softly,

Neither of them seemed to have noticed that Jean-Guy had also slipped into the kitchen but he didn't say anything. Realising what this chance meeting could mean, he moved silently across next to Kathy and caught hold of her hand.

Piers put his arm around his sister and hugged her close. "I didn't play for a long time. I joined the Air Force, learned to fly and made a whole new life for myself with a new name and a made-up history."

"New name?" she questioned in disbelief.

"I haven't been Ciaran Maloney since I was sixteen. I left the family, left my past life and that meant I had to leave you too." He didn't let go of Roisin but there was a hardness to his voice that dried his sister's tears. "I changed my name to Piers Buchanan. I left the Air Force to work as a commercial pilot and until about a month ago I hadn't been near a piano since you and I did that last recital in Coleraine." He looked at the other three in the room. "Then I met some people who showed me that music isn't about what it had always been about before. So I thought maybe I owed them something. Piglet is one of the best violinists I have ever heard and knew just how to persuade me to play again. I still don't know how she did it. Jean-Guy I'm not sure about. I think he's going to turn out to be more of a tyrant than you."

Roisin looked at the young man with the dark eyes and the brown curly hair and remembered. "Oh, my God. Jean-Guy Dechaume. How did you get out of Czechoslovakia?"

"I ran," he said simply. "For now I am in hiding."

The wife of a Soviet Cultural Attaché was only too aware what that involved.

"Which means," her brother told her, "you have now joined us in our lies and deceit and you will have to play the game too. Jean-Guy will one day be free to be famous but I can never be known as your brother again. Maybe you could claim me as some distant relative one day, but not yet. Now, blow your nose on something that isn't already soggy and it must be lunchtime. I'm assuming you'll stay?"

Roisin Thompson drove back to London after lunch. Kathy could tell the Professor was impressed with the way Piers had handled the situation and together they had all agreed that Roisin had had a meeting with the editor of her revised book, she had heard a piano trio play, and she still no longer had a brother called Ciaran. He didn't offer to stay in touch with her and she didn't ask. But he didn't want to play any more after the meal and went up to his room accompanied by his faithful cat.

"Is that it then?" Jean-Guy asked the Prof. "Will he play again? I would have liked to have tried him out as an accompanist just once."

Petr Mihaly thought about that. "Tell you what. We'll leave him alone for today but tomorrow we'll set Kathy to work on him."

The two men looked at her and Kathy had a feeling she was blushing. "What do you mean?"

"He means," Jean-Guy explained as though to a child, "that you have that man wrapped round your fingers. He said it himself to Roisin and if anyone can get us playing as a trio, it is you."

Kathy really wanted to protest at that but she knew the other two would never agree with her. It was true that she and Piers had an understanding which meant she pushed the boundaries with him more than she ever had with any man she hadn't slept with. She knew she hadn't misjudged him. Piers would play along with her, let her push those boundaries but any time he chose he would push straight back and somehow, subtly, let her know she had gone far enough. No man had ever been so close to her and yet so distant from her. She realised the other two were now wondering why she hadn't spoken.

"Don't be silly," she told them. "But I'm sure I'll have fun trying."

By half past two in the morning Kathy hadn't managed to get to sleep with so many thoughts whirring in her head and she was very hungry, so she groped her way through the dark house to the kitchen in search of food. She was not expecting to find the kitchen light on and Jean-Guy guiltily stuffing a bowl of Cornflakes at the table.

"You too, huh?" she asked and started making herself a peanut butter and grape jelly sandwich. "Want a cup of tea?"

"Yes please. How can you eat that stuff?" Jean-Guy had tried peanut butter once and never touched it again.

The two sat and ate in silence for a while, neither of them wanting to say what was in their mind.

"So where does this leave you now?" Kathy asked as a gentle opener when she couldn't stand the silence any longer.

Jean-Guy looked at his empty cereal bowl and his voice gave away how troubled he was. "We just have to trust her not to betray either of us, no matter how accidentally."

Kathy reached across and took his hand. She knew that she had the least to lose of any of them if Roisin told anyone that there were in effect two fugitives hiding out in the Prof's house. "What on earth was the Prof thinking of?"

Jean-Guy seemed to be thankful to have something more practical to talk about. "Well, it is because half his life is writing the books and reviews. That is his public life if you like and the one that meant he had to accept her in his house. His other life is the hidden one where he helps people like me and has all sorts of safety measures and hotlines in the house."

Kathy now felt more confused than ever but had a feeling some things were going to start making sense at last. "What do you mean?"

"There is a phone in a drawer in the study which is a different line from the phone on the desk. The hidden one you just pick up and it goes straight to whoever is in charge of all this in this country. There is also a radio set that works the same way in case the phone line is out. And that piano piece, *La Campanella*? Well there is a cassette of it in a machine next to the phone and if we are in danger then someone has to pick up the phone and play the piece of music. No spoken message needed. That is the signal."

Kathy remembered Emma's reactions when she had heard that piece being played and now it all made sense. Her friend had known all about it for years and never told her.

Jean-Guy looked at the frightened woman sitting at the table with him. "I'm sorry, but against the judgement of the other two I think you need to know too."

"It's not real," Kathy whispered, even though she knew it was. And it was a terrifying thought to realise she was living so close to a world of shadows and secrets. "I'm a violinist from Wimbledon. Things like this don't happen to me."

"Is that what you said when your relationship turned abusive?" was the compassionate question.

Kathy put her sandwich down half eaten. "Yes. I kidded myself for years that there was nothing wrong. Even when he had the knife against my neck I thought it was my fault."

Jean-Guy came to kneel beside her and put protective arms round her. "This time there really is nothing wrong, and knives scare the shit out of me in case I lose a finger so I never use them. But I think in the end you will worry less if you know all the facts. And one fact is that by letting Roisin into what is going on, we have exposed ourselves just a little bit more to what is out there."

She turned towards him. "And what is out there?" He didn't answer her straight away but the warmth and strength of his arms consoled her. Their faces were very close together now and part of her was screaming inside that this was the perfect moment for him to kiss her. She wanted him to. This wasn't going to be a hot and steamy fling like she had had with her driving instructor. This was a vulnerable man who had let down his defences and shown her just how he felt. This wasn't a man who would have sex with her until neither of them could think straight. Or maybe he was. She was standing on the edge of something and it could be the best thing she had ever done or one of the worst. He was so close she barely had to dip her head so she could brush a soft kiss onto his lips. "I know you're scared. Maybe even more scared than me as you know more what is going on. But we can look after each other, can't we? At least I'm not facing this one on my own,"

Jean-Guy couldn't believe she had done that to him. Couldn't believe that this beautiful, scarred woman would trust him like that. His breath caught in his throat and he returned her gentle kiss. "I don't know what's out there, and that's the truth."

Kathy looked into his troubled, dark eyes and knew deep inside she had done just what she had been told not to do and had fallen in love again. She had taken that step into the unknown but instead of falling as she had before, this lovely man had caught her and held her and was going to keep her safe for ever.

Kathy got up with a vague intention of making some tea but Jean-Guy stood with her, holding her close against him without speaking. Kathy didn't even care that she was only wearing her nightgown and Jean-Guy was in his pyjamas. She wrapped her arms round his back and thought he flinched a bit at her touch but he didn't move away. This time when he kissed her she felt the heat of his body against her own as they stepped into the labyrinth together and were no longer journeying alone.

He cupped her face in his hands and gave her more kisses, each one longer and harder than the one before it and he felt the fire of her response. Kathy tipped her head back for him so he could explore her throat and she began to hope that maybe he would get so carried away they would make love right there and then on the kitchen table. She started on the buttons of his pyjama jacket and couldn't believe it when he stopped her.

"Good idea," he said hoarsely. "But also very bad idea unless you have something with you or are on the Pill."

She went back to the buttons. "I'm not, and I haven't," she breathed in his ear. "But I know who has."

They exchanged a quiet smile and then he caught her by the hand and let her lead him upstairs.

It was daylight when Kathy woke and this time there were no dread thoughts when she looked over her shoulder and saw Jean-Guy was sleeping in her bed. His back was towards her and her eyes could just make out what her fingers had felt. Uneven skin on his back where once he had been flayed for being a traitor to the State. Five lashes while his wrists were bound and tied to a wall. They hadn't touched his hands. He had been expected to take his punishment, mend his ways and go on to be an ambassador for Czechoslovakia and the greater Soviet Union with his music. The wounds on his back had only been half-healed when he had run from the country of his birth and hadn't stopped until he got to Suffolk. She softly kissed his shoulder without waking him then put on her nightdress and dressing gown and went out onto the landing. A quick glance to the right and she saw the door to the large back bedroom was closed which meant Piers was almost certainly still in bed. She felt a bit sorry for him this morning. Even though she liked to think of him as the independent free spirit, her big brother with the wicked sense of humour, he was still a flesh and blood man who had had an emotional reunion with his sister yesterday and she hoped he hadn't been woken during the night.

As usual only the Prof was in the kitchen and there was no sign of the Cornflakes and the half-eaten sandwich from last night.

"Sleep well?" he asked her as he often did.

"No, not really." Kathy replied thinking maybe he had heard her last night too. "I was thinking about Piers and Roisin and wondering if they will ever play together again. How much would you pay for a ticket to a recital where he is her accompanist?"

"Everything I own and twice as much beside."

"Will it ever happen?"

"Can't see it, can you? There's no way he's ever going to give up flying for a music career."

"Have you any idea how much the average commercial pilot earns?" asked a cheerful voice as Piers joined them. "More in a month than a crappy accompanist would get in a year."

"Don't you ever call yourself a crappy accompanist," Kathy told him. "Not until Jean-Guy had turned you to mincemeat anyway. Or are you abandoning us now?"

Piers gave her one of his lovely smiles but his voice was weary. "I was awake half the night just churning it all over in my mind. Yes, it was a hell of shock meeting Roisin like that. More for her than for me as she thought I'd been dead for over twenty years. Yes, it brought back some memories I thought I'd buried too deep ever to be dug up again. But the short answer to your question is 'not yet' and that's all I'm saying. And now I'm off to get a paper. Fancy a walk to the shop, Piglet?"

Kathy saw the glance between the two men. "I'm guessing maybe you two have already talked about this so I won't ask you to go through it all over again. Yes, I'll come for the walk with you, it'll help clear my head but can I get dressed first?"

Piers looked at her searchingly but all he said was: "Nah, we'll have a pyjama party on the way."

"Aren't you a bit overdressed then?" she challenged.

His smile widened and he was clearly vastly amused now. "You want me to go out in my pyjamas? Have you seen my pyjamas?"

Kathy wasn't sure whether he would be a traditionalist or sleep in a T shirt and shorts. "No, is there something special about them?"

He was laughing as he handed her the mug of tea he had made for her. "They're invisible."

"Oh!" she exclaimed and felt herself starting to blush at the thought of that beautiful man sleeping naked. She buried her face in her tea and nearly scalded her tongue.

"Still want me to join your pyjama party?"

"Um, no, thank you," she squeaked and fled back to her room, nearly slopping her tea as she raced up the stairs with it.

Kathy and Piers set out along the coast path once she was dressed, both inhaling the softer air of early spring. They were about half way to the village when Piers hugged Kathy tight to him with an arm round her waist and said, "OK, you little tart, spill."

She had been happily dreaming about the man who had shared her bed last night and for a scary moment wondered if the one walking so platonically beside her had some kind of mind-reading talent. "I have no idea what you're talking about," she tried desperately. His arm was snug round her waist now and she wished she didn't like it quite so much. It didn't help her peace of mind when he leaned a little closer to her and almost breathed in her ear.

"So I didn't hear you and lover boy going downstairs in the small hours, didn't hear you both talking and then sneaking back up?"

Kathy knew Piers' sharp hearing hadn't let him down. "Um…"

"And it wasn't Jean-Guy raiding my cupboard for the supplies I need when I meet Sarah, and it wasn't your food all over the table that I cleared up last night? And don't get me started on the sounds I heard coming out of your room."

To her profound relief this was her big brother still teasing her, not some thwarted potential lover wanting to know why he had been thrown over for someone with outwardly much less to offer. "You and your rabbit ears! Have we no secrets from you?"

"Probably not. I assume you've seen the state of his back?"

"Yes, but how did you?"

"He showed me, that time I wound him up about his defection. So I got the whole story and was generally made to feel a bit of a shit. He also told me probably just a hint of your story, so I hope he treats you well or I'll have to do my big brother bit on him. But if you're going to make a habit of it I may need to start sleeping with ear plugs in. And you need to buy him some supplies while we're in the shop so he stops nicking mine."

"I can't," Kathy said appalled. "I mean it's Sarah. She's known me since I was about ten. Won't you…?"

There was a hard edge to his teasing now. Her big brother wasn't going to be any kind of a pushover. "No I bloody won't. You want to go around yelling the house down with your nocturnal activities you take responsibility for it."

"I don't yell," Kathy protested. "I grant you maybe I'm not the quietest in bed…"

"I've heard less racket taking off in Concorde," he interrupted her and she wasn't sure if he didn't want to hear any more in case she lost her little sister image or in case he got a bit too interested. "And if you make me buy them I'll only shout at you across the shop asking what size you want. And if you hide behind the shelves I'll make you choose a flavour too,"

Kathy looked up into his laughing eyes and believed he wasn't interested in her in that way. He had Sarah now and he was content. "You would too, wouldn't you? God, I'm only glad I didn't have you as a brother when I was a teenager."

To her disbelief, the annoyingly handsome Concorde pilot literally snorted with laughter and let rip with the most infectious laugh she had ever heard so she

181

joined in until her ribs ached and the two of them were nearly crying.

"Tell me?" he pleaded wheezingly. "Please tell me all?"

Kathy broke away from his hold. "No chance," she laughed. "There are some things brothers and sisters just don't share."

"Please? Just a hint?"

She stopped and turned to face him and thought he had never looked more stunning than he did when his eyes were laughing like that. She fondly batted his nose. "No."

His reactions were quick and he caught her hand while it was still next to his face. He looked hard into her eyes and his laughter died. "You've made your choice," he acknowledged. "I was an idiot, left it too late and now I've lost you."

She tucked her hand through his arm. "Not as a friend," she reminded him as they resumed their walk.

His voice was tinged with the bitterness of regret. "Not as a friend," he agreed.

The cleaned and refurbished shop looked much brighter and bigger since the reorganisation and the stock was starting to reflect the impending summer season rather than basic essentials for the locals.

"Good morning," Sarah greeted them cheerfully and abandoned the counter for a kiss and a cuddle with Piers. "It really feels like the first day of spring today."

"What makes you say that?" Kathy asked and wondered if she had given something away.

"You two. It's the first time you've come here not wrapped up like two abominable snowmen. Barry was in earlier and he said he can't let us have another practice barrel as he can only spare one per team so we'll just have to hope it goes well on the day. Have you thought any more about what you're all going to wear?"

"Hm, North Sea, back end of March. Two sets of thermals and a hot water bottle," Piers told her.

"You craze me sometimes, you know that? Mum's said she can make costumes for us if you like? Ian and Trevor have done it before so they're all sorted. She's already been asked to make for at least two of the other teams." Sarah turned to Kathy and announced proudly, "Mum's well known for her sewing. She used to make stage clothes before she inherited the shop. Worked in one of the big London theatres."

Kathy was duly impressed. "I wish I'd known, I've got a couple of concert gowns that need altering. I really like them but because I'm so short I've either got to hold the skirts out of the way when I walk or wear six inch heels."

Piers was clearly not happy about this. "Do we have to?"

"You've seen the photos," Sarah pointed out stubbornly. "And that's exactly what we all do."

Piers turned to Kathy. "Help me out here. Do you want to go in to the sea wearing ten petticoats and a corset?"

"Doesn't bother me," she told him and then realised he was going to barter doing her shopping for her if she backed him up. "You do sell condoms, don't you?" she asked Sarah.

Piers understood perfectly. He looked at Kathy. "You cow," he said pleasantly which confused Sarah even more.

Sarah looked from one to the other. "What are you talking about? Have you run out or something?" Her eyes widened as a dread thought started to process in her mind. "Are you two…?"

Piers knew where that thought was going and it wasn't one he wanted to encourage. In Sarah or in himself. He sighed and sounded slightly irritated. "They're for Kathy and Jean-Guy. Do you think I'm totally immoral?"

Sarah flushed unhappily even though she wasn't sorry to realise Kathy wasn't the threat she had seemed to be. She rather liked the idea of Kathy and Jean-Guy getting together. "I never know where I am with you," she snapped back at Piers as she didn't like his tone. "You've got the mind of a butterfly and I can't keep up. It's not my fault I'm stupid."

He gathered her into a repentant cuddle. "Don't ever call yourself stupid."

"Why not?" she retorted. "Everyone else does."

Piers cupped her face in his hands and gave her a gentle kiss. "And that, my love, is because they don't know you."

She looked up into his eyes. "What did you call me?" she asked softly.

He tapped a finger on her lips. "Well it wasn't stupid."

The bell over the shop door pinged and a large family group all came in. "Caravan park opened today," Sarah remembered and the moment was over. "Going to be busy."

Kathy turned her best 'help-me' look on Piers.

"Oh, no," he told her. "Go and choose your own. I'm sure Sarah will wrap them in a nice brown paper bag for you."

For the first time since they had arrived, Kathy and Piers met other people on the coast path and although they were outwardly friendly with their greetings the two found themselves checking that nobody saw them go through the gap in the hedge.

"Caravan park's open," Kathy told the Prof who was sitting at the kitchen table quietly having a post-breakfast cup of coffee.

"Good and bad news," he acknowledged. "But it'll still be quiet for the next month or so. Easter is late this year and the main traffic won't start until after then. More people for your concert though, so I think maybe it's time we worked out a date."

"Any news from the Home Office?" Kathy asked and started making coffee for Piers and herself while he got on with the toast.

"Sadly, no. But there is some interesting chatter out there. Messages are coming in that Jean-Guy's sister is now on the run too. Apparently their parents have moved to Moscow from Prague as his father has got a new job at the Music Conservatoire there and at one of the stations on the train ride to the Soviet Union young Marianne got off the train and didn't get back on again."

Kathy sat at the table. "Goodness. Deliberately?"

"Unlikely to have been accidental."

Piers finished making the coffees and joined the other two at the table. "That can't be good news for the parents. Is Marianne as valuable to the state as her brother is?"

"No. She's a musician too but not in his league."

"Oh? What does she play?" Kathy asked.

"She's a rank and file violin in one of the orchestras in Prague. I mean, she's good but she's never even wanted to try as a soloist or ensemble player."

"With a brother with his talent, nor would I," Piers commented and sounded rather bitter. "Have you told him?"

"Not yet. I'm waiting for updates and it may be she didn't mean to miss the train and will turn up safely in Moscow. So today I suggest you do some work on your concert pieces. Unless, of course, any of you fancy digging over the vegetable plot for me?"

"Good session on the Franck?" Kathy asked.

"I'll go and find my hand armour."

Audrey had soon learned that if she went for the feet she was quite likely to get trampled or get a paw squashed under a pedal. Piers had soon learned that if he opened the top of the piano to stop her sitting on it she would just stalk up and down the keyboard. They had all learned that if they shut the cat in another room she would howl like a banshee and at a loud enough volume to put them off. So the piano top stayed down and Audrey reigned supreme.

Kathy watched Piers take his shoes off and settle at the piano, with Audrey keeping a strict eye. "Why do you play in your socks?" she asked.

"Habit," he said vaguely and played the A for her to tune. "I did a concert in bare feet once but I was only nine at the time. No don't stand there, I can't see you."

"If I move any further over I won't be able to see you."

"You don't need to see me, you're the soloist."

Kathy moved about six inches forward. "You haven't played instrumental works before have you? We play sonatas and trios as equals, no matter how bossy Jean-Guy gets. You only ever become more of an accompanist if you're covering the piano reduction for a concerto. And if you ever fancy doing that then Jean-Guy and I will love you forever."

"So which concerto do you want to learn?"

"Well, I don't like Sibelius so it would have to be the Shostakovich One. Now, are you going to play or not?"

Piers looked at the score in front of him. "Sorry, my start isn't it. How fast do you want to go?"

Kathy lightly smacked him on the head with her bow. "No, what was I just saying? You set the tempo. If I don't like it, I'll let you know."

Jean-Guy sat on the stairs as he had done once before and listened to Kathy playing her violin in the sitting room. He wanted to take her back to bed when he heard her playing like that. And then the piano part wove its own magic with hers and he didn't know how two people could play like that and not give in to the carnal desires that the music was stirring in his mind as well as his body. His rather obsessed imagination visualised Kathy and Piers getting very intimate to the music even though rationality told him that was physically impossible so long as they kept playing.

In his study, Petr Mihaly forgot all about the book he was supposed to be editing as he listened to the beautiful music pouring from the sitting room. More prosaically he couldn't wait to hear what would happen when the pianist was up against the formidable talent of Jean-Guy Dechaume in the Grieg Sonata.

Jean-Guy took advantage of the musicians' break between movements to slip into the sitting room. "Don't mind me," he instructed and settled himself on the sofa. He listened as the two went over some technicalities and worked on getting a couple of the more syncopated passages work better then, to his surprise, Kathy plonked herself next to him on the sofa.

"Your turn," she told him.

"But you've only played one movement."

"Yes, but this way you get a turn before Piers' fingers are totally wrecked. He really needs to practise more."

Piers soon found out that Kathy had been kind to him. Jean-Guy's talent was internationally famous and he was a demanding and exacting musician who expected equal perfection from his pianist. They didn't quite come to an argument at the end of the first movement but Audrey sensed her human didn't want to play the hand game any more and went to keep Kathy company on the sofa.

Kathy was impressed by the music being played by the two men. She had heard the playing of Jean-Guy Dechaume on the radio and on record but she had never heard him play live. The tone and volume of the cello were almost overpowering in the sitting room and she wasn't surprised when Piers took a couple of seconds to open the top of the piano now there wasn't a cat on it any more. She shifted herself on the sofa so she could watch the performance that then took place. They went for the second movement which was breath-taking in its gentle lyricism but it was also a magnificent clash where Piers, without a cat to distract him, battled on equal terms with the celebrated Jean-Guy.

"Third movement," the cellist ordered at the end of the second.

"Give me a break."

"It is a short movement. I like to play it at slightly above the marked tempo."

"Piglet, come and page turn for me, please or I'll never keep up."

Kathy shot off the sofa to sit next to Piers on the piano stool and she could feel his concentration like body heat. Jean-Guy was sitting just in front of the piano so the two could see each other quite easily and she saw the way they exchanged frequent glances, keeping the tempo and rhythm in total perfection right to the end. The tension in the room snapped as the last note was played and Kathy just had to applaud the playing even though she was now having some serious self-doubts.

Jean-Guy steadied his breathing. He didn't think he had ever played that piece with such a brilliant piano accompaniment and he was emotionally and physically exhausted. He quietly put his cello on its side on the floor then went and briefly took the hand of the man who sat at the piano looking slightly dazed as though he couldn't believe he had just survived such a musical ordeal.

"Thank you," Jean-Guy said and his voice was unsteady. "Now tell me why you waste your talent flying silly aeroplanes?"

"And when you've told him, you can explain it to me all over again," Petr Mihaly said as he came into the room with four mugs of coffee on a tray. "Gentlemen, I would like to say that I have just heard a truly outstanding performance, even if the first movement was a bit of a battleground. And I'm sorry I ever suggested a little concert in the village hall. It would be like asking

Margot Fonteyn to dance on a school stage. I will find somewhere better for you."

"I'm not doing the concert," Kathy said in a small voice and the other three looked at her in disbelief. "I can't believe you'd make me play with you two."

To the Prof's amusement, there was suddenly a three-person squash on the piano stool with Kathy in the middle and both men hugging her. He noticed it was only Jean-Guy who kissed her though.

"Kathy," the Prof said to her as sternly as he thought he should, "Where did you get that idea from? I heard your Franck earlier and it was exquisite."

Kathy sat on the piano stool feeling wretched and useless. She felt as though the other two had just been humouring her and letting the silly little woman play along for a while then when she was out of the way they unleashed a force that was greater than anything she could have imagined.

"Piglet, listen to me. That bloke of yours has gone. He's the one who has made you feel useless and second best, not us. I've heard what you and Jean-Guy did to get rid of him and I just wish I'd been there to see all of it. And if you can do that, you can do anything. Now, come and drink your coffee then ask the Prof if he's got a copy of the Shostakovich One."

"You can play the Shostakovich One?" Jean-Guy asked sounding impressed.

"I used to think so," Kathy said miserably. "Just not very well."

"Can't do any worse than me trying to be a whole orchestra."

"Oh, shut up!" Kathy snapped. "For a bloke who hasn't played for thirty years that wasn't exactly a mess of wrong notes, was it?"

To the surprise of the other two men, Piers didn't snap back but spoke quite calmly and gently. "Sorry, didn't phrase that well. If you will let me, I will be honoured to be your orchestra."

Kathy looked up at him and began to recover a little of her self-belief. "Really?"

"Really."

"Emma has the Shostakovich, I am almost sure of it," the Prof said regretfully. "But I have the Sibelius."

"I'm not allowed to play Sibelius, it's too erotic."

"The man who told you that is gone," Jean-Guy told her. "And if you can make Sibelius sound erotic I'll, I'll bake you a cake. A more cold-hearted composer I just can't imagine. Too much Finnish snow."

"You can bake?" Piers asked and it was his turn to sound impressed. He got up to take a mug of coffee from the Prof.

"Never tried," Jean-Guy admitted.

Kathy suddenly had to laugh. She had taken possibly the biggest step away from her past that she could and she had done it with the help of the two most absurd friends she could have imagined. And one of them, she thought as she drank in the soft kiss Jean-Guy gave her, was now so much more than a friend. "OK I'll try the Sibelius. I studied it in my last year at college so I hope it won't be too bad going back to it." She turned to the man sitting next to her on the piano stool "Go on, you choose a concerto too. We need to keep Ratty on his toes."

The wickedness of his smile was worthy of Piers. "Oh, I will choose Prokofiev *Sinfonia Concertante*, of course. They say it is the most difficult piece a cellist can attempt and even I can't manage all of it. Sadly I couldn't bring any of my music with me so I have no score."

"I'll get you a score," the Prof promised. "You must tell me if there are any other works you would like. It can't be too much longer before you are playing concertos again."

Kathy thoughtfully picked up her mug of coffee. She couldn't remember the last time she had really challenged herself as a player. She would never get to the standard of the man who had shared her bed last night but it was time to break free of the shackles that had held her for too long. She offered Jean-Guy her hand. "Erotic Sibelius in exchange for a chocolate cake?"

He accepted the challenge. "Done."

It hadn't occurred to Kathy that Jean-Guy would sleep anywhere that night other than with her even though neither of them had said anything and she was quite surprised when he turned to go into smaller bedroom at the front when they were on the landing. Piers had already gone to his room and the door was closed but he had headed off with the piano part for the Sibelius so the other two guessed he wouldn't be going to sleep for a while.

"No Sarah for him tonight," Kathy remarked. She opened her bedroom door then looked at Jean-Guy. "I got you some supplies when I was at the shop this morning."

Jean-Guy hoped his rising excitement wasn't too obvious. "Seriously? You know he heard everything last night?"

Kathy had been thinking about that. "I have a plan for Rabbit-ears," she smiled.

A delighted Jean-Guy followed her into the bedroom and watched as she took two balls of cotton wool out of the glass jar on the dressing table and held them up with a triumphant smile.

"Good idea," Jean-Guy approved. "Want me to take them along?"

"No, I'll do it."

"OK, but don't get his hopes up."

Kathy was still smiling as she tapped on Piers' door. "Only me," she said softly. She guessed he must have been getting ready for bed as his shirt was undone giving her a nice look as his smooth, remarkably pale chest. "Oh, sorry," was her immediate reaction. She held up the cotton wool. "Thought you might appreciate these."

He took them with a rather wry smile as he realised what she was looking at. "Thank you. I'll look forward to a better night's sleep." He knew she wanted to say something so he spared her having to think of some diplomatic words. "Something else the Little People gave me, luminous Irish skin. Which is why you may very occasionally see me in short sleeves but you will never, ever catch me in shorts. Now, goodnight. Don't keep him waiting."

He moved his right arm to close the door and Kathy saw something odd. "Have you got a tattoo?" she asked as she tried to get a better look at the dark lines on his chest.

"I lost a drinking game a long time ago."

"Let's have a look."

Jean-Guy arrived behind her as a reluctant Piers held open the right side of his shirt to give her a proper look at the dramatic drawing of a leaping panther.

"What's it jumping on?" she asked, seeing something else there and really wanting to touch it.

"Oh, for Christ's sake, what's a bloke got to do to get to bed round here?" Piers grumbled and sounded as though he meant it. He took his shirt off completely so the others could see the panther was swatting at a skilfully drawn swallow-tail butterfly on his right shoulder at the front and then he turned to show them a whole flight of many different butterflies going across his shoulder, upper arm and back, heading for an exquisitely drawn hibiscus flower between his shoulder blades. From the flower several skeletal butterflies, which seemed to become ever more disintegrated, tumbled down his spine to his waist.

Kathy felt there was something disturbing about the image, it was intricately drawn and quite breathtaking in its artistry but it wasn't at all the gentle scene you would expect from flowers and butterflies. It was as though the butterflies were escaping from danger only to throw themselves into destruction.

"Go to bed," was all Piers said. "Both of you. And thank you for the ear plugs." He politely but firmly closed his bedroom door in their faces.

Kathy and Jean-Guy settled together in their bed both thinking of the somehow violent image of the tattoo. "Was I the only one who found that scary?" she asked.

"I'd like to know what Sarah thinks of it," Jean-Guy said and gently kissed her neck. "And, no, I'm not going to get a tattoo."

March continued to bless them with warm weather. A collection of music including the Prokofiev came for Jean-Guy and the Prof really rather enjoyed hearing the music being played in different rooms of the house. It was always the piano in the sitting room, always with Audrey playing the hand game, learning to sheathe her claws and not minding the gloves at all. The violin and the cello were usually in the bedrooms upstairs, the musicians each absorbed with their own difficulties. The Prof was quite well aware that Kathy and Jean-Guy were spending the nights together but he didn't say anything. He was just grateful Kathy had made her choice and hadn't gone for the other one. Piers, they all noticed, still went off to the village occasionally to visit Sarah but he was always back by midnight and never made any attempt to bring her home with him. Kathy wondered just how much her parents knew. She hoped in a way that this wasn't just going to be a bit of a holiday fling on Piers' part, but she couldn't see a future for the shop girl and the Concorde pilot.

Nobody was expecting the evil switch of the wind from the balmy southwest back to the bitter north. Direct from the Arctic and blasting the daffodils and early blossoms that had dared to presume winter was over.

Kathy couldn't believe it when she got out of bed one morning and the air in the bedroom hit her like a bucket of cold water. She threw on the warmest clothes she had brought with her and went downstairs hoping to find some warmth in the kitchen. To her relief, the Aga was putting out some heat again and the Prof had just made the habitual pot of tea and was making a start on some porridge. Something he hadn't done since the weather warmed up.

"Ah, good morning," he greeted her. "Anyone else stirring yet?"

"Thought I heard Piers thumping about but Jean-Guy's still out for the count."

"Good. I need a word with our pilot."

"Is he in trouble again?"

"Not this time."

The two settled to their tea and porridge and Kathy had nearly finished hers by the time Piers wandered in looking as though he hadn't woken up properly and with an odd flush on his usually pale face. None of them had mentioned the tattoo since they had seen it, but Kathy would sometimes watch him and visualise it under his clothes even though she tried not to. Somehow the secrecy of it bothered her more than the scars on Jean-Guy which were now quite familiar to her.

"Sleep well?" the Prof asked.

Piers yawned. "Sorry. No, not really."

"Well, drink your tea, then read this." The Prof slid a folded piece of paper across the table to him.

"Am I in trouble again?"

"Not this time."

Piers read the brief note he had been given. To Kathy's alarm he screwed it up then slumped forward with his head on his arms on the table.

"What on earth?" she asked and put an arm across his back, trying not to think she was touching those desiccated butterflies through the soft wool of his moth-holed sweater.

His whole body heaved and he started sneezing. "You're asking me to fly just as I feel like crap."

"Sorry," the Prof said. "I hope you haven't picked up this flu that's going round."

"Probably. But I won't get it badly as the airline makes sure all crew get the vaccine."

"Can you fly today?"

"Well, no reputable commercial airline would let me anywhere near a flight deck feeling like this. Can you give me forty eight hours?"

"I'll pass the message on. It's not ideal. Go back to bed."

Jean-Guy arrived in the kitchen at his usual hour to find Kathy and the Prof were still sitting at the table and there was no sign of Piers. There was something odd about the atmosphere in the room and nobody spoke as he helped himself to the porridge keeping warm on the Aga.

"We have a slight problem," the Prof told him as he sat at the table.

"That can't be good."

"It's Marianne. She did defect from the train and is now in hiding in West Berlin. I was told Piers is to go and get her but he has just gone down with flu and isn't fit to fly today. So she will have to wait for another day or so."

"Can't they get her out by land as I was?"

"No. Our best hope is to fly someone in for her."

"And he is the only pilot in the country who could get her?" Jean-Guy asked cynically.

"No, but they want to test him. I can't tell you anything really but I have made comments to you about him being useful and, if you want to put it in terms he would understand, he is back on their radar since he got mixed up with you two so they have carried out their vetting on him and he has been cleared to go. Of course he has been told none of this but he is not a stupid man and he will be aware of what is going on. It will be an easy trip but it won't be one he wants to do."

Kathy felt she was peeping into that awful chasm again. "So why make him do it?"

The Professor sighed. "I don't know. And that is the truth. I tell you more than I should but in this case I genuinely have nothing I can tell you. He is known in my world from a long time ago and I understand they have been trying for years to get him back. There is something in the background and even I have not been told what it is."

"Does he know?"

Petr Mihaly pulled a wry face. "As I said, he isn't stupid. He will know something. He will know there are hundreds of pilots who could do this trip and he will have a good idea why they have chosen him. But he will go. He has been trained to know that to refuse would be worse."

Kathy looked towards the window and wished this whole thing wasn't going to happen. It felt like the start of something and it wasn't going to be good. "Will Marianne come here?" she asked to deflect the topic "I imagine Jean-Guy will be pleased to see her."

The Prof was glad to get back to practicalities. "Initially just for a day or so until we can move her on. So, I'm sorry but it's separate rooms for you two. Jean-Guy, you will have to go back in with Piers. But I don't want any gossip on the circuit about you two. And while he is away I need one or both of you to go and warn Sarah to stay away too. No personal relationships on show while Marianne is here. There is something about her story which doesn't stack up and I don't like it."

Kathy looked across at Jean-Guy but he wouldn't look at her. She had a bad feeling that he somehow thought this was his fault. Just for a few treacherous seconds she had to agree.

Dangerous Errand

As Piers had predicted, forty eight hours later he was over the worst of his symptoms and he left the farmhouse in the Land Rover too early in the morning for Jean-Guy to be out of bed but the other two saw him off. Kathy couldn't help noticing an air of quiet resignation about him that she had never seen before. It seemed the Prof had told her the truth and even the thought that he was going to be flying again was no consolation to the man who had been trained to obey orders.

Petr Mihaly looked at the sad woman who sat at the breakfast table with him but didn't seem to want to pour herself some cornflakes from the box she was holding almost defensively in both hands He spoke softly to her as though he was afraid of frightening her even more. "I have said to you over the last few weeks maybe more than I should so now I will tell you the whole of it. Part of what I do for this country is to give a room to passing defectors. But I am sure you have worked out I am also involved in other activities for the British security services and I have now been told that Piers is going to be recruited sooner or later. I spoke to him last night and, as we guessed, he is fully aware of this but also we were right in our assumption that he doesn't want to go. He told me things that made me realise this flight is not the first link in the chain they are using to pull him back in."

"They can't make him go, can they?" Kathy asked feeling quite angry on Piers' behalf. "Why him anyway?"

The Prof kept his tone quiet and calm, still trying not to worry her too much. "He has a unique set of knowledge and contacts from his past, from Northern Ireland to South America and the Caribbean. He is known and liked by people and in places where our services wouldn't dare to send agents. The airline have had their instructions which is why he holds licences to fly several kinds of plane and other strange things that breach normal practices. Even while he has been here they have made sure he keeps his licences and I have no doubt it won't take him long to adjust to military flying again. Still, at least you took my advice and chose the other one." He saw the look on her face and knew he had failed. "Please don't worry about Piers."

"How can I not now?" Kathy demanded.

"Because the people I work for are not in the habit of deliberately putting their employees in mortal danger. If, and it's a very big if, they ever did succeed in getting Piers, he would be most use to them as a courier, taking and bringing information as he flies round the world. With his regular visits to the USA he would be a very useful link with the CIA and they will be looking at him too on this little trip. Not for one moment do I think he would ever be used for anything more involved than that."

"And they've got to persuade him to go first," Kathy pointed out. "Somehow I don't think that will be easy."

The Professor wasn't smiling. "If they want him enough they will get him. But let us move on now. We can only wait to see what happens. Breakfast and then don't forget to go and see Sarah as soon as you can."

Kathy and Jean-Guy set out for the village after breakfast, dawdling along the coast path, deserted again in the biting northerly winds and with the occasional squall of rain making them glad they were dressed for the weather.

"Be nice to see Marianne again," Kathy began after a lengthy silence. "After what the soldiers did to her, I'd say she'll be glad to get away."

Jean-Guy was thoughtful. "You know, that is a very odd thing. I saw what it did to you. I can still sometimes sense in our bed that it haunts you. Marianne was never like you."

Kathy didn't like to think any woman could ever lie about such a thing. "It affects different people in different ways. My attacker was my ex, on his own, in our flat. She went through something quite different."

"True," he had to acknowledge. "But there is something odd about the whole thing. The Prof thinks so too. And why Piers when there must be a hundred suitable pilots?"

"Now that I do know, but I think maybe the Prof should be the one to answer that for you. In the meantime all we can tell Sarah is that he's got the flu and he's out of bounds for at least ten days. How long do they think he'll be?"

"You ask me a question which I can't answer."

"Here's one you can answer. Shall we buy a cake for tea?"

"Yes. Definitely."

They were surprised to find Sarah's mother in the shop which was oddly empty of customers.

"Good morning," she greeted them cheerfully. "If it's Sarah you were hoping to see I'm afraid she's in bed. Gone down with this duzzy flu that's going around. I don't think you'll be seeing her for at least a week. How are you getting on with the knitting wool?"

"Loving it," Kathy replied. "I hope she gets better soon. We've just popped down to let her know that Piers has gone down with it too."

Sarah's mother smiled indulgently. "They're such a lovely couple, aren't they? I must say with her track record I thought she'd never find a man to marry her."

Kathy and Jean-Guy looked at each other. "I didn't realise he'd asked her," Kathy said before she decided to be discreet.

"Oh he hasn't, love. But I'm sure he will. I mean I know he's divorced and all that but we're all allowed to make one mistake in our lives, aren't we? I hope it won't be a long engagement as they're neither of them getting any younger. I've been telling her for years it's time she made me a granny. But she's thirty eight now so they need to get their skates on. Of course, we'll have to persuade the vicar to marry them as he's divorced."

Kathy could feel a headache coming on and edged her way towards the cakes. "Oh, you've got a Victoria sponge. My favourite. I'll have to get one of those."

"Which reminds me, I hope I got this right but Sarah said you were going to ask me if I'd make you a concert dress. I'd be more than happy to, been a while since I made a decent evening gown. I've got some patterns for you to choose from but they're next door. I've done your costumes for the Race but I'll need you both to try them on. Of course, I've finished the one for Piers but I wasn't going to have him stripping off in front of Sarah so he hasn't tried anything on. It will really suit him, but most things would, wouldn't they? I keep telling her she's lucky to get him. Anyway, is it just the cake for you today?"

Kathy and Jean-Guy escaped from the shop with mild headaches, the sponge cake, a bag of apples and a bar of fruit and nut which Kathy was determined to save as a treat for Piers. The two munched apples on the way back and went cheerfully into the kitchen planning on doing some work on their parts to the *Ghost*.

The Prof was at the kitchen table where they had left him and was looking at Audrey, sitting on a kitchen chair and yowling such as only she could.

"What's the matter with her?" Kathy asked and put the shopping on the table.

"I have no idea. I heard her when I went upstairs and there she was on Piers' bed going round in circles and howling the house down. She followed me down but won't let me near her to see if she's in pain."

Kathy sat next to the cat who stopped her noise and stepped across to Kathy where she reached up and put paws round her neck as she had done to Roisin. Kathy took the opportunity to check Audrey as best she could but her touch didn't seem to bother the cat. She couldn't see anything wrong with her paws and Audrey even let her look at her teeth which the men thought she was very brave to even contemplate doing.

"Well, I can't see anything wrong with her," was the best she could offer. "But we'd all better keep an eye on her in case she's eaten something. Are the others all OK?"

"Fine, except they don't let her near them while she's being so noisy."

"Perhaps she's missing her human and the hand game," Kathy suggested. "But I'm not going to put the gloves on and set myself up as target practice. She still puts her claws out occasionally."

"Me neither," Jean-Guy announced. "In fact I am going to put in some work on the Prokofiev so I'm ready for him when he gets back. Are you going to work on your Sibelius?"

"Not straight away. I'll sit with Audrey for a bit. She's quieter now so perhaps she'll settle."

"Maybe she has the flu," the Prof suggested. "She wouldn't leave Piers alone when he was ill."

Kathy waited until she was alone with the Prof and a silent cat. "Just how dangerous is this errand you've sent him on?"

"In theory it is a simple exercise to see if he will abide by the rules. No matter how useful he is, they can't have a maverick in the system. He has been trained in the forces, he'll do as he's told. I believe they are providing him with a two-seater military craft for the flight so he will be happy."

"I hope Sarah's over her flu by the time he gets back. He was out of control after an hour in the little thing at Ipswich." An absurd thought crossed her mind. "Must be quite nice to fly. Can you imagine it? All the way up in the sky and looking down on the clouds?" Practicality returned. "Oh, well, I'll never be able to afford flying lessons unless I can persuade Piers to teach me for free and I can't see that happening. Right, time for a bit of Sibelius. You have no idea how much I'm enjoying playing my choice of music again."

"Have you and Jean-Guy thought of running through the Ravel *Sonata*? You won't miss the pianist so much then and I'm sure I have it in my collection."

Kathy was failing to put Audrey down as the cat seemed suddenly to have turned into a silent octopus with eight barbed legs and no matter how many legs she disentangled there seemed to be lots more threatening to wreck her borrowed raincoat.

"What a lovely idea. But first I have to get rid of the cat."

"Just take her with you. She'll get bored eventually. The music is on the shelves in the sitting room."

Kathy was mildly surprised that Jean-Guy wasn't keen on the Ravel although she could see he liked the idea of an unaccompanied duet for them to work on. He seemed to be in as odd a mood as Audrey that day and Kathy wasn't sure how to get through to either of them. Although Jean-Guy came to her bed that night as he habitually did, he pleaded tiredness and just rolled away from her, where he lay perfectly still although she knew he wasn't asleep. She looked at him and wondered if there was something in his past that Marianne knew and he didn't want anyone else to know, He certainly hadn't been at all pleased to hear she was coming to stay even if it was for only a few days.

"Tell me what it is?" she asked softly.

To her relief he rolled back to face her but she could tell from the way he spoke that he had been crying. "I ran from my life in Czechoslovakia," he began hesitantly, "I don't know why Marianne is coming after me. She has never been unhappy there so far as I know."

"Even after what the soldiers did to her?"

Jean-Guy gathered her into his arms at last and his tears were hot on her neck. "I ran from my past. And now it is running after me. I am afraid of what will happen when it catches me."

Kathy didn't know what to say. "We'll look after you," she whispered in the darkness. "Me and Piers and the Prof. We won't let anyone hurt you ever again."

He didn't reply, just held her close and Kathy lay awake until the small hours listening to Jean-Guy's steady breathing and thinking of Audrey now curled round alone on Piers' bed. She wondered if cats could cry.

It was like the first few days they had been there when they didn't know what was happening and they had mostly sat around in the sitting room occasionally talking about nothing much in particular. But the recent music and laughter had gone from the sitting room and the piano was silent, with a discarded pair of shoes next to it. For two days Audrey refused to leave Piers' room. If anyone managed to get her off the bed she would fight and scratch until they let her go again. On the second day they gave in and put food, water and a litter tray in the bedroom for her so she could go back to her vigil on the bed.

The wind continued hard from the north, whipping the trees that had decided maybe they wouldn't put their leaves out just yet after all. On the third day, they couldn't help noticing that Audrey hadn't eaten anything although they thought maybe she had had some water and she just lay on the bed curled round and defensive. Not even Kathy was allowed near her.

On the fourth day Kathy and the Prof were having a silent breakfast when there came an odd sound from the sky as though two clouds had hit each other a long way out to sea.

"Oh God," the Prof said. "I hope that wasn't the power station."

The two rushed to the landing window as that was the only one in the house that faced that way but all seemed as normal.

Jean-Guy came out of Kathy's room looking half asleep and dishevelled. "What the hell was that? Has the power station gone up?"

"Looks OK," the Prof assured him but anything else he would have said was drowned out by a military jet aircraft screaming overhead, coming low out of the North Sea like a demon from hell. They were all convinced the pilot dipped one wing as the plane passed just their side of the power station.

"What on earth..." Kathy started to say. She turned towards Jean-Guy and fell over a small tortoiseshell cat who streaked down the stairs and out to the kitchen. Jean-Guy managed to catch her before Audrey toppled her down the stairs and suddenly all three were laughing with relief.

"I think he's back," the Prof said for all of them.

Piers walked in through the back door late in the afternoon. Only the Prof was there, preparing the evening meal and he looked round on hearing the door open.

"Kathy! Jean-Guy!" he yelled into the house. "They're here." He addressed Piers' companion in Czech. "Hullo, Marianne. Glad you got here safely."

"Didn't think I was going to get here at all," she said gracelessly. "I should have been out a week ago."

Kathy arrived in the kitchen first and noticed Piers was dressed in what looked like military fatigues and a leather flying jacket from the 1950s. She gave him a hug.

"Missed you," she told him. "But not as much as Audrey has." She turned politely to his companion, a tall brunette young woman who was staring round the kitchen as though she had landed on another planet. "Hi, you must be Marianne. I'm Kathy."

The new arrival glared at the woman who had just shown such affection to the pilot and turned to the Professor. "Am I staying here?" she asked in Czech.

"Just for a day or two."

"Why? You have held my brother for weeks."

"Marianne," he explained politely, "we speak English in this house out of respect for those who don't speak Czech. Come upstairs and I'll show you your room."

She still refused to speak English. "Thank you. Where is Jean-Guy?"

"I'm here," he told her in English as he came into the kitchen from the house. Brother and sister exchanged an awkward embrace and neither seemed particularly pleased to see the other.

Marianne looked at the Professor. "I'd like to have a bath before I eat," she said curtly.

"Of course, follow me. Did you bring any luggage at all?"

"Very little and I'm going to burn it all tomorrow as it reminds me too much."

"Then you will have no clothes to wear," the Professor pointed out mildly.

"So she can go and buy me some clothes. Nice clothes. I don't want to be seen looking like a refugee."

The Professor took this bad-mannered guest upstairs hoping she was just tired, and Jean-Guy and

Kathy looked at Piers who had slumped in a chair at the table.

"What was all that about?" Kathy asked Jean-Guy. "Anyone want tea?"

Two teas were requested and Jean-Guy gave them a rough translation of what Marianne and the Professor had said. "How did you get on?" he asked Piers.

"I thought I'd met my share of difficult women but none like her." He idly cuddled a loudly purring Audrey who had climbed onto his lap.

Jean-Guy sat with him. "What the hell happened?"

"Apparently I was late. And she doesn't like English people. So I told her I'm Irish and she tried to hit me in the face. Turns out she doesn't like men either. Just screamed at me that we're all rapists even if only with our eyes and ripped a bloody great hole in my shirt asking me how I liked it. So I said there was no way I was going to be shut in an aeroplane with her as she wasn't safe."

"What did they do?" Jean-Guy asked.

"We reached stalemate. They made lots of phone calls and in the end a female USAF pilot flew that cow back in my plane and I got to bring hers back. We met up at one of their bases where they all found it the funniest thing in years and gave me some clothes they reckoned even she couldn't rip. Believe me, she tried. How the hell I didn't drive off the road on the way here I'll never know." He gratefully accepted the mug of tea Kathy gave him. "How's Sarah?"

"She's got your flu. We saw her mum in the shop and she reckons the poor thing won't be up to receiving visitors for at least a week."

"Damn. Cold bath for me tonight then."

Kathy felt a smile inside her. She hadn't even thought that maybe Piers was serious about his relationship with Sarah. That maybe they would somehow find a future together.

"Me too," Jean-Guy said sadly. "There is to be no mixed sleeping while she is in the house."

"You mean I've got you kicking me to death again tonight?"

"At least I don't snore."

The Professor came back into the kitchen. "Car keys please," he asked Piers. "I've explained there's no way Kathy is going to go and buy clothes for her so she will have to wear what she brought."

"It's not locked. Am I going to be safe in the house with her around or should I go and see if Sarah's family will put me up?"

The Prof hadn't been expecting that to be an option and he started to wonder, "I'm sure she'll calm down soon," he assured the other man rather than tell him flat-out he couldn't go. "I've seen them more hysterical than that. Just try not to be alone with her. But I think for tonight I'll let her eat in her room. By the way, was it you making that godawful noise this morning?"

Piers smiled then. "Yup. They gave me a US jet fighter to fly. So I just had to take it the long way round so I could go through the sound barrier out over the Bay of Biscay. Annoyingly misjudged it and was a bit too close to the coastline here when I came out of it again." He saw the way they were all looking at him. "And yes, I got a bollocking for that too. Apparently the wings should have fallen off." He had that wicked smile on his face again and they weren't sure whether to believe him or not.

Kathy kissed his cheek. "I have so missed you," she told him happily.

Jean-Guy grinned hugely. "Me too. Can I have the jacket? I've only got one coat."

"Idiots," he said fondly. "How's the erotic Sibelius coming on?"

"Do you smell baking?" Jean-Guy asked.

The Prof smiled to himself as he went out to the car. The unbroken circle was strong again but now it was under the greatest pressure it had ever known.

Phantom of the Winds

It was all so reassuring in the morning. Kathy came downstairs in time to find the Prof and Piers sharing the paper again and generally not talking much over their breakfasts. The fatigues and leather jacket had been replaced by the habitual jeans and sweater and he looked a lot better.

"Good morning," the Prof said brightly. "Sleep well?"

"Better than I expected," she had to smile. "Back to the music today?" she asked Piers.

"Hope so, or I'll be forgetting where all the notes are. When do you reckon I can go and see Sarah?"

"Oh dear, you have got it bad. Well, I'm supposed to be seeing her mum at some point to discuss my concert gown so we could walk along and see how she is."

They were eating toast together when Marianne came into the kitchen. She was dressed in a bright yellow and white polka dot dress that was cut quite low at the front and Kathy wondered how she wasn't cold as although it wasn't as bad as it had been it certainly wasn't summer dress weather. Her dark hair had been brushed until it shone and she wore it tied back with a jaunty white ribbon which showed off the silver earrings she wore. She had a silver necklace with a moonstone oval charm on it and it looked very fetching against her olive toned skin which, Kathy guessed, would go an enviable shade of brown in the summer and Kathy started to feel dowdy in her striped rugby top and plain blue trousers. Marianne's eyes were more hazel than the darker brown of her brother but she had the same smile. Her accent when she spoke English was much stronger than her brother's had become over the weeks of incessant use.

"Good morning. I am sorry if I was rude yesterday but I hope you understand how desperate I was to get away." She leaned artfully over Piers to kiss him on both cheeks in greeting and was clearly making sure he could see down the front of her dress. "And thank you for coming to rescue me. Did you enjoy your ride home in the Phantom?"

Kathy had no idea anyone could make the word phantom sound so sensual.

"Lady pilot said you must have flown it like demon to get back in time you did. I wish I'd been with you. It must have been so exciting riding your phantom of the winds."

"Would you like some toast?" the Professor asked her politely.

A jealous Audrey landed on the table and hissed a warning at this new menace.

"No toast, just coffee. I don't eat breakfast." Marianne picked the cat up and plonked her on the floor. "And I don't like cats," she announced.

"Well there are a lot of them here," Kathy told her and went to comfort an indignant Audrey.

"And this one's mine," Piers snapped at Marianne and took Audrey back from Kathy.

Marianne just looked at him as though he was out of his mind and helped herself to some tea from the pot without waiting for any coffee to be made for her.

After breakfast Kathy and Piers got ready to go out on their walk to the village. Marianne would have gone with them but the Professor told her in no uncertain terms she wasn't to leave the house for the few days she

214

would be there. The leather jacket was hanging up in the hall and Kathy was surprised Piers took down his battered old waxed cotton coat to wear.

"Not putting on your nice new coat?" she asked him.

"No point, I've got my old RAF one at home somewhere. You can wear it if you like but it'll be too big."

The brown leather jacket totally swamped Kathy but she wore it anyway and was really very warm by the time they got to the shop.

It was still Sarah's mother behind the till. "My goodness, you got over this duzzy flu quicker than Sarah has," was her greeting to her daughter's sweetheart. "Do you want to pop next door and see her?" To Kathy's hidden amusement any hopes Piers may have had were dashed. "She's still quite poorly but she can show you the patterns while you're there. Door will be open, just go on in."

"I feel like your chaperone," Kathy muttered to her companion as the two went to the house next door to the shop. They didn't like to barge in unannounced so Kathy tapped on the door as she opened it and called down the hall, "Sarah? You in?"

Sarah came into the hall from the back room and saw she had two visitors. "How lovely to see you!" she cried and then coughed like a barking hyena. "Sorry, can't seem to shift this cough."

"I'll risk it," Piers smiled and kissed her.

"Thought of you yesterday," Sarah told him. "There was this really loud bang and we all thought the power station had gone up, but one of our customers said it was a plane breaking the sound barrier over the sea.

Which made sense as straight after it this really loud jet plane shot across, ever so low."

"Some lucky sod from one of the bases," Piers said rather resentfully.

"You'll get back to your flying soon," Sarah consoled and kissed him lovingly. She turned innocently to Kathy. "He's told me about his breakdown and how Emma said he could come and stay here for a bit."

Kathy caught on to the lie but didn't dare elaborate. "Well, if Emma had any ideas about the two of us getting together she's going to be very disappointed. Your mum said she's put out some patterns for me to look at?"

Sarah looked at her with a surprising shrewdness at the obvious change of topic. "I know that," she said and Kathy thought she meant it was because Piers had chosen her. "Anyone could see you would choose Jean-Guy. Even when you first brought him here and he bought *Winnie the Pooh* you'd already chosen him." Kathy was a bit thrown by that. She hadn't had any idea herself at that time. But Sarah barely paused for breath. "Come on in. Dad's at the wholesaler so we've got the house to ourselves for an hour or so." She cuddled herself against Piers. "But don't you go getting any ideas. I can hardly get in enough breath to walk at the moment, never mind the antics you get up to." As if to prove her point, she had a coughing fit as soon as she had sat on the sofa in the back room.

"You do sound terrible," Kathy sympathised.

"I feel it," she agreed and tucked a crocheted blanket round herself. "Make us some tea, please?" she asked Piers. "Yours is always the best."

"Flatterer," was all he said but he went out of the room and Kathy presently heard noises of kettle and mugs so she guessed he knew his way round the house.

The room was warm so she took off the leather jacket then sat on the floor next to the coffee table to look through the patterns spread out there and winced to hear the other woman's really rather nasty cough. Sarah had managed to get some air into her lungs by the time Piers came back with the tea.

"I like your jacket," she said to Kathy. "Looks warm."

"It is," Kathy assured her and paused as one of the patterns caught her attention.

"Is it new?"

"New to her," Piers told her as he risked the germs and sat with Sarah on the sofa. "We found it in a box in the loft. God knows how long it's been there. I wanted it too but she arm-wrestled me for it and won." Sarah just looked at him and he smiled at her in that twinkly-eyed way he had. "Bloody strong these violin players. It's all that bowing."

Sarah had learned that little smile on his face meant he was only teasing her. "I used to play the trombone," she admitted a shade wistfully just as her guests had taken mouthfuls of tea. "Oh, now you're both laughing at me, I knew you would. I don't know why I told you."

Kathy wasn't sure how neither she nor Piers had choked on their tea at such an unexpected revelation but she saw him put a hand up to his nose so she guessed it hadn't all gone down his throat.

"Trombone's good," she rushed to assure Sarah before she got too upset. "Was this at school?"

217

"Yes, just for a few terms. I was never very good at it, then this kid called Tom came along and he wanted to play the trombone so they took it away from me and gave it to him."

"Well, that was mean of them. Piers, stop laughing. I know several women who play the trombone."

Piers mopped his streaming eyes on his cuff and gave Sarah a very repentant kiss. "I'm sorry, I don't know why I found it so funny. Just wasn't expecting it." He put his arm round her and she, mollified, leaned against him. She spoiled the effect rather by having another coughing fit.

"What about this one?" Kathy asked, showing her chosen pattern to Sarah. "Do you think this would work? I don't want anything strapless while I'm playing and puffy shoulders are out as they'd just get in the way."

Sarah leaned forward and looked at the simple, elegant evening dress with spaghetti straps over a voile yoke and falling into a shift dress that only the petite Kathy could get away with. "Oh that is lovely. Do you want to try on your Smugglers' Race dress while you're here? It's upstairs in the sewing room. It'll probably fit, Mum's good at working out sizes."

Kathy felt a bit awkward about going round the house while her hostess was trapped under a blanket on the sofa, but she really wanted to see what the dress would look like. "Are you sure you don't mind me wandering all over your house?"

"No, you go on. It's not like we've got anything to hide. Come down here when you've got it on and I'll have a look at you."

Kathy got to her feet. "Five minutes," she told Piers.

"It'll take me ten to unwrap her from this chastity blanket," he replied and Sarah laughed so hard she started coughing again.

It was slightly more than five minutes before Kathy came down again as she had had to admire the dress in the full-length mirror in the sewing room. It owed a lot to Hollywood's idea of pirates with its laced-front bodice and mock undershirt billowing white along the neckline. Fortunately there was a zip in the back so Kathy didn't have to wrestle with laces and the skirt ended perfectly just above her ankles. The bodice and sleeves were a shade of dark red she would never have dared wear before and the skirt was of dark green and red vertical stripes which ought to have made it look Christmassy but it didn't and there were so many petticoats under it she rustled as she walked up and down the room for a few minutes. It showed off a bit more of her chest than she was used to but after seeing Marianne in her yellow spotty dress, Kathy was relieved to realise the bodice was too well cut to reveal anything it shouldn't. Feeling like a whole new woman starting out on an adventure, she galloped down the stairs and twirled into the living room

"What do you reckon?" she asked, aiming the question at Sarah as she didn't want Piers to make any of the comments she just knew were forming in his mind.

Sarah fished her hand out from under Piers' shirt and looked at her. "You look lovely," she said. "I can't wait to see Jean-Guy's face when he sees you in it. Mum's put you in the red and green and I'm in a kind of orange and blue. And mine's about ten sizes larger," she finished quite cheerfully.

Kathy was buoyed up by the sensation of her new dress and wished she could wear it home. "Does his tattoo feel funny?" she asked. "I really wanted to touch it when he showed it to me." She realised her mistake when Piers looked as though he could cheerfully have throttled her and Sarah stared at her as though she was a madwoman. There was nothing for it, she was going to have to brazen it out. "How can you not have seen it? The things you two have been getting up to in the stockroom?"

Sarah had moved slightly away from the man on the sofa. "What tattoo?" she demanded angrily. "People I know just don't have such things. It's what whores and sailors do. Not respectable middle-aged men who fly Concorde."

"No, it's what young RAF men do when they're stationed away from home and lose a drinking bet. And did you just call me middle-aged?"

Sarah wasn't in the mood for his joshing. "Show me. Now."

"I'll get you back for this," Piers told Kathy as he took off his sweater and got his right arm from its shirt sleeve.

Sarah looked as though she was about to cry as she pushed him round by the shoulder to see the images on his back better. She also did what it hadn't occurred to Kathy to do and checked just how far down his back those skeletal butterflies went. "That is disgusting!" she declared and turned furious eyes on Kathy. "Have you seen it properly? All of it?"

"Well, I thought I had," she started.

"Show her," Sarah told him. "And then I'd like to know what she thinks of it."

Kathy wasn't sure she wanted to see what was apparently so abhorrent but Piers stood up, turned his back to her and hooked his waistband down so she could see that the skeletal butterflies crumbled into a dust which was forming a human skull right at the base of his spine. She gave in to curiosity and touched his unexpectedly smooth and cool skin. "That is beautiful," she told him. "I have no idea what it's all about but it's quite beautiful now I see all of it."

Piers shrugged his shirt back on again and started doing up the buttons.

"I can't bear to look at it," Sarah mourned. "Just get dressed and go away." She turned her face into the sofa and started coughing and crying at the same time. She sensed Piers was getting closer to her and held out a hand to keep him away. "Get off me," she told him and pulled the blanket over her head. "I don't know how anyone can say it's beautiful."

"I'll get changed," Kathy muttered to him and shot back up the stairs. She left the pirate's dress in the sewing room then galloped downstairs again to find Piers waiting for her in the hall and he had her coat and bag in his hands.

"Are you taking the pattern?" he asked her.

"I'll just pop it next door to her mum. 'Bye, Sarah!" she called. "Hope you get rid of the cough soon. And I'm really sorry they gave your trombone to Tom."

"'Bye, Kathy," came the unmistakeable use of the singular. "Pop round any time you're passing."

Piers stood outside the shop while Kathy went in to show Sarah's mother her chosen pattern.

221

"Oh, yes, that'll be perfect for you. I'll get some fabric samples for you."

"And Sarah told me to try on the Race dress and that's a perfect fit. So thank you for that."

"You're very welcome. Piers still with her?"

Oh, no, he's outside. I'm afraid they've had a bit of a falling out."

For a moment Sarah's mother looked totally crushed. "Well, I suppose it had to happen sooner or later."

"I'll let her tell you all about it," Kathy said and made her escape feeling guiltily that it was all her fault.

The coast path was still cold and windy and the two walked along in silence for a while.

"I'm sorry," Kathy said, unable to bear his moodiness any longer. "It didn't occur to me you'd managed to keep it hidden. It could have been worse, she might not have seen it until your wedding night."

He smiled grudgingly. "True. That would have been a mess." He looked at her then and even his eyes were smiling. "What wedding night?"

Kathy just laughed. "So what is it all about anyway?"

As he had done once before, he offered her his arm and she took it, guessing herself forgiven. "The panther is...I don't know what you want to call it. Creation? The butterflies, maybe freedom, hope, dreams, whatever. The panther chases them into the flower which destroys them instead of giving them nectar to live."

"So are you saying life just turns freedom and hope and happiness into death?"

"Basically."

"Just how drunk were you after losing that bet?"

"Sober enough to tell the tattooist what I wanted and not quite drunk enough to block out the pain. It was a long and sweaty night in Hong Kong."

"It's very well drawn."

"Yeah, she was a good artist. She was actually from Lithuania of all places. Some of us found our way back there and bought some of her drawings on another trip round the back alleys. I've still got a couple hanging up in my house. Managed to keep them as part of the settlement."

"What did your wife think of it?"

"She was one of the ones holding me down when the pain was at its worst. She was in the RAF too, that's how we met. I'd got a commission and she hadn't but that didn't bother us at the time. Then after that I had the job out in the Caribbean but she wasn't happy so I went into commercial flying. Started with Air France but she still wasn't happy so I switched airlines. Didn't help the marriage."

Kathy was curious to learn more about this woman. "What did she do in the RAF?"

"She was a nurse. Probably still is."

Kathy realised that particular line of conversation was closed. "So when were you going to show Sarah the tattoo of despair?"

"Hadn't actually thought that one through."

Back at the house, he opened the back door for her and they went in to an empty room but could hear Jean-Guy wrestling with the Prokofiev in the sitting room.

"Time for some music, I reckon," Kathy remarked. "And I really am sorry I messed things up with you and Sarah."

"I daresay she'll get over it. Maybe."

"Another butterfly of hope through the treacherous hibiscus of life on its way to destruction?"

"Something like that. You know your flowers, most people called it a lotus."

"Been on display a lot has it?"

"Twenty odd years ago. I try to forget about it these days."

"You are getting middle-aged."

Jean-Guy stopped his playing when the other two came into the sitting room and Marianne tossed down the book she had been reading.

"Where did you get to?" Jean-Guy wanted to know and sounded a bit put out. "I was hoping to do some work on the Grieg today."

"Went to see Sarah. Had a row and split up."

"Oh, sorry. You want to play?"

"Yes, we need to sort out the first movement."

"Want a page turner?" Kathy offered.

"I'll turn pages," Marianne cut in brightly. "I had to leave my violin behind and I miss music." She went to the piano and put the top up ignoring Audrey who had just tried to jump from the sofa to the piano but landed on the floor instead. Marianne watched sceptically as Piers got himself settled to play and commented, "So you take shoes off and put gloves on. What kind of crazy pianist are you?"

"A bloody good one," her brother told her. "Just turn the pages and keep quiet. Right, pick it up at rehearsal mark F and let's go through to J. I'm not happy with your passages there, you rush the semiquavers and the rhythm was definitely out at G. Which meant when you hit the sixes at H you didn't stand a chance in hell."

"I have never rushed a semiquaver in my life."

Marianne settled herself on Piers' left and Kathy picked up Audrey so the two of them could sit in the armchair by the fire and watch. She thought Marianne had the strangest technique as a page turner as she somehow managed to lean across in such a way her right breast nearly hit Piers on the nose. Kathy wasn't surprised that he made a total hash of the piano solo at letter G.

"What the hell are you up to?" Jean-Guy almost shouted at him.

"It's actually quite hard to read music when someone's shoving a tit in your face," came the scathing response. He turned to Marianne. "Just back off will you? Either turn the pages properly or I'll do it myself."

The Prof came into the room and somehow sized up the situation in one glance. "Problems, gentlemen? Perhaps I can help. Marianne, you are excused duties, I will sit with Piers."

Marianne was smiling as she walked out of the room, the page-turning fell to the Prof, and Piers made even more of a mess of the piano solo. He put the top of the piano back down and Audrey triumphantly took up her position and waited for the hands to start dancing again.

"Just take it a bit more slowly for now," the Prof advised gently. "You are rushing the semiquavers at F which puts you in trouble at G. So by the time you get to H you have lost it."

"Sorry, not been a good day. And I don't rush semiquavers."

With the calming influence of the Prof beside him and Audrey playing the hand game again, the music

225

settled down and the troublesome bars were sorted out. Kathy was fascinated to watch as the three worked their way through the movement, pulling apart any parts they weren't happy with. She had no idea the Prof could teach so well, so knowledgably and so patiently; she thought he just wrote reviews. He also turned pages without getting in the pianist's line of vision.

"And now, gentlemen," the Prof declared, "I think it is lunch time."

Much to their surprise, Marianne had prepared lunch while they were rehearsing and there was the smell of baking in the kitchen.

"I like your stove," she told the Prof. "We had one like it in one house in Praha. But not so many ovens." She had found an apron which she had tied over her yellow dress and which covered her chest a bit more. "I have made you apple tart."

"Thank you, Marianne," the Prof said courteously as they all settled at the table.

Marianne smiled almost coquettishly as she sat next to Piers and placed an artful hand on his thigh. "I'm sorry I distracted you from your playing too," she apologised. "But you are very beautiful man and I am sorry to hear you don't have girlfriend any more."

He picked the hand off again. "I'm not giving up on her. I'll go round and see her later."

Marianne's behaviour was impeccable for the rest of the meal. The tart she had made was excellent but she waved away their compliments.

"It is what good women do. We look after our men. Now I make coffee then I will wash up so you can all play music again."

226

"Shall we go and look at the Ravel for a few minutes?" Jean-Guy asked Kathy after coffee.

She guessed what he really wanted. "Good idea. We can go to my room which leaves the sitting room free for the piano."

The two of them went upstairs with their instruments but didn't dare do anything more than have a bit of a kiss and a cuddle.

"What happened with Sarah?"

"She saw the tattoo. It was my fault in a way but it never occurred to me she hadn't seen it. But the best bit is it all goes down to a skull on his bum which I hadn't realised."

"Do you mean to tell me you and Sarah have been looking at…?"

"Oh, not really. It's just about there," she said and poked him. "Anyway, she wouldn't look at it. She told him to get out and so now I suppose he's free for Marianne to get her claws into. Just what is she playing at?"

"She wants something. I don't know whether it is as simple as she is going to try to get him to marry her for his nationality or something else. Perhaps she will talk to you about it. If she starts to talk, try to tell her nothing but get her to confide in you. Just do whatever you can because it's been a long time since I heard him play the piano so badly."

"He's just split up from Sarah and had that flight out to Germany and back as well as the flu. I'm sure it'll all get better."

"I hope so. Because the sooner she's out of the house, the sooner I can get back in your bed and we will all be happier."

227

Kathy looked at the bedroom door but there was no lock on it. The only upstairs room with a lock was the bathroom. "Want to help me wash my hair?" she asked and took hold of his hand. "I often find the best way to do it is to get in the bath."

Marianne was still in the kitchen just finishing off the washing up when Kathy went back downstairs with her newly-washed hair bundled in a towel on top of her head.

"Tea?" Kathy asked politely.

"No. Thank you. How long have you been having sex with my brother?"

Kathy hoped that the abruptness of the question was due to Marianne not being as proficient in English as her brother was and she remembered the Professor's warning about not wanting any gossip about her and Jean-Guy on the network. She kept her tone light and curious. "What makes you think we have?"

Marianne was not to be fobbed off, but there was a moment's hesitation before she persisted. "Is he good?"

Kathy could hear Emma's voice asking the exact same question, but Emma would also understand the full implications of Kathy having a serious physical relationship and the idea of Emma asking her that made her smile. "I wouldn't know," was all she offered in return. She wasn't best pleased when Marianne sat at the table with her.

"I had lover once," Marianne began sounding rather regretful. "Soldier in Red Army. It started when I was about sixteen. Sometimes his friends liked to be there too. Then I told him I thought I was pregnant so he threw me away. I was so angry I made up rape story to spite

228

him. And his friends. They sent him to prison. Of course there was no baby in the end."

Kathy sat at the table, slightly appalled that Marianne had been so calculating and just a bit grudgingly envious she hadn't stitched up Richard in a similar way. "And Piers?" she asked, still keeping it lightly curious. "What are your plans for him? I've seen you looking at him and he is very handsome."

Marianne helped herself to a gulp of Kathy's tea. "Do you think maybe he will marry me now he has no girlfriend any more? I can get message through to Russians and tell them that I have Irishman for them to train to work for us. They thought at first he was someone else but he will do."

Warning bells were ringing so loudly in Kathy's brain she thought Marianne could probably hear them. "Sorry," she said and sounded perfectly genuine. "But why would he want to go and train for the Russians? And who did they think he was anyway? And who thought he was someone else?" So many questions were pounding round in her head and she didn't realise she had spoken the first three aloud.

Marianne stopped pretending. "There was British special agent known as Palach. If you look quickly Piers is much like him. We had hoped it was him. But it isn't and Piers is not who they thought he was but he is not so stupid he would die rather than refuse me."

Kathy had gone so far beyond shocked, it was all starting to feel very real. She thought of poor coughing Sarah, hiding under the blanket on the sofa with all her dreams destroyed and knew she had to do something with them all under such imminent threat. She tried to think what she would say to Emma if she had just announced she was going to steal another woman's boyfriend. "He may get back together again with Sarah," she tried desperately while her mind raced and in her imagination another butterfly of hope was crushed to dust while the demonic notes of *La Campanella* mocked her.

"No, once he has had me he won't want another. And if he refuses me, which he won't, I will use a knife on him. But now you should stop sleeping with my brother. I am taking him back to Moscow with me very soon as our parents are so worried for him. I came just for Jean-Guy and now I have Piers too as bonus."

Kathy began to feel as though she was drowning. "So you're not here for asylum?"

Marianne looked at her as though she was mad. "No. I am here to take back to Soviet Union what belongs to them. A great cellist and man who can fly American fighter plane after only one lesson. Pity he wasn't Palach, but he will do." She closed a frighteningly strong grip round Kathy's wrist. "And you will tell Jean-Guy you don't want him any more without telling him what I have just told you. Although I think maybe he will be glad to go home. Piers may take a little more persuading but he will agree in the end if only to stop me hurting you." She smiled, amused that she had now clearly terrified this blonde Englishwoman who had thought she would get to keep the famous Jean-Guy Dechaume.

Kathy could quite believe her. She looked around the kitchen as though one of the cats might suddenly help her but all she could see was a cloud of butterflies slowly turning into dust.

From Stone to Thorn

Marianne took off the apron and pulled the front of her dress down just a bit more. "Let's go," she said quite politely. "You must end with Jean-Guy."

Kathy was still trying to think of a way forward. "But there's nothing to end," she protested and tried to sound convincing.

"He thinks there is. I have seen how he looks at you. Go and tell him. He won't want to come with me if he thinks he is going to have you. And keep away from Piers too."

Kathy could only hope that the peculiar understanding she had with Piers wouldn't let her down now she needed it. "I'll tell him, but he won't understand why. And I certainly don't fancy Piers in that way."

"Yes, you do," Marianne laughed at her. "You sleep with my brother but you really want Piers in your bed. And he wants you too. Anyone can see it in the way you talk to each other. I think maybe Jean-Guy won't be surprised to hear what you have to say to him."

Kathy thought Marianne's assessment of the situation was way out. Even Sarah had read the situation better. She went ahead into the sitting room where Jean-Guy was now slowly working his way through Roisin's book while Piers was at the piano cursing over one of the trickier passages in the *Ghost* that still gave him problems.

Kathy sat next to Jean-Guy on the sofa, sitting sideways so her back was towards Marianne and both men would see her face. "Can you do something for me, please?" she asked him perfectly calmly then looked up at Piers who stopped playing but his expression didn't change. It was as though he was just mildly curious.

"Maybe. Depends what it is," Jean-Guy hedged, not having the other man's intuition.

"Will you please tell your sister that you and I aren't having sex with each other, that we don't want to and that you and I aren't more than friends?"

Jean-Guy wasn't quite quick enough to do as she asked and realised his mistake, so he winged it. "Hey, once we did it. After the pub. Was I so bad you don't want it again?"

Kathy was impressed by that piece of improvisation. "Oh, yes. After the pub when we were both drunk. Can you honestly say that was the best sex you've ever had?"

Marianne caught her breath and looked from the two of them to the man at the piano who was now grinning hugely. "That is not true!" she protested. "You are more than that to each other."

Piers gave her a very enticing smile. "Oh, trust me, that's true. I was driving the car while they did it. Come on, it was the drunk fumbling of a couple of kids. Mean to tell me you haven't done something similar?"

Marianne couldn't believe a man who smiled like that would lie to her. "So she is not whoring with my brother?"

Piers hoped the choice of words was due to a poor command of English. Otherwise it was unforgivably brutal. "Only in his dreams. Hey, Piglet, this one's for you. And remember I don't lock my door at night." He idly played a few chords on the piano and then let rip with a full-blooded rendition of *La Campanella* which startled the others and was loud enough to be heard in the study.

Jean-Guy got to his feet at the end of the performance. "You play much too loud," he said. "I am going to give this book back to the Professor, it is too hard for me." He stalked out of the room and the others heard him open the study door and then it closed firmly behind him.

The residents of the house were aware that there was only ever to be one circumstance under which that piece was to be played all the way through, but Marianne, not understanding the nuances, flirtatiously complimented Piers on his playing. Kathy knew Jean-Guy and the Prof would have picked up on Piers' warning signal and would now be waiting for her to find a way to tell them what was really happening.

Kathy gave Marianne a smile as if to confirm her part in the plot. "He's always showing off playing that piece but it is a beautiful work and I wish he would play it more often."

"Incredible playing," Marianne agreed and tried to catch Piers' eye but he didn't raise his eyes from the keyboard and his face looked even paler than usual.

With a suddenness that startled the two women, Piers dropped the lid of the piano harder than he needed to and said, "Sorry, don't feel too good," then walked quickly out of the room.

Marianne looked at the closed door then at Kathy. "What is matter with him?"

Kathy wasn't sure whether to say he probably had a headache, was feeling upset over Sarah or had eaten something that disagreed. Before she could decide which excuse to use the Professor had come into the room.

"Where is he?" he asked and didn't sound very pleased. "I have told him many times not to bang the piano lid like that."

"Think he's gone upstairs," Kathy offered. "He said he didn't feel well."

"I will go find out," Marianne offered sweetly.

"No, I will go," the Professor corrected her and turned to leave the room. "I don't care how old he is or what he is, as long as he is here he is in my care."

Not wanting to talk to Marianne now they were alone again, Kathy got her knitting out and curled defensively round in one of the armchairs. Marianne sat on the sofa and watched her silently.

The Prof was back in a surprisingly short time. "He is unwell," he agreed. "I will take him up some water. Marianne, he says did you put something like nutmeg or cinnamon in the lunch?"

"A little clove on the apples," she admitted defensively.

"Ah, clove. You have made him sick as he can't eat some spices. He was calling you some not very nice things."

Kathy bent her head over her knitting pattern as though she needed to study the sleeve shaping for Jean-Guy's sweater. She had no idea whether that story was true or not but she was glad it had got Piers out of Marianne's way.

Piers came downstairs to join them in the kitchen at tea time, looking drained and only managed half a cup of tea then just about got into the garden in time to bring it all up again. If that was an act, Kathy thought, it was a very good one. The Prof abruptly ordered Piers back to bed and sent him off with a bucket, and Audrey followed

234

behind to keep him company. Kathy was silently relieved Marianne was so pleased with how she had handled things so far she didn't suggest that as they were such good friends now it would be a nice idea if they shared a bedroom.

On the morning of Marianne's third day in the farmhouse Kathy got up just before four o'clock, flushed the toilet, clicked her bedroom door shut and went down the silent stairs. They all knew the sound of the toilet was enough to wake Piers in the night and she silently apologised to him for disturbing his sleep after the rough day he had had. Hoping Marianne would have heard the bedroom door shutting again and believe she was back in bed, if she had even been woken, Kathy went out of the back door and along to the derelict cottages that were soon going to be inaccessible as the brambles and nettles were beginning to stage their annual takeover. It was still dark, but there was enough ambient light from the power station for her to see her way through the rhododendrons. She braved the thorns and the stings and made her way into the cottages where she sat on what had once been a stone windowsill and waited.

"Piglet?" asked a soft voice just a few minutes later. "What the hell's going on? I thought you'd gone back to bed then I heard the door."

Kathy had never been more thankful for Piers' hearing. With her mind a confused mess, she just flung herself into his arms and sobbed, "She's going to marry you and if you won't then she'll kill me."

Marianne triumphantly sprawled half on top of her Irish lover in his bed and let her fingers trail slowly

235

all down the tattoo on his spine. His perfect body fascinated her and she pushed the covers away so she could admire him as he lay there, quiet now and with the afternoon sunlight coming through the south window of the room, creating a warm light on his cool, pale skin.

Piers lay flat on his front, with his face among the pillows and felt her hot, dry touch on his aching back. He hadn't seen any sign of the threatened knife Kathy had told him about but guessed it was somewhere to hand so he had been the submissive one, letting her be in control even when her rather brutal lovemaking nearly put his left hip out of joint. He felt slightly sick and knew it wasn't cloves this time, but at least Kathy had now had the chance to talk to the other two. He just wished he knew where that knife was so he could use it himself. Marianne tucked one arm round his waist in a lazy movement as though she was going to roll him towards her and he heard the click of a blade flicking open.

Downstairs in the study the other three were deep in conversation and all relieved to know that Marianne was due to be moved on to another safe house but this time with her story blown and plans were being put in place to send her back to Moscow, alone and thwarted.

"He's done well," the Professor remarked. "He's managed to keep her up there a good two hours. If he can only manage it for another hour the car will be here to take her away. We will still all have to be careful. I don't know who she has been in contact with, but the immediate threat will be removed."

Kathy was huddled tight into Jean-Guy's embrace in an armchair but she couldn't stop shaking. "She's not really going to use a knife on him, is she?" she pleaded and looked into his worried dark eyes.

"He has his wits about him and his training to help him," the Prof tried to reassure her. "At least he knows to expect it."

Kathy put a hand to her throat where there was a tiny scar that most people didn't notice. She lost her battle against her tears and let Jean-Guy rock her gently in his arms as she tried not to remember the feel of the blade as a man forced himself on her.

The Professor listened a bit harder. "They are on the move, I think going into the bathroom. I will go and make tea, as that is what I do at this time of day. You two go into the sitting room. I guess they won't be upstairs much longer."

The tea was made and the Prof made a point of calling Jean-Guy and Kathy in a little too loudly but it was a while before the other two joined them. Kathy was almost amused to notice that Piers seemed to have hurt his back again and she wondered briefly if he had some peculiar technique in bed. She noticed he visibly winced as Marianne sat herself on his lap and twined her arms round his neck.

"Backache?" she asked sympathetically and handed him a cup of tea.

He smiled ruefully. "Something like that."

Marianne snatched the cup from him and drank the tea herself. "He has bad back like old man," she said and there was no humour in her laugh. "He says aeroplane seats are bad for him so he has back trouble." She gave Piers a soft kiss on the lips and he didn't try to fend her off. "But I found out all his secrets. He has many." Her hazel eyes were cold as she looked across at Kathy. "What did you think when you kissed him? I know you have. He told me so. He has told me everything about the two of you."

Kathy guessed Piers would have made something up to protect her and Jean-Guy, and didn't know what to say. So she said nothing.

"You thought it best kiss you have ever had. I thought same but now I know how. He is very good."

Kathy noticed Piers wasn't looking at her as he was watching the Prof pour another cup of tea and no doubt hoping he would get to drink this one.

"Cute trick to get women in sexy mood," Marianne said. "Did you not think so?"

Kathy remembered a drunken snog in a pub car park. "I thought he was sucking a sweet," she said naively.

Marianne snorted in disbelief that anyone could be so gullible. "Show her," she instructed Piers and took the second cup of tea away from him. Realising he wasn't going to do as he was told, she drank the second cup too.

There was a loud knock at the front door and the Professor tried not to sigh audibly with relief. "Marianne, it's time to move you on. You always knew you wouldn't be here for long."

"I can't go now."

"I've received my orders," was the only explanation the Professor gave her.

"Oh, no," she protested. "I am going nowhere without Piers. He is my best lover ever."

Piers didn't look at all pleased by the compliment. He stood up with a few clicks from his joints, and unwrapped her arms from his neck. "I can't come with you," he told her and sounded as though he was really sorry about that. "Not yet. The same people who are now telling you to go have told me to stay. But I will find you. They can't keep us apart for ever."

Marianne looked at him as though she couldn't quite believe it had been that easy. "You promise?"

His blue eyes were guileless as he kissed her. "I said I would, didn't I?"

"You did," she agreed and looked triumphantly at Kathy. "So now he is promised to me. But you can kiss him just once more to find out his secret." The door knocker banged again and the Professor went to answer it. "Go on. You say you aren't with my brother so he can watch you and then you can tell him the secret too."

Kathy felt trapped. She could now either kiss Piers in front of Jean-Guy or she could try to get out of it. Neither option seemed particularly good.

"Hang on a minute," Piers cut in. "I've just said I'll be with you. Why the hell would I kiss her?"

Marianne's eyes never left her brother's face. "Because someone is lying to me."

Piers gave her a filthy look. "Well, it's not me."

"I know it's not you."

Kathy realised that if Jean-Guy so much as looked at his sister the wrong way their whole story would come crashing down on their heads. "Oh, for pity's sake!" she exclaimed and didn't give herself time to think about it. She put her hands on Piers' face and pulled his head down for a kiss. To her relief, he joined in with the charade and he even fooled her for a moment, "Happy now?" she asked the thunderstruck Marianne.

The other woman looked as though she was about to explode into a violent temper and lashed out at Piers but he saw it coming and dodged. "You!" she screamed at him. "You are Palach."

"Who?" he asked innocently.

"Palach in Russian. In French it is 'le bourreau'." Marianne looked at her brother. "Translate for him. My English isn't so good."

"The executioner," he replied. "Or someone who causes pain to others."

"Yes," she agreed. "Exactly."

Two men arrived in the kitchen with the Professor and one of them spoke to Marianne in Czech. She smiled and gave Piers a hard kiss on the lips. "I will see you very soon. You must tell these people to let you go. I think you will like life in Russia."

They all went with her to the front door and watched the car take her away barely able to believe she had finally gone. The Professor closed the door, Piers grabbed the first available jacket and wrapped it round himself suddenly cold and walked quickly ahead of the others into the kitchen so he could finally get his cup of tea.

He poured tea from the pot and gulped half a mugful of it before anyone spoke.

"You did very well," the Professor complimented him. "Are you sure you wouldn't like some fresh tea?"

Piers finished off the mug and held it out. "Yes please. And who the bloody hell is Palach anyway?"

The Professor didn't want to have to explain. "He is an old operative. He retired in the late seventies and doesn't work any more. We won't talk of him. He was not a nice person."

While the Prof provided more tea, Kathy looked at Piers, rather incongruously wrapped in her knitted jacket which although oversized on her was way too small for him, and saw him shiver. "You OK?" she asked sharply.

"Not really," he admitted. "You were right though. That bloody cow sleeps with a knife under her pillow. Thank Christ you'd warned me about it."

"So she didn't stab you?" Kathy checked.

"Oh, she tried. But I was armed with several lethal pillows."

Comforted by his smile and the feel of Jean-Guy's arms round her, the shadows of her past life slipped away again. To distract her mind she asked curiously, "So what is the secret to your kissing? You can't always be sucking a sweet."

Piers necked a second mug of tea and gave her one of his lovely smiles. "Missed your chance to find out," he laughed. "I've only ever lost two drinking bets in my life. Both times in Hong Kong and still itching from the tattoo when I lost the second one. Haven't taken one on since." He opened his mouth and rolled back his tongue to show the others the silver hoop pierced through the webbing underneath. "That was the only place the lads reckoned the medics would never find it."

Jean-Guy's stomach heaved. "And did they?"

"Nope. And now, I have to see Sarah and tell her why I can't ever go back to her."

"Does she need to know about you and Marianne?" Kathy asked. "It's not like you cheated on her. She had just thrown you out of the house."

Piers took the jacket off and got control of his emotions. "I feel as though I have. It's how I screwed up last time."

Kathy had a feeling she knew what he meant and wasn't surprised when he explained in almost disjointed sentences as though the memories were hitting him like physical blows.

"My marriage. It was me that broke it up. I had an affair. Didn't last long and I got found out. I ended up divorced and broke; which I'd guess you'd say I deserved. I'm not even married to Sarah and what have I done?"

Kathy, if she had been truthful, was shocked and sympathetic in equal parts. So far as she knew she had never met an adulterer before and realised that ever since she had known about it, she had assumed Piers' marriage had broken down because of something his wife had done.

The Professor put his hands on Piers' shoulders. "You did what you had to do. I've known men go into situations not as bad as that and they'd had a full briefing. I'm afraid I will have to take you through a formal debriefing and it will have to be taped. Do you want to do it now?"

"No bloody way. Don't even want to think about it right now. Let me get it sorted in my head and I promise I'll go through it with you calmly and sensibly tomorrow. But right now I can't face it. So I am going to change my sheets, have the longest, hottest bath I can cope with and then go and tell Sarah I've fooled around with my best mate's sister. I don't expect her to forgive me."

It seemed to be a long, quiet evening in the farmhouse. Unusually, Petr Mihaly joined the other two in the sitting room and they listened to a concert on the radio. He asked them if they wanted to talk over what had happened the last few days but they, like Piers, said they didn't. So he had to apologise to Kathy and explain that he had to conduct the taped debriefing with her too and he hated to see the look in her eyes as she acknowledged that it must be done. Out of sympathy for her, he agreed that Jean-Guy could sit with her while she talked. He knew he would have to submit those interviews and his own report on how Piers and Kathy had so skilfully handled Marianne. And, even worse, he had to report how well those two had worked together. The people he worked for would be happy to hear that the man they had been monitoring for so long was proving himself ever more suitable. And now it seemed they also had a likely candidate in the petite blonde violinist from Wimbledon. Petr Mihaly had fiercely protected his own daughter from that dark world, and he would do the same to safeguard those two who had become like children to him. But he had his orders to fulfil and he was bound by agreements which gave him no option.

Nobody felt like going to bed until they knew what Sarah said, so at about 10:30 they went into the kitchen and the Prof made a rare treat of some cocoa. He had barely poured it into the mugs when Piers came into the kitchen and silently joined them at the table.

"Cocoa?" the Prof asked him and held up the saucepan. "I've made too much as I always do."

"Please. I haven't had cocoa in years."

"Is that it then?" Kathy asked kindly. "All over?"

He put his hands on the table so they could see he had a silver puzzle ring on his wedding finger. "I underestimated her," he admitted sounding a bit dazed. "It seems we've just got engaged. This ring is one of hers and she said that if I take it off before she's got a wedding band on me then she will tattoo a ring on my finger herself. Do you suppose it'll be safe to take her somewhere to buy her a ring?"

The Professor wasn't happy about this turn of events. "I didn't think you were that serious about her," he said. "What did you do?"

"I told her, in front of her parents, what I'd done to my marriage and that I'd done the same to her with Marianne. She said it wasn't the same at all as we weren't married so I asked her if she'd like to be and next thing I knew she was licking my tonsils and her dad had got the sherry out. Forgotten just how much I hate sherry."

"Were you serious?"

"Yes." Piers finished off his cocoa. "Not going to talk about it. I'm a grown up and perfectly capable of screwing up my life without any help."

The Professor still wasn't convinced but Piers did have a point. "I would suggest Norwich. It's a bit further than Ipswich but it has some good jewellers. I hope you have a lot of money in your bank account because I think Sarah deserves something good, don't you?"

They made plans to go to Norwich the next morning after Piers and the Prof had had their official talk. Piers rang Sarah at about midnight and the others had been half way up the stairs when he was speaking to her but they heard her shrieks of delight.

"I can't believe she took him back like that," Kathy remarked to Jean-Guy as they lay quietly together in bed that night.

"Nor can I. I can't see you taking me back if we have a row and then I go off and sleep with Roisin."

"I think Roisin would probably smack you round the head, tell you where to go in two languages and send you back."

"I think you're probably right. I don't seem to attract women the way he does."

Kathy gave him a hug. "You attracted me. Right from the moment I saw you at Ipswich station with your snotty cold."

"So you chose me, with my cold and my cello over him? Why? I am curious to know."

"There was just something about you. Something a bit lost and helpless."

"Ah, so it was pity love?"

"Maybe. Once. But not any more. There was never really a choice to make. I like him, of course I do. Love him in a way I suppose. But he's like a crazy big brother with the bonus that we can flirt a bit knowing it's not going to go anywhere." She gently stroked his face and smiled. "I don't know when I really fell in love with you. You just kind of sneaked up on me."

"I know when I fell in love with you. You were standing on the stairs, holding your blue dress and you were angry with me for not being in bed."

"That seems so long ago now," she murmured drowsily.

Jean-Guy watched her lovingly for a while before he settled against her in the bed and thought to himself that he may not be the annoyingly handsome one with the glamorous job, an enigmatic tattoo and a secret silver ring in his mouth, but he wasn't the one sleeping alone that night.

They were ready for their shopping trip soon after breakfast the next morning. Piers had spent quite a while with the Prof who needed to make notes on what had happened yesterday but they found the time for that before breakfast. Piers went back to the study after breakfast to tell the Prof that they were going and the other two were slightly puzzled when the Prof closed the door of the study for a few minutes and all they could hear was a much muffled conversation with no discernible words. But then Piers joined them with a roguish smile and just said:

"What do you reckon? Do I offer her diamonds?"

"I thought the idea was she chooses it," Kathy remarked.

"Have you seen that pinny she wears in the shop? Woman of no taste. I've told her so several times."

"Says the man with girlie butterflies all down his back."

"Piglet?"

"What?"

"Just shut up and be nice for one day."

Jean-Guy was about to remonstrate but then he realised it was just their crazy English backchat again and he would probably never understand it.

There were quite a few local ladies outside the shop when the Land Rover arrived and from the way Sarah was blushing madly as she came out to get in the car, those inside it guessed she, or more likely her mother, had already told the whole village that there was going to be a wedding. Sarah got in the front seat of the car, the ladies all swarmed into the shop and they could well imagine the gossip that would be flying across the counter.

246

To Kathy's great relief, Sarah gave her betrothed a lovely kiss and put her hand over his on the steering wheel. "Not changed your mind then?" she asked as though she couldn't quite believe it.

He returned the kiss. "Not yet. You?"

"No chance."

None of them had been to Norwich before and they got a bit lost in the various streets and alleyways between the car park and the shops but eventually found a cluster of quite high-class jewellers. Sarah was going to head off to somewhere less expensive but Piers told her they might as well have a look in the window anyway just to see what there was.

Kathy and Jean-Guy stood next to each other and looked too. The prices appalled Kathy.

"Some of those cost more than I would expect to earn in a year."

"So if I was a Concorde pilot and not a penniless musician and I was buying you a ring, which one would you choose?"

"I wouldn't," she said firmly before this engagement idea started getting contagious. "I love you so much, I will walk to the ends of the earth barefoot over hot coals for you, but please don't ask me to marry you."

He knew to back away. She had been attacked on the eve of her wedding so he could understand she had no intentions of making plans for another one. He didn't mind at that moment. She had chosen him and that was all that mattered for now. "OK, so which one would you wear while you were walking all over the coals?"

Thankful he hadn't asked any questions, Kathy looked again at the jewellery on display. Richard had bought her a large diamond cluster set in yellow gold and she had hated it. So she dismissed all the yellow gold and sparkling stones, and moved further down the display where there were some much less ornate rings.

"That one," she told him quite truthfully. "White gold Celtic knotwork. That's only about six months' wages."

Jean-Guy looked sadly at the simple ring and realised that for all he could afford it, it may as well have cost a million pounds. "That is a very beautiful hot coals ring," he agreed. "But look, there is one that has the coals on it."

Kathy followed the line of his pointing finger and saw the one he meant. A plain, narrow band of tiny baguette-cut rubies. Classy, elegant and everything she wasn't. "Now that is the perfect hot coals ring," she agreed. "But there's no price on it and we're not even going to discuss it any more." She looked across to the other two and thought they looked so sweet standing there with their arms round each other.

Sarah turned away from the shop window and caught them looking at her. "We're going to go inside," she told them. "Want to come too?"

So they went into the shop where the man who came to serve them was too professional to look as though he knew they couldn't afford any of his goods. Sarah picked a ring out from the tray taken from the window and tried it on but it was too small for her fingers.

"It can be altered," Kathy pointed out to her, looking over her shoulder and personally thinking it was one heck of a garish lump.

"No, I want something I can take home with me and I've got such fat fingers."

Kathy saw a beautiful sapphire ring in the bottom row on the tray. Square cut between two diamonds, the ring looked fairly large to her eyes. "That's a nice one," she suggested.

"Do you think so? Mum always says I need big jewellery because I'm so big."

"Try the sapphire," Kathy encouraged.

The sapphire looked much better and was actually a bit too large.

"I like the colour of it," Sarah admitted.

"Would Madam care to see some more sapphires?" the shop assistant asked.

"Are there any more?"

"We do have others."

Sarah and Kathy bent over the tray of sapphire rings and didn't know where to start.

"Which one will you still like in fifty years' time?" Kathy asked her.

Sarah closed her eyes, then snapped them open and went instinctively for an emerald cut, a deep dark blue that seemed to glow almost golden in the shop lights, flanked by trilliant diamonds. Her hands were shaking as she took it off the tray and found it was the perfect fit.

Kathy smiled at her. "See, it chose you in the end."

They looked across at the two men who had by now completely lost interest in ring-buying and were talking about something on the other side of the shop.

"Found one," Sarah told them. "And it fits."

Piers and Jean-Guy dutifully came across to admire the ring now sparkling on Sarah's finger as though it belonged there.

"Good choice," the groom-to-be approved. "Want to get your wedding ring too while we're in here? I can't imagine your mother will let it be a long engagement."

"Can we?" she asked and looked as though she was about to cry.

The sales assistant didn't falter. "Would Madam like platinum to match?" He looked at the prospective groom dressed in a tatty waxed coat and scruffy jeans. "Will you be paying by card, cheque or cash, sir?"

The others caught something in his tone and Piers smiled slightly. "Card. I assume if we spend a lot of money you will ring them up to check my credit is good?"

"Company policy, sir."

Piers fished a rather expensive-looking wallet from his coat pocket and took out an American Express Gold card. "Want to check it out now? Make sure it's not stolen?"

Jean-Guy took Kathy by the arm. "Shall we wait outside? The smell of all this money is making me hungry."

Kathy laughed and followed Jean-Guy out of the shop. "I never knew he had an Amex Gold card. No wonder he's buying her platinum and sapphires."

"I offered, you refused. I thought that was a very nice hot coals ring we found in the end."

"It was lovely. But unless you're going to get a sideline flying Concorde it'll be somebody else wearing it to the ends of the earth, won't it?"

He got the message and didn't say any more on the matter.

"Now where?" Piers asked as he and Sarah joined them a surprisingly short while later.

Kathy guessed he had come a long way from the near-bankrupt state he had been in and the card hadn't been refused as Sarah was wearing her sapphire and diamonds and looking so happy Kathy couldn't help but feel her own mood lifting. She really had liked that ruby ring though. The red of the stones had reminded her of her pirate's dress and the sense of freedom she had had for the few minutes she had worn it.

"Get your wedding bands?" Jean-Guy asked.

Piers handed him a small bag. "Yes, and as you've just been appointed best man, you can look after them."

Sarah was looking round and she grabbed Kathy's arm. "Look! Pizza Hut!"

"Lunch time!" Kathy exclaimed and thought it had been a long time since she had had a pizza.

Kathy was quite surprised they dropped Sarah off back at the shop and although she and Piers said their affectionate goodbyes, they gave no clue when they might see each other again. It was a very odd sort of relationship, she thought, and was glad she was sharing a house with the man she loved.

There was no sign of the Prof or tea, although it was about the time of day he habitually made some so Kathy and Jean-Guy set about making the tea and Piers went to fetch the Prof from the study.

Tea made and still no sign of the other two, Kathy went to remind them, guessing they had got engrossed in musical chat. She was about to go into the study when from inside she heard a clicking sound she recognised from somewhere and then something was put down on the desk.

Piers came out of the study and almost bumped into her. "Tea made yet?"

"Yes, just coming to get you both." She couldn't see past him into the study and knew if she asked he wouldn't tell her.

"Go on, move. I can't get out with you standing there."

"Sorry," she smiled. "Just thinking."

"Well don't. It doesn't suit you."

Half way through her mug of tea Kathy remembered where she had heard that clicking noise. It had been in a film on TV she hadn't intended to watch but had got engrossed in the plot. She looked up, startled, and caught Piers looking at her. He just gave her a secretive smile and tapped his nose as he had done once before. She dawdled over her tea drinking until she was alone with the Professor.

"Did you send Piers out with a gun today?" she asked him.

He didn't seem at all baffled that she had worked it out. "He has been in the armed forces. The key word there is 'armed'. He has been weapons trained and we still don't know exactly how Marianne has been operating."

"But you can't just whip a gun out in the middle of Norwich. You might shoot someone."

"It was a calculated risk. I presume you heard him take the magazine out to show me the weapon was clear?"

"Yes. I remembered the noise from a film."

"Oh, Kathy, I wish you would come and work for us. But all you want is music. Would you even consider the basic training?"

"What? No! I'm a violinist from Wimbledon. Please don't ask me again."

Kathy shot out of the kitchen and into the sitting room where Piers was working on the Prokofiev *Sinfonia Concertante*. To her relief, Jean-Guy wasn't in the room so she sat on the piano stool next to Piers and turned the page of his music even though he hadn't got that far.

"Oi," was all he said and batted the music back.

Kathy gave Audrey a tickle under the chin. The fingers were moving slowly but Audrey wasn't going to be distracted; sooner or later they would speed up again. "The Prof just tried to recruit me."

He didn't even stop playing. "Not surprised. I'm guessing you said the same as I've said for ages, just a bit more politely."

"I just want to go back to where I was before Emma got married and all this kicked off."

He stopped playing then and looked at her. "No you don't. Running scared from your ex for one thing."

"True. I just feel life has gone all crazy and I don't know where it's going to end."

"Go and get your fiddle out, that'll help. Want to do some Sibelius?"

"Well maybe just a bit on the slow movement. That'll confuse Audrey."

"Nothing confuses her. She is just waiting and plotting."

"Like all good cats do," Kathy assured him as she took her violin from on top of the piano.

Jean-Guy had just come out of the bathroom when he heard it. The violin and piano playing the Sibelius slow movement. Playing it like he had never heard before. He sat on the stairs again and listened to the harmonies that seemed to have a living pulse to them the way those two played it and it was as though he was with Kathy again for the very first time.

Audrey sat on top of the piano and watched for a while as her usual targets moved across the keys with a quiet gentleness that really wasn't conducive to pouncing so she hunkered down and waited. Kathy had her eyes on her music but her mind was letting in that beat of the rhythm and she felt her breath catch in her throat as she remembered her first time with Jean-Guy.

"Last movement?" came the enquiry from the pianist.

"Please," she replied with her mind still distant.

Audrey was happy, the flying fingers were back and it was game on.

Piers had to applaud at the end. "Well done, Piglet. Play it like that on the concert platform and you'll bring the house down."

Kathy slowly came back to reality. "Can you smell something?"

"Not really, but it wasn't me whatever you think it is."

"Someone's baking."

The next morning it was the sound of the rain that woke Kathy from her blissfully exhausted sleep. As she always did these days, she looked over her shoulder and saw Jean-Guy was lying facing her and looking so sweet she could feel herself falling in love with him all over again. The chocolate cake had been pretty good too considering he'd never made one before. And that had been one hell of an erotic dream she'd had about him last night. She reached out her right hand to touch his face and froze in something between abject horror and total delight. There was a ruby and white gold ring on her middle finger and she had no idea how it had got there but it went long way to explaining that dream she had had.

"How the hell?" she started then gasped as Jean-Guy's eyes flicked open.

"Happy hot coals day," he whispered to her. "And I didn't steal it either."

Kathy was later than usual going into the kitchen and only Piers was there finishing off the dregs of his coffee and trying to fathom out a clue in the cryptic crossword. She slapped her right hand on the table and said, "OK, spill."

He picked up her hand and admired the ring. "Suits you."

"How did he afford it? And don't give me any of that Irish flannel of yours."

Piers let go of her hand. "Offered me his cello as collateral. If he doesn't pay me back in a year, the cello is mine."

Kathy sat at the table and tried not to think of the consequences if that happened. "But that cello is all he has in the world. Would you really take it?"

"Won't need to. As soon as he's legal he'll make the cost in months if not weeks."

"And if he doesn't?"

"I'll lend it straight back to him. I wouldn't sell it as it's been in his family for about four generations. But he wanted to get you the ring and this way his pride is intact."

Kathy really wanted to cry that her adorable Moly had pledged the only thing he owned in the world, just to make her happy. Trying not to give in to her emotions, she started to make herself some coffee.

"Skindiver," said the man at the table.

"What?" Kathy asked, a bit sorry he had interrupted her lovely thoughts.

"Last clue in the crossword. Got you, you little sod." Piers got up from the table and stretched the stiffness out of his back. "Are we playing today?"

"Depends on your plans with Sarah."

"Haven't got any."

"You're engaged to the woman and you don't have any plans even for today?"

"Well, she'll be working from six this morning until nine tonight by which time she'll be knackered and just want to sleep. Same again tomorrow and then we've got the Smugglers' Race so I probably won't see her until race day."

"Is she going to keep working after you're married?"

"Her plan is to start having babies as soon as we're married. She's always wanted lots of kids so God knows how many we'll finish up with. Mind you, with multiples in both our families perhaps she'll just have a litter and get it over with." The phone rang at his elbow so he answered it and an odd expression crossed his face. He held the receiver out to Kathy. "I think it's Emma, but she sounds like she's swallowed a mouse."

Jean-Guy had been in, had coffee and breakfast and gone out again and it was nearly half an hour later before Kathy went into the sitting room where she could hear the Prof was coaching the others on the Prokofiev.

"Emma wants to speak to you, Prof. She's got some, um, rather surprising news. Good news," she added quickly seeing the look on his face. "She's still on the phone."

The Prof went out to the kitchen and Kathy sat on the piano stool so she was between the two men. "That was the weirdest conversation I have ever had with Emma and that includes our drunken teenage soul-searching. When she'd finished squeaking long enough to get her words in order it turns out Derek's dad has come into an inheritance. Some dim distant relative he'd only vaguely heard about and never met passed away and so his estate goes to Derek's dad as the nearest living family member. Apparently it's taken his solicitors and executors quite a while to get things sorted which is why they've only just been notified." She suddenly laughed. "It's really quite ridiculous. The 'estate' is literally that. A big old house and several acres out in Somerset and it comes with a title. Which means that when it's Derek's turn to inherit our kid from communist Czechoslovakia will become a bona fide English Countess."

She didn't quite get the reaction she was expecting. Jean-Guy was looking at her as though she was speaking a language he didn't understand and Piers just made a funny noise somewhere between a sniff and a snort. She guessed Jean-Guy was genuinely confused by the English legal and social system so she dug her elbow in Piers' ribs. "And what's that supposed to mean?" she asked feeling a bit cross that they hadn't joined in the joy and ridiculousness of it all.

"I'm Irish," he reminded her. "Want me to be happy your friend is going to become part of the repressive upper classes that take the native land away from those that have lived on it for generations?"

The genuine venom in his voice shocked her for a few moments. She turned startled eyes on Jean-Guy who had finally grasped a concept he could understand.

"I didn't realise such things happened in England," he began, trying the innocent tack hoping that would avoid any confrontations.

"They don't," Kathy replied. "Well, not for a few hundred years anyway. And you can't go getting ratty with Emma about it. She didn't ask for it."

Piers just shrugged in that way he had and rubbed the top of Audrey's head. "True. Just don't ask me to shake the hand of an Earl and not have a wash afterwards."

"You'll like Derek's dad, he's got the same mad sense of humour as you have. And, as I remember, he did his war service in the Fleet Air Arm as a mechanic. I bet even you've never flown an aircraft off a ship."

"Do you know what? I don't think I have. Flown float planes and flying boats."

Jean-Guy tossed down his cello bow. "You two have lost me. Again. What the hell is a flying boat?"

By supper time that day, Jean-Guy had learned so much about aircraft and the English social system he felt he had spent a day in school. He was still confused how the wife of an Earl could be a Countess, and really didn't understand that Derek's father's surname would now be the name of the title he had inherited which meant Derek's name would be different from that of his father. Seaplanes of all sorts he could cope with.

"How about Snape Maltings?" the Prof asked, apparently at random part way through their evening meal. He looked up and saw their expressions. "Sorry. I was thinking out loud. For your recital?"

Only Kathy understood. "No, that seats over eight hundred people. That would be ridiculous. We'll never attract that big an audience."

The Prof gave her a knowing look. "I think the name of your cellist will fill the hall twice over. I was thinking about September time as it should be fairly easy to book it that time of year once the main concert season is over. I'll ring them tomorrow and ask about available dates."

Jean-Guy was starting to get a bit excited about the thought of an eight-hundred seat concert venue. "I have heard of it, of course. Britten made it very famous in the music world but I have never seen it. Can we go to a concert there and see what it is like?"

"Not sure what's on at this time of year, but if we are thinking of booking it I'm sure they will let us look round. And I'm also sure you'll have your status confirmed by then; it'll be six months away after all. In fact, I think maybe we'll promote it as your English debut."

"My first concert as a free man," he mused. "I like the idea of doing it with my friends."

"And I'll get to wear the dress Sarah's mum is making for me," Kathy enthused. She and Jean-Guy exchanged looks and smiles feeling both excited and just a bit nervous. Kathy had played in small ensembles before, including string quartets, but never publically in anything as small as a trio and the musician in her was anticipating the challenge.

"I will need to launder my concert clothes," Jean-Guy thought out loud. "They have been squashed in a bag for months. It is white tie and tails so will look good with your dress."

They finally thought to look at the one person who hadn't spoken.

"You OK with September?" Kathy asked him. "I'm sure they'll give you a day off to come and play. And you've said yourself you get lots of days off between flights so we can still meet up and rehearse as you only live a couple of streets away and we have Emma's piano for you to use."

He sighed once and looked at the happiness and hope shining in their eyes. "Why not? But I'm not dressing up like a bloody penguin. In fact I may not even wear any shoes."

"Wear your pilot's uniform," Jean-Guy teased him. "You will look so smart. But shoes, yes. You must wear shoes on the concert platform."

"I wonder if I could persuade Audrey to sit on the piano," was the only reply

Stone Litany: runes from a house of the dead

The Smugglers' Race was due to be held at about midday to coincide with the high tide which gave the barrel-haulers a bit less land to cover between the beach and the pub. Kathy looked out of her bedroom window that morning to see March had decided it would rather belong to winter than spring, the fir trees were lashing in a vicious east wind and the rain was almost horizontal.

"Surely they won't do the race in this weather?" she mused out loud. There was no reply from the man still sound asleep in the bed.

Down in the kitchen only the Prof was at the table. "They can't do the race in this weather, can they?" she almost pleaded with him as he gave her a mug of tea.

"Oh yes. I believe they will do it in anything including gale force winds. I've only known them to cancel it once and that was when the beach was so full of jellyfish it wasn't safe. You're only going a few feet out to sea. And if you've got any sense you will send the men into the water and you and Sarah will take up the rope when the barrel is on the beach."

"Are we completely mad?" she asked.

"Yes. Just make sure none of you damages your hands."

Kathy gratefully sipped her tea. "Where's Piers? He's usually here before me."

"Right behind you," said his voice and she jumped. "Sorry, didn't mean to scare you."

She gave him a fond smile. "It's bad enough having a house full of ghosts without you scaring me as well."

"Do you really believe in the ghosts?" he asked curiously and made himself some coffee.

"Part of me does. I've felt odd things too often over the years for there not to be something in it. They say this place is so haunted the locals are too scared to come here except as a dare for Halloween."

"They have said for years it is," the Prof explained. "It's one reason I bought it as its history keeps people away. It has only had its present name for about two hundred years. Before that it was known as Dead Man's Farm. A local author wrote a book about it several years ago and I have a copy of it. I think I read about half of it then could read no more for laughing. If there are ghosts in this house then I have lived with them for over twenty years and they have never shown themselves to me." He looked at the clock. "Well, we should have Emma and Derek here in about half an hour if they left London when they planned to."

Piers wasn't surprised Kathy believed in the ghosts, or that the Prof didn't. "How are they getting on in Somerset?" he asked to get away from the topic.

Kathy had to laugh. "Well, Ron wanted to give Derek the title of Viscount, apparently he can do that, but Derek just said he's not going to be named after a chocolate biscuit so Emma doesn't get a title until Derek inherits. Meantime, they're spending a lot of time in Somerset because the house is a bit of a wreck and the grounds aren't much better. The plan is to sort it out a bit then make it earn its keep as either a tourist attraction, or maybe a hotel. But if it doesn't make money her father-in-law will have to sell it. And he says if anyone calls him by his title, he'll clock them. His name is Ron and that's it."

"You're right, I like the sound of Derek's dad," Piers agreed.

Emma and Derek arrived nearly an hour late, and those in the farmhouse had been starting to get worried thinking of fallen trees on the road, car crashes and all sorts of other imaginable horrors. When she did arrive, Emma gave Kathy a hug and said:

"Sorry, I know we're late but I thought I'd stop by the flat for any post as I was coming this way and there was a policeman on the doorstep. It's awful. All the flats in the house have been burgled. I did explain about us and flat 3 and they let me have a quick look and I could only see a few things missing. I couldn't see your diary or your passport but I expect they're in your bag as they always are. The housekeeping cash had been taken from the tea caddy, the TV and record player have been taken and the whole place was a complete mess. I've got your spare fiddle and viola in the car too, guess the thieves didn't know what they are. The landlady's hopping mad as the thieves totally smashed all the locks and doors, and the police told her the house security needs to be improved a heck of a lot. So she's served notice on all her tenants and said she's going to sell the place."

Kathy forgot she was due to haul a wet barrel out of the North Sea in about an hour's time. "What?"

"Yes, she's given three months' notice to quit. I am really sorry. I mean, I can arrange for the piano to be shipped down to Somerset and you're welcome to come and sleep on our sofa bed in Southfields but we'll be moving ourselves soon as we've decided that we're most useful getting the Somerset estate going properly rather than staying on in London and carrying on with our jobs."

Kathy put her hands to her face and didn't know where to start. She looked at Jean-Guy but he was still trying to catch up with Emma's frantic gabble and didn't quite seem to have grasped the concept that the two of them were shortly to be homeless.

A familiar arm gave her a hug across the shoulders. "Don't worry about it, Piglet. You know my house has plenty of room so you can both move in with me if you want to. Can't offer you rent free, but it'll all help towards the mortgage. Now, it's time for us to turn ourselves into smugglers, or pirates, or whatever the heck we're supposed to be and go and get a bit wet."

Kathy was beginning to think she was spending a lot of time recently getting wet and bedraggled. She had tied her hair out of the way, but it had escaped from its plait and was lashing her face as she hauled on her side of the barrel. The shingle was hurting her feet, her arms and shoulders were burning with pain, but there were only five out of ten barrels left in the race and the team from the pub wasn't going to quit without a fight. She looked up briefly from her post at the side of the barrel. Ian and Trevor had their shoulders against the rear of the barrel, she and Sarah had grabbed the rope tied round the middle of it to steer more than anything else, and Piers and Jean-Guy were hauling from the end of the rope at the front of the barrel. There was a crowd of people round the remaining teams, all yelling advice and encouragement but Kathy hardly heard them. Her head was down and she just concentrated on keeping that slippery barrel under control. Her beautiful dress was probably ruined as the petticoats were plastered to her legs and she was sure one of the shoulder seams had ripped. The barrel jerked to a halt and she nearly fell backwards.

"It's stuck!" Ian yelled from the back. "Kathy, tip it towards Sarah, we've hit something."

Kathy tried to push that cold, wet barrel away from her but it wasn't moving. A loud howl went up nearby so she guessed the teachers had done something similar but their barrel was now broken.

"Is it still OK?" Trevor bellowed above the noise of the wind and rain and the baying of the crowd.

Kathy looked and couldn't see any obvious leaks but everywhere was so wet, she couldn't be sure. She just nodded briefly and kept trying to free the barrel. Suddenly a hand with a puzzle ring on one finger clamped over hers, she felt Piers' body almost moulding against her own and the two of them managed to roll the barrel just enough towards Sarah to free it. Piers went back to his rope, whistles and cheers from the crowd told them they were on their way again and she just hoped there wasn't much further to go as she thought her arms were going to snap before too much longer. Her feet told her that the sharp sand and cutting grass of the dunes was now past them and there was only the coast path to cross then they would reach the finish line at the edge of the pub car park. Ian and Trevor were pushing as though their lives depended on it but they were the only ones of the team looking forwards towards the pub and knew how far they had to go. She had no idea where the power station team were but she was quite sure she could hear Emma's voice, bawling like a proverbial fishwife above the din of the crowd.

265

To her great relief she saw a white line painted on the ground under her feet and then with one final shove, the brothers got that barrel over the line and the noise of the crowd got so loud she wondered if they had actually won. She managed to straighten up a bit but then she, as the smallest member, found herself being squashed in a group hug with so much body heat coming off it she could have sworn they were steaming. Barry from the pub came over to check their barrel. He was sensibly dressed in waterproofs and boots and didn't hurry his job. The spectators went suddenly silent.

Barry grabbed Trevor's wrist and raised his arm up to the leaden, pouring skies. "Barrel intact!" he shouted. "We have a winner!"

The power station team were only about a yard behind them but were magnanimous enough to come and congratulate the winners then everyone went into the welcoming warmth of the pub and nobody seemed to care that the sodden competitors were making puddles of rain and seawater all over the floor.

"Get the beer going, Barry!" Ian shouted at the landlord.

Kathy didn't dare look at Jean-Guy but Ian and Trevor got themselves one each side of her and hoisted her to sit onto the bar.

Barry gave her a kiss on the cheek and handed her a silver cup full of beer. "Get that down you," he laughed. "Then you won't feel the cold so much."

So she took the first gulp of the beer, then the cup was passed round the rest of the winning team. To Kathy's vast amusement, the future Countess put four fingers in her mouth and whistled as loudly as anyone else in that riotous bar as the village celebrated getting the trophy back.

Kathy's arms were still aching when she rolled out of bed the next morning and the sunlight coming through the gap in the curtains hit her in the face like a badly adjusted stage light. Jean-Guy was lying on his back, snoring gently among the tumbled sheets and the eiderdown was in a heap on the floor all tied up with the blankets. He had slept badly that night, kicking her in his sleep and whimpering as he tossed and turned but he hadn't woken so far as she knew. It bothered her more than she would ever tell him that he sometimes had these nightmares that made him so restless, but he never remembered his dream in the mornings. Or, if he did, he wasn't going to speak of it. But something in his past was haunting him, and unlike her own fading shadow it wasn't going to show itself so it could be beaten.

All was quiet in the kitchen when she went downstairs but the back door was open so she looked out to see Emma and Piers standing quite close together in the garden with their mugs of coffee. She was glad to think her two dearest friends finally seemed to be getting on so well, so she made her own coffee and then went out to join them.

"Morning," she said, squinting in the light.

Piers threw the remains of his coffee over the nearest flower bed. "I'll leave you ladies to your gossip," he said. He gave Kathy a kiss on the cheek in passing. "Bruised legs?" he asked but he had gone into the house before she could answer.

The two women settled at the rickety old patio set in a sunny corner of the garden and Emma admired the ruby ring on her friend's hand. "So you chose the musician?" she asked gently and Kathy was glad her oldest friend could be so happy for her.

"Wasn't really a choice," Kathy replied and couldn't help smiling. "It was always going to be him ever since you introduced us at the station. If anyone was going to get me over the ex it was someone even more damaged than me."

Emma leaned close to her and said conspiratorially, "When I saw that other one wrapped round you in the Smugglers' Race yesterday... well, I don't know how you can share a house with him and behave yourself. I'm pretty sure I couldn't."

"You'll have to fight Sarah for him now."

Emma smiled. "Yes, I saw the tacky ring. It's a bit obvious, isn't it? Anyway, he's lent me his house key and asked me if I would check on it. I think he's a bit bothered after your burglary which I can understand. I shall resist the temptation to lie on his bed and think things I shouldn't. I did suggest to him that if you and Jean-Guy do move in then it might make more sense for the piano to move with you rather than go to Somerset. Leave you all to discuss that and let me know? Suits me just fine if you want to keep your trio going as I don't need it down there. Do you want to see some photos of the place in Somerset?" Without waiting for an answer, she took a wad of photos out of her jacket pocket and started going through them one by one.

Emma and Derek had to leave in the morning and a thankful Piers reclaimed his room at the back of the house as he hadn't got much sleep in the room at the front with only a thin wall between him and the sounds of Jean-Guy having a nightmare.

None of the three barrel-racers felt like playing any music while over-used muscles recovered from the exertions of the previous day, so in the afternoon they went back to their books in the sitting room and the house was quieter than it had been for a long time. Kathy had gone back to Roisin's autobiography which she hadn't finished, and Piers had borrowed the Prof's book of ghost stories while Jean-Guy had borrowed a book in Czech which he was finding extremely funny.

Kathy looked up from her book and had to smile to notice that Piers had gone to sleep over his book, sitting in one of the armchairs with his head resting peacefully on Audrey who was over his shoulder again. Jean-Guy himself was lying on his back on the sofa and giggling periodically, reading his book with a speed he didn't show in English.

"What's the book?" Kathy asked quietly out of respect for the sleeper.

"*The Good Soldier Svejk*. I haven't read it for years. You should try it sometime."

"In Czech?"

"Maybe one day I will translate it for you. I presume Rabbit-ears is fast asleep?"

"Yes, and looking really rather adorable." She saw the look he gave her. "You don't need to be asleep. You're always adorable. We really should find out if he was serious about us sharing his house. It won't be easy with all our crazy jobs."

"I think it would work. Should we wake him?"

"No, don't think he got much sleep last night."

"Oh, I'm sorry. Was I dreaming again? I know when I have had the bad dreams as I wake up more tired than I went to sleep but I never remember them."

Kathy was thoughtful. "Do you think it would help you if you did remember them?"

"No," he replied quietly. "There are things in my past I don't want to have to remember and I think they are what sometimes make me sleep so badly."

"Is it something you could talk to the Prof about? I'm sure he would understand."

"Yes, he would understand. But I don't want to break his trust in me."

Kathy wasn't sure how to reply to that and she would have been relieved that the Prof came into the room at that moment but the look on his face made her worry even more. "What's happened?" she asked anxiously and her voice was loud enough to disturb the man asleep in the chair.

Petr Mihaly looked at the three of them and wished he didn't have to do this. "I am sorry," he began and chose his words very carefully. "I am sure this is nothing to worry about, just another scare by those who want Jean-Guy back but a message has come through to London to say your parents have been taken by the State and are going to be tried for intellectual crimes. This has to mean they're pretty sure you're in the UK and they have probably stopped looking in Paris and Bonn. I'm keeping the radio channels open and I'll keep you updated."

"How reliable is the source?" Jean-Guy asked as a bleary Piers tried to get his brain into focus.

"Not the best," the Prof reassured him. "As I said, my hunch is it's a scare tactic to flush you out, but I just wanted to let you all know in case it does come to something."

270

"Where is Marianne now?" Piers asked sounding a bit more awake. "Could she have got something out?"

"She's in another safe house in the UK," the Professor replied.

"So they won't have told her Piglet has grassed her up and she'll still be thinking I'm going to track her down and let her help herself to Irish citizenship?"

The Prof gave him a sharp look. "That is true. Maybe it's time you showed her how sincere you are and asked me to contact her with a wedding plan."

"I have no idea about weddings," he replied, seemingly missing the point. "Sarah's doing all of that. She and her mother had a go at the vicar until he agreed to marry us in the church, which is what they want, and they've booked the date. But it's only going to be a very few in the congregation; probably just you three and Sarah's parents plus her friend Alison who recently moved back from Cambridge."

"Let me write it all down," the Professor requested. "But we'll leave out Sarah's side of things. I need the date, I assume it'll be the local church and vicar. She may complain it's an English church service but I think it should keep her quiet for a bit longer."

"You have a date?" Kath asked. "When were you going to tell us?"

"Sarah only told me yesterday."

Kathy loved a good wedding and, just for a moment, forgot why the Prof had originally come into the room. "So? When is it?"

"April thirteenth," Piers told her.

"That's too soon," the Prof replied without thinking. "Marianne may well still be in England at that date as we are having problems negotiating a trade for her and we can't risk her trying to come back here to find you. Tell her May or June by which time she will have been deported."

"No, it really is April thirteenth. Nine o'clock. It's a Monday but that doesn't matter as Sarah said her parents will get cover for half an hour or so for the shop. We're having just enough of a ceremony to make it legal, no bridesmaids and no flowers. Sarah's not buying anything special to wear and all she's asked me to do is not turn up in jeans. We weren't going to marry so soon just to make things a bit more believable, but that business with Marianne has stirred up things I don't like which is why I went along with Sarah's idea."

Kathy was horrified. "No! That can't be right. Just what are you getting yourself into?"

Piers removed Audrey from his shoulder, holding her gently against him while he got his thoughts in order and decided how much to tell them. "Sarah wants kids, she doesn't want a husband, and her family are totally complicit in the whole arrangement. She has promised she will put me on any birth certificates and she and any kids will take my name, but she's not going to be dependent on me in any way as her parents and her friend Alison will support her. She said I'll have as much access to any kids as I want but I don't think she'll encourage it. She's been honest with me from the start and she's leaving it up to me to decide if I want to make an excuse and end the marriage formally or we just carry on and pretend we're making it work with my job in London and her staying here."

"But where the hell does that leave you?" Kathy demanded, upset for a friend, and thinking there was something very wrong with the whole idea.

"She didn't know how my marriage ended until I told her last week and, if you want to put it this way, my part of the deal is I don't have to be faithful to her."

"So your whole relationship with her has been a total sham? And the marriage isn't going to be any better?" Kathy asked not sure whether she was sad there wasn't going to be a happy ever after, or annoyed that he had duped them all so successfully.

"Yeah, pretty much. I mean we like each other and get on well together, enough to fool people anyway. And she really does hate tattoos. And as I don't ask you two questions about your love life, no matter how noisy it gets, I don't think we need to discuss mine any more. Do you? You've got enough problems with what's happening with Jean-Guy's parents."

"I think I will go and make tea," the Professor said very carefully as though he was trying not to lose his temper. "Piers, as you are taller than me, please come and get the new packets of biscuits down from the pantry shelf for me."

The two men left the room and as Piers was if anything a couple of inches shorter than the Professor, Kathy and Jean-Guy knew an excuse when they heard one.

The kitchen door closed and the two left in the sitting room didn't even like to speculate.

"He's an idiot," Jean-Guy announced.

Kathy cuddled up against him on the sofa, now more concerned about his future. "Do you think it's true about your parents?"

He laced his fingers with hers and gently kissed the ring she was wearing. "To speak the truth, I don't know. I think the Prof is right, those who want me back have narrowed their search down to England and sending Marianne was their way to confirm and our mistake not to see it. So long as she is held here then we are still that one step away from discovery."

A letter came for Jean-Guy a couple of days later. It had been forwarded to the Professor from the Foreign and Commonwealth Office and it was written in Russian. These days the Prof always opened his post in private in the study as he could never be sure what the postman would bring, and his heart was heavy when he saw the envelope. He had so enjoyed the company of these three people in the house and just wished there was a way he could have kept them there forever. But somehow he knew this was the beginning of the end.

Inside the official envelope was the one that had been handed in at the British Embassy in Moscow with a request for it to be forwarded to London and so the British had done what was requested and sent it on. The letter had been opened and he had no doubt it had been read in the Embassy and in the Foreign Office and then it would have been photocopied and sent to other departments in the system as well.

It wasn't a long letter; he wasn't sure he believed most of it, but he knew he shouldn't give in to temptation and destroy it. He was tempted to hide it for a few days but also knew that delaying matters wouldn't help to resolve them, so he went to find his house guests who had become his new family. He would miss them so much when they went. Just outside the study, he paused. The house was quiet which usually meant they would be in the sitting room with their books, although they had found the old Monopoly set yesterday and had persuaded him to join them in a few games. They had also found dominoes and playing cards so although they were finding things to amuse themselves with, he was sorry they were playing so much less music. With Jean-Guy's future looking so uncertain, they seemed to have lost their soul and their will to play music together.

With lots of thoughts suddenly stirring in his mind he went back into the study again and shut the door behind him.

Piers lifted his head from the ghost story book and half wished it would stop sending him to sleep. Some of the stories were quite fascinating. He had heard the Prof come out of his study and then go back in again which was a bit puzzling. Looking across from his armchair by the fire he could see Kathy and Jean-Guy were stretched out on the sofa in an intimate cuddle but with books in their free hands as though it was all quite innocent really.

"Come on, kids, either go upstairs or play music," he told them almost sharply.

Kathy looked at him over her shoulder. "What music?"

Muttering several rude words under his breath, Piers started looking along the shelves of music and took down the first thing he found. He tossed the violin and cello parts at them. "Mozart."

Jean-Guy lazily looked at the music. "Nah, I only like the B flat one."

Piers muttered a few more rude words and carried on along the shelves where the music wasn't in any sort of logical order that he could work out. "Piano, piano, violin solo, piano. Who the hell needs so much piano music?"

"Someone who plays the piano?" Kathy offered

At the exact same moment Jean-Guy replied quite forcefully, "You."

"Here's another trio. Never heard of it. Dvorak. Something in Russian." Some more music was hurled across.

Jean-Guy picked up the cello part and suddenly sat upright, inelegantly dislodging Kathy from her comfortable position on top of him. "You've found the *Dumky*. Now we're talking."

"Yes! Love this one!" Kathy enthused and half fell onto the floor in her eagerness to get her violin out.

Piers put the piano score ready and shook his head as though at the antics of a couple of toddlers. He flicked ahead a few pages and hoped his sight-reading had improved with all the playing he had done recently. Before Kathy and Jean-Guy had got their instruments ready, Audrey came hurtling in from the kitchen and was on the top of the piano in one spectacular leap from the back of the sofa.

"That cat is a witch," Kathy declared and rubbed Audrey under the chin.

"Just been reading that," Piers told them as he played the notes for them to tune to. "Superstition says there used to be a witches' coven meeting round here in the fourteenth century. They were burned alive and buried in what is now the back garden. Builders found their remains when they built the seventeenth century extension to the farmhouse."

"Gross," was all Kathy said. "Shut up, I don't want to hear any more."

Jean-Guy said what the other two could only assume was swearing in Czech as the C string peg on his cello kept slipping, but it made Kathy think of something a lot more pleasant than buried witches.

"Are we going to give our trio a name?"

Jean-Guy got the troublesome string in tune. "Good idea. But do we pick a Czech name, an English one or an Irish one?"

"Why not call it Dodman?" Piers suggested.

The other two immediately recognised the name of the farmhouse. "I like that," Jean-Guy approved. "Good, simple name. And appropriate for us."

"You know everyone's going to ask us who Dodman is, don't you?" Kathy asked.

Piers put his gloves on as Audrey got into pounce mode on top of the piano. "It isn't anyone. It's commonly believed to have been taken from the original Dead Man name, and it's also a Norfolk dialect word for a snail but not unknown in Suffolk."

Petr Mihaly didn't want to go into the sitting room when the Dvorak started to be played. He lingered in the doorway of his study and listened with respect to the way those three could play together. He hadn't heard that trio before so unless they had played it through while he had been out shopping they could all be sight-reading it. He listened a little more critically and realised one of the three was missing bits out so he didn't get left behind and really needed to do some hard work on his sight reading. The Prof smiled, but knew he couldn't put it off any longer.

He went into the sitting room with the letter in his hand, but the musicians were all concentrating and didn't notice him at first. Audrey was determinedly batting at Piers' hands on the keyboard as she had done so much Kathy had had to knit more gloves. Piers himself looked

277

a mess with his neat haircut all grown out and his shirt sleeves rolled up. Kathy had whirled her long hair on top of her head and pushed a pencil through to keep it in place and her bright pink sweatshirt was in a heap on the floor so she was playing in a scruffy denim skirt and a vest top. Jean-Guy took advantage of a few bars rest to peel off his sweater and he saw who had just come into the room. He also saw the Professor had a letter in his hand and something in the other man's demeanour made him miss his entry and the trio stopped abruptly, the other two wondering why the impeccable Jean-Guy would do such a thing.

You have a letter," was all the Professor said and he held out the envelope to Jean-Guy.

The younger man took it. "Have you read it?"

"Yes, it's from your mother."

"Excuse me," Jean-Guy said politely to the others and took his letter out to the kitchen so he could read it alone.

"Give him five minutes," the Professor advised. "We can discuss your upcoming programme. Having heard your Dvorak I'm thinking that maybe you should do that instead of the Beethoven. Gives our star cellist more prominence too, and a much lighter work for a late summer evening."

"You have a date for it?" Kathy asked eagerly.

"The Maltings is free in the evening of September eighth. They have said we can go any time to look round, all we have to do is ring the caretaker and book a day and time. It would also be a good idea to build up your repertoire so you could do a series of concerts and maybe some recordings. Jean-Guy has a lot of orchestral soloist work lined up and I am working on his diary. I hope you don't mind, Kathy, but I have put him on the books of your agent and she is happy to take you on as a trio as well."

"We've decided to call ourselves the Dodman Trio," Kathy told him. "Apparently it's a dialect word for a snail."

"How charming," the Prof acknowledged. "I always thought it was just a more euphemistic way of saying the Dead Man name. And I think you should bring in a few more modern pieces as well. You're working on the *Dumky* which is always a crowd pleaser and I have always liked Henze's *Kammersonate* myself."

"Love the Henze," Kathy agreed. "Such a cross between tuneful and totally mad. I think the Dvorak will suit us very well when we have worked on it a bit. I'd love to work us up to Mendelssohn." She turned to the man at the piano. "You OK with that?"

"I have no idea what you're talking about. I grew up accompanying song cycles."

The Prof sighed to himself and thought that the Dodman Trio may have a technically brilliant pianist but his repertoire still needed a heck of a lot of work on it. "I think you'll find the Henze on the shelves. I'll take you through it now, the piano part is very demanding in places. Kathy, it may be a good time for you to go out to the kitchen while I give Piers a lesson. And please take Audrey with you, I don't know how you can cope with her while you are playing."

Kathy took the mildly protesting Audrey out to the kitchen and she just heard the Prof's remark of, "Now take those silly mittens off as they don't do your playing any favours and just be grateful I'm not making you put shoes on yet."

Jean-Guy was sitting at the table, the letter was open in front of him but he was just looking across the kitchen with his eyes more focussed on the dresser than anything.

"Audrey and I have come to make some coffee," Kathy said quietly, not liking to intrude. "Am I allowed to ask?"

Jean-Guy didn't answer her immediately but listened to the first blast of piano playing from the sitting room. "He is playing the Henze. I played that as a student at the Prague Conservatoire. Piers will need to do a lot of work on it to get up to standard." He took his glasses off now he had finished reading and said, "The letter is not what the Prof was told, it's from my mother. Posted in Moscow to the British Embassy there two weeks ago. It confirms my father's appointment in the Conservatoire and she is asking me to come home. I have a series of recitals booked in April, including a couple in the Kremlin, and she says if I come to join them in Moscow now then there will be no reprisals. The Soviet and Czech press will just put out that I have been on a rest for the sake of my health."

Kathy could feel her heart rate was going up. He spoke so calmly, so emotionlessly almost that it told her just how his feelings must be all confused and churned up inside him. She tried to think logically; "What about that news of arresting them for intellectual crimes?"

"She doesn't mention it directly. Just that comment about reprisals. I think I may have to go back."

Kathy sat at the table and knew what it meant when novels talked about a cold hand gripping your heart. She looked at the man sitting opposite her and suddenly felt she didn't know him any more. He sounded as though he had made up his mind, for the sake of his parents he would risk going back to the very place where he had been held and tortured. "What? Are you completely mad? You've risked your life once to run away and now you sit there and say perhaps you should go back? What the hell is the matter with you?" She hadn't meant to sound angry but she didn't know how to break down this wall he had put up round himself.

Silence fell in the kitchen broken only by the sounds of a pianist making a total mess of some music and a cat scratching at the kitchen door as she wanted to go and join him.

Kathy tried again, doing her best to keep her voice level and practical. "They flogged the skin off your back and sent your own sister across to trick you. Why would you go back? Especially to the Soviet Union?"

He wouldn't touch her or look at her which did nothing to comfort her. It was as though in his mind he had already turned and walked away. For the first time since she had fallen in love with him she began to wonder if this was the real Jean-Guy. The one who would turn his back on her for something in his past. He had known his parents would be at risk when he defected. He, and they, had had to accept that. But there was something else behind this stubbornness. Something far deeper and more complicated than a family tie.

Jean-Guy was also clearly struggling to remain unruffled about all this. His voice was tetchy and Kathy could sense he was on the verge of losing his temper, if not at her then at something else that was driving him to these desperate measures. "Because they are my family. I can't leave them like that. That makes me worse than a traitor." He folded up the letter and put it in the back pocket of his jeans. "The Dodman Trio needs to get a new pianist. He can't play that Henze and wants to insult the audience by not dressing properly."

Kathy acknowledged his misplaced anger. She put her arm across Jean-Guy's back, thankful he didn't shrug her off and feeling as though she was fighting for their relationship as well as the future of the Trio. "Give him time. He coped well with sight-reading the Dvorak and, as he said, he hasn't done instrumental work before. He's got a lot to learn."

"Time is what we don't have. I will give the Professor two days to find out what is going on in Moscow and the same time for him to play the Dvorak. The Henze is way beyond him and always will be. If we are to go ahead as a trio we have to take it seriously."

Kathy thought of that performance of *La Campanella*. "Well now you're just being unreasonable. I don't know how the Prof's contacts work, but I'm sure if he had any news he would tell you."

"Then I won't wait two days. Don't make me any coffee." Jean-Guy went out of the kitchen leaving the door open so a delighted Audrey streaked back into the sitting room where the music wasn't getting any better.

Revelation and Fall

Jean-Guy shut himself away in the small front bedroom which he hadn't used for quite a while, refusing lunch as well as coffee. After a silent lunch, an anxious Professor went into his study to try to find out what was going on which left Kathy and Piers with a long afternoon ahead of them.

They cleared away and washed up after lunch, then Kathy made them more coffee as they didn't know what else to do and they sat back at the table.

"Walk into the village?" Kathy suggested half-heartedly.

"Nah, too much wedding talk going on, I'm staying out of it." Piers knew what was in her mind. "No, we're not going to talk about my love-life. Not unless you want to talk about yours first. Like what the hell you're going to do if he does go back."

Kathy realised that this man could somehow tap into her feelings. Whether it was all part of the training he had had over the years or a deeper intuition she didn't know. What she did know was that this wasn't someone who could be fobbed off with a flippant remark and feigned insouciance. "I don't have a clue," she admitted. "I suppose it was something I never thought would happen. Do you think he will?"

He didn't immediately reply. "Tricky one. My gut tells me he won't. I think the Prof will see if the security services can get someone in on a fact-finding mission. What good would it do Jean-Guy to go back there? The Prof knows the business inside and out and if he reckons it's a ruse to get their delinquent cellist back then I believe him. Please don't worry about it." He saw she wasn't consoled. "Shall we take our coffees into the garden? Seems a shame to waste the good weather."

"Why not," Kathy replied and the bitterness inside her bubbled to the surface. "I think I'd be wasting my breath if I tried to talk to him right now."

"Yes, I rather think you would," he agreed. "Come on, let's go and find a patch of sunshine to sit in for a few minutes then we can do something rash and foolish like baking a cake for tea. Have you any idea how to make a cake?"

Kathy was somehow comforted. This was a man who treated her as an equal. Showed her respect and yet at the same time protected her. Even if Jean-Guy ran back to Russia, Piers was her friend for life now. "Taught at school but I'm not very good at it." She watched as he took off his puzzle ring and put it on the kitchen table. "Are you trying to get your finger tattooed?"

"No, but it irritates like hell. Christ knows what it's made of but there's certainly no hallmark on it. I'll put it back on before I next see her."

"Jean-Guy showed me the rings you and Sarah chose. You're not going for the matching pair then?"

Piers half smiled. "Oh, I'd have had one to match hers as there's hardly anything of it, but she wanted me to have some ridiculous thing about an inch wide. Which apparently is the fashion. So I said I wouldn't wear one at all in that case and we had a bit of an argument in the shop and in the end the bloke serving us suggested the one for me. I think he just wanted to shut us up before we emptied the shop of customers."

Kathy knew he wouldn't take offence. "It was, um, not what I would have expected of you. I thought

284

you'd have gone for something a bit more classy and subtle. Like its wearer."

He acknowledged her attempt at levity with the ghost of a smile. "I don't like it but I'd been backed into a corner by the pair of them." He shrugged. "Still, if Sarah and I stick to our plans I won't be wearing it for long."

Kathy picked up something in his tone. "I'm sure Sarah won't mind if you decide you'd quite like to stay married to her."

"Don't," he requested. "Please, just don't get involved."

Kathy knew when it was time to back away. "Come and sit in the garden. But we'll put you in the shade so you don't get sunburn."

"Used to get sunburn so often as a kid," he said as he followed her outside. "Just couldn't understand why all the others were getting browner and browner and there was me and Roisin still a pair of snow-babies. There was one kid I remember, Connor O'Malley, I swear the sun only had to come out and he changed colour."

"Did you like school?" Kathy asked as they settled in the garden in the shade of the old crabapple tree and several cats wandered out to join them.

"Not really. Half the kids were scared of me and Roisin as we were Maloneys and the other half sucked up to us. Don't think either of us made any friends at any of our schools. I suppose you were the class swot?"

Kathy finished her coffee and lay down on the grass. "Yup. Straight As all the way through. Not. Do you think that cloud looks like a teddy bear?"

He lay down beside her. "Nah, it's a pig. One day I'll take you flying and you can see the tops of the clouds.

It's pretty incredible up there." He nudged her with his elbow and pointed at a small cloud. "Milk bottle?"

"Wine bottle. Being chased by a dragon."

It was surprisingly warm in the spring sunshine with the rhododendrons shielding the garden from the wind and even a few early bees were seeing what there was in the way of food. Kathy shivered as she was getting chilly and opened her eyes to realise she and Piers had fallen asleep in the garden which was now in a deep afternoon shade and the grass was starting to get a bit damp. Neither of them was wearing a watch but she guessed they had been out there quite a while. Slightly more embarrassingly she had woken up half rolled on top of him with her head cushioned comfortably on his shoulder.

"Please move," he said without opening his eyes. "I think you've squashed all the feeling out of my arm."

Kathy sat up and picked grass out of her hair. "Sorry, how long was I asleep for?"

"God knows, I've only just woken up myself." Piers sat up beside her and started shaking his right arm trying to get the circulation going again. "Come on, let's go and see what's happening in there."

They went into the kitchen where all was reassuringly normal. The Prof had just made tea and Jean-Guy was sitting at the table marking a score with some pencil annotations.

"Ah, good," the Prof greeted them. "I was going to give you another few minutes then come and get you."

"Where's my ring?" Piers asked. "I left it on the table."

The Prof shrugged apologetically. "Wasn't here when I came out to make tea. Maybe one of the cats has knocked it off."

They all spent a few minutes checking the kitchen floor but there was no sign of a silver puzzle ring.

"You are so going to get your finger tattooed," Kathy told Piers seeing he looked genuinely cross and hoping to console somehow. "I'll tell her it was the cats if you like."

"Sit, please," the Professor requested before those two got going again. "While you two have been sleeping like babies in the garden and Jean-Guy has been working hard on his music, I have been busy in my study. There's only one way we can find out what is going on in the USSR and that is to send a couple of people in. There is a joint US and British diplomatic and trade mission going out on Thursday and one of you is now going to be flying the aeroplane that takes it." He shot Piers a look that not only silenced him, but the other two as well. "Good, no arguments this time. I am now going to tell you all more than I should at this stage as it will stop Kathy and Jean-Guy nagging me for information. Do you remember Kerryanne who flew Marianne back? She has worked for the CIA for years and will be in charge of the operation. Your role is that of support and it is really just to test you and see how you cope in a very minor capacity and we are lucky the Americans have given us the chance to slip you in. She is captaining the aircraft, you are going back into military uniform, although I believe they are promoting you to Wing Commander, and you will be her co-pilot. Did you buy yourself a decent wedding ring in Norwich?"

"Um, yes," Piers managed, feeling as though the walls of the farmhouse were falling in on him, and trying not to lose his temper as he realised that particular bullet which he had been dodging for the last twenty years had now finally hit him. He didn't want to play this game again, but because he had been there before he knew to refuse would be worse.

"Good. As that tawdry trinket Sarah gave you is lost, I need you to wear it as Kerryanne has requested you go in as a married man. Kathy, you are to take Piers to the meeting point in my car and then drive back here taking a different route home returning about four o'clock. If anyone in the village, including Sarah, asks we have to tell them Piers been called back to work. We will agree the reason before you go. Now go and get your wedding ring as we need to make it look as though you have been wearing it a few years."

"When do I go?" Piers asked and sounded oddly resigned to what he had guessed was going to come. Kathy felt so sorry for him but she began to realise there was a much deeper agenda for this man. A much darker one, and that was why the Prof had warned her off him. She hoped this would never happen to her.

The Professor was thankful this most unwilling of participants was not going to make a fuss as he had been dreading. "You leave at about six tomorrow morning, meeting Kerryanne in a service station just off the M1. She will have the official car with her. Full briefing will take place tomorrow and you will both fly the delegation out on Thursday from London. And no questions, as I am not providing any answers. Now, you have a couple of hours until our supper time so I suggest you go and play some music. Do not sit and chatter, I will be listening."

Jean-Guy went to fetch the ring and brought it to the sitting room. He handed across the box and said awkwardly," This is my fault. They are sending you into God knows what and it's my fault."

Piers didn't immediately put the ring on. "No. It's not. Not really. What has happened with you is just the final excuse they needed. But I'm not going to let them keep me. I'll do this for you and then that's it."

He put the ring on and looked at the triple band of platinum, with a polished centre between brushed outer bands. "Funny, I didn't wear a ring last time. Perhaps I should have done."

"Suits you," Kathy complimented him, even though she thought it was far too chunky for his hands and guessed Sarah was making a point. "But it does look very new. Better let Audrey have it for five minutes."

"Music, please!" the Prof bellowed from the study. "I told you not to talk about it and I can hear you gossiping like a load of old women."

The Prof drove an unremarkable white Ford Fiesta which he usually only used to go to the supermarket and back for his weekly shop. Kathy was glad to see he had a full tank of petrol in it and wasn't sorry when he gave her some cash to buy more petrol if she needed it. She felt oddly nervous driving with Piers in the passenger seat but that was what they had been told to do and it was barely daylight when they left. The Professor and Jean-Guy had both got up to see them off but there were no emotional farewells just a quiet departure from the house that had been their sanctuary for so long.

The route out to the A12 took them through the village and already Sarah was outside the shop getting set up for the day and she was talking to a couple of men who worked on one of the nearby farms. She looked up, saw the Professor's car coming along the road and stepped across the pavement.

"Now what?" Kathy asked.

"You'll have to stop a minute, we've got to start the story going."

Sarah put her head in through the passenger window and exchanged a gentle kiss with Piers who had already tucked his left hand out of the way under his legs. "Off on a day out?" she asked curiously.

"Been called in to work," he replied quite calmly. "Just a few days' training."

"Wouldn't have thought you needed any training," Sarah smiled teasingly.

He gave her another kiss. "It's all your fault. You've helped me so much I'm starting to feel ready to fly again. I'll see you when I get back, OK?"

"OK, love. Take care of yourself. Just make sure you're back before the thirteenth."

"Wouldn't dare not be," he replied and sounded as though he meant it.

Kathy drove on again; her passenger clearly wasn't in the mood to chat but just looked out of the side window. She felt it was going to be a long journey. "So what do you know about Kerryanne?" she encouraged.

They were early getting to the meeting place which was a surprisingly small and underused service station a few miles north of Leicester. The car park was quiet with about six lorries and two cars in it and the two got out of the Fiesta, pleased to be able to stand up and have a bit of a stretch.

"Where are you going to go for the day?" Piers asked and looked at the two cars that were parked there already. One was a bright blue Hillman Avenger and the other an even less restrained coral pink Alfa Romeo Alfasud. He couldn't imagine an American intelligence officer driving either of those.

"I think it'll probably take me most of the day to get back if I take the route out to Peterborough and then drop down through Cambridge. I can always kill a bit of time in Stowmarket or somewhere if I need to as I know that's just over an hour from home." Kathy looked across at him but his face gave nothing away. "Aren't you just a bit scared?"

"I can't quite decide whether this is better or worse than facing eight hundred people at Snape Maltings. Probably about the same."

A sleek black Mercedes swept elegantly into the car park and pulled up next to the Fiesta. Kathy could feel herself staring as the most beautiful woman she had ever seen in her life got out of the car and flicked her long honey blonde hair back over her shoulders. She was tall, slim and didn't appear to be wearing any make up. Her perfect skin was lightly tanned and her eyes were more green than hazel. She was simply dressed in a white trouser suit with no blouse under it and the heels on her white boots were at least four inches high. When she got closer to them, Kathy realised she wasn't as young as she appeared but with those legs and that figure she didn't suppose anyone would care.

"Hi," she greeted Piers with a handshake, as though assignations in car parks were something she did all the time. "Good to see you again and without that hellcat trying to kill you." She bestowed a dazzling smile on Kathy and held out her hand then continued in her pleasant, well-educated American tones. "Hi, I'm Kerryanne and I'm now going to steal your man away from you with no dramatic goodbyes. Just go use the bathroom in there, buy yourself a coffee or something and by the time you get back to your car, we'll be gone."

Kathy briefly took the hand that was cool with a surprisingly strong grip. "Pleased to meet you," she managed to say. Kerryanne didn't speak again so Kathy locked the Fiesta and walked away towards the building feeling as though she was the frumpiest woman on the planet. Kerryanne had been wearing a perfume that smelled of mimosas and lemons and all her jewellery matched. A silver watch on her left wrist, silver bangles on her right and what looked like platinum and diamonds on her wedding finger. She could well imagine that once Piers had been tidied up a bit and those two had got their flying uniforms on they were going to make quite a dramatic couple. She didn't turn to look as she felt, rather than heard, the Mercedes purr almost silently away on its mission.

She got back to the farmhouse at just after four o'clock and sat in the car for a few minutes letting her mind settle then took a deep breath and went round the side of the house and in through the back door.

Jean-Guy shot up from the table and rushed to give her a hug. "Everything go alright?" he asked her and she guessed he had passed quite an anxious day.

"Yes, fine. We met Kerryanne just as you said and they went straight off. I came back the long way round and stopped off in Stowmarket to do a bit of shopping, which wasn't the best plan I've ever had as I have no income but you didn't see her."

"See who?" Jean-Guy asked as the Prof set about making the tea.

"Kerryanne. She would make Miss World look like the back end of a bus. And she flies fighter jets, speaks Russian and German and God knows what besides. I tell you, if the flight crew are going to be part of the diplomatic envoy they're going to be turning a few heads."

"They will be in the background," the Prof explained kindly as he put teapot and mugs on the table. "Although I believe they will be attending one function where evening dress is required as obviously having an Anglo/US crew is all part of what the delegation is about."

Kathy and Jean-Guy simultaneously shouted with triumph. "So he will have to 'dress up like a bloody penguin' after all?" Jean-Guy laughed.

The Prof had to smile, he could see how much these two were missing their third. "Sadly not. He will be in RAF mess uniform. But he will hate it just as much I have no doubt."

After tea, Kathy and Jean-Guy went into the sitting room as they habitually did and looked at Audrey sitting on the piano, patiently waiting for the music to start. "Want to play something?" Jean-Guy asked.

"Not really, but I suppose we should. We can't spend the next however long moping around and getting worried."

They tried playing two parts of a Mozart trio for a while but it didn't sound right so they switched to the Ravel.

"We cannot spend the next week like this," Kathy announced. "This is ridiculous. Let's give ourselves the rest of the day off then draw up a rehearsal schedule and stick to it. Otherwise we're going to be picking things up and putting them down again and not getting anywhere."

"True. Do you think we will ever work as a trio? If Piers is back to flying Concorde we can't book a diary of gigs and expect him to be available. We will have to work with his flying days as that earns him so much money."

"I think we'll worry about that when it happens," was all Kathy was willing to say.

Petr Mihaly took pity on the two lethargic people at the supper table with him. "I can give you a small update. Kerryanne and Piers are now at their UK base and he has finally had a haircut and tomorrow will be out on the parade ground."

"Why?" Kathy asked.

"Because he is supposed to be in the military and won't have been drilled for over ten years. He has to be convincing as an RAF Wing Commander as it is unlikely such a mission would be flown by civilian pilots. Kerryanne has her own agenda out there and I don't know what Piers' involvement will be. It is likely to be minimal but they will have to work closely together on behalf of both countries. It will not be easy for them and they will both have to go through UK and US debriefings on their return and that may take several days."

Kathy was starting to worry now. "But he'll be back in time for his wedding won't he?"

"I really hope so as I don't think Sarah will cope too well with being jilted."

Piers had been away for three days when Kathy and Jean-Guy thought that perhaps they should walk along to the village to see Sarah. There were several people on the coast path, some with dogs, some in family groups and all clearly tourists. The two who had begun to consider themselves local felt a bit resentful of all these others on 'their' path.

"I never thought I'd want to see this place in winter again," Jean-Guy said to Kathy as she tucked herself against him to let a family group pass by going the other way.

She put her arm round his waist. "I never thought I wouldn't want to leave," she admitted.

He hugged her close. "Well, why don't we ask the Prof if we can stay? We know all about his second life anyway so he needn't worry about keeping secrets from us."

"But there's no point in us relocating to Suffolk. We need a base in London for work and travel," Kathy pointed out while at the same time seeing the exciting simplicity of such an idea.

"Yes, and Piers has said we can share his house which you say is plenty big enough for us all. Do you have much in the flat that you want to keep?"

"No, not really. I'll keep my pink mug with the daisy on it but the rest of the kitchen stuff came with the flat. The bedlinen and towels are mine and I have some music there. Most of my things stayed in Wimbledon as I kept moving round so much avoiding my ex."

He stopped walking and turned her to face him, taking both of her hands in his and sounding as madly excited as she felt. "Emma has keys to your flat and to Piers' house so we could ask her to box up our things and move us across as soon as she can. Do you think she would?"

"I'm sure she would. Or, knowing her, she'll get Derek to do it while she supervises. But don't you think we should ask Piers first? We haven't really worked out any details with him. And there's the piano to organise too."

"Have you not seen how lonely he is? Every night he sleeps alone and he is now marrying a woman who doesn't want him just so she can have babies. I don't understand him at all but I think he will be happy to share."

"So you think he's lonely too? It seems such a shame as he's such a lovely person. Do you suppose he could do the same as us and live here when he's not working?"

"With his flying I don't think he will have much time when he isn't working. Just maybe odd days and it would be a lot of travelling between. And also he has the best room in the house and the Prof will need it for his defectors."

The same thought occurred to them both at the same time. "The cottages!"

They walked on again, forming happy plans and almost sorry to reach the shop which was very busy again.

Both Sarah and her mother were working behind the counter and from the look of them it had clearly been a hectic morning. Kathy and Jean-Guy felt almost as though they were intruding.

"Hullo, loves," Sarah's mother greeted them as her daughter was busy with a customer. "Sorry, it's a bit mad in here at the moment. Go and get yourselves a coffee on the beach and I'll get Sarah to pop across if she has a moment."

The two went back out into the street and saw a pavement sign pointing towards the beach and indicating there was a café open there. What they had assumed was a boat house had opened the panels on its sides to show windows, the sea-facing huge double doors were open, there were tables and chairs inside and out and the easterly breeze was blowing a delicious scent of coffee and cakes towards them.

"I never knew this was here," Kathy remarked as they wandered towards the mirage, following their noses and the chatter of people sitting outside round the pastel-coloured tables. Inside the boat house it was painted a fresh white with a glass-fronted display case showing cakes and traybakes of a dozen different varieties. There was a sandwich menu on the wall behind the counter and a list of coffees that made Kathy think she was back in cosmopolitan Earl's Court.

There seemed to be only one woman running the café. She looked to be in her thirties, she had brown hair cut in a short, mannish style and was dressed in a checked shirt and dungarees under her crisp white apron.

"Morning," she hailed them cheerily. "What can I get you?"

Kathy and Jean-Guy had a quick count-up of their change and just managed to afford an Americano, a mocha and a slice of coffee and walnut cake.

"I never knew this was here," Kathy said apologetically. "I've been coming here for years and I never knew."

The woman laughed. "That's because it wasn't. This is my first season. It was mostly Sarah's idea as she's got a sharp business head under that fluffy hair of hers." She looked at them a bit critically. "You are Kathy and Jean-Guy? Friends of Sarah's fiancé?" Upon receiving a confused affirmative she positively beamed at them. "So pleased to meet you. Now put your money away and tell me all the gossip about him. I'm Alison, by the way. Old friend of Sarah's."

Oh!" Kathy exclaimed. "Yes, Piers mentioned you. He said you're coming to the wedding. I thought he said you lived in Cambridge."

"I did. I was running a café there but Sarah said she'd managed to find a way to have the kids she wants so why not bring the business down here as this is really a prime spot." More customers came in. "Go and find yourselves a couple of seats and I'll stop by when I've got a minute. Americano, mocha, walnut," she said to herself just before she greeted her next customers.

"Shall we sit inside?" Jean-Guy suggested. "It's a bit quieter."

They sat on pink and yellow cushions on a wooden bench at a scrubbed wooden table in a corner of the cafe and Kathy looked round at the whitewashed walls hung with beach-themed paintings and photographs. The whole place was calm and relaxed and it really didn't matter that there was sand and shingle on the floor along with the wet footprints of children.

"This has such a happy feel to it," Kathy remarked. "I'm so glad Alison has come here. And if today is anything to go by she's onto a winner with all this trade."

Alison rushed across to their table with their order. "Sorry, bit of a madhouse. Catch up soon."

Jean-Guy got to his feet. "I will help you. I have worked in restaurants before."

"But, you can't just do that," Alison exclaimed and tried not to sound too pleased.

"Yes, I can. I did it a lot when I was a student. But your coffee machine scares me so I will be your waiter and wash up."

With the work force doubled, the queue was soon worked through and Kathy had to admit Jean-Guy was certainly quick on his feet and good at remembering which customer had ordered what. She began to feel she was the only one of them who didn't have any other talents. She drank one of the best mochas she had ever tasted and resisted the temptation to eat all the cake so there would be some left for Jean-Guy.

The two workers took advantage of a slight lull to sit with her for a few minutes.

Alison took a gulp of her own latte and said, "So, does he really fly Concorde?"

"Oh, yes, quite a few years now," Kathy replied, not having thought about Piers at all as she had been so busy watching Alison and Jean-Guy working as such an efficient team. "Are you going to be open all year?"

"Probably not. I mean the main tourist season is Easter to kind of Septemberish. Sarah said I may be able to keep going for a bit longer, maybe into October with soup and rolls but really this place is dead November to February. But if I can pull in trade for six busy months and two or three quieter ones then I can make a go of it."

She looked round but the inside customers were all talking and there was no queue at the moment. "Why is he doing it?"

"Doing what?" Kathy asked.

"Marrying Sarah. What kind of bloke will agree to marry a woman just to give her kids? I mean what's in it for him?"

"I really don't know," Kathy replied. "He told us she doesn't want a husband and then told us to butt out of his love life. We don't know what their agreement was but he said she doesn't expect him to be faithful to her. So I suppose the marriage doesn't mean anything to either of them and it's just some kind of legal thing so she can have kids."

Alison still didn't seem convinced. "He lives in London doesn't he? What's to say he's not going to make her go back there with him?"

Kathy was puzzled that this woman should suddenly appear rather hostile and tried not to sound too argumentative. "He works out of Heathrow so he has a house in London for convenience as much as anything. Why don't you ask Sarah?"

"I did. She said they haven't talked about it. They're going to wait until she gets pregnant and then decide." She looked round as more customers started arriving. "Be a love," she said to Jean-Guy, "and clear some tables for me. Looks like the second wave."

Trade had dwindled to nothing by two o'clock in the afternoon and the wind off the sea was getting cooler sending the tourists back to their holiday homes and caravans. Both Kathy and Jean-Guy helped Alison by bringing in the tables while she cleaned down the working area and wrapped up the few leftover cakes which she gave to them to take home. Alison had closed the window panels and just locked up for the night when Sarah walked across to join them.

"Hi," Sarah called. "Busy day?"

"Frantic. Thanks for sending across the cavalry. I really am going to have to employ staff though. Can't rely on these two, even if you did send me an ex-pro of a waiter and one of the best sandwich makers this side of the A12."

Kathy and Jean-Guy felt slightly embarrassed by the praise. They were even more embarrassed when, right in front of them, Sarah and Alison exchanged a long, slow kiss on the lips.

"We'd better be getting back," Kathy managed to say while the shock still filtered through her system. "Thanks for all the cakes."

"You're very welcome," Alison told them as though she and Sarah hadn't just staged a very clear revelation of their relationship even if it was only the other two who could have seen them. "Don't suppose you fancy popping along tomorrow to help out?"

Kathy and Jean-Guy looked at each other.

"We can do," Jean-Guy offered cautiously. "I have my cello work to do but I could find time for a day or so as we can't practise trios while Piers is away."

"I'm only open ten to two at the moment. So see you about nine thirty?"

"OK," Kathy agreed then she and Jean-Guy turned and set off for the coast path neither daring to say out loud what was in their minds as somehow speaking it would make it all seem too horribly real.

The Prof was in his study when they got back but they made themselves an early cup of tea and settled at the kitchen table.

"I don't know where to start," Kathy said feeling a bit shaky now she had had time to digest the full implications.

"Well, I think we now know why Sarah doesn't want a husband," Jean-Guy told her. "And from the way Piers ate our heads off I'm guessing he knows why too. And I don't even want to think about how they are doing things in bed. So, shall we work out our living plans while it is quiet then you can ring Emma and we can speak to the Prof about what we would like to do?"

"What would you like to do?" the Prof asked from the doorway as he came in with at least four cats stalking his feet. "I thought I heard you coming back. You have been out for quite a while."

"We've been helping at the café on the beach. It's run by Sarah's friend Alison."

The Prof helped himself to some tea from the pot and unwrapped one of the foil packets on the table to find a piece of marble cake which appealed to him. "Ah, cake. Yes, I remember hearing about Sarah and Alison many years ago. But you know what village gossip is like. Alison went away to Cambridge, and now Sarah is flaunting not only a remarkably handsome fiancé but also a very shiny new ring, I think that has killed off that gossip."

Kathy stuck her finger in marble cake crumbs then licked them off. "It's not gossip."

"I think you have more news for me than I have for you, so I will tell you mine first. Piers and Kerryanne flew out of Gatwick this morning with the British Foreign

Secretary and the US Secretary of State in their plane along with several dozen members of staff and cabin crew. Perfect flight to Moscow and they touched down about one o'clock our time. We may hear more later but first they have to make contact with our people in Moscow. Of course it is more complicated as they are crossing UK and US business but it really is a remarkable piece of co-operation between our two countries. Now what do you have to tell me?"

He listened quietly to all their plans, as well as what they had seen Alison and Sarah do then proposed a walk down to the cottages without saying anything else.

The nettles and brambles were slowly winning but they managed to get across to the remains of the building.

"As you can see," the Prof pointed out, "from the roofline and where the doors are, this was once two cottages. If you put them together it would make quite a good size house if that is what you are thinking or you can keep them as two which will be a lot less structural work. I must admit I had a more selfish hope that you two would stay in the farmhouse with me and the ghosts and cats."

"How would that work?" Jean-Guy asked curiously as a madly excited Kathy clutched his hand.

"At the moment, you would just live here when you aren't working and we will be company for each other. As I get older it will console me and Emma to know there will be someone around to look after me more and arrange my care. Then when my time comes I will bequeath it to you for you and your children."

Kathy thought she had had a beautiful dream and it had come true. "But, what will Emma think of that idea? This is her house too."

"Emma has never wanted this house. She grew up here yes, but she finds it dark and old-fashioned. She hates the way the people walk past the hedges and she hates the way it is so isolated. She has always said that when the house is hers all she will do is sell it."

"It's still her inheritance," Kathy tried, but not very enthusiastically.

"She now has several acres in Somerset, a title and probably a much greater fortune to inherit from Derek's family. I am sure even when it is yours you will always make her welcome here. I will speak to my solicitor about it and also Emma as it will mean altering my Will."

"Where will that leave Piers?" Kathy wanted to know. "I don't suppose he can stay too, can he?"

"Piers is marrying Sarah and he has his home in London but he will always be welcome. Judging from what you have said, I have a strong feeling Sarah will prefer him to take the option of ending the marriage once she has had her family, her friend Alison will move in to console her for her husband's treachery and they will live outwardly respectably together as two old maids and bring up the children together."

Jean-Guy thought of a possible problem with the plan. "They may not have any children, then what happens? He didn't manage it with his first wife."

"I don't know we should be talking about this. But I asked him exactly that and it will save you asking the poor man the same question. When he and his wife failed to produce they both had all sorts of tests. The problems were hers, not his. By the time that was confirmed, their marriage was already breaking down so she decided not to do anything about it. Don't worry about him. What with his airline duties and what the people I work for have lined up for him, I would recommend you seriously think about finding another pianist if you want to continue as a trio. There will already have been great pressure put on him to go back into the RAF with the prospect of promotion to Group Captain within the year. In fact, I must be truthful, and point out it is very likely he will take up that option and not come back to civilian life and us after this mission."

Kathy refused to believe it. "No," she protested vehemently. "He loves playing our trios with Audrey on the piano. I don't care if he wants to play at the Albert Hall in his bare feet, I'm not giving up on him like that. And I bet Sarah won't either now she's so close to getting what she wants."

The Prof had to admire her fidelity. "He can still marry her, if that is what they agree to do. She will then become the wife of a serving RAF officer and she will choose not to go on any postings with him," he pointed out kindly. "In so many ways his going back into the Air Force will suit her much better."

Jean-Guy gave her a loving cuddle. "Kathy, you must realise that his isn't the world of music like ours is. All he has known all his adult life is flying planes and being in the military. For him it would make so much more sense than to try and mix together flying Concorde one week and then playing piano trios with us the next. He doesn't know our repertoire and can you honestly see him having time to work on it when he is flying again?"

Kathy wanted to scream with frustration that these two didn't understand what she felt in her bones. Piers would never leave them.   He would never leave her. Then she thought about it. Piers didn't need her in the same way Jean-Guy did. Piers would manage without her and she would learn to manage without him. It was as though something shifted inside her and she knew he was going to go. The anger and frustration drained away and all she wanted to do was cry as she saw her dreams falling like those doomed butterflies, turned to dust as they thought they had found happiness. There would be no more laughter in the farmhouse as the Dodman Trio were pestered by a persistent tortoiseshell cat. There would be no fun recital in Snape Maltings. She looked back to where the farmhouse was hidden behind the hedges and realised that she would have to let it go. She and Jean-Guy had a future together and she knew she should be happy.

She sighed just once. "I can see your points. But I'm not going to agree to look for another pianist until Piers has told us himself he wants to quit. I don't care if he has to do it from a public phone box in the middle of the Scottish highlands. I want to hear him say it."

The Door of the Sun

Kathy and Jean-Guy reported for work at the café promptly at nine thirty the next morning. The Prof didn't say anything but he wasn't happy to see the renowned cellist wander off along the coast path with the love of his life to spend his day waiting on tables rather than working on his music. He knew Kathy wouldn't stand in the way of Jean-Guy's career and he just hoped that this unsettled time in their lives would soon be over. He didn't think either would ever give up their music but it was as though part of them was missing while Piers wasn't with them to make up the whole. Audrey, on the other hand, didn't seem the slightest bit concerned that her human had left her again, although she did scoot into the sitting room from time to time and sit on the piano waiting for the music to start.

Alison didn't mention kissing Sarah so they didn't mention it either but got on with putting out the tables and chairs for those who wanted their drinks and cakes outside. The weather was cooler that day but April had blown in on a mild wind and by the time the café officially opened at ten o'clock there was already a small queue forming. Alison had made the cakes at home that morning and they looked very tempting to the two extra workers who had got up late and missed breakfast. There was a lull in customers about half past eleven so Alison made them a coffee each and sat with them at one of the outside tables.

"Been a couple long?" she started as though genuinely curious.

"Oh, not long," Kathy offered. "In fact we didn't meet until January when Emma had us both arrive at the house on the same day."

"I don't know how Sarah thinks she can put up with it but it's the only way we'll get to have any children," Alison commented and the other two realised she was steering the conversation where she wanted it to go.

Jean-Guy fished a drowned insect out of his coffee and played along. "We don't know why Piers would put up with such an arrangement. It leaves you and Sarah playing happy families and him on his own again with another failed marriage on his records."

"She's never tried to deceive him," Alison defended her friend.

Jean-Guy backed away from an argument. "No, she hasn't. He was the one who deceived us until a few days ago when he told us about their arrangement. And just as you are happy for your friend, you must understand we are worried about ours."

Alison was silent for a few minutes. "Yes, I can appreciate that. Sarah told me how close the three of you are so I can understand your worries. But she says neither of them wants to live with the other. Of course, I've never met him as Sarah kept him all to herself if he was around when I was getting set up here but she does seem genuinely to care for him. Which I don't understand at all. Still, they've come to this agreement and Sarah won't give me the details of it, so I suppose we'd better let them get on with it. I don't expect he'll be around much if he's working in London. They've pissed off most of the village by having such a small wedding, which I suppose is his idea."

"So far as I understand it, the small wedding was a mutual agreement," Kathy corrected her as kindly as she could, wondering where all this was going. Alison seemed to be as much in the dark as they were.

"We see the same problem two different ways," Alison conceded. "I hear it from Sarah, you hear it from Piers, and neither of them is telling the full story. The version I got is that he doesn't want to get married in a church at all but she does so he eventually gave in and said OK but just the barest legal minimum. When I asked her why she told me he's not a Christian and then wouldn't say any more."

Kathy thought of the way Piers would wolf down the Prof's bacon pudding so that ruled out Judaism and Islam and probably a few others as well. "He's never mentioned religion to us. Well, not to me anyway."

The women looked at Jean-Guy who hadn't said anything yet. "Um," he began. "He is Pagan." The other two just stared at him. "He... he, um, has a pentangle on his body and I saw it one night when we were sharing the room."

Kathy and Alison were now highly curious as Jean-Guy seemed to be rather embarrassed.

"Another tattoo?" Kathy guessed.

"No, I can't remember your word but it was burned onto his skin so now it is a scar. It is horrible. I asked why and that is when he told me of his faith. I have never been more pleased that I have no faith of my own."

Alison looked very sceptical. "I thought Pagans just danced naked round trees."

"He explained it as perhaps the oldest faith, they have no God as other people know it but it is all about living in harmony with the spirits that are in and around us."

"Yeah, right. And he earns his living carting rich people about in a luxury jet? Something doesn't stack up there. There's a hell of a lot doesn't stack up with that one and the sooner Sarah gets rid of him the happier I'll be."

Kathy bit back her fury before she was goaded into indiscretion. "Please don't judge him until you've met him. You couldn't meet a lovelier person." She looked at the man sitting with them. "Well, perhaps one other."

"Can you believe her?" Kathy squeaked indignantly to Jean-Guy as they walked home along the path at the end of another busy day in the café.

"Yes. I listen to her defending Sarah and I listen to you defending Piers and you are both speaking the same language just different words." He hugged her to his side as they walked. "We have to accept Alison as part of Sarah's life. We may not like it but that is how she lives."

"I suppose." She sighed and changed the topic. "I'll ring Emma tonight. Ask her to move out the few bits I've got in the flat. It'll all go in one box so won't be a problem. The piano, I don't know. I'll have to talk to her about that."

Her mention of the piano sent Jean-Guy off on his own train of thought as he had been feeling guilty about taking a whole day away from his cello. "I suppose we could put together a quartet rather than a trio. Then we wouldn't need regular players and if we had to you could play the viola part and we could bring in a couple of violinists."

Kathy was slightly horrified that he would be so callous even though the musician in her could acknowledge he was just being practical. "Are you making plans for what to do without Piers?" she asked. "Well, I've said my piece. I'm not going to decide anything until he has told us what he wants to do."

Jean-Guy gave her a kiss and a cuddle right in the middle of the coast path. "Kathy, you are the nicest person I know and so faithful to everyone. OK, I agree. We will wait and ask Piers what he wants to do. I would like him to do the concert at Snape even if that is the only concert the Dodman Trio ever does. Just think, if he goes back to the RAF he can wear his uniform on stage and then he won't have to be a penguin."

Kathy didn't have a Somerset number for Emma so she was glad to find her at home that evening.

"We've just got back from another trip down there," Emma told her and sounded very weary. "So I hope this won't be a long chat? I'll ring you tomorrow for a proper gossip and keep you up to date with what's going on. But remind me to give you the phone number down there before you hang up today."

Emma listened quietly while Kathy explained that she and Jean-Guy were definitely going to be sharing with Piers. She knew the Prof hadn't mentioned anything about her and Jean-Guy staying on at the farmhouse with him as he wanted to get all the legal niceties sorted out and make sure there was still an inheritance for his only child, before he put the proposal to her.

"I've got your stuff here," Emma consoled. "Wasn't going to leave it in that place with no security was I? So long as you're sure he really won't mind."

"It was his idea in the first place. Have you been round there yet?"

"Yes, I popped round a couple of days after he gave me the key. I hope that's his Ferrari in the parking space." There were some background noises and Kathy deduced Derek had just brought his wife a cup of tea. Emma gulped some of her drink. "Oh, Kath, you're going to love living there. I know you said you've seen the kitchen but isn't that little Aga just adorable? Weird shower room at the front on the ground floor where any normal person would have a dining room, but the shower head alone is the size of a dinner plate. Something he inherited when he moved in I would think. Enormous bedroom on the first floor at the front which I'm guessing is the spare as the bed in that one wasn't made up. Huge living room on that floor too looking over the garden. I mean, his own garden in Earl's Court. It must cost him a fortune."

Kathy thought this all sounded very promising and didn't like to mention that she knew Piers had taken out a very scary mortgage on it. "He told me the bit over the car port doesn't belong to him so he's actually only got half a house."

"That explains why it all feels a bit lopsided. I thought maybe it had been flats as the whole place is so oddly arranged. With a lot of work on it, it would be a really lovely home. And can you imagine ever owning all of it?"

Kathy had a sudden horrible thought about what might happen if the owner of that house went back into the military. There was no way she and Jean-Guy would be able to afford it. But she wasn't going to change her plans with Emma now. "And did you go and lie on his bed and think things you shouldn't?"

"So tempted but I couldn't in the end. There are three rooms up on the next floor and it looks as though he sleeps in a tiny box room at the back. Probably because it's so quiet up there. Attic is just two totally empty rooms and there's hardly any furniture anywhere so I don't know how he'll cope with you and your messy ways and knitting wool all over the place."

Kathy ignored the insult, she'd heard it too often before. She couldn't help feeling that the lack of furniture was because Piers' stretched finances didn't go that far. She took a deep breath and went for it. "What about the piano?"

Emma hesitated. "Well, if you're absolutely sure. I mean I'm happy for it to move with you as Derek's dad has inherited two that we've found so far. Shall I ask around? It'll be a hell of a job to get it into the living room but loads of space once it's there."

Kathy really hoped this would all come off. Did serving RAF officers even need their own house? She had no idea. "OK, find out if it's possible and what it will cost and let me know?"

"I'll get Derek onto it, he's the one with the brains. Do you suppose there's any deposit to come back to me, since I paid it when I first took on the lease on the flat? Although knowing that mean old bat she'll blame all the tenants for the damage and keep all the deposits. Anyway, better go. I'll talk to you about the piano next time we chat."

Kathy felt a bit sad and lost as she went to find Jean-Guy in the sitting room. "Emma's on the case. We're going to be moved out and gone and probably taking the piano with us. I never thought that would be the last time I saw that flat when we came up here."

They had been helping out at the café for five days before the Professor interrupted the silence of their evening meal by announcing, "I have another bulletin for those of you who wish to hear it."

Jean-Guy and Kathy immediately stopped eating and looked at him.

"I don't get much information through but all seems to be going well. Our perfect flight crew have kept out of the limelight as needed apart from one evening function where they were presented to President Brezhnev as an example of co-operation between two major military superpowers."

"So has the puppy been brought to heel?" Kathy wondered out loud.

The Prof smiled at her. "He is back in military uniform, years of training have kicked in and if you put a piano in front of him right now I could guarantee you he would keep his shoes on. The good news is they are on schedule to leave Moscow tomorrow morning and I believe they are flying into Schiphol first as the Secretary of State and his entourage are changing to a flight direct to Washington. Then Piers and Kerryanne bring the British contingent on to Heathrow and should get in fairly late tomorrow evening. Debriefing is estimated to take another two days. And that will be all I can tell you."

"Mission accomplished?" Jean-Guy asked. "Did he make contact with my parents or just with Leonid Brezhnev?"

"Not with your parents. If anyone has met with them it would have been Kerryanne. Piers is not getting directly involved in the actual operation as he isn't trained. The report said your parents are safe and well in Moscow and that is all I can say."

"So what the hell was all that about them being arrested?" Jean-Guy snapped. "Just another lie to get me out into the open? Will I even be safe once I have asylum here?"

Kathy laid a hand on his arm and the Professor spoke to him as soothingly as he could. "What we are hoping for you is Indefinite Leave to Remain which is the most secure status you can have. You will need to apply for British Citizenship in order to have full rights in the UK, but that is several years away."

"Or I could marry you," Kathy offered rashly; nervous but resolute as she looked at her sweet Moly.

The two men looked at her but neither spoke.

"Think about it," she said as the idea started to make more sense in her head. "It would solve a lot of problems."

"And create a lot more," the Professor told her. "It is not an easy option. I know Piers is going into a very strange marriage arrangement but I would advise you not to do the same. Especially as you've only known each other less than three months. That won't convince anyone at the Home Office."

Jean-Guy gave her a gentle kiss of gratitude. "And it is also what you have said you don't want."

Kathy looked into his eyes and thought how tired he looked. "I don't want to lose you even more than I don't want to get married. Did that make sense? I know what I mean."

"Eat your suppers," the Professor advised. "I just thought you'd like to know that it looks like Piers will be back with us in a few days and then you'll know where your trio is going."

Alison was putting out the fresh cakes again the next morning when Kathy and Jean-Guy arrived at the café at nine o'clock and her smile of greeting was genuinely warm so they wondered what Sarah had said to her.

"Quick chat before we open today," she told them. They sat at one of the indoor tables this time and she didn't offer them a drink. "I've been so grateful for the help you two have given me, but we can't go on like this. I've advertised for a couple of official paid summer helpers by putting a note in the shop window and I've had four people call by already this morning. You will always be welcome to come here, but the takings have been about four times what I thought they would be so it's time to get staff organised. Unless, of course, either of you wants to apply for the job?"

They exchanged a look. "No, it's just as well in a way," Kathy explained. "We should have Piers back in a couple of days and we really need to work on our music."

"Well, two of my prospective employees can start as soon as I want them to, so I asked them to call by later today for a trial shift. I'd like you two just to give me today and tomorrow if that's alright then if the new ones are as good as they ought to be I can let you go after close tomorrow." Alison looked at them shrewdly but kept her tone pleasant. "Have you heard from him at all while he's been away?"

"Not a word," Kathy replied truthfully.

"It's just that he does seem to have been away for a very long time."

"He hasn't flown commercially for two months," Kathy explained trying to remember what Piers had said over the last few weeks. "He needs to go through all sorts of training and accreditations before he can get his full licences back. He has classroom work and simulator work as well as flying while he's being observed. It all takes a long time but they have to make sure he's safe."

"Oh, OK. That's not how Sarah put it but she seems happy to trust him."

It seemed to be forever until the café closed even though it had been another busy day, and then they were free to be on their way back along the coast path with not many leftover cakes at all as business had been so brisk.

"That bloody Sarah," Jean-Guy muttered to Kathy. "She must have been gossiping with Alison. Thank Christ she has no idea where he has really gone. The sooner he stuffs her with babies and gets out of that relationship the happier I'll be."

"Me too. And Alison's not keen on it either. Thing is, Sarah's a gossip like her mother. Always has been. I think it's working in the shop that does it."

"I'm sure that's all it is, but gossips can do a lot of damage. We're going to have to be so careful. We don't know how many people here now are tourists so anyone could be some kind of enemy and if Piers is going into the Prof's line of work then we can never trust anybody ever again or we could betray him."

"Which is probably reason enough for the Prof to want to keep us here," Kathy mused. "No, that makes it sound like a punishment. I just hope Emma isn't upset by his idea as I never thought I could be as happy again as I've been here with you and Piers."

Jean-Guy was thankful to hear her say that. It meant she was looking forward and, in her own way, getting ready to move on. "So in your happy little world, where will we all be when we get ready to go on stage at Snape Maltings in September?"

Kathy thought about that for the rest of the way home. As they went into the garden she stopped and said determinedly, "You and I still won't be married but we'll be so happy together everyone will hate us. I don't think I want us to have kids just yet but maybe in a couple of years or so. Emma will have had a beautiful baby boy so the family line will be secured and they will be making plans to have at least another two. The Prof will have decided he's had enough of his secret life and will be engrossed in writing Roisin's biography with a load of other commissions coming up. Roisin herself will be in the audience with her charming Russian husband and their three no doubt incredibly beautiful children."

Jean-Guy waited but she said no more. "And Piers?" he prompted gently. "What is his fortune? Go on, what would you have happen to him in your perfect world?"

Kathy almost laughed. "Well, I'd make him want to give up flying so he could be part of our trio for ever and perhaps even be Roisin's accompanist again and I'd give him the most tender loving reunion with his first wife so he can ditch Sarah and still have the happy ever after."

"She made death threats against him in front of their divorce lawyers."

"I know. But you asked what would happen in my perfect world. My own little happy place where the hibiscus feeds the butterflies their nectar after all and doesn't beguile them then crush them to death."

"What the hell are you going on about now?"

"His tattoo. It's bothered me ever since I saw it. He sees himself as the flower who destroys hopes and dreams."

"You have a very vivid imagination. So if I tell him to get another butterfly put on which has escaped the flower, you will be happy?"

Glad to have been teased out of her mood, Kathy smiled at him. "Good luck with that. And just where is that burned-on pentangle you saw anyway?"

"It is on his left hip. He was undressing for his bath one night and I was working on a score at the dressing table but looked up to ask him something and just saw it quickly in the mirror. It was so terrible it made me swear. I think he was a bit embarrassed too."

They went into the kitchen where the Prof was preparing the evening meal but seemed to be even more absent minded than usual.

"We have a problem," he greeted them rather abruptly.

Kathy was still in her happy place and thought for a minute one of the cats had eaten the sausages. "Oh? Anything serious?"

"I hope not. The diplomatic mission is delayed in Moscow. Some kind of problem with the paperwork of one of the crew. We can't find out which one but I think they will manage to plead diplomatic immunity and it'll only be a short delay but they have lost their flight path to Schiphol because of it and have to wait to get clearance again."

"So we can't let our breath out just yet," Kathy remarked. "Do you want any help with supper?"

"Perhaps today yes, thank you. Can you peel some potatoes for me, please?"

And that acceptance of help worried Kathy more than anything. The Prof would normally never let her help in the kitchen.

Alison's two summer staff turned out to be a middle-aged village lady and a young local lad who had left school last year but was taking some time off before going to University in the autumn. They were both perfectly good and capable workers so Kathy and Jean-Guy switched from being unpaid temporary staff to customers having a free drink and cake by the middle of the morning.

They sat at one of the outside tables and looked across the beach to the sea.

"What's Moscow like?" Kathy asked curiously. "I've never been."

"It is a strange place. So many beautiful things in it and at the same time so much hard reality. One day I will take you to Red Square and you can see the churches with the onions on top. I think as a city I prefer Leningrad. But the best place of all is Prague. If ever we got married we would honeymoon in the Old City there and watch the stars in the sky from Charles bridge. There are some good walks along the Vltava too, especially in the autumn."

Kathy realised he had mentioned marriage and she hadn't panicked at the thought of it. There was a flicker of hope in her that maybe, just maybe, one day. She focussed on something else he had said instead "The what?"

"Vltava. It's the river that goes through Prague."

"Say it again. It sounds such a pretty name the way you say it."

"You must know your Smetana? Have you never played the piece? It's called after the river."

"Yes, but it sounds nicer the way you say it. So how do you say 'hello' in Czech?"

"Seriously? You want a Czech lesson now?"

"Why not. It's either that or think about delayed flights."

Alison was afraid she was going to have to ask them to move on as they were taking up a perfectly usable table while they chatted but before she really needed to they got up and slowly wandered off along the beach and she just caught a snatch of Jean-Guy speaking something foreign that wasn't French while Kathy watched his face very attentively and her love for him shone out of her eyes.

Both Kathy and Jean-Guy were aching from laughing at her attempts to speak even the most basic Czech when they got back to the farmhouse.

"Ah, good," the Prof greeted them. "You are in time for lunch today, I wasn't sure you would be. Some good news for you. The night flight from Moscow landed in the early hours of the morning at Schiphol so as soon as the crew have had their regulation rest period our diplomatic mission is expected to fly in to Heathrow at about tea time today. Apparently the first officer is far better qualified to bring a large passenger plane into Heathrow than is the captain so he will be taking off and landing for the last leg of the journey. And it seems our American friends got a bit careless and came back with one extra cabin crew member which is what caused the delay in the paperwork."

"Can you get a message across to Piers once they're back in the UK?" Jean-Guy asked and Kathy wondered what he was plotting.

"I expect so, if it's something important. I understand the debriefings will take place in London."

"I think I can honestly say that Kathy's happiness depends on it," Jean-Guy said and tried not to laugh.

"I'm telling you, he'll never agree to it," Kathy told him, having worked it out.

"Want to bet?"

"OK, if he does then it's my turn to bake. I've had lots of tips from Alison so I'll make whatever cake you like."

"Lemon drizzle?"

Kathy offered her hand. "Done."

The two shook hands and Jean-Guy realised he was starting to get the hang of this English backchat. It would take him a while to get to Piers' standard but it was a definite start.

"What are you talking about?" the Prof asked, confused but glad to see them so happy.

"Butterflies," the other two said in unison.

They didn't hurry lunch that day and as they ate tinned peaches for dessert, Kathy, trying to sound as nonchalant as she could, asked the Professor, "What do you know about Piers' wife? First wife I suppose we'll be calling her in a few days' time."

"Quite a lot. She had to be vetted too before he could work for us. But without her knowing she was being vetted. No problems with anything. In fact I gather she is a perfectly charming woman."

"Did she marry again?"

"Kathy, what are you scheming now in that head of yours? Chantal went back to her maiden name of Montgomery after the divorce and she has never remarried. Also soon after the divorce she changed from working in Casualty to became a paediatric nurse. She is now at Great Ormond Street as a critical care specialist nurse and her reputation is second to none. She has no children of her own but has helped bring life back to so many for other people, and when asked by a very sympathetic operative working undercover she said she feels her life is blessed. She regularly attends the local Pentecostal church in Tooting where she has lived since her marriage was dissolved. Her ex-husband paid her off in a lump sum so she receives no alimony and she hasn't heard from him or of him since they walked out of the divorce court and she said many bitter things to him in the heat of her anger. She has made her peace with herself and with her God and I think we should leave it there, don't you?"

"She sounds lovely," Kathy said wistfully and really wished there could be a happy ending for the nurse too.

"You are such a dreamer," Jean-Guy told her lovingly. "The Prof has just told you, a little more politely than Piers did, to butt out of his love life so I think you should respect that, don't you?"

"It wasn't an easy marriage even in the best of times," the Prof cautioned. "But I know what that look on your face means so to satisfy your curiosity, I will tell you what I have been told. Chantal's father was in the RAF during the war which is why that was all she ever dreamed of doing. So, along with her older brother she booked herself a ticket on the *Windrush* and came over from Jamaica in 1948 and as soon as she was old enough she signed up for the Air Force. Mixed marriages are not easy even now and back in 1954 when they married it was virtually unheard of. They both got abused for what they had done and I think it was probably a blessing in the end that they didn't have children. The fractures had started before his commission was up and he didn't renew it. They tried living with her family in Jamaica but their marriage was pretty much over by the time they came to the UK, and that would have been sometime in the mid seventies. I think they tried so hard to make it work, but the external pressures were too much."

Kathy wiped a tear from her face and hadn't realised she was crying. "But that's horrible. Why couldn't they just have been left alone to be in love with each other?"

"Kathy," Jean-Guy reminded her gently, "it wasn't Chantal who finally broke up the marriage."

"I know," she admitted sadly. "But that's what would happen in my perfect world."

"Dreamer," the Prof smiled. "Who wants some coffee?"

They knew the diplomatic flight had landed at Heathrow but then the radio waves went silent again and the early days of April ticked away. By the middle of the second week, Jean-Guy and Kathy didn't dare go into the village in case they met either Sarah or Alison who were going to want to know why there was still no sign of the bridegroom with just a few days to go until the wedding. Eventually the vicar rang the farmhouse to ask what was going on as he liked to hold a rehearsal even for such a small wedding, and it wasn't going to be the same if the bride used her friend as a substitute for the groom at the rehearsal and he just turned up on the day.

Reluctantly, on the Friday before the wedding day, Jean-Guy and Kathy reported to the church where not so long ago Emma had got married and had to tell the vicar that the groom still wasn't around but they were convinced he would be and that they would tell him what he had to do.

The vicar was going to call off the wedding but Sarah's mother took him aside for some words and he very reluctantly agreed it could go ahead as it was such a minimal ceremony. Sarah already knew that Piers' first wedding had been a military affair, conducted on an airbase somewhere overseas and was clearly furious to find out just how brief a stripped-back church wedding was going to be. But, to Kathy's admiration, she didn't ask the vicar to sneak more prayers and blessings back into it.

With icy politeness Alison asked them if they would like to come across to the café for coffee but Sarah stormed off back to the shop saying they were very busy. With some vague idea of soothing the angry friend of the bride, Kathy and Jean-Guy followed her through the village and into the café where the outside tables were busy but it was quiet inside. Alison didn't quite slap their drinks on the table in front of them but there was certainly no cake on offer.

The two sat next to each other feeling like a pair of scolded children and didn't dare say anything while they had their drinks and wondered what they could do to start making things a bit better.

"Is this seat taken?" a familiar voice asked and the two looked up into the twinkling blue eyes of the man with neatly cut raven-black hair, who didn't wait for a reply but thankfully dumped his bag and coat and sat at the table with them.

"Where the hell have you been?" Jean-Guy hissed. "You've just missed the wedding rehearsal and I think either Alison or Sarah is going to hang you upside by the toes."

Kathy loved it when Jean-Guy didn't quite get his English phrases right. "What happened?" she asked a bit more warmly and she could feel the smile of relief on her face.

"Total balls up with the paperwork. It looked at one point as though Kerryanne was going to be arrested. The Soviet police had her in for questioning at any rate."

"Why her? I can't believe she'd be so careless."

"She wasn't, but as the captain of the flight she is responsible for knowing who is on board and logging the flight plan. They'd managed to get one of their own out and thought they could just hide him among the cabin crew but the Soviets did a head count before we took off and found it didn't add up."

Alison came across to the table. "Can I get you anything?" she asked politely as she didn't know who this customer was after all. She just saw a very good-looking man in a scruffy blue shirt that needed ironing and what looked like jeans that had seen better days and extremely battered walking boots. He had thrown a tatty waxed cotton coat over the back of the chair and dropped a canvas kitbag on the floor before he sat down and he didn't appear to be wearing any jewellery.

"Oh, thanks. Just an iced latte please," he requested.

"Alison," Kathy said, realising the other woman didn't know. "This is Piers. The nearly runaway bridegroom."

"Where the hell have you been?" she asked angrily. "We thought you'd reneged on your deal with Sarah."

"It's not a 'deal'," he pointed out coldly. "So far as I can tell I'm getting damn all out of it."

"Except permission from your wife to sleep around. Have you spoken to her yet?"

"Not that it's any of your bloody business but yes I have. I've just been into the shop to tell her I'm back and she told me I'd find these two over here. She also told me to expect a bloody hostile reception from you which, quite frankly, I don't think you have any right to give me. Now please may I have that coffee and I'll get in another round for my friends. Thank you. And I'll also thank you to stay well over by your counter and butt out of our conversation."

Kathy found this unseen side of Piers rather intimidating and wondered if all Wing Commanders were so brutal. She wasn't surprised when Alison sent the young lad over with the drinks and she could almost see the steam coming out of Alison's ears at being spoken to like that.

"She says these are on the house," the lad offered and almost ran away into the kitchen where sounds of washing up could then be heard.

Kathy and Jean-Guy looked across to Alison and smiled their thanks which seemed to help a little but Piers turned his chair slightly so his back was towards the counter.

"Sorry," he said shortly. "But the mood I'm in right now I could cheerfully kill someone and that bloody bitch is first in my firing line."

To Jean-Guy's unspoken admiration, Kathy took hold of Piers' hand that didn't have a ring on it any more and just asked him gently, "What's happened? Here, try the mocha, they really are good. And then just take a couple of deep breaths and tell us what's got you so wound up."

He took the breath then obediently tried the mocha. "Yup, that's good," he agreed and sounded a bit calmer. "Well, good news first, your parents are fine. But I thought I was never going to get away. I've had an Air Vice Marshall of all things, as well as some bloke in a suit both trying to recruit me separately and together, and it wasn't pleasant to put it mildly. They stopped just short of physical violence but the mind games and threats were getting bloody serious towards the end. It finished up with an official warning that if I put so much as one toenail out of line they'll have me up on so many charges under the Official Secrets Act I'll never see the outside of a prison again. Then they got me to sign so many secrecy agreements I was beginning to wonder if I was spelling my name right."

"So what happens now?" Kathy asked.

He finally smiled. "Well, on Monday I'm getting married, then after a decent length of time with my bride, let's say Wednesday, I'm cleared to go back to London and to work. Retraining, accreditations and more training but should be back to full duties by the end of the month. And I believe I have a concert to play in on September eighth. Come on, drink up, I need a decent night's sleep in my own bed."

Back in the sanctuary of the farmhouse it was as though Piers shed a prickly outer layer. Some lunch and a snooze later he joined the other two in the sitting room still in his scruffy clothes but minus the walking boots and sat at the piano. He dumped a couple of parcels on the top of the piano but didn't comment on them.

"Start with the Dvorak?" he asked and they bolted to get their instruments while a delighted Audrey took up her post next to the parcels.

Kathy and Jean-Guy could not believe how much Piers' playing had improved. He tossed off the most technically demanding parts of the work as though they were pieces for a beginner and the three ran straight through the piece without stopping.

"Bloody hell," Jean-Guy said at the end. "What the hell has happened to you?"

"Two things, which I can tell you now there are no public ears flapping on the sideline. Firstly our Russian hosts put me and Kerryanne in a suite in what had been some kind of imperial palace, and in that suite was a grand piano. They said we were to ask for anything we wanted so I asked for the music to the Dvorak. I had many hours to kill while Kerryanne did whatever it was she was doing in Moscow, so I did a lot of piano practice. Got out and about a bit with the official guide for a propaganda-fuelled look at Moscow with some of the other delegates. One of the Soviets looking after us is a bit of a pianist himself so we got talking with his bad

English and my zero Russian and some communal sign language, and he told me the piano in the suite used to be in the Tsar's palace and it was rumoured the royal children had played on it. They can't have tuned the thing since those kids last played it but funnily enough within twenty four hours a piano tuner had been in. And secondly, our friend Andrei got Kerryanne in on a masterclass at the Conservatoire as one of his friends is studying piano there. She told me not to go because of my connection with you and there is always a chance I could go back to the Soviet Union quite openly as a musician. Which was kind of annoying as I wanted to go but I had to pretend I was sick and I'm sure you can guess who was taking it?"

There was a kind of startled gulp from the man sitting behind the cello.

"Yup. A gentleman by the name of Professor Karel Dechaume. Kerryanne went and talked to him after the class and told him her co-pilot was a piano player. What else she might have told him, I don't know but she must have somehow implied I knew you musically. He knew she'd come in on the Anglo/US diplomatic mission and he is a very smart man so he somehow managed to ditch Andrei and took Kerryanne along to his study for some tea. Which was just as well as Kerryanne and I were quite aware our suite was bugged both aurally and visually so there was no way we could have talked with him there."

"How is he?" Jean-Guy hardly dared ask.

"Missing his children. They've guessed but don't know you're in the UK and she couldn't tell them. Once you've got some kind of asylum then you can tell them yourself." He looked across at their violin player. "Piglet,

330

what is going through that tiny brain of yours? You look as though you're about to explode."

Kathy couldn't contain her laughter any longer. "It's just that with you and Kerryanne sharing a suite, and with all the monitoring equipment and things in your room…"

He understood where she was going. "Sorry, Piglet. Signed the secrecy agreement on that one."

"Is that going to be your get-out clause for everything from now on?"

"Yup, pretty much. Fancy a bit of Mozart to calm us all down?"

So they played Jean-Guy's favourite *Trio in B flat* and then Piers said to them, sounding a bit disappointed, "I was quite sure you two would be bugging me for souvenirs by now and you haven't said a word."

"You haven't exactly been on holiday," Kathy pointed out. "But did you bring us something then?"

"Of course." He picked up the parcels from on top of the piano and handed them out. "Can't lie; I had some help with these."

Kathy unwrapped a knitted lace shawl in the finest grey yarn she had ever seen and it was the softest thing she had ever touched. Inside the shawl was a bottle of perfume with a rather classy French name.

"According to Kerryanne that is an Orenburg shawl made using hairs from goats in the Ural mountains and just what you need to keep out the Siberian wind round here. Turns out she's another knitting person like you. And that's a bottle of the perfume she wears. I saw the look on your face when you met her so I asked her to get me some via the US Embassy diplomatic bag."

Jean-Guy looked a bit puzzled by the paper bag he had been given then he opened it and for one slightly frightening moment Kathy thought he was going to cry. "What is it?" she asked.

"Tea," was the rather surprising reply. "It is a blend my mother makes up from about four different kinds of tea and to me it is the smell and taste of my childhood and home. It is the best thing you could possibly have brought me. Thank you, but how did you manage it?"

"Your father handed it in at the place we were staying and said it was for Kerryanne as she had complimented him on the tea he gave her and, in the spirit of the mission that had brought her to Moscow, he thought she might like to take some for her family. The shawl she knitted while we were out there." He suddenly laughed. "She can knit like a crazy thing, never seen needles move so fast." He turned to Kathy. "She got the yarn out there and when she'd made it gave it to me and said it was for you. I think she thought you're my girlfriend but I doubt if we'll see each other again so not going to worry about it. Something else for you too."

"What?" she asked, still enchanted by the shawl.

"You didn't, did you?" Jean-Guy asked catching the other man's eye.

"Bloody did too. I'm on the promise of a lemon drizzle here."

Kathy caught on and shot across to the piano. With more disbelief than dignity she hauled up the back of his shirt. Heading towards his left shoulder, flying determinedly away from the flower was a beautifully drawn delta-wing moth.

Monday morning was a perfect spring day on the east coast of Suffolk. Nine o'clock was late enough in the morning for the early-rising birdwatchers to have bought their takeaway coffees and gone and too early for the main gathering of visitors so there were eight people who reported to the church as Alison felt she could leave her two staff members in charge for half an hour. Sarah's parents decided to close the shop just for that half hour rather than pay someone to be there and they too joined the small group in the church. There were several curious villagers outside but nobody followed the bridal party inside.

Kathy had no idea a church wedding could be such a simple affair. Sarah Francesca Strowger and Piers Kyne Buchanan made a quiet exchange of vows and rings, were declared man and wife then the register was signed and it was all over. Her parents went back to the shop and the Prof gave his excuses and went home which left the other five to go across to the café where Alison had made a little two-tier wedding cake and had laid one of the inside tables with a white cloth and some flowers.

"My gift to you," she told the newlyweds. "It's the only kind of reception you're going to get, you poor sods. It just seems so wrong to be drinking your health with coffee."

"Oh, don't worry," Sarah smiled and admired the rings on her finger. "Barry's expecting us all down the pub this evening. Oh, and, Kathy, he said please can you wear your red dress and dunk yourself in the sea before you go there as he'd never seen anything so sexy in all his life."

Kathy had never been called sexy before. Even Richard hadn't used that word and she could feel herself getting hotter and hotter with embarrassment.

"She looks a bit flushed to me," Jean-Guy remarked. "Do you think maybe a cold dip in the North Sea will cool her down?"

She just knew that given half a chance those two men would have had her down the beach and into the sea, dressed in the one good skirt she had brought with her. "Don't you dare!" she warned them and looked like a startled deer about to make a run for it. To her relief they just exchanged a look and a smile and clearly couldn't be bothered to interrupt their coffees.

After the reception, the bride and groom wandered through the village to her house, Alison went back to work as trade was building up and Jean-Guy and Kathy returned to the farmhouse along the coast path taking with them a sizeable chunk of wedding cake for the Prof.

"Barry's quite right, you know," Jean-Guy told her as they meandered quietly along with their arms round each other. "I'd never seen anything as hot as you in that wet dress either. Please wear a red dress in September."

"At least you didn't say a wet dress," she laughed. "Sarah's mum is making me a blue one."

They stopped and exchanged a few gentle kisses. "I'm sure she could make you a red one too?"

"I'm sure she could," Kathy agreed. "Do you know what? That really was a lovely wedding. No fuss like Emma had, no messing about with dresses and hair appointments. No bridesmaids, hundreds of pounds worth of flowers, two hundred guests all over the house and a string quartet nobody was listening to or anything like that. I mean I know it's not going to be a proper marriage but that really was a truly beautiful wedding. Just a simple ceremony and you could tell those two really do love each other. I hope they find a way to make it work."

Jean-Guy wasn't totally convinced about that but he saw an opportunity and took it. "Would you have one like it?"

"Maybe," she agreed dreamily. "One day. But not just yet."

They went into the kitchen by the back door as they had done so many times before but although the Prof was in the kitchen he wasn't alone. Sitting at the table with him were a middle-aged man and a woman who had such a sense of serenity about her even the cats were sitting in an orderly row in front of the Aga.

"Oh," Kathy exclaimed. "Didn't know you were expecting visitors. We've brought back some wedding cake."

"Thank you, that was thoughtful of Alison. This is Chantal Montgomery and her Pastor, John Stevens."

Kathy felt as though a block of ice was sliding down her insides. "It's lovely to meet you. But I'm so sorry, he just got married a couple of hours ago."

Chantal smiled at the two in the doorway. "I know. I haven't come to marry him. I've prayed for guidance many times over the last few weeks as I've felt I needed to see Piers again if only once and now I've come to make my final peace."

Kathy didn't want to hear what this lovely, gentle woman was going to say next and she could feel the tears at the backs of her eyes.

"I have breast cancer and my prognosis isn't bad but it's not that good. The treatment is going to be long and hard and I know my God wants me to say some kind of goodbye."

"He's only at Sarah's. If we phone him now and he borrows her dad's car he could be here in ten minutes," Kathy offered.

"No, sweetheart, let him go. It's probably better this way. Even after all my prayers I'm not sure I have the strength to see him again now I'm here."

Kathy knew how Piers would feel about this. "Don't you think he might like to say goodbye to you too? He loved you so much once and if we tell him you came and then left again you'll break his heart."

Chantal's smile was warm and somehow sad at the same time. "No, he'll understand. He did much the same to me in the early years of our marriage." She realised they deserved a bit of an explanation. "He had headaches so bad they would make him sick for days and the medics thought it was a brain tumour. He was twenty three and they told him he could die of it. Fortunately tests and a different doctor diagnosed migraines so they said he wasn't going to die of it but he couldn't fly any more. I think he'd rather have died. We were in Hong Kong at the time, we both loved it there, but if he couldn't fly then that would be the end of the posting and probably his career in the RAF." She looked at the others. "You don't need me to explain what that would have meant to him. So I did some research of my own and, against the advice of the MO, took him to an acupuncturist in Kowloon." She got to her feet and started buttoning up her coat. "Does he have the headaches now?"

"Never known him to have one," Kathy replied. "And he's still flying so guess not."

"Good. The acupuncturist said it would work as long as he kept the stitches in his ear. Anyway, we must be on our way. The Pastor and I are due in his brother's church in Colchester for lunch. I'm sorry in a way to have missed Piers but I think it's for the best." She paused and smiled the saddest smile Kathy had ever seen. "Please give him my love and my blessing," she said to her.

There was a lengthy silence in the kitchen while people tried to understand things that were so unfamiliar. Petr Mihaly almost visibly shook himself back to reality. "When do you start your treatment?" he asked, quietly practical.

Chantal recovered her smile. "I'm having the initial operation in just a couple of days. They're not sure how extensive the tumour is and if it's gone through to the spine or lungs then I will be on palliative care. If God has seen fit to spare me, it will be a mastectomy and then chemo and radiotherapy but it will be a long course of treatment."

"I think you're so brave," Kathy said and, even though this woman was almost a total stranger, she really wanted to give her a hug and cry. "Will you let us know how you get on? Either way?"

Chantal seemed a bit surprised that someone she had only just met should be so caring. "Yes, of course. Thank you." She seemed to wonder if she wanted to ask the next question but she was naturally curious. "Who is it he's married today?"

"Oh," Kathy exclaimed, somehow not expecting that. "She's a lovely local girl called Sarah. They only met a few months ago so we were all a bit surprised."

She knew it wouldn't be a good idea to tell this childless woman that all Sarah wanted out of her new husband was a family.

Chantal's smile became a small laugh. "That sounds like him. Well, I hope he'll be happy this time. We had to wait until he was eighteen and then it was a mess as he had no family so he had to be made some kind of Ward of Court with the RAF as his legal guardian." She shook her head at the memory. "My family thought I was out of my mind too but we were young and just didn't care. Is Sarah quite young?"

"Mid thirties, I think," Kathy offered. "I've only ever known her as the girl in the shop. But she's really very nice when you get to know her."

Chantal thought about that too. "Well, we survived twenty years married to each other but I think if you offered us the chance to do it again, we'd both refuse."

"Do you still love him?" Kathy wanted to know then thought that was probably a bit forward considering she'd only just met the other woman.

This time Chantal did laugh. "Oh, yes. He's an easy man to love, a hard one to live with and an even harder one to leave. Anyway, we really must be on our way. My problem is I'll stay and chat for hours."

The Prof had to return her smile. "You will always be welcome here," he told her. "And if Piers says otherwise I'll remind him whose house it is." The three residents walked their guests to the front door and the Prof opened it for them. "I hope all goes well for you," he said to Chantal. "And even more I hope we'll see you again."

"Yes," she said thoughtfully. "It's so beautiful here." Chantal turned back and looked into the house that had been such a sanctuary, and impetuously kissed Kathy on the cheek. "Look after him," she said quietly, then stepped out into the sunlight.

Resurrection

The day after the wedding Kathy and Jean-Guy walked along to the beach café, not sure if they hoped to see Piers or not. The Prof had suggested, and they had agreed, not to phone Piers on his wedding day to tell him his first wife had turned up. He would be back soon enough now he was due to return to work and the Prof would give him the news then. When they got to the café they could tell Alison was in a foul mood and they were grateful it was the quiet but efficient Steph who brought their order across to the table where they sat outside enjoying the April sunshine.

"Word to the wise," she said very softly. "Someone is hopping mad today."

"Is it because Sarah has got married?" Kathy asked.

"I think that's something to do with it, but when she's in that mood I don't ask too many questions."

Kathy and Jean-Guy didn't chat much while they drank their coffees and weren't sure what to say when the reportedly 'hopping mad' Alison came across to their table as Steph and Josh were perfectly able to cope.

"Hi," Alison said pleasantly enough as she sat with them. "So what did he tell you about this marriage? Sarah told me it was just a piece of paper to legitimise their kids and he wasn't going to be hanging around once he'd done what he had to do. So maybe they aren't going to assume it'll happen on their wedding night but he knows the terms of the deal. Gets her pregnant then clears out."

Kathy was rather taken aback by the brutality of that. "But how was it ever a 'deal'?" she asked, thinking she'd have one last try. "I mean what did he get out of it?"

"You mean apart from my girlfriend?" Alison asked cynically and her eyes never left Kathy's face. "He gets ten grand out of it."

"What?!" Kathy exclaimed, not wanting to believe her but somehow now it all made some kind of horrible sense.

"Her parents paid him to marry her. They and Sarah explained about the entail of the shop and how illegitimate daughters can't inherit."

"But isn't there a law against that kind of thing?" Kathy asked, appalled but somehow not surprised Piers would do something like that.

"In old-fashioned terms, his wife came with a dowry. If she dies before they have children he can't inherit the shop as her family estate is entailed down the female side so it would all go to her cousin Margaret who currently lives in Tasmania."

"And have they paid him yet?" Jean-Guy asked thinking that although the explanation made the marriage make more sense, he disliked it more than ever.

"Half on marriage and the other half on a successful pregnancy." Alison said coldly. "I didn't know the full terms myself until I got Sarah to tell me all about it just before she walked out of the house to marry him."

"So has he taken the first payment?" Kathy asked.

"Yes. Her parents had it wired through to his bank account yesterday afternoon. Can you believe he banks with bloody Coutts? He said it was something they used to do for RAF recruits. Bloody snob. They've both said they don't want to live with each other which at least means as soon as she has our daughter he'll get the hell out of all our lives and stay out."

"I can't believe it," Kathy protested faintly. She didn't want to believe it as she had thought Piers and Sarah were getting quite fond of each other. Or maybe she had just seen what she wanted to see.

"Oh, believe it," Alison said nastily. "At least the mercenary little bastard has been doing what they've paid him to do."

Kathy saw the genuine hatred on Alison's face and somewhere inside her a warning bell was starting to ring.

The residents of the farmhouse didn't see Piers again until he came on Thursday morning to pack up his things ready to be at the airport for work on Saturday.

"How's married life suiting you?" Kathy asked him a little more bluntly than she had intended when he walked into the kitchen as they were having their morning cups of coffee.

Piers just shrugged and wouldn't sit at the table with them but stood leaning the small of his back against the Aga as though trying to ease an ache in his spine. "OK I suppose. Anyway, back to work tomorrow. So, Piglet, I'll have to take the Land Rover back with me which I'm afraid leaves you on the train." He half smiled at her. "I'm assuming you've got clearance to leave too?"

Kathy looked at the Prof who gave her a vague smile. "Piers has been cleared," he explained, "but he is being monitored. If we don't pick up any signs he's of interest to anyone then I hope you'll be able to go home in a week or two."

Kathy was almost sad to hear that. It was as though the best holiday ever was coming to an end. "I've got a gig at the end of the month which still stands so far as I know. Will it be OK to ring Jane? I'd guess if she's got bookings for me then that's it. I can go too." She distracted herself with practical things. "Now Jean-Guy and I are living here at least part of the time I can leave behind most of the stuff I brought so the train will be fine for me."

"And that's another thing," Piers remembered. "Prof, is it OK if Audrey stays with you, please? I don't think she'd have much of a life in London."

Petr Mihaly glanced at the little tortoiseshell cat who was on top of the Aga and rubbing her face adoringly on Piers' sleeve. "Of course. But you'll be back here, won't you?"

Piers looked faintly astonished. "Well, no. I mean it's been good of you to put me up, but I've got no reason to be here. I'll come up here a few more times and stay with Sarah until she's sorted out but I won't need to come to Suffolk after that as it's been made perfectly clear to me that I won't be wanted." He almost smiled but his voice was bitter. "So that'll be two marriages I'll have screwed up. I think I'll regret ending the first one more." There was a heavy silence in the kitchen and he saw the way the other three exchanged a look. "What?"

It was the older man who told him. "I knew about you by reputation but I was given my instructions and now I have got to know you better I am glad to have had you live here as I think it has done you a lot of good. I like to hope that maybe you will think of us as your family as I have to give you some news and I don't know how you will cope with it." He had got the full attention of the other man now and continued kindly, "We had a visit from your ex-wife on your wedding day. She traced you through the airline who contacted those I work for and the message came through here. I gave consent for her to be told this address thinking perhaps she would just write to you."

Piers sounded more suspicious than happy. "So how is she? I hope she's well and happy. I don't expect her to have forgiven me."

The Prof sighed and thought this wasn't getting any easier for either of them. "Chantal wasn't here long and I'm not even sure she wants us to tell you what she said but I honestly think you need to know."

Kathy watched Piers very closely as he listened to what the Prof had to tell him about Chantal but his face gave nothing away.

Piers was silent for a long time after the Prof had finished. He looked away from the others towards the window where the April sunshine was lighting up the garden and he sniffed a bit and blinked but didn't speak. Kathy reached out to touch his hand but he snatched it out of her reach.

"We're so sorry," she offered. "I don't know if you want to get in touch with her after all that happened between you? I mean she did come here presumably to talk to you but she didn't ask for us to even tell you she'd been."

"No, she wouldn't have," he said quietly. "Please excuse me, but I have to go and pack."

He left the room and the three at the table looked at each other.

"Not good," the Prof muttered half to himself.

"He's pretty upset," Kathy agreed. "I'm surprised."

"What are we going to do?" Jean-Guy asked in general to the other two.

"What do you mean?" Kathy replied, genuinely not understanding.

"I have listened to what Piers has been saying and it is not what I had been thinking would happen. I liked your flat in Earl's Court and I'm sure we will be very happy sharing Piers' house but now he speaks as though he is going to go out of our lives again. I think I will go and talk to him."

"Is that such a good idea?" Kathy asked. "The Prof has just given him some pretty shattering news about the woman he used to be in love with and from the way he's gone off like that I'm guessing maybe he wants some time to work things out in his own mind."

"I have to agree with Kathy," the Prof added. "I think we leave him for now to sort out what he wants to do. I hope we don't lose him. But there is a chance we may."

They didn't see Piers again until nearly supper time when he came into the sitting room where Jean-Guy had gone back to his cello practice and Kathy was knitting. Jean-Guy was running through his part to the Grieg Sonata and he didn't stop as the other man went quietly across to the piano, found the music and picked up the piano part in the middle of the second movement without saying a word and without interrupting the soloist.

Movement over, Jean-Guy stopped playing and looked at his accompanist. "Thank you for that. It makes so much more sense with the piano. Have you made decisions?"

"Yes," came the positive reply. "As you know, Chantal and I split very acrimoniously. I tried to talk to her but she told me to go to hell. She'd filed for divorce within the month and I didn't contest it. She took pretty much everything we had and then demanded a financial settlement too. My solicitor told me to declare myself bankrupt as I wouldn't then be legally obliged to pay her but I couldn't do it. It would have been like cheating on her all over again. So I paid her in instalments as agreed between our solicitors. I was cold and hungry and I honestly felt that she had sent me to the hell she believed I deserved. Finally paid her off and got the Decree Absolute. Not long after that I won a settlement in another court case which got me out of the godawful rental I'd been in and paid the deposit on my house and I started getting my finances back on track. I'm hoping that her visit means that maybe she has found some kind of forgiveness. So I'm now going back to work in London. but I'll need to visit here until Sarah's had her baby, then she and I can decide what we're going to do long term. Problem is, I have a feeling she's not going to want to stop at one, even if the firstborn is a girl. So, in spite of what you've been thinking, I'll still be available to be your pianist, and we'll just have to see where it all goes."

"And Chantal?" Kathy asked before she could stop herself.

He smiled, but there was no humour in it. "Yes. My ex and first wife. I'll return the politeness she's offered and when I'm back home I'll ring her brother I've no idea where she's living now and if he's moved then that's the end. But I'll give her one shot and that's it." Audrey leaned across from the top of the piano and gave him a loving head-butt and a loud chirrup. "I'd just like to talk to Chantal now there are some years between us, and hope we can make some kind of peace."

Kathy and Jean-Guy exchanged a glance across the room as they realised that their third was still in love with the woman he had cheated on all those years ago and her reappearance in his life was cracking open some old and very deep wounds.

Consoled by the knowledge that Piers would be back with them, it wasn't so hard to say goodbye to him on the Thursday but it did seem odd in the farmhouse with his room clean and tidy with the bed stripped and none of his possessions in the house. It was a beautiful day on the Friday so Kathy and Jean-Guy walked into the village breathing in the soft sea air and neither of them envying Piers being stuck in an aeroplane cockpit and having to concentrate on his job while they were free to enjoy the air and the walk. But both did realise that he was probably perfectly happy to be back where he belonged and really wouldn't care that he was smelling aviation fuel rather than the salty North Sea.

They went into the shop first and found only Sarah in there, busily putting stock out while she didn't have any customers to serve for a few moments. She looked round when the shop door pinged and smiled broadly in greeting.

"Well, good morning to you two. Piers get off alright yesterday?"

"Yes, fine. He's got to do a lot of retraining but we got the distinct impression he couldn't wait to get back there."

Sarah's smile became a little wry. "Yes, I thought that too. Oh well, at least Alison isn't in such a grump with me now he's gone off for a while. I don't know what's the matter with her. This is something we've talked about for years, even before she went back to Cambridge."

Kathy put two packets of custard creams and a jar of peanut butter on the counter. "What do you mean?" she asked curiously.

Sarah looked towards the door but there weren't any signs of approaching customers. She sighed quietly, just once. "Alison and I have been together for years. I knew my mum wanted me to have children, so Alison told me that I should get myself a husband then I could kick him out and she and I would live together. This was years ago. I said I couldn't be that horrible to anyone so we had a row and that's when she went back to Cambridge saying I was being horrible to her."

The warning bell ringing so loudly in Kathy's brain she thought the other two could probably hear it. "Hang on. Are you saying this whole sham marriage thing is Alison's idea?"

"Well, almost. I mean she and I thought I'd cope with marrying some local farm worker or another and I'd just use him for what I wanted, then she'd tell him to go away." She stopped and looked down at the counter. "But then," she continued unhappily, "I met Piers and so I rang Alison and said I'd found a man who would do what we wanted and she wanted to know all about him. So I told her and she said I couldn't have him."

"Why?" Kathy prompted, liking this story less and less the more it went on.

"Alison said he's too smart. He'd work out it was just a plot and he would never agree to it." Sarah looked back up at them and her eyes were swimming with tears. "But there was one thing we hadn't thought of. I was stupid and I got fond of him so I told him the whole truth and he was really shocked I'd even think of doing that to him. But I knew I'd never find someone else and he was going to walk out on me but I begged him not to and that's when Mum said she'd pay him to go through with it. He got really angry, I didn't think he had such a temper on him, so I was crying and Mum was crying and it was awful. So I rang Alison and she said 'good' and I was to get rid of him and she'd find me someone in Cambridge and bring him with her. This all happened while Piers was still with me and when I told him what she'd said he just went all quiet and said he'd do it. Alison hates him but I've told the two of them they've at least got to be civil to each other while we're together. He hates her just as much too. He accused her flat out of bullying me so she threw a plate at him. Fortunately she can't throw straight but from the look on his face he could have killed her." Sarah rang up Kathy's purchase on the till. "Never mind, he's away for a while now so Alison has settled down a lot. Piers and I could never live together properly anyway so I hope we'll sort something out that suits us all."

Neither Kathy nor Jean-Guy felt like going across to the café after that conversation but they walked back along the path for the most part in silence, not sure what to say. The only thing they did decide was to tell the Prof all about it and it was some comfort to see that he clearly wasn't happy about Sarah's revelations either.

"My advice," he offered in the end, "is to do exactly what Piers told us to do at the beginning and stay right out of it. I will monitor things as best I can officially but I have no idea what else we can do. They're all grown-ups, it seems young Piers knows exactly what he is letting himself in for and at least Sarah had the courage to be totally honest with him."

"It smells bad," Kathy told him.

"Yes, it does. There is something very wrong with the whole set-up and I don't like it any more than you do. But I have a feeling that underneath all the training and calmness, Piers is still a very volatile Irishman and it sounds as though Alison is scratching her way through his armour and I don't want to think of what will happen if she really provokes his temper. He will laugh about it with us, but just think for a moment. His father and uncle were training him to fight for their cause. He has skills and secrets in his past that he has buried for a long time and I don't want to see them come to the surface. I just wish there was a way we could warn Alison to back off and leave him alone."

There was a silence between the three of them for a while and it was Jean-Guy who spoke for all of them. "Well, I hope Sarah has her daughter very soon and then perhaps it will all be over and I will get my accompanist back. Because I am not letting that one go now I have found him."

Nobody in the farmhouse was expecting Piers to ring them on the Tuesday evening of the next week.

350

Kathy answered the phone as she had been passing the one in the hall when it rang.

Piglet, hi. Glad I've caught you. Don't suppose you and Jean-Guy fancy a trip to London to suss out your new home do you?"

The excitement began to bubble up inside her. "Am I free to leave now too?"

"I'd guess so. Check with the Prof but I've been notified I'm no longer being monitored so there's something changed in the background. It's just that I've had Emma on the phone to say the piano's moving across on Thursday and I'm not going to be here."

"I'll check with the Prof, but it's sounding promising."

"Emma and Derek are hoping to come up tomorrow so I've no idea how that will work out as I've only got one spare bed and I'm sure all four of you don't want to share it."

"Could be interesting," Kathy agreed. "But you must have got a sofa we can sleep on?"

There was a quiet snort of laughter. "Yes. If you're five foot nothing and don't mind a few lumps."

"Hey, I'm only five foot two on a good day. I'll fit. OK, one or both of us will be along tomorrow, depending on what the Prof says."

"Thanks, Piglet. Just got back from the airport and I'm bloody hungry."

"Been flying?"

"Oh, yes. New York and back in two days. See you tomorrow."

Somehow Kathy wasn't surprised that Jean-Guy was advised to stay hidden but Kathy was cleared to go.

351

The Prof offered no details and they had learned not to ask.

It was odd to leave Earl's Court Tube station and without going straight up Hogarth Road and Kathy was quite pleased with herself for even remembering how to get to Piers' house from the station. She knew it was the right place as in the car port were the black Ferrari and Derek's Ford Capri and she could see the faithful old Land Rover was back home with the neighbour. Just for a moment she paused on the pavement and looked up at the house that was going to be her latest home. The whole building looked tired and shabby compared to most of the others in the street and it didn't match the others in the row which all had two downstairs windows with a central front door while hers had one big window and an extra-wide door at the front. She could see that at one time there had been quite a large window beautifully positioned in the centre of the building on the first floor but it was now boarded over so she had no idea where that was on the inside. The half of the house over the car port looked even shabbier as the windows were filthy and there was ivy growing out of one of the roof gutters.

She went past the cars in the car port and knocked on the side door, impatient now to be inside her new home.

Piers opened the door and looked past her. "On your own?" he asked and didn't sound particularly hopeful or disappointed.

Kathy kept her voice level and practical as, now she was on her own with Piers, things weren't quite so clear any more. "Yes. The Prof's making phone calls but he reckoned Jean-Guy was best advised to stay away a bit longer."

Piers smiled and stood back to let her in. "Well, glad you made it. Come in."

Kathy stepped into the kitchen which was as large and airy as she remembered and she could hear there was someone walking about upstairs. "Emma?"

"Oh, yes. Making herself quite at home." Piers held out some keys to her. "I've had an extra set cut so you and Jean-Guy can each have your own. Square ended key is the street door and the other one is this side door. No point in giving you a back door key as you can't get to it from the outside as the gate at the back of the car port belongs to the other half of the house. Go and explore and I'll get the kettle on for some tea."

"What?" she asked lightly trying not to show her disappointment. "No guided tour?"

He sighed with mock resignation. "Come on then." He pushed open the door from the kitchen to the front of the house and Kathy saw a huge room well lit by the one big window but there wasn't one single piece of furniture in it. "Remember I told you a disabled gent lived here? This was his main room so he had his bed and chair and things in here and this," Piers slid open a wide door next to them, "was his bathroom."

"That is weird," Kathy assessed as she looked at the well-appointed wet room that still had its grab rails and a drop-down shower stool in it and was not at all what she would have expected to find in the main reception room of a house.

"Yup. Watch this kitchen door as it opens both ways so don't smack anyone in the face with it." Piers

353

took her back into the kitchen and opened the door to the box staircase she had seen before.

"Careful here as it's only a very small landing," he warned her.

Kathy stepped in behind him and saw the way one set of stairs plunged quite steeply down and another set went up at an impossible angle. "What's in the cellar?"

"Damn all. No, not quite true. A few brick shelves and alcoves which I guess used to be cold food storage and, for some reason that the estate agent couldn't explain, a gun cupboard. No guns in it, but the last person to shut it left the key in the lock so if ever I get a gun I've got somewhere to store it. Anyway, please be careful on the stairs. They're the original back stairs for the servants so they're pretty steep and narrow."

Kathy admired him from behind as he went ahead of her up the stairs and they popped out on a landing that was blocked off at one end.

"OK, room at the front is the one with the bed in it and Emma and Derek have claimed it for now but I'm guessing it's the one you and Jean-Guy will use."

The door of the room flew open and Emma rushed out to hug her oldest friend. "Kath! You are one lucky cow coming to live here! If I didn't love you so much I'd hate you."

"I'm sure you can visit any time," Kathy said and peeped round her friend to see a huge room with what she hoped was an en suite in it rather than a large cupboard.

"That was the carer's bedroom," Piers explained. "It's got its own bathroom so there won't be any fights for the shower. I'm guessing they took the main stairs out when the house was split so that's one hell of a room now. Downside is, we've only got the back stairs. Room opposite is what was the carer's living room."

Kathy and Emma both went into the back room which spanned the width of Piers' side of the house and Kathy stopped in the doorway just to look at it. The room was if anything too big and the few items of furniture looked small and lost. There were two windows which went almost floor to ceiling and a very dramatic, if dusty, cut glass chandelier that seemed to have been there so long it had spread roots into the ceiling. The curtains were an outdated 1950s graphic print in unfashionable shades of red and yellow but looking at the amount of material in them, Kathy guessed Piers couldn't afford to replace them. Either that or he had no taste when it came to interior decorating. There wasn't much in the room. Just the sofa with its back to the window, a TV in one corner so anyone who wanted to watch it would have to sit sideways on the sofa and a bookcase in one of the alcoves next to the fireplace which had been rather crudely boarded over with pegboard. The room was clean enough and the wooden floorboards had once been stripped down and varnished but the whole house felt tired and neglected somehow.

"I'll go and get the kettle on," Emma offered. "Getting a bit too pregnant now to cart myself up and down all these stairs. Now I really don't envy you those. You'll have thighs like tree trunks living here for too long."

Kathy put her bag down on the sofa. "OK, where to next?"

"Up another floor," was the reply from her landlord.

Back to the stairs and another steep climb brought them to the second floor of the house where there were three doors. Piers opened the one at the front of the house first.

"I guess this is another bedroom," he offered.

Kathy looked in and saw another large, airy room with big windows but no curtains at all.

"This whole top half was closed off," Piers explained. "There was a door across the stairs on the floor below and nobody had the key so I had to take it off its hinges after I'd moved in. No idea what I'd find up here."

"Oh, OK." Kathy thought this room was smaller than the one below and there was no sign of an en suite. She wasn't surprised that one of the two back rooms was a bathroom but it seemed to have been frozen in time in the 1920s and was rather glamorous in a monochrome Art Deco kind of way. "Nice bathroom," she remarked.

"Yes, but the shower decides what temperature it wants to be so I usually use the one in the wet room all the way downstairs. Bath's OK though." He saw the way she was looking at the one door he hadn't opened for her. "That's my room. You don't go in there just as I don't go into yours. OK?"

Kathy wasn't quite sure whether he was telling her he would respect her privacy or warning her off. "OK," she agreed. "I think maybe you and I need to set a few house rules, don't you?"

"Yes," he agreed. "What have you in mind?"

"I don't know when Jean-Guy will get his clearance to join us." Kathy paused. This wasn't going to be harder than she had thought.

Piers briefly touched her arm. "It's OK," he smiled wryly. "One of us has to say it flat out so I'll do it. We share the house, you two will pay a token rent to keep things legal but you and I aren't going to get involved physically. Is that what you wanted to say?"

"Yes," she admitted, relieved. "But if Jean-Guy and I don't work out…"

"You will," he interrupted her. "Any idiot can see that."

She returned his smile. "Housework?" she asked more practically.

"Cleaning stuff is kept in one of the kitchen cupboards. I haven't got any carpets so there isn't a hoover. I just mop the floors."

"Good. I hate hoovering. Garden?"

"Not a lot to do. It was designed for the bloke in the wheelchair so it's all concrete paths and raised up flower beds full of bushes. Gardening isn't my thing but that one's no trouble. You really want to look in my room, don't you?"

Slightly annoyed that she was so transparent to him, Kathy could feel herself blush. "Um, yes. Sorry, just being nosey."

"Go on then, one nose then out, OK?"

He pushed open the door and it made a slight whooshing sound where the base brushed the floorboards and leaned back a bit so Kathy could peep round him to have a quick look. She was quite surprised to see he slept in a single bed. There was a bookcase which seemed to be full of diaries and a few what looked like text books, a single wardrobe and a chest of drawers that didn't match. No mirror or dressing table that she could see and the bedside table was an old two-drawer wooden filing cabinet with a lamp and a library book on it.

"Cosy," she offered politely.

"By which you mean it's very small. Yes, it is. But it's also the quietest room in the house and, as you may have noticed, I have bloody sharp hearing which isn't always a good thing when you're trying to sleep during the day. And to save you asking and sneaking in here, those aren't diaries with details of my love life in them, they are my pilot log books. To anyone who's not a pilot they are probably the most boring books on the planet and I don't want you, or anyone else, to touch them. Understood?"

"I wouldn't," Kathy replied truthfully. "That's your room and I respect your privacy. I'm just thankful you offered to take us in or I don't know what would have happened."

"You two would be in some rat-infested bog hole of a basement and I'd be rattling round here with all this space to myself."

"Yes, we probably would. What's up in the attics?"

He shrugged. "Couple of empty rooms. The rooms and walls in this place don't tally up somehow so I'd guess the other side of the partition has the lion's share of the space. Never been in it, don't even know who owns it. But it's not been let the whole time I've been here. Just occasionally I can hear mice, or rats or something in there but so long as they don't come into my half I'll live with them."

"Tea's made!" Emma bawled up the stairs and the two on the landing realised they were actually standing

358

very close together as Kathy had leaned round him to look into his room.

"Sorry," she said and backed away.

"We're going to have to be careful…" He stopped abruptly as they heard Emma stumping and puffing up the stairs to find them, and no doubt thankful she didn't have to live with those stairs.

Emma saw her oldest friend was standing a bit too close to her incredibly attractive landlord but there was a kind of gentle intimacy between them which she didn't like to break. She had thought Kath was happy with Jean-Guy but now she wasn't so sure. "Tea," she managed to pant as she got her breath back.

"You didn't need to come up here," Kathy told her. "We did hear you."

"Well you didn't say anything so I thought you were out of earshot in a place this size. Come on, down you come. I've even found the biscuit tin. Seems to be full of custard creams." She went ahead of them all the way down the stairs to the kitchen where Derek had already got the mugs of tea organised.

"Didn't know how you take yours," he said to Piers. "So haven't put anything in it."

"That's fine. I don't tend to drink milk as it seems to give me indigestion. What time are we expecting the piano tomorrow?"

"I'm meeting the removals people at Hogarth Road at eight," Derek told him. "Emma's staying here to meet it this end."

"Well, I'm leaving about seven so it's all up to you lot. Try not to knock any walls down. I'm guessing it'll go in the living room at the back somehow. Does it come with any music? I didn't bring anything down from Suffolk."

"Only Kath's fiddle music," Emma replied. "You mean you're going to carry on playing? I was sure you'd stop just as soon as you could."

"No, I'll carry on a bit longer," Piers replied vaguely. "I'm sure it's doing me good and I have a feeling Jean-Guy is going to be packing out my cases with music the next time I see him."

"Ah, yes," Emma smiled. "The dictator. You've heard about his reputation with accompanists?"

Piers did smile then. "Oh, I have. But he hasn't heard of my reputation as a pianist."

Emma returned the smile. "Uh-huh? And what's that?"

He raised his mug of tea to her. "If he upsets me I just walk away and refuse to play any more. I don't need the money, I'm not putting up with any crap, so if he wants me to hang around he's going to have to be nice to me."

"You two," Emma told him, "are going to be a musical match made in heaven. Please don't go off in a huff. I want to know what happens next."

The four settled with mugs of tea and custard creams and Piers genuinely couldn't remember what it had been like to sit there alone and lonely. It felt good to have some life in the place now. Something crossed his mind as he decided two biscuits were quite enough. "Funny thing is I've actually got one piece of music in the place. I found it inside the sofa of all ridiculous places and the sofa I found in a skip."

"You mean you just helped yourself to a sofa?" Kathy asked.

"No, I'm not that dishonest. I knocked on the door and asked if I could have it. Think they were a bit surprised. Nice couple just a couple of doors down were doing a bit of refurbishment so they let me have their old sofa out of the skip and this table and chairs too. And that old bedframe in the front bedroom. I only got round to putting a mattress on it last week when I knew you were moving in. And the bedlinen is stuff I took from the old marital home so it's been in the airing cupboard for years."

Emma looked at him. "You're a bloody Concorde pilot, how come you're so hard up?"

"I'm not now, but I was then. Just never got round to doing anything about the place. Couldn't see the point with just me in it. And Concorde doesn't pay extra, that's just a myth."

Kathy didn't want Emma to upset her landlord so soon after she had arrived. "What was the piece of music?"

"Bruch, *Kol Nidrei.* I expect it's somewhere around still."

"Cello arrangement?" Kathy asked.

"No idea. Didn't even look at it. In fact I think I may have stuffed it back in the sofa."

Kathy remembered that conversation as she lay on the sofa that night and thought how quiet it was in the house compared to the noise of Hogarth Road even though it was only a few streets away. The sofa had turned out to be just the right size and quite comfortable for someone of her height and she happily settled for sleep in her new home and was just dozing off when she remembered the music. She put a hand down between the back of the sofa and the cushions and pulled out the sheets of paper quite easily. Peering at it in the dim light offered by the street lights outside she saw it was the cello and piano reduction and she smiled as she smoothed it out and put it carefully on the floor. The annulment of vows she thought to herself as she felt herself falling asleep. In so many ways, the preparation for a new beginning.

By the time Kathy got downstairs for her first breakfast in her new home, the Ferrari had gone from the car port but Emma and Derek were already in the kitchen making toast and trying to work out the coffee machine.

"Sleep well?" Emma asked as her father so often did.

"Funnily enough, yes. That sofa's surprisingly comfortable. Piers gone to work?"

"Yes, just came down in time to catch him dashing off looking even more delicious than ever in his uniform. I give you a week before you've jumped into bed with him."

Kathy got the coffee machine worked out and deliberately wouldn't look at her oldest friend. It had been a strange night on the sofa in the end. She had dozed fitfully at first, her mind returning obsessively to those few minutes she had stood on the landing with Piers and felt that maybe she had made the wrong choice.

Emma was a bit concerned that the other woman hadn't immediately replied to her comment. "Oh, my God. You didn't, did you?"

Feeling slightly irritated by Emma's assumptions, Kathy started making the drinks. "No, I didn't. I've made my choice and don't look at me like that. You may think I'm completely potty, but I don't want to go to bed with him."

Emma bit into her toast. "And if you and Jean-Guy don't work out?"

Kathy gave her friend the most mischievous smile she could manage. "Well then, maybe I'll change my mind. I'll let you know."

Emma laughed. "I have so missed the old Kath," she mused. "Going to go across to Hogarth Road with Derek just to say goodbye?"

Kathy looked at her pink mug with the daisy on it. "No point. You've already brought everything across for me and I hate saying goodbye."

"True," Emma admitted. "No matter how many times you and I went our ways I don't think we ever actually said goodbye to each other in so many words, did we?"

By the middle of the morning, the removals firm had brought the piano across from Hogarth Road and realised they had a bit of a problem. But they had got bigger pianos into smaller houses and by lunch time had manoeuvred the piano into the back sitting room. They left it between the windows so there was maximum light on the keyboard and it looked as though it had been there for a hundred years.

The two women stood in the living room telling each other that one day this would be a lovely home; full of music and laughter and tales of concerts and audiences, grumbles about rehearsals and conductors and gossip about fellow musicians.

Emma sighed quietly. "I really do envy you," she admitted. "It's going to be so strange now not having a

London base but just being stuck in Somerset surrounded by babies. I'm going to miss all the gossip and the gigs."

She sounded so wistful Kathy gave her a hug and tried not to feel too smug. "I'm sure you can stay here any time you like," she consoled.

"I'm sure we could," Emma agreed and the old lights came back into her eyes. "Right, that's it. Let's go and get a copy of *Loot* and *Exchange and Mart* maybe even the local paper and see if we can't get some furniture in this place before he gets back. Because, quite frankly, the whole place is a disgrace. Still, at least it's clean."

Kathy looked at her watch. "That doesn't give us long."

"Kath, this is us. 'Long' isn't something we're used to."

By the time Kathy shut the side door of her new home and exchanged hugs with Emma and Derek they had been busy in the house. For not a lot of money they had found a 1930s wooden double bedframe for the front bedroom on the second floor, and a battered set of Edwardian bedroom furniture for Kathy's room. They had struck lucky at a house clearance and returned triumphant with two unmatched fireside chairs, a selection of clean eiderdowns and blankets which they had dumped on the bed up on the second floor and they had also managed to get a rather handsome Fortnum and Mason wicker basket which they had loaded with Kathy's knitting wool stash and parked in the sitting room so it made a kind of coffee table. An eclectic selection of bedside tables and lamps had completed their haul and they all went off to their homes feeling rather pleased with themselves for achieving so much in one day.

Kathy was having serious misgivings about bringing in so much stuff without asking first but guessed Piers could probably afford to hire a skip now if he wanted to get rid of it all again. It had certainly made the house look a lot more lived in and given it a rather welcoming, shabby air as though you could just turn up, kick your shoes off and make yourself at home. It appealed to Kathy after the stiff formality of the house she had grown up in where rules had to be obeyed, floors were carpeted and furniture had to match.

She had made up her mind to see if her car would start after its long rest in a parking space a couple of streets away and as she settled into the familiar driving seat she told it that she was going to give it six goes to start and then she was going to abandon it again and go home to Suffolk on the train. The car sulked at her tone then startled her by starting the second time she turned the key. She almost fondly patted its steering wheel and she was smiling as she set off on the familiar route to Suffolk. She had done this journey dozens of times and often told herself that her car could find its own way there if she just asked it. The roads were fairly quiet and she got back to Suffolk about tea time.

"Piano arrived alright?" the Prof checked as he paused in his tea-making to give her a smile of greeting.

Kathy took off her coat and almost sighed audibly with relief that she was safe at home again. It had been strange to be out and about again and she almost hadn't liked it. "Oh, yes. They had to take a window out to get it in but it suits its new home. We brought in some new furniture for him too. Hope he doesn't mind but there really wasn't much in there."

The Prof smiled. "I'm sure he won't mind at all. As you are here without phoning for a lift I assume you brought your car?"

"Oh, it's outside. Started surprisingly easily. I don't know what I'll do with it now as I'm sure Piers said he's not supposed to put two cars in the car port as it's shared with the other half of the house, but it's all double yellow lines in his road so I may have to risk it for a while. Be nice not to have to hunt the streets to find a space."

Kathy looked round as Jean-Guy came rushing into the kitchen and wrapped his arms round her in an enveloping hug of pure joy. "Did the Prof give you my news?" he asked eagerly.

Kathy just about got her breath back but Jean-Guy hadn't let her go. She looked into his dark eyes and thought she had never seen him look so happy before. "Oh, my God," she realised. "You've heard from the Home Office."

"Yes, yes I have," he laughed and gave her a short but very heady snog in front of the Prof. "They have granted me Indefinite Leave to Remain, effective immediately. So that's it. I am free to stay. I can stay as long as I like and you and I have a future together and, and, I don't know what else."

Petr Mihaly was just as delighted and it warmed his heart to see the innocent joy of the couple in front of him. Kathy had walked away from the temptation of the handsome, enigmatic Piers and had clearly made her choice in the gentle musician who held her so close in the farmhouse kitchen. "Yes, it is the best news. I have told your agent and she is now confirming bookings for him. Give it a while and he will be able to apply for British

Citizenship but for now, you two have a way forward at last."

Kathy caught Jean-Guy's hand and the two exchanged a look and a soft kiss. "Yes," she agreed. "I have no idea what will happen next but I guess this is the start of our new lives together."

The story continues in *Fractured Sonata*

Acknowledgments

Thank you for reading this first story of Kathy and her friends. I hope you will continue to follow what they all get up to in the future stories in this series.

My thanks to those who have helped me in this long journey to a completed novel, right from its very first beginnings when it really was 1981 to its resurrection during the first Covid lockdown of 2020. To my human family: Raymond, Ben and Becca for not minding too much if mealtimes got erratic and the housework wasn't done, and to my feline family Bailey and Calamity who helped with the typing. To the many musicians I have ever met or worked with and also to the helpful people on the Heritage Concorde Facebook page who provided answers to my most obscure questions.

Finally, huge thanks to the annoyingly talented artists who conceived the front cover. Picture by Paul Saunders, based on an original idea by Jess Ford.

And finally, a little bit about me

I live near the east coast of Suffolk but grew up in London, like Kathy, at the end of the District Line. I trained as a shorthand typist, didn't like that so became a librarian. After some time in the care industry I am now quietly winding down towards retirement putting in a few hours a week in a local coffee shop.

When I am not losing myself in writing novels, I can be heard making a lot of noise on a bass trombone in the local brass band, or trying to behave myself in the viola section of a local orchestra. I hate gardening, am useless at cooking and share my chaotic home with a very tolerant husband of over thirty years, two beautiful and talented children and a couple of extraordinary cats. I couldn't do this without you.

Printed in Great Britain
by Amazon